GOLD TOWER, RED TOWER

BOOK ONE OF THE MAGIC TOWERS

CHARLES DAVID EYER

The characters and events in this book are purely fictional.
Any similarity to real persons, living or dead, is coincidental.

Copyright © 2020 by Charles David Eyer
All rights reserved.

Gold Tower, Red Tower
Book One of the Magic Towers

Eyer, Charles David, 1966—

ISBN: 978-0-9826273-2-7

**Library of Congress Control Number:
2020913922**

Fiction
Fantasy Novel
Wizards, Dragons, Elves, Dwarves, Goblins, Tooskers

Artwork by the author
Map at the end of the book

Published by:
Mossy Noecy Books, Olathe, Kansas
an Imprint of Zannalornacopia Inc.,
a division of Pandooni Biblioteka Inc.,
& in Arcadia by Throg Anvel Press.

Printed in the USA

1
PORTERVILLE

Friday morning and Keith Brenner tossed a pop-tart in the toaster before running downstairs to his basement bedroom. He pulled on his clothes and then stopped to admire his books, even though he had done this a thousand times before. The only newness came from having lived here only a few months, but all these books had been laboriously moved from the house he had grown up in. He had half-filled the built-in shelves that lined one wall, for he was an avid reader and compulsive book buyer, and he ran his fingers along the spines, hardcover classics and cheap paperbacks, each like an old friend. The fantasy and science fiction titles occupied the place of honor on the shelves behind his desk. He thought to pull one out and take it with him, as his greatest fear was to be stuck somewhere with time to kill and nothing to read, but then he thought better of it. He would wait for the new book he would buy after school.

Turning, his eyes fell on a blue robe hanging on a peg in a corner, and he went to it. It had a hood and was covered in arcane symbols like a proper wizard's robe. Rubbing the thick, soft material between fingers and thumb gave him a thrill of pleasure as always. He shrugged on his backpack and bounded up the stairs, kissing his grandma on the forehead as she slept in a living room recliner.

He gulped down his milk. Pop-tart in hand, he went outside where he saw the rake lying in the yard where he had left it, the leaves still unraked. The garage door opened behind him, and he heard his father curse when the car door banged against the stacked boxes in their cluttered garage.

"Keith! We're cleaning this garage and throwing some of this junk away this weekend." His dad could barely squeeze into his car.

"Great. There goes my Saturday."

Keith climbed aboard the yellow bus that took him across the river and north to the other side of town, where it disgorged students at Porterville High School. Keith's bus came the furthest so it was last in line. He watched a long line of luxury cars drop off the kids from the west side, and by the time he finally got off the bus eveyone else was inside. He knew he should hurry to make class before the first bell rang, but he sauntered. The bell rang, but still Keith stopped at the open library door. Large collections of books had that effect on him. The librarian smiled at him and pointed at the clock. Keith slowly moved on, a fantasy in his head, and showed up after geography class had already started.

Keith joined several of his friends at a large table. Ms. Garcia was talking and without missing a word walked over and thrust a fishbowl in front of Keith's face. There was one slip of paper in it. When he took it out, it read: UZBEKISTAN.

He daydreamed while Ms. Garcia's voice droned on for awhile. When the other students made rustling noises he came back to reality and attacked the project in front of him. Using an atlas as his guide, he drew the long sinuous borders of this strange country on a big sheet of paper. A colored pencil provided the big red dot for the capital, Tashkent. Sitting back to admire his work, he thought Uzbekistan looked like a dragon leaping over Turkmenistan, its forelegs landing on Afghanistan. Its misshapened head was ready to breath fire and turn Kyrgyzstan into a smoking ruin. Red Tashkent was the dragon's malevolent eye. Feeling inspired, Keith used the colored pencil to draw flames coming out of Uzbekistan's 'mouth.' He rechecked the atlas, noting again the long names of these central Asian countries.

He looked over at TJ's work. His big friend had gotten France for his country and was struggling to draw squiggly rivers. He was making the Loire too short, the Seine too far north, and he left the Garonne and Rhone Rivers off entirely. A pretty blonde girl named Holly Hudson came over from her table to help him, giggling at his struggles. TJ was a great football player and the biggest kid in Porterville High, with shoulders so wide you could park a school bus on them. He played on the varsity squad despite being only a freshman, and he was smart too but couldn't draw for beans. He and Holly had begun spending a lot of time together.

"Put the Eiffel Tower right here," said Holly.

"Holly, let TJ do his own work," Ms. Garcia said as she came by. Holly went back to drawing cute koalas in eucalyptus trees on her map of Australia.

"Don't forget to draw some taipans slithering under the trees," Keith said, and she smirked at him. She was a newcomer to their circle, and he had been standoffish at first but had warmed up enough to joke with her.

Then there was brown-haired Woody Brunswick, Keith's closest friend, a serious look on his face as he concentrated on drawing the Amazon River basin, complete with colorful macaws. On the far side of the table sat three girls. Maya was an African-American girl with dreadlocks and artistic pretensions, populating massive snow-white Canada with Eskimos alongside igloos in the north and bright-red maples along the southern border. Her drawings were always creative and intricate. Danielle was a tall brunette with dark ringlets framing her pretty face and brown eyes. She was drawing pyramids alongside her bright blue Nile. Holly and Danielle were best friends, but Danielle now had to compete with TJ for Holly's attention. The third girl was Paula, a tall redhead with beautiful blue eyes, known for her good hands and dry humor. She played basketball and volleyball, but right now she was drawing Mt. Fuji on her Honshu Island.

Lastly there was Dominic, the school misfit, in only his first year in the Porterville school system. Shy and quiet, he was the great grandnephew of Old Man Putnam, and the only person Keith ever met who read more than him. He sat at the end of the table and read, ignoring the assignment until Ms. Garcia walked by, closed his book, and tapped his blank paper with her finger. Dominic opened the book back up as she walked away. Keith read Dominic's slip of paper: CHINA.

"I'd start with the Great Wall," Keith whispered to him. Dominic smirked at him and went back to reading.

Eventually the bell rang. "Those who haven't finished, or haven't even started"—she glared at Dominic—"can take their countries home and finish drawing them this weekend," Ms. Garcia called out above the noise of twenty freshmen high schoolers scrambling to leave. "I know tomorrow night is Halloween, but you should still have plenty of time for homework."

She stopped Keith at the door. "And erase those flames from Kyrgystan, young man. I won't have you burning up any countries."

"It's the dragon that did it, Ms. Garcia," Keith said.

She smiled at him. "There are no dragons in the real world."

"But mapmakers always write *Here There Be Dragons* on their maps."

"Not in my class they don't."

Kido and Dahlia fell in together in the hallway. He pointed to her hair. "I like your curls."

"They're Mary Pickford curls. She was an actress from the Silent Era of Films. You're still coming to the party, right?"

"I think so."

"You better. I read your horoscope. You're supposed to go with the flow today."

"Fabulous. Is Mercury still retrograde?"

"For you always, Keith." She gave him a wink and briefly touched the back of his neck with her warm hand before walking off."

Keith stood and watched her walk away, his feelings in a turmoil. He had gone out three times with her before she broke it off saying she wasn't ready to get serious. But he had kissed her, and he had a crush on her still.

Classes, lunch, more classes. Keith daydreamed his way through algebra class, still fantasizing about the Uzbek dragon burning its swath of destruction through Central Asia when he wasn't thinking of Dahlia. Woody got his attention, mouthing the words 'fifteen minutes' and pointing at the clock while Mr. Lemuelson droned on about the Pythagorean Theorem.

Finally the bell rang and the kids swarmed out of school. Woody's mom drove them to the store which she owned with Woody's dad. On the way they passed Betty the Bag Lady, a fixture of Porterville. Bundled in old clothes, she was pushing a shopping cart full of her wordly possessions down the sidewalk past the imposing marble facade of a bank. "That poor woman," Mrs. Brunswick said, shaking her head.

At the store, many younger kids were there trying on Halloween costumes, but the boys headed back to the book shelves and Magic case.

"Boys, how was school?" Mr. Brunswick said from behind the glass counter. Woody's dad had his long silver hair up in its usual ponytail and was wearing a tie-dyed shirt. While he talked to his son, he handed Keith a brand new book, book four in the *Goozer War* series by Trent Trout, which Keith excitedly flipped through. He had been waiting months for it to come out.

"School was boring," Woody said as he studied a nearby rack of comic books.

"Good thing you only have ten more years of it," said Mr. Brunswick with a chuckle.

"Ten? Dad, we graduate in less than four years," said Woody.

"He's counting college," Keith said, looking up from his book.

"That's right. You need college if you don't want to work forever in retail or fast food," Mr. Brunswick. "Unless you're going to join the military or learn a trade."

"Fat chance of that," said Woody.

"Or maybe medical school," said Mr. Brunswick with a big smile for his son.

"I know, dad," said Woody with a sigh.

Mr. Brunswick leaned on the counter. "How about you, Keith? What are your plans for a career?"

"I don't know, Mr. Brunswick."

He took on the serious look of paternalistic concern. "I know you're only a freshman but these days you have to start thinking early about careers. I know you like to read."

"I love to read."

"You've probably bought more books from me than the rest of Porterville combined."

"I've thought about becoming a teacher. Or a writer."

"Teaching's a noble profession. You won't get rich, but you can make a real difference. Writing's a tough racket, unless you're the next Stephen King or something." He laughed at that.

Keith was too busy scanning the items in the glass case to answer. Not that there was anything new here, just the usual figurines of dragons, trolls, and fairies, a few samurai swords, and the assorted gaming paraphernalia. But then amongst the brightly-colored dice and joysticks, Keith saw a strange box. The worn cover, adorned with a large dragon and four colored towers, declared it to be a board game called "The Magic Towers."

"I've never heard of that," Keith said, pointing at it.

"Oh, that. *That* is an old board game, very rare," Mr. Brunswick said. "So rare I've never seen one before."

"Can I see it?"

"Sure." He brought it out and placed it on the counter and carefully lifted the lid. Keith watched him set up the board, placing a tall plastic tower in each corner, each tower a different color—gold, red, green, and black. "There are more pieces, but I don't want to get it all out."

Woody came over. "Wow, that looks cool."

Mr. Brunswick said, "Just got it today, second-hand. I'm betting some collector will pay a pretty penny for this baby."

Mrs. Brunswick joined them, saying, "Someone probably had

that in their basement for years. Looks like it's in good condition, though."

"Old Man Putnam's great-nephew brought that in."

Dominic, Keith thought with surprise.

"Old Man Putnam's still alive?" asked Mrs. Brunswick.

"If he is, he must be a hundred by now," said Mr. Brunswick.

"How much is it?" Keith asked, still enthralled by this novel game.

"Oh, I bet I can get $200 for it, maybe more. Make me an offer."

Keith looked at the rumpled twenty dollar bill his mother had given him. "I guess I'll have to wait."

"Sorry, son."

Mrs. Brunswick nudged her husband, shoulder to shoulder. "Let the boys take it home for the night and play with it. They won't hurt it. Will you boys?"

They nodded enthusiastically. Mr. Brunswick studied their bright faces while he weighed the suggestion. He then boxed the towers back up and carefully handed the game over. "Just for tonight. You bring it back tomorrow, and be careful with it, boys. That's my retirement in your hands."

Mrs. Brunswick drove the boys to Keith's home where Woody was staying over.

Porterville was an exurb in an outer ring of suburbs clustered around a teeming metropolis in the Midwest. Most of the town sat north of the lazy Archet River as it meandered on its merry way towards some distant inland sea. Crossing the bridge going south over the Archet one may turn left toward the trailer court or continue straight on to Putnam Lane and the last two houses inside city limits. Keith's family had the house on the left, Old Man Putnam on the right. Beyond was the endless prairie.

Keith got out clutching the board game and as Woody said goodbye to his mother, Keith looked up at his neighbor's house across the street. Old Man Putnam was the oldest living person in Porterville, living in the oldest house in Porterville, said to be 300 years old. Built like a castle out of reddish-black stones quarried from some far away place, it had towers at each corner, just like the four towers in the board game, Keith realized. Below the battlements, the windows were always covered with drawn curtains showing no light. An old black wrought-iron fence of spear points circled the house, and an old cemetery hiding on the far side held the graves of generations of Putnams. No one had seen the old man in years, only his ancient manservant could be seen occasionally doing yardwork or driving an old truck on errands. The land around Porterville is quite flat, the only hill being where Putnam Castle stood overlooking everyone else. The creepy architecture combined with the owner's ecentric behavior gave rise to all sorts of rumors. Keith's family was suspect in the eyes of some just for being neighbors, not that they had a choice.

Keith called his friends to invite them over to play the board game but they all had other plans. "We used to always play games together, but now everyone else is into sports or cheerleading," he said.

"They're too grownup for fantasy games," said Woody. "High school changes everything. I should be studying chemistry or algebra myself."

"Yeah, if you're going to medical school."

After supper, Keith set up the board on his bedroom floor while a supine Woody read the background story written on the inside cover of the lid:

First there was nothing. And then the World Fabricator just happened to be in the neighborhood and decided this place needed something. So he rolled up his galaxy-sized sleeves and made a dragon, a huge and powerful dragon he called Tiamat. And he didn't stop there. Next other races popped into being: elves, dwarves, humans, even goblins (apparently created during a night of binge drinking by the World Fabricator before going off to nap for a few centuries). But Tiamat set to work eating everything she could and what she couldn't eat she flamed to a crisp. In alarm, the other races banded together to kill her, but farmers, fishermen, and hedge fund managers were no match for the might of Tiamat. Then out of the wilderness came four men of Magic, wizards of great power who would destroy the beast, saving the Known World. Dragon, as everyone knows, tastes like chicken, so they sent out for butchers of renowned skill to carve the beast up for a celebratory feast.

But when Tiamat was opened up, her body revealed she had been carrying four eggs. Tiamat had been pregnant, although no one could explain how her eggs had been fertilized. It was, to say the least, an immaculate conception. Anyways, one egg was given to each of the wizards to take as a gift. Three of the wizards were human and the fourth an elf. Each retired to their separate homes in the far corners and raised their hatched dragons. They each built a tall tower at the spot where their dragon was hatched, using the residual embryonic Magic residing inside the eggs to create shields of enchantment for protection. And inside their Magic Towers they concocted their first batches of golden ichor dust using the blood of Tiamat gathered at her place of demise. Thus there were four towers and four dragons and four vats of dragon blood. Wizard wannabes flocked to the towers to become apprentices.

The four dragons were called the Prime Dragons and were named: Ramyre the Red, Pangma the Gold, Mazunga of the Shadows, and Sanshinar the Green. Each dragon operated as a totem to the wizards and their towers. But the dwarves were angry that the elves had a dragon and humans three, but they had none. So they used some of their great mined wealth to bribe a zealous apprentice wizard named Antares to create a dragon for them using ichor (elves cannot be bribed). The dwarves liked their dragon so much they paid for three more. The elves, fearing they were falling behind, created several new dragons of their own, and the humans followed suit. Soon there was a dragon escalation that spiralled out of control until hundreds of them filled the skies. They were of course not Prime Dragons but Juvies, or Juvenile Dragons, too young to yet breath fire but still possessing claws, teeth, and great strength and cunning. Paranoia and greed abounded. The races went to war over territory and wealth, each backed by flying squadrons of dragons. More blood soaked into the ground.

Finally the World Fabricator woke from his nap and when he saw what had happened, he became peeved. He put Antares in time out for 1000 years. All dragons, Primes and Juvies, were banished to a specially-controlled dimension called Sporu Angosta, to be kept there until all the races would grow up and behave themselves. There was nothing left for the races to do now but hunt down all the goblins found above ground. But that failed to assuage their frustrations until the rumor was passed around that great wealth also lay inside Sporu Angosta. Huge mounds of gold and silver coins, gems, and jewelry, they said. A golden throne of Infinite Power, they said. And tall Magical-looking doors were discovered in the Mountains of Meb. Each race scurried to send teams of adventurers to pass through this portal. They wanted back their dragons! They wanted all that treasure! They wanted to sit on that golden throne! And most importantly of all, each race wanted to deny the others of victory! They were going to outflank the World Fabricator, but alas, all such attempts ultimately failed.

Now it is your turn, player, to play the game of The Magic Towers. Choose a tower to defend and try to win all the gold for yourself and defeat your opponents. Be the first inside Sporu Angosta! Good luck!

Woody put down the lid. "This is going to be so cool." He sighed. "Although I should be doing my homework."

Keith picked up the dice. "Let's roll to see who goes first."

The game was meant for four players so they each picked two towers and played against each other. The game tokens had several human warriors in armor with swords and several wizards in robes with staffs. There were four elvish tokens and a pair of dwarvish ones but strangely no dragon tokens. The colored path their tokens took led through mountains and over a river. It winded across a desert and a tundra, with separate paths leading to each tower. There was a stack of cards for actions when landing upon special squares and yellow plastic pots of gold to be won. They found a folded white plastic sheet which unfolded to reveal a large black oval labeled "Teleport Rock," and a plastic marble which activated the teleportation. The game sucked them in and they had so much fun they lost track of time.

Keith's dad knocked at the door shortly after midnight. "Hey, are you guys still up? It's late."

"We're playing a new game, dad."

"It's so much fun, Mr. Brenner."

"Is it? Well, don't be too much longer. Remember tomorrow...er today now I guess...is Halloween. Get some sleep."

"We will, dad."

They were clearing the board when Keith said, "I don't see any spot called Sporu Angosta."

Woody searched with him. "I hadn't noticed but you're right. There is no Sporu Angosta." They flipped the board over but it was blank.

"And we never teleported anywhere either."

"And we never saw any dragons."

They went to bed happy but confused.

"What are they doing down there?" asked Mrs. Brenner when her husband came back upstairs. She was half asleep and fully reclined in bed.

"They're playing a board game."

"At least they're not drinking beer and consorting with slutty girls," she said in a sleepy voice.

He snorted with humor. "Good point, my dear."

2
HALLOWEEN

On the morning of Halloween, the first thing the boys did after waking up was to get the board game out and search again for Sporu Angosta, thinking it might've Magically appeared overnight but to no avail. None of the cards mentioned teleporting either. They rode their bikes north after breakfast to return the game to the Brunswick's Book Store. Woody's father was happy to see it back safe and sound and kissed the box.

Back outside the boys biked down the street and took a shortcut through an alley between a strip mall and a wooded lot.

"Are you going to the Halloween Party tonight?" Woody asked as they pedalled side-by-side.

"I don't know."

"Your mom went to all that trouble of sewing your blue wizard's robes."

"I know. I hate to disappoint her, but I don't feel like a party tonight. I don't feel like I belong in that high school or with our friends much anymore."

"We used to do everything together, but now TJ has his sports and Holly her cheerleading, and Danielle her theater and her dance, and Maya her church and charity work. You and I are the only ones who still like fantasy and gaming."

"And you've always got homework to do," Keith said. "You've gotten boring."

"Oh yeah! Race you to Oak Street!" Woody yelled and took off, racing ahead. But Keith was more athletic and soon passed Woody.

Then suddenly an older teenager on a bike came around a corner to block Keith's route. Keith recognized the crew cut hair and hard face of Eddie Patterson. Behind him were Troy and Nick on their bikes. Eddie was the town bully and would have been a senior this year if he hadn't been kicked out for bringing a knife to school. He worked in his father's auto repair shop, and rumor had it he carried that knife tucked in his sock and dealt drugs on the side. Eddie, Troy, and Nick called themselves the Black Scorpions and liked to terrorize younger kids. They always wore black t-shirts and dark shades.

Behind Keith, Woody spun around and biked away furiously, saying over his shoulder, "I'm going for help."

Eddie jumped off his bike, letting it fall with a crash and grabbing Keith's bike. He lifted his shades. "Well, lookey here. If it ain't my old pal, Keith. You got any money for me today, Keith?" Eddie used to steal lunch money from kids before he'd been kicked out. He had victimized Keith several times last year, and Keith would've gone hungry if not for Woody's donations.

"Let me go. I'm not giving you anything," Keith said, struggling to get his bike out of Eddie's grip. Eddie was big and strong, if a bit roly-poly. Troy and Nick rode up to box Keith in. Troy was red-haired and bucktoothed, with a big Adam's apple on his long neck. Nick had bad acne and dandruff flakes in his slicked-back black hair.

"Turn your pockets inside-out or else, Keith." Eddie got in Keith's face, saying his name with cold venom.

Keith thought of the tweny dollar bill in his pocket that his mother had given him out of her savings. He wasn't letting Eddie have that. "No!" he said, feeling bloth defiant and afraid.

"We'll see about that," Eddie said as he bent to reach for something in his sock.

"You're in trouble now," Troy taunted and Nick laughed. Troy shoved the back of Keith's head.

Just then there was a crash of shrubbery and a shopping cart came through to plow into Eddie's derriere and knock him over.

"Watch where you're going!" an old woman yelled. It was Betty the Bag Lady.

An angry Eddie got up with a butterfly knife in hand, flipping it to bare the blade. "I oughta stick you, you dumb ol' broad."

Betty didn't back down. "Oh, you think you might, do ya?" And the old woman pulled out a huge dagger and waved it in Eddie's face, complemented with several loud yipping noises. She flicked it and cut a shallow slit in Eddie's right cheek. The action was over before Eddie knew what hit him. He yelled and put his hand to his face in shock. His fingers came away bloody.

"You die!" Eddie shrieked. He made a move towards Betty as did Troy and Nick. His bike now free, Keith pedaled and hit Eddie, knocking him on the ground again. Troy approached Keith with balled fists. The whelp of a siren interrupted everything as a police cruiser appeared at the alley's far end, lights flashing.

Eddie cursed as he pulled Betty's cart over before retreating to his bike. "I'll make you pay next time, Keith," Eddie threatend as he mounted up. The Black Scorpions rode off, looking back several times as Betty waved her dagger at them, yelled gibberish, and jumped up and down. She hastily put her dagger away with a glance at the cop approaching with Woody and Mr. Brunswick.

A surprised Keith sat on his bike and regarded Betty. She had scraggly gray hair and was missing some teeth, but kindly blue eyes stared back at him. "That was amazing. How can I thank you for helping me?"

"I hate mean people like that," she said. Keith helped her, piling old clothes and junk into the cart she had put back upright. In went a toaster and hair dryer, a musty sweater and worn sweatpants, a doll missing an arm and a giant plastic candy cane. Keith grabbed the last item off the ground and turned the box over.

"Hey, where did you get that board game?" Keith asked.

"It's the Magic Towers!" Woody read the cover as he came up.

Keith gently handed it over to Betty as she said, "I've had it for years, since I was a little girl. Don't play it, though. Don't want to break it." She wrapped it in pink parachute pants and reverently laid it in her cart.

"Imagine that there are two of those board games in this town," said Mr. Brunswick.

"It doesn't work though. No teleporting," Keith said.

"You just need a key," Betty said.

"There was a plastic key that came with the game," Woody said.

"No, you need a *real* key," Betty insisted.

The boys were confused. "What do you mean?"

Woody's dad had gone off to where the cop was filing a report.

"I'll show you." With a wink and a grin, Betty unrolled a long panty hose taken from the cart's depths and reached in to pull out a small box. She lifted the lid to reveal a small spherical object of swirled color, like a large marble. It gave off a whisp of something like smoke or steam, and there was a strange not unpleasant smell. Keith felt a tingle. She snapped the lid shut and handed it to Keith. "You take this one. That leaves me with only one left." She turned to Woody. "Which means you get none." She patted the panty hose. "I'd give it to you, but I need it to get back."

"Back where?"

She cackled. "Wouldn't you like to know." She winked and pushed her cart down the alley, singing in an off-key voice, "*If I was walking in your shoes, I wouldn't worry none. While you and your friends are worrying about me, I'm having lots of fun.*"

Coming back, Mr. Brunswick asked, "What is Betty up to?"

"I don't know," Keith said, having shoved the box in his hoodie's pocket.

Back at Keith's house, the boys went to the kitchen in search of lunch. Keith took out a bowl of butterscotch pudding, his favorite desert, but then decided they needed sandwiches first. Hoagy buns were slit open and slathered with mayonnaise before piled high with sliced turkey and lettuce. But the cheese drawer was empty, nary a slice of baby Swiss or provolone, not even American.

Woody found the note. "Your mom is going to the quilting store and then the grocery store. Maybe she'll be back soon with cheese."

"Nah, she takes forever when she's in the quilting store."

"I can eat mine without cheese."

"Dunderfunk, I say."

He could see his grandma napping in a recliner in the living room. They had been living in this house for only three months. Before that, the Brenners had had a nice house on the fashionable west side of town, but then Keith's dad had been laid off when his company 'downsized.' His dad eventually found another job but it paid a lot less and so they were forced to move. Then his sick grandmother moved in with them. Pill bottles now clustered on the kitchen counter next to the toaster and medical bills covered the dining room table. Their current house was much cheaper, being where it was. It was an old ramshackle affair stuck in the no man's land between the trailer park and Putnam Castle. No one else would live here. And in those three months no one in Keith's family had visited their neighbor. His parents in fact had gone to great lengths to keep him away from the wrong side of the street. But once in awhile Keith liked to do what he was told not to as some kind of morale imperative. Standing with his cheeseless sandwich, Keith got an idea.

"Let's go borrow some cheese from the Putnam's," he said suddenly.

"I should go home and study chemistry," Woody said, and then he realized what Keith had said. "What?" he said in shock.

"I bet they have a fridge full of cheese."

"They can keep it. I'm not going over there." The tone in Woody's voice left no further room for discussion.

"Oh, Woodmeister. What am I to do about this timidity of yours?"

"What humidity?"

"Timidity! Never mind. You stay here, and I'll bring back some cheese."

"If you're not back in ten minutes, I'm calling the police."

It was a cool fall day with a breeze that kicked the leaves around. With a powerful aversion towards yardwork, Keith tried to ignore the leaves. Across an empty street and up the grassy parking, he found the iron gate so widely ajar that he could slide through without moving it. Along a narrow weed-choked sidewalk and up crumbling stairs to a wide covered porch he went like a condemned man on his last walk, his courage shrinking with each step.

The front door opened as he approached it, and he found himself face-to-face with Dominic sporting camouflage pants and a Bauhaus t-shirt.

"Hello, Dominic."

"Hello, Keith."

The boy looked down at Keith's hands and Keith followed his gaze, realizing for the first time that he had managed to carry his sandwich all the way from his kitchen to the Putnam's porch without knowing it. He wouldn't have believed it except that it was still lying there spread open in his hand, waiting to receive its cheese.

"I wonder if you have any cheese I could borrow for my sandwich," he said, feeling sheepish all of a sudden.

"Cheese?"

"Yes. You know, baby Swiss or whatever."

A pause and then, "Sure, come on in."

Keith found himself standing in a tall foyer of dark wood, lit by a single Tiffany table lamp. Looking around he saw old things: furniture, family pictures, rugs. On a table was a photo album with the Putnam name written in calligraphy. On the wall to his left was a poster of an old blue car, one of those right out of the Great Depression. Bonnie and Clyde probably drove one. JORDAN BLUE BOY SOMEWHERE WEST OF LARAMIE, the poster said. Below it a silent jukebox stood, all bright lights and chrome. To the right, a wide stairway climbed up into the gloom. The air smelled stale. The whole impression was one of a house little changed by time.

"The kitchen is this way," Dominic said and they turned that way but came up short as an older, bald man dressed in gray pants and a red vest over a white shirt came towards them. His lidded eyes held no emotion but mild curiosity.

"This is Fishworth," Dominic said to Keith before explaining it all to Fishworth. Kido recognized him as the manservant sometimes seen outside in the yard.

Before Fishworth could say anything, a barely-audible and nasally voice called out, "Is that company, Dominic?" The voice came from a darkened arch behind them, and there was a hint of pleasant surprise in it.

"Yes, Great-Uncle."

Fishworth hurried into the darkness. Soon a light came on and Keith was ushered in with Dominic to find a very old man lying in a hospital bed. Only a few gray strands of hair clung to a bare head covered in age spots. Pale white skin was drawn tight over cheekbones and thin white fingers clutched at the bedcovers, but bright blue eyes sparkled from their deep sockets. The room had a stale, medicinal smell. Fishworth left for the kitchen.

"This is my great uncle, Gerald Putnam XXIII," Dominic said. "The last in a long line of Gerald Putnams."

Keith introduced himself and then said, "We played your board game last night, the one called The Magic Towers, from Mr. Brunswick's game shop."

"Oh, that old thing? Did you like it?"

"Yes, it is so much fun. We couldn't stop playing."

Old Man Putnam seemed pleased to hear this and sat up with help from Fishworth. "I designed that game when I was much younger." He spoke slowly and with great effort.

Keith said, "One thing though. We couldn't find Sporu Angosta or do any teleporting."

The smile on Old Man Putnam's face melted away like snow on a sunny day. "There are a few flaws in the game, I admit. Maybe that's why it never sold well."

Keith felt instantly sorry for the criticism. "Maybe someone can fix the flaws and start selling the game again?"

Old Man Putnam waved a feeble hand. "No, no. The game is quite unfixable. There is no hope, for you see the whole game is based on the adventures of our family patriarch many years ago. I come from a long line of Putnams. You would not believe the stories I could tell you." It took awhile to get that all out.

"Really? Like what?" Keith's curiosity was on point.

But the old man sank back into his pillows, and he turned his head away with a long sigh.

Fishworth had returned. "Talking wears him out. You'll have to leave for now, sir," he said and handed Keith two cheese slices wrapped in plastic.

Out in the foyer, Dominic said, "You really played the game?"

"Yes, Woody and I."

"Woody, too?"

"He was too chicken to come over here."

"And you couldn't teleport?" Something in Dominic's demeanor changed. He seemed animated by some energy.

"No. The game had a teleport rock and a key but it never had us use them."

"It's just a game anyways. Tell me, Keith, would you like to see a *real* teleport rock?" Dominic's eyes twinkled with mischievous mirth now.

"You know of one?"

"There's one here in the house, on top of the tallest tower. Wanna see?"

Keith didn't know what to think, but he decided to play along. "Sure."

"Follow me." He turned like an imp and bounded up the stairs. Keith raced after him.

Upstairs, a long hallway presented itself and Keith saw Dominic far ahead. He ran to catch up, portraits of stern old pioneers glaring as he flew past. There were many closed doors and a few old lights in sconces, fleeting impressions of the second floor. A faded green runner led along the wooden floor to a door, which Dominic opened to reveal a narrow, steep stairwell climbing up. Keith followed the disappearing tennis shoes, round and round, up and up. Small windows let in the autumn light and showed them rising high above the ground. At the top was a trap door in the ceiling and Keith climbed through to stand on top of the tallest crennelated tower of Putnam Castle. Before him was a teleport rock, maybe twenty by forty feet in dimensions but only four or five inches high. Made of some shiny black stone, its flat and smooth surface looked dark and forbidding.

"Here it is," Dominic said without fanfare.

"A teleport rock? That's what this is?"

"Yeah. I said it was up here, didn't I?"

Keith thought about the absurdity of the situation. The rock looked totally out of place, but then the whole castle was out of place for a place like Porterville. And he was out of place for being here.

"How come I've never seen you before this year?" Keith said.

"I used to live in Chicago, but my parents sent me here to live with my great-uncle while I finish high school. I got bullied a lot at my old school."

Keith wasn't sure what to make of Dominic. "How does it work?" He gestured towards the rock.

"Apparently, you stand on it and drop a teleport key and a portal opens up."

"In the rock?"

"I guess."

"Sounds simple enough. Have you tried it?"

"No. I didn't know about it until Fishworth told me yesterday. This is only the second time I've ever been up here."

"Has Fishworth tried it?'

"No."

"Has your great-uncle?"

"No. Fishworth said he was always afraid to."

"Well, when was the last time *anyone* used it?"

Dominic shrugged. "I think it hasn't been used since the family founder, Gerald Putnam the First, came back with all that gold three centuries ago. Everybody since has been afraid to use it."

Clearly the boy was crazy. "Afraid of what?"

"The stories."

"Stories of what?"

"Oh, just dragons, goblins, and evil wizards, the things that can kill you on the other side."

"Well, why don't you let me try it? I could use some gold."

"You wouldn't survive by yourself."

"How do you know? Besides I have some friends I can take along." Keith was making a game of this and was thinking of dragging Woody, TJ, Holly, Danielle, Paula, and Maya into it. Then he remembered they were all too busy to do anything with him anymore. He stepped over and kicked the edge of the rock to find it felt solid enough. Leaning over, he placed a hand and felt its smooth surface and a cool sensation flowed into his hand, and for a moment, he thought he felt the presence of another world, an alien place full of Magical creatures. He blamed it on his hyperactive imagination. "Where are the keys?"

"Great-uncle had one, but I don't know what he did with it. I can't find it anywhere."

"So the teleport rock is useless then?"

"Pretty much."

"You don't talk much do you, Dominic?"

"No."

Keith began to feel that the rumors about Putnam Castle might be true. "I think I better go. Thanks for the cheese."

"If I find the key, we could try it someday. If you want."

Near the front door, Keith encountered Fishworth again, who said, "What did he show you?"

"The teleport rock."

The old man sighed and shook his head. "You must understand that Dominic has an overactive imagination and his parents have overindulged him in everything. Please don't think too unkindly of him despite his wild fancies."

"The rock did look real."

Fishworth gave him an appraising glance as his eyelids raised like shutters on windows. "Do you think it's real?"

Wanting only to get away and backing blindly towards the door, Keith bumped into the jukebox that then began playing a song he'd never heard before. With a backdrop of jaunty country music, a group of male voices began singing in harmony:

I've been hearing you're concerned about my happiness. But all that thought you're giving me is conscience I guess.

Keith realized how surreal this all was. "No, of course not."

Fishworth looked around and then bent to unplug the jukebox so that the music ground to a halt. "Thank you for stopping by. Dominic has no real friends, but he stands to inherit everything when my master passes on." Another sigh and the old manservant shuffled back through the darkened arch.

When Keith got back home he described his visit to Putnam Castle to Woody. Without looking away from his video game, Woody said, "Keith, I think you're spending too much time daydreaming. You can't tell the difference between fantasy and reality anymore."

"The telepoprt rock was real though," Keith said between bites of sandwich. "What if it really worked?" he said but Woody wasn't listening. He put down the controller.

"I gotta go home and study chemistry."

Keith went down to his bedroom and finished his sandwich sitting at his desk with song lyrics running through his head.

I've been hearing you're concerned about my happiness. But all that thought you're giving me is conscience I guess.

Keith searched the internet for the song lyrics, found a video online, and listened. He quickly realized the song he had heard on the Putnam's jukebox was the same song Betty the Bag Lady had been singing. The whole thing felt too creepy to Keith.

3
Let's Teleport

The slats over the window broke up the afternoon sunlight into bars of light and shadow. Keith brushed sandwich crumbs off his desk and reached behind to pull some random book off the shelf. He opened it to a random page and read a scene about dragons fighting each other in the skies over some mythical city. *The Dragons of Kharthula*, a favorite book. But his eyes wandered off the page, focusing on the blue wizard's robe he didn't feel like wearing, and he thought about the Halloween party he didn't feel like going to. He didn't feel like he belonged at that high school, but he wasn't quite sure where he did belong in this world. That's why he liked escaping into his books. It was only in mythical worlds that he felt at home. He put his head down and let his mind daydream. The daydream became a nap, and the bars of light and dark slowly drifted across the book spines while the corner where the blue robe hung deepened into shadow.

When Keith awoke his room was dark. Ignoring his unfinished map of Uzbekistan, he donned his blue robe and went upstairs. His father had already gone to his second job, and his mother was at her book club meeting. Grandma slept in her living room chair while the TV played some old show. He kissed her forehead and walked out onto the porch. Night had fallen and the air was cold enough he could see his breath, but a warm light showed in a window in Putnam Castle. He wondered why he had put on the robe. It was certainly too late to make the school party now. He suddenly realized that his costume was missing a staff, and what is a wizard without his staff? He made do with the best substitute he could find back in the foyer.

Umbrella in hand, he walked across the street and knocked on the door but no one answered. The door opened easily. Save for a light in the butler's pantry and the jukebox, all was dark. He didn't bother calling out but crept through the arch to where Old Man Putnam's door was closed. He rapped softly. "Mr. Putnam? It's Keith from across the street. I'm just checking to see if you're okay." No answer. He opened the door and a foul reek assailed him.

The room was partly lit by the yard light out back coming through the window. The first thing he saw was the empty bed where Old Man Putnam should have been, and then with an icy shock he realized he was not alone. Two humanoid creatures were lurking on the far side of the room. One was crawling out the open window and the other stood waiting its turn. The second one turned and gave a gutteral sound at him. Keith got a quick impression of black skin covered in warts, a long nose, pale scars on its forehead, and red eyes full of menace. It clawed the air, but Keith was already running away as fast as he could. Fearful the creatures would catch and eat him, he tore out the front door and down the path, through the gate and across the street. Pausing in his front yard to look back, he saw no creatures following, and with heart pounding, he entered his own house.

His grandma was still asleep and he shook her shoulder. "Grandma, I saw monsters in the Old Man Putnam's sickroom."

"That's nice, honey," she mumbled and turned her head to the other side.

He called Woody and told him the same thing.

Woody said, "Keith, I'm trying to study Chemistry."

"You don't believe me, do you?"

A pause and a sigh. "What was the last thing you read?"

"*Dragons of Kharthula*."

"In which there are monsters. You're just projecting your fantasies into your real life to compensate for how boring your real life is."

"Dunderfunk! That's ridiculous."

"That's escapism. I know you, Keith."

"Come over here tomorrow and we'll go see. I'll show you monsters. Bring the rest of the gang, too."

"You're organizing a snipe hunt? They won't believe you either."

Keith told him about Betty's gift in the alley.

A pause, then Woody said, "I would like another crack at that game."

"It's not a game piece, Woodmeister. It's real."

"Right, for the *real* teleport rock in Putnam Castle?"

"You didn't go to the party."

"I'm going to medical school instead. You didn't go either."

"Are you coming over or not?"

"We'll see."

As he hung up, Keith realized he had dropped the umbrella inside Putnam Castle. "I gotta go back for it. Tomorrow. Not tonight."

The next morning, Keith was sitting on the porch contemplating Putnam Castle, baseball bat in hand, when his friends pulled up in two cars. They could see he still wore his blue robe as he stood to meet them.

"Guess who didn't come to the party last night?" said Danielle.

"So the party's coming to you," said Holly.

"What's this about monsters, Keith?" TJ asked.

"I told you they wouldn't believe you either," said Woody.

"I believe Keith," said Paula.

"You would. You still think there is a ghost living in your attic," TJ snickered at her.

"I've seen him!"

"Sure, you and no one else."

"You went into Putnam Castle last night?" TJ asked.

"Yes, I'd been there once before, but last night I saw two goblins climbing out a back window where Old Man Putnam used to sleep," said Keith. He described the entire encounter.

"Did Old Man Putnam see them?"

"He wasn't there."

"You're sure they were goblins?" asked Danielle.

"That's what they looked like," said Keith. "Black goblins, smelly, and ugly."

"Goblins are green."

"These were black."

"Black like me?" asked Maya.

"No, blacker, like obsidian."

They all turned and silently contemplated the Castle.

"Did you see any of the Putnams there last night?" Woody asked.

"No."

"Did you see any pools of blood on the floor?" Holly asked.

"No."

They exchanged anxious looks until Woody said in all seriousness, "I don't believe in goblins."

TJ laughed and broke the ice. "Come on, let's go see. It can't hurt to take a look."

TJ led the way, wielding Keith's bat. The seven freshmen crossed the street and went up to the still-open front door of Putnam Castle. Quietly they crept inside, ready to run back outside at any sound or movement. But there was no one home. No Putnams, no goblins. They crept to the bedroom and found it empty.

Everyone relaxed.

"Well, this was waste of time," TJ said, lowering his bat.

"Where'd they all go?" said Danielle.

"Maybe they're all upstairs taking naps?" said Maya.

"Maybe they're all dead," Woody said.

"I got a bad feeling about this. Let's go," said Paula. "We're trespassing."

TJ looked up at the ceiling and then at Keith and asked, "Is that where this so-called teleport thingy is at? Upstairs?"

"Yes, on top of the tallest tower."

"Where else would it be?" Woody mumbled as he found himself at the end of the group climbing the stairs.

On the second floor, they found Dominic playing Joy Division in his bedroom, the door open. "Where is your great-uncle? Keith asked.

"Come on. I'll show you."

They ascended the tower to the teleport rock.

They spread out around it with puzzled looks.

"So this is it?" TJ said. The others were silent, but Woody now gushed in joyous surprise.

"Wow, it looks amazing!" Woody came forward and bent to place both hands palm down on the smooth, cold surface. "It looks real, like the one in the game would look if it were real. You weren't lying, Keith."

"Of course not. Would I lie about something like this?"

Woody shot him a look. "Well, sometimes you exaggerate a little."

"Guys, it's just a rock. A funny, strange rock but still just a rock," said Danielle.

"It's weird," said Maya.

"This whole castle is weird," said Paula.

"It's still just a rock," said Danielle.

"It's not what it *is* but what it *does*," said Keith.

"What does it do?" asked a nervous Holly, standing close to TJ.

"It teleports people from Porterville to a Magical Land of dragons, wizards, elves, and dwarves," he said it as simply as if he were talking about sports or the weather.

There was a pause and then everyone burst out laughing except Keith, Woody, and Dominic.

"Oh, Keith, you act like you're still in junior high," TJ said when he stopped laughing.

"I think I've seen enough," said Danielle as she turned to leave. Most of the others followed, but Dominic, Keith, Woody, and Paula still stood at the rock.

"You want to see my great-uncle?" Dominic said to Keith.

"He's up here?"

"Follow me." They went past the rock to the far side of the tower and peered out between two merlons. Dominic pointed down at a fresh mound of dirt at the back of the Putnam family cemetery. "There he is."

"When did he pass away?"

"Last night. It was sudden. Fishworth and I buried him."

"That was fast."

"It was how great-uncle wanted it."

"Where is Fishworth?"

"He left after the burial. Just handed me great-uncle's will and left in his truck. The castle is mine."

"Did he tell you where the key is?"

"Unfortunately not."

"Maybe he took it with him."

"Maybe, the sneaky bastard."

"I have a key."

Dominic looked sharply at him. "You do?"

"Yes. Betty the Bag Lady gave it to me."

Dominic's look said it all. "Betty gave it to you."

"I say we try it."

"I'm game. Let's teleport into the Magical Land and have an adventure."

"Lets."

"It's better than going back to school. Do you have the key right now?"

Keith dug into his pocket and brought out a small box that he held aloft as he turned and yelled, "Guys, you want to see how the teleport rock works before you go?"

They all stopped and turned back around.

"Keith, we're not kids anymore. If you want to play a kids' game, that's your decision," said TJ.

"Are you chicken?" Keith said.

That got TJ. TJ didn't like his courage being questioned and his face became serious. "All right. We'll do this one time." And he came back to the rock, trailing Holly. "You got two minutes. What do we do?"

Keith looked at Dominic. Dominic said, "Stand on the rock."

TJ without hesitation stepped up and planted his large feet on the teleport rock. After a brief hesitation, Holly joined him. So did Keith, Woody, Dominic, and Paula.

Danielle and Maya were still at the trap door watching all this, but finally they came back and got up on the rock.

"Ok, big guy, you got all of us. Now what?" TJ said. "What's in the box?"

Keith took something out of the box and brandished the small key triumphantly. To the others it looked like he was holding a large, colorful marble that emitted a wisp of smoke. Those closest could catch a scent of something strange but not unpleasant.

"What is that?" TJ said impatiently.

"A teleport key."

"Whatever. Now what?"

"He drops it and activates the teleportal," said Woody. "And if this were real, we'd be Magically transferred to a different world."

"Oh, it's real all right," Keith insisted. He was enjoying the moment, holding all his friends in suspense.

Maya laughed and Danielle rolled her eyes. TJ snorted and made a *please continue* motion with his hand. Holly clasped her hands and closed her eyes as if to pray. Paula and Dominic stood stoically while Woody wore a bemused look.

"Okay, here goes," Keith said.

"If Magic be true," murmured Woody.

"If dragons be real," murmured Paula.

"Shh." Keith wanted to show them something, to get his friends attention and make them admire him. He wanted their validation, even though he didn't really think the rock would work.

He dropped the key, expecting it to bounce and roll along the rock's hard surface. So did everyone. Instead, it hit with a *plop* noise, and with a strange ripple of the surface it disappeared like a stone dropped into a pond. There were gasps and shocked expressions.

"Where did it go?" asked Danielle.

"It disappeared!" said Woody.

"Cool," said Paula with a smile.

They stood waiting in expectation for several seconds but nothing happened.

"That's it?" TJ said. He looked around. "This Magical Land sure looks a lot like Porterville."

"The little marble did disappear though," Holly said.

"So what? Nice Magic trick, Keith," TJ said, "but I gotta go." He turned to leave but found his feet had frozen to the rock. He grunted and tried harder but to no avail. "I can't move!"

Everyone tried but they were all stuck. And then the surface of the rock began rippling. Keith felt himself slowly sinking, as if in quicksand. They were all sinking and began crying out in fear. Instinctively they all took a deep breath and held it as the sinking motion accelerated and they all plunged under. The world turned marine blue and through this medium, Keith could see his friends as nearby ghostly figures flailing around as if they were drowning in some ocean. He turned to reach out to Woody through the thick liquid-like environment, for it felt like he was underwater, but his friend was too far away. Instinctively he tried swimming with his arms, for they had freedom of movement, unlike his feet, but he could not resurface. He felt like he was drowning and started to panic when he noticed light filtering down from above. The liquid became thinner and its blueness lighter in color, his friends more visible.

They all popped up into the air until they were entirely out of whatever blue liquid they had passed through. Keith looked down at himself and others, expecting to see dripping clothes and damp hair, but everyone looked completely dry. He felt his shirt and hair, but they were dry. Then he lifted his eyes and was shocked at what he saw.

4
THE GOLD TOWER

They found with relief that their feet were no longer frozen in place, and turning around they took stock of their situation. They were standing on a teleport rock identical to the one on top of Putnam Castle, but they were no longer in Porterville. That was for sure. The rock sat in a small leveled area cut into a hillside in some large clearing. Downhill they could see a vast forest stretching away as far as the eye could see. In the direction Keith was facing were several barn-like wooden buildings with an attached pen holding pigs. Beyond he could see horses in another pen. Turning behind him, he saw more forest. And to the uphill side was what had taken his breath away.

The hillside climbed a hundred yards from the teleport rock and there at the summit stood a Magic Tower, sunlight gleaming off its golden surface. Like a skyscraper back home, it reached up very high into the cobalt blue sky. The air had a clean country smell, and it was so quiet. No cars, planes, or trains could be heard, as if the modern world had been left behind.

For a moment they stood in shock. Paula was the first to break the silence. "Cool. You did it," she said in a hushed voice to Keith. "You teleported us."

"Yeah, but where?" said Danielle.

"Wow," Woody softly exhaled.

"This cannot be real," said a shocked TJ.

Dominic was the only one who didn't look surprised, but he stayed silent.

They saw no inhabitants. "Where is everybody?" Maya asked.

Holly was shaking her head. "Let's not find out. Take us back home, Keith."

"Can we go back?" asked a doubtful Paula.

"Sure we can. We just need to find that little marble thingy. Wherever it rolled to," said TJ as he began walking bent over and searching. Holly, Danielle, and Maya took their cue and joined him while Keith, Woody, and Paula stood transfixed.

"I don't think it came with us," said Paula.

"I think it's gone. I think it gets used up in the teleport process," said Woody.

Paula said, "Is that right, Keith?"

Keith looked at Dominic.

"Its Magic is used up, and we have to find a new one to get back," said Dominic.

TJ straightened up. "How do you know, Dominic?"

"I know."

"We're all here because of you and Keith."

"You came willingly."

"Stop fighting. Dominic, where do we find a new marble...er, a new key?" said Danielle.

They all looked around like a sack of teleport keys might just be sitting anywhere in the open. They also noticed they weren't alone anymore. A figure appeared in one of the pigpens, herding swine. Then a large group of figures exited the tower and ran downhill towards them.

"There's probably some in that Magic Tower," Dominic said.

"I think we had better get into the trees," said Woody, and they scuttled for cover.

Two tall wizards, one in a gold robe and the other in a black robe, watched a second gold-robed wizard feed a dog-sized gelatinous blob that didn't move so much as it slowly oozed around inside a wide, shallow stone basin. Pieces from what looked like a blue cake of soap were broken off and tossed into the basin one at a time and the blob oozed around absorbing them all, a sparkle of energy cascading throughout its translucent blobiness with each morsel. A fourth wizard, in black robes, stood standing at a large open window. All were older, bearded men.

Their wizardly titles were the Gold Mage and Gold Rook, along with the Black Mage and Black Rook. Their names you will learn later. They all held tall wooden staffs in their hands.

"Marnoch will be here any day now with his precious army." said the Black Mage.

"I know," said the Gold Mage. "Our quest is nearly at hand." They talked in soft voices.

"But why wait? We should try it now, today, before it is too late," said the Black Mage.

"We are not going over this again. We need his soldiers," said the Gold Mage.

"Not if we do it right. They will just be in the way, and then we'll have to share what we find with them."

"Shall I retrieve the vial then?" said the blob feeder, casting the last blue soap piece into the basin.

"No," said the Gold Mage.

"Yes," said the Black Mage.

An uneasy silence reigned. The three wizards watched the blob ooze around in vain for another morsel.

Suddenly the Gold Mage said, looking around, "Do you smell Magic?"

A bright, quick flash of something golden-orange whizzed in the air over their heads, and they ran following it to the window.

"Strangers on the teleport rock!" Pointing, one of them cried out, and they all ran outside.

"Call out the guard!" ordered the Gold Mage after what he saw.

The kids had hidden behind trees and peeking out saw armed men running towards them. Then several horsemen quickly appeared and came on fast. The kids broke and ran deeper into the woods, but the horsemen dodged through the trees to cut them off, and the footmen came up from behind until they were caught in a ring of spears and swords. They were escorted into the tower and made to stand before a table of four seated, robed men, their hoods up.

"And what have we here?" asked the Gold Mage.

No one dared answer.

"Well?" His voice raised a notch, a note of anger creeping in.

"Sir, we are travelers who came here by mistake," said TJ. "We are sorry to trespass."

"We'll be happy to leave," said Holly. The others nodded enthusiastically.

"You're not going anywhere," said the Gold Mage.

The kids stood there nervously, dressed in their anachronistic fashions, blue jeans and khakis, t-shirts and polos. All except Keith, who still wore his blue Halloween costume robe.

The Gold Mage got up and walked over to stand in front of Keith. "You do not look like you belong from around here, and yet you wear the robes of a wizard or priest. What town do you hail from?"

"Porterville, sir."

The wizard took down his hood so Keith could see his dark eyes under bushy eyebrows, and his long drooping nose hanging over thin lips. He leaned over Keith and breathed his bad breath that smelled of pickles and onions.

"I have never heard of that town. Which kingdom is it?"

Keith hesitated, confused. He did not want to admit he was from another world. So instead of saying the Midwest or the United States, he said the next word that came to mind. "I come from the Kingdom of Uzbekistan."

"Ooze-bek-uh-stan." The Gold Mage repeated the strange word. "And where in the Known World is this Kingdom?" The wizard's eyes narrowed in suspiscion. "Your accent is neither Pandooni nor Arcadian. It is as if you come from across the sea."

"That's right, sir. We did." Keith thought it best to agree.

"The Never Sea, I suppose?"

"Yes, sir." Keith was happy to have his lie supplied to him.

The wizard straightened up and crossed his arms. "How interesting. How interesting indeed." He returned to his seat. "Are you all from the lands on the other side of the Never Sea?"

"Yes, sir," the kids said in unison.

"I see." He stroked his beard and regarded them some more before sending them away.

After the kids were gone, the wizards unhooded. In deep concern, they talked rapidly.

"They are spies," the Black Mage flatly declared. He had a triangular face and a goatee hanging off his pointed chin.

"Possibly," the Gold Mage said, stroking his own, much fuller beard.

I'd say there is no doubt," said the Black Rook, a pale-faced man with cold eyes.

The Gold Rook turned his florid face to his counterpart from the Black Tower."But sent by who?" he asked.

"The Bloody Hoods most likely," said the Black Rook.

"What are those of the Red Tower after?"

"Perhaps the elves sent them?" said the Gold Rook. "They hate us."

"They don't care enough to hate us. They wouldn't come near enough to be able to spy on us," said the Black Rook.

"Oh, the forests of Alfheim are full of elvish eyes and some are turned our way, but the elves wouldn't use human spies," said the Gold Mage.

"They are young for spies," said the Black Mage. "The two girls with flamboyant hair could be witches."

"I agree. The one with the color of dragonfire and the other the color of gold, clearly witches. We must keep them out of the tower," said the Gold Rook.

"We will," said the Gold Mage.

"Shall we burn them at the stake?" asked the Gold Rook.

"That will draw too much attention at this delicate stage in our plans," said the Gold Mage. "We do not need such extreme measures. Rather we will sell them to the Slave-King instead. Young and healthy slaves will fetch a good price in Z Town."

"The one in blue is a wizard," said the Black Rook.

"An apprentice wizard perhaps," answered the Black Mage.

"But what is the meaning of his strange robes?" asked the Gold Rook. "Could he be instead a priest of some cult beyond the Sea?"

"He is a wizard who teleported them all in," said the Gold Mage. "We all saw the Guffin and smelled the Magic."

"A blue robe means he is then a wizard of the Blue Tower," said the Gold Rook.

"But there is no Blue Tower," said the Black Rook.

"Perhaps it is there in Ooze-bek-uh-stan," said the Gold Rook.

"Legend has it that there once was a Blue Tower, many centuries ago," said the Gold Mage. "Some still search for its ruins."

"And Akasha is its totem dragon," said the Gold Rook, nodding his agreement. "She is listed among the Sporu Dragons."

"We do not believe these myths," said the Black Mage. "No one has ever found this Blue Tower. Perhaps the Blue Tower lies across the sea after all, but who cares?"

"Perhaps, but what if you meet Akasha inside Sporu Angosta?" the Gold Mage asked.

"Hmmph. I am more worried about what this might mean for our own plans. It is quite the coincidence to have young wizards and spies teleporting in on your teleport rock right before we are to begin our special quest," said the Black Mage.

"Nothing has changed. You are just overreacting," said the Gold Mage.

"Am I?"

"The Quest is still on."

"But what will the good King think of your visitors? He could be coming up the hill from Z-town with his precious Dragon Guards even as we speak."

"You let me worry about the King. He won't even know about these young trespassers. I am not worried about any of them, except perhaps the one in blue robes. He had an aura...." The Gold Mage's thoughts trailed off.

The kids were placed in a small wooden building behind the pig sty. Looking around in the gloom, they perceived a single room with no furniture. A small high window covered in dust and cobwebs let in little light.

"Well, this is turning into a real fun adventure," said Holly as she sat on the straw-covered floor.

"What do we do now?" asked Maya.

"It's cold in here," said Paula.

"You're always cold," said TJ.

Keith jiggled the door latch. "Locked."

TJ grabbed the latch and shook it violently, but it held.

"Probably a guard out there anyways," said Woody.

Keith looked up at the window. "If I were a wizard I would fly up there and smash the glass, then drop a rock or cinder block to knock out the guard."

"Except you can't fly, and there's no rocks or cinder blocks in this room," said Woody.

"Too bad you're not Spiderman. Then you could just shoot up a web strand and climb up that," said Paula.

"This ain't a comic book we're in, Paula," Woody said.

"Is there any other way out?" asked Danielle.

They searched the walls for holes or gaps but found none.

TJ went over to Keith. "That marble key-thing that got us here, you only had one?" he asked.

"Betty only gave me one."

"And we need another one to get back home?"

"Yes."

"You brought us here with no way to get back." It was not a question.

"I didn't think it would work."

TJ doubled up his fist and Keith cringed, but Holly stepped in and begged her boyfriend not to fight. TJ took to pacing in front of the door.

"Does anybody feel different?" Danielle asked.

"Yes, I feel older," said Paula.

"You look older," said Holly. She looked around. "You all do."

Everyone looked at everyone.

"We all look like we're four or five years older," said Danielle.

"I felt something when we came out of that blue water, but everything happened so fast," said Maya.

"It's like we're no longer high school freshmen, but college freshmen," said Woody.

Everyone nodded in agreement.

"The teleportal changed us as we went through?" Keith asked Dominic.

"I think so," Dominic said.

They were brought food and water and then left alone to spend a sleepless night lying on the straw. The guards came in the morning to march them out into the blinding sunlight. Blinking, trembling in fear, looking disheveled with straw in their hair, the kids were a sorry sight.

They were lined up and surrounded by guards in front of the tower. A slight stoop-shouldered man sat before a small wooden table upon which was placed a large, closed book, an ink pot, and a quill pen. The man wore plain gray robes and wire-rim spectacles. Next to him stood a short, barrel-chested and powerful-looking man with whiskers and piercing eyes. He wore a sword and a white tabard bearing the gold tower sigil, and his bare arms were knotted with muscles and covered in tattoos. He spoke in a loud voice:

"My name is Lancemaster Phineas, and I am in charge of security at the Gold Tower. I serve the Gold Mage. And now so will all of you. You no doubt have strange and vile names which are unacceptable. Therefore you shall be given a tower name by the Tower Clerk Dulcinata." They were forced to line up.

First came TJ. He was made to speak and spell his name and place of birth. Dulcinata looked up at the huge young man blocking out the sun. "Trailhog," was the name he bestowed.

TJ misheard him. "Trailhawk?" he suggested hopefully.

"Trailhog!" It was the Lancemaster who answered, jabbing two meaty fingers into Trailhog's chest for emphasis.

Trailhog grew angry. "Trailhog! That is a stupid name!" He tried to flip Dulcinata's table but four guards wrestled him away.

Dulcinata gave a dignified harumph as he enter the name in his register, and with a scratching of the quill pen, TJ Estes of the Kingdom of France became Trailhog, slave of the Gold Tower.

And then:

Holly Hudson of the Kingdom of Australia became Holly Hawk.

Danielle of the Kingdom of Egypt became Dahlia Truelove.

Maya Knight of the Kingdom of Canada became Misha Night.

Paula Fletcher of the Kingdom of Japan was now Pyra Flamestar.

Dominic Putnam of the Kingdom of China was now Domingo.

When Woody spoke his name the guards laughed. Dulcinata did not bother looking for a tower name in his book. Woody Brunswick of the Kingdom of Brazil was dubbed Kerwood Dunwood. The guards found this strangely amusing.

Keith's turn was last.

"Say and spell your old name."

"Keith Brenner. K-E-I-T-H."

Dulcinata flipped through his book. "Your Tower Name is now Kido, spelled K-I-D-O, Kido Bremen in full."

"The way you spell it, it sounds like Kid-do."

Phineas stepped forward until Keith gagged at the man's bad breath. "No, it's Kee-do, pronounced like Gree-do."

"Greedo?"

"Yes, Greedo. Only you're Kido. This ain't Mos Eisley, kid."

"But—"

Phineas nodded at a soldier who used his spear butt to move Kido along.

And thus Keith Brenner of the Kingdom of Uzbekistan was now Kido Bremen. They all had new names, and their old identities were stripped away in the process. Kido was forced to surrender his blue robes. They all were forced to undress and put on homespun breeches and tunics for the boys, dresses for the girls. Their clothes looked used though laundered, all in drab shades of gray and brown.

Escorted to the blacksmithy on the far side of the stables, they were horrified to find themselves fitted with iron collars around their necks. Trailhog fought hard and it took four guards to hold him down until an extra-large collar could be snapped and welded shut.

"Don't hurt him!" Holly yelled.

In shock and humiliation, they were again addressed by the Lancemaster after having marched back before the tower.

"Having been found trespassing on tower property, and obviously not being lawful citizens of either the Kingdom of Pandoon or the Kingdom of Arcadia, you are hereby declared property of the Gold Tower, subject to the authority of the Gold Mage and the Order of Wizards, for the period of twenty years or until said Mage releases you, whichever comes first."

"Twenty years!" sputtered Trailhog, and the rest cried out too.

"Silence!"

Several wizards in both gold and black robes came out of the tower to observe them, the Gold and Black Mages marked by their staffs. One of the gold wizards was much shorter than the others. Kido observed more wizards watching from a balcony high up on the tower. The wizards stood in silent contemplation while the kids chaffed under such scrutiny. The Gold Mage and the short figure exchanged whispers and there was some pointing. More whispers between the Gold Mage and the Lancemaster indicated some decision had been reached.

And then the guards prodded everyone with spears back towards the pig barn except Kido, Domingo, and Woody. They were forced to go to the tower. The kids cried out at being separated but to no avail. Kido turned for one last look at his friends before the tower swallowed him up.

5
THE RUINATION

Once inside the Gold Tower, Kido, Woody, and Domingo found themselves servants in a special world where time no longer mattered. The days blurred together and only by counting sunrises could they have any sense of moving forward. Their days were spent doing menial chores. Woody usually worked in the kitchen and Domingo in the laundry. Kido was a personal slave to the short wizard they had seen outside. When unhooded, the wizard turned out to be a black-haired teenager with a round face who looked a few years younger than Kido. He spoke in a flat monotone.

"I am your new master and my name is Orthus," he told Kido that first day. "I am training to be a wizard, and one day I shall succeed my father as the Gold Mage. You will do as I say. If you are disobedient, I will have you beaten. If you try to run away, I will have you beaten. If you steal from me, I will have you hung. Also, do not go anywhere near the gates of Sporu Angosta. If you do, I will sell you to the Slave King in Z Town. In fact, you shouldn't even touch the gates for they have a Magical power that would turn you into a slug. Do you understand all this?"

"Yes, but where are all my friends?"

"A simple yes or no answer was all that was required. You are not allowed to ask me a question without my approval, but just this once I will not have you beaten since you are more ignorant than impudent. Your friends are agricultural workers for the tower, though very soon they will be taken to the slave market in Z Town, and then they will be scattered all over Pandoon, for the need for slave labor is great. Take my advice and forget about them. Remember, you are my property now. First thing I want you to do is clean my bathroom. Scrub it thoroughly. I will be back to inspect it in an hour. If you displease me, I will have you beaten." Orthus had a dry and dull personality, but Kido hoped he was not cruel. Kido decided to do as he was told and avoid any beatings.

And so it went, days filled with menial labor. But Kido kept his eyes and ears open for any opportunity. He hoped to learn Magic somehow. This was after all a Magic Tower. Somehow he had to find a teleport key, free his friends, and get them all back home. It seemed about a month after his arrival that he had his first chance when special visitors arrived at the tower. From the talk he overheard, Kido learned that the king of the next door kingdom was here after a long journey.

On that day, Kido was bringing laundered clothes to his master's room. The guard let him pass like any other day. In the outer sitting room, the open shutters let in bright sunlight to reveal a room that was richly decorated: marble floors, fine taspetries, and ornate furniture. Kido bet that centuries of great wealth had built this Gold Tower.

The door to the inner bedroom was on the far side of the room, but Kido lingered, his attention drawn to something besides clothes. Over on the large desk of polished swaple wood, he could see a big book lying open. He crept over to have a look. Orthus, he knew, was outside with his father and their distinguished visitors. Kido was all alone, safe to snoop.

The book was thick, with gilded edges and heavy pages of the finest paper, lined with black-inked hand-written lines of Magic. This was the spellbook of Orthus. Kido leaned over to read, flipping pages but keeping the open spot marked with one hand. Kido had only been living here for a short time, but he had heard that a stranger could not open a wizard's closed spellbook. But Orthus was a careless boy who often left his open. Stopping on one page, Kido read an intriguing spell, silently mouthing the words and feeling something stir inside of him. He pretended he was a wizard. He knew a wizard's pride and joy was his spellbook. Kido wished he had his own. And then he saw his reflection in a mirror mounted on the wall. He saw a young man with brown hair and earnest brown eyes. But it was the iron collar around his neck that drew his attention. It was no ordinary collar of a common slave but one stamped with the icon of a tower painted bright yellow, marking him out as a slave of the Gold Tower. The cruel reminder of his servitude made him doubt if he could be a wizard in this strange world.

With a sigh, he abandoned the spellbook. Just then Orthus unexpectedly burst in and took his sword and another book lying on his bed which Kido hadn't noticed. "The wizards are fighting a giant! You must come see, Kido."

Kido followed Orthus out onto a south-facing balcony high up on the Gold Tower and under a beautiful cobalt blue sky. Woody and Domingo were already there. Below them, wizards and soldiers surrounded a hundred-foot tall giant.

"Where did the giant come from?" Kido asked.

"From the Magical land of Sporu Angosta," said Orthus. But the fight seemed over. The giant was lying motionless on its back. Orthus still held the sword and the unknown book, as if he had intended to help with the fight.

"Can we go down and see the giant, master?" Kido asked Orthus eagerly.

"No, a quick look is enough for you slaves. You should be happy I gave you that. Now there is work for you to do."

"I still need to put away your clothes."

Orthus said, "Do that later. First I want you three to tidy up the Wizard's Study."

"Us? Now?"

"Yes. You three. Now."

"We're not allowed in the Wizard's Study, master," said Woody.

"I give you permission. Besides, there is such a mess and all of father's wizards are busy."

"But we want to see the giant up close."

Orthus handed a surprised Woody the unknown book. "Too bad. You're my slaves and must do as I say. Now get. I'm going down to look at the giant by myself. And don't open that book or it will turn you into slugs." Reluctantly the three boys turned away and went inside. They went up two stairways and down deserted hallways.

"I can't believe we're allowed inside the study," Woody said.

"I'd rather go see the giant," said Kido as he opened the heavy wooden doors into the Magical inner sanctum.

"I'd rather get rid of this book. It's heavy."

The study they were in had a very long swaple table running down the center of the room with book cases on both sides and a large window at the far end, where it faced north. The only thing to see in that direction was a thicket of aspen and swaple trees and the tall cliffs and mountain peaks of Meb beyond. The table was littered with papers, tomes, half-burned candles, and ashtrays full of cigar butts and ashes. Burning candles illuminated it all. The room was stuffy and Woody opened up the window to let in fresh air.

Kido pulled out one of the over-sized chairs and sat in it, prop-ping up his head in his hands and staring glumly at the books opposite. "How are we going to figure out what spellbooks will help us get back home?"

"I think we need to run away from this tower, get off these iron collars, and find the others." Woody grabbed his iron collar and pointed at Kido's.

"We need to find the others before they're sold as slaves," said Domingo.

"If they're still here. In the meantime, help me put these books away."

Kido sighed one last time and got up. Grabbing a book from the table he looked for an open slot on the bookshelves and slid the book in. He was going to grab another book when he got an idea. Standing with arms crossed, he closed his eyes, visualized levitating books, and spoke the spell words he had learned from his master's spellbook. He felt a funny, wonderful feeling. Opening his eyes, he saw a book gliding through the air without any help. He guided it onto a shelf, although it took several tries to line it up. Sitting down, he lazily levitated books with a casual wave of a finger while a surprised Domingo watched with mouth agape. Soon there were none left to reshelve on their side. Woody by contrast had many left. Then Kido noticed how tall the shelves were and wondered what was in all those books. Craning his neck back, he saw the top shelf was mostly empty, just a few books. He could see it was darker away from the window. Walking deeper into the study, he saw one big book sitting by itself in the far corner on the topmost shelf. He saw that Woody was too busy reshelving books to notice, and Domingo was occupied searching a cabinet for teleport keys.

Now any other kid would leave an unknown book alone, especially a book in the Wizard's Study in the Gold Tower. But Kido loved to read and being a slave boy, he was denied reading. He was willing to sneak a peek and read surreptitiously. And here was a chance to read a giant book of Magic. He levitated it down. It was so big and so heavy that he had trouble and nearly lost his concentration on the spell. He got a strange feeling from it as it landed with a loud thud on the table.

"Kido, you're supposed to be putting them away, not taking them out," Woody said. "You're going to get us in trouble." Woody came over and took the book into his arms.

Kido said, "Too bad we can't open it and see what it says."

"Read a book of Magic? We can't!"

"I know. Only the wizard who owns it can open it."

Woody shook his head. "I mean we shouldn't. Do you know what they'll do to us if we're caught? Remember, we're only slaves."

"No one is here to catch us. They're all out with the giant."

"They can have the giant."

Kido would not be put off. "Let me just take a peek."

"Why?" Woody eyed him suspiciously and clutched the book to his chest.

"C'mon, Woodmeister. Let me have it."

Woody began backing away, clutching the book to his chest, his lips trembling. "I dunno. You think there might be something in here that could help us get back home?"

Kido crept after him, his arms outstretched "I bet there is. Let me try."

"I dunno." Woody took another step and fell as his foot slipped. The spellbook fell with another loud thud.

Kido laughed. "You clumsy boy. You should be more careful with spellbooks, Woody. Let's just read what's inside."

Fear replaced the awe in Woody's eyes. "Read it! Are you crazy?"

Kido looked at the large spellbook still lying on the floor. "I am going to open it up."

"You are crazy."

"Well?"

"Wait. I thought it was impossible to open another wizard's spellbook," said Domingo.

"Is it impossible or just dangerous?" asked Woody.

"Maybe both," said Domingo

"Maybe that's a lie meant to scare us," said Kido.

"We'll learn what it's like to turn into slugs if you open it." Woody bit his lip and rolled his eyes, which he always did when thinking. He groaned, then sighed. "I know when you get like this nothing I can say will stop you anyways, even though I'm sure to regret this. But hurry up and remember, if anything happens, it's your fault."

"Sure, Woodmeister."

They went over and knelt on the floor before the spellbook. The thing was huge, seveal inches thick, bound in some strange animal hide."

"What animal has skin that color? It's—"

"—butterscotch. We'll call it the Butterscotch Book!" Kido said.

"Why butterscotch?"

"The hide's color reminds me of the color of butterscotch pudding."

"Just hurry up with whatever you're going to do."

"I wonder if it can tell us how to make teleport keys."

Woody was having second thoughts. "Why don't you just open a few pages and read 'em like you said before, and then let's put it away quick and finish up and get out of here. I'm getting nervous." Woody was always nervous about something.

Kido tried lifting the heavy cover. "It won't budge. Just like I figured."

Then the hide parted and a large amber eye opened suddenly in the front cover to glare at them.

"It's alive!" They gasped and backed off. "Whoa!"

"Let's leave it alone," said Woody.

"We can't leave it lying on the floor," said Kido.

"I'm not touching it."

Kido said, "Maybe we can talk to it."

"You can't mean that."

"Yes. It's alive. It'll report us to its owner now. We're already in trouble so let's take a chance."

"Kido, I'm a scared kid who has no interest in Magic, and you shouldn't either. Let's just reshelve the rest of the books and get out of here."

"Magic is what is going to get us home. You don't believe I can do Magic?"

"Of course not. You're just a kid from Porterville like me. Where would you learn it?"

"Orthus always leaves his spellbook open. I memorized a spell from it."

"How can you read Magic?"

"It was in the MotherTongue."

"How can you read their language?"

"I taught myself to read it."

"Me too. I've learned enough to read at the high school level already," said Domingo.

Woody groaned. "What was the spell?"

"*Levitate*."

Woody stared at Kido. "Dunderfunk. Orthus will have Phineas spear you if he catches you reading his spellbook. And just reading a spell doesn't mean you can do Magic."

"I've already done it. I've levitated several things. I can do Magic."

"I saw him levitate books just now," said Domingo while he still searched for keys.

"Ha! Prove it."

"Stand still." Kido backed up several steps and closed his eyes.

Woody crossed his arms and eyed his friend with skepticism. "Kido, we're wasting time—"

"Sssh." Kido raised his arms and murmured something.

Woody opened his mouth to complain and suddenly felt his body lift off the floor. Too shocked to speak, he watched Kido and the bookshelves fall below him. Looking up he could see the ceiling getting closer.

"Kido, umm, stop please."

Kido wiggled a finger and Woody stopped to hover in mid-air, twenty feet off the floor. "Kido, please put me down."

"I can levitate myself too. Watch." Kido said nothing and made no gesture, yet he slowly rose until he was floating next to Woody. He crossed his legs and sat on a cushion of air looking smug.

Woody gasped. "But how? You're just a kid from Porterville."

"It's fun to do Magic." The two bobbed a little, as if riding a gentle air current.

"Kido, you've been made a slave like me. They won't let you learn Magic. This is bad. You'll just end up in big trouble and me with you if we're caught. I don't see how any of this is going to help us get back home to Porterville."

Domingo turned around after failing to find any keys and saw his two friends floating high up near the ceiling. He walked over beneath them. "You actually did it."

"It's easy." said Kido.

"Can you levitate me?"

"Sure. Hold still." Kido said several strange words and pointed a finger at Domingo. Now all three floated together in the air.

"See? Magic is what we can use to do all that. This is a Magical world we're stuck in. I'm going to read every spell I can from Orthus's spellbook. I've been sneaking books out of the library and teaching myself to read at night. I want to learn elvish too. I have to figure out how to become a wizard and stop being a slave."

Woody shook his head. "How long is that going to take? I've already missed a chemistry test back home."

"I don't know," Kido admitted.

"Don't forget that we have to find everyone else too."

"Hopefully they're all in Z Town still. They say that's close by."

"They could be anywhere."

They heard a voice calling from beyond the closed study door.

"Orthus!" Woody whispered in fear. "He can't see us like this."

"Follow me," whispered Kido.

"What?"

Quickly Woody and Domingo felt themselves pulled out the window like kites driven by a strong wind.

Orthus burst in and looked around. "Kido? Woody? Domingo? Where are those lazy slaves?" He looked under the table and went to peek out the window. "I bet they went outside to see the giant after all." Shaking his head, Orthus left.

Hovering outside the tower and above the window, Kido, Domingo, and Woody waited. "Good thing he didn't look up," whispered Kido.

"Now he knows we left the study and didn't finish the job."

"So, since we are already in trouble, let's make it worthwhile. Let's visit the gates to see if we can get inside."

Woody deadpanned, "Going to the Gates, the Gates of Sporu Angosta. That's your next suggestion."

"You do sarcasm very well for a slave boy."

"Put us back in the study so we can take our lumps."

Gently floating side-by-side, Kido leaned over and whispered to Woody, "To the gates first."

"Maybe the gates will be open and we can find keys inside," said Domingo.

Woody groaned as they floated to the ground, and he followed his friends around the tower until they came to a huge opening at its base where it faced towards the gates. The hole was at least a hundred feet wide and a hundred feet tall. The ground in front of it was smooth dirt where no grass grew. They peered inside and saw a cavernous chamber full of dark shadows.

"What is this place for? It's big enough for a truck or RV. Several trucks in fact," said Woody.

"I don't think these people have discovered the internal combustion engine, yet," said Kido. "In all the time we've been here I haven't seen or heard a single car, truck, plane, or train. Have you?"

"No, this world is very quiet. Everyone rides horses or walks. They don't even have bikes."

"Yeah, they're still waiting for the Industrial Revolution. Let's go."

With one last look at the hole, they tramped away from the tower and through the trees under that cobalt sky, where some clouds were rolling in.

Orthus rushed through the tower's main door, but the three slaves were not out there. Instead he watched as soldiers tied the lifeless giant to a huge wheeled flatbed with thick ropes. The giant wore blue pants and red suspenders over a naked muscular torso pierced with dozens of arrows, scarred by spear thrusts, and blackened by Magic burn marks. Its long blonde hair flowed off the front end of the flatbed and its bare feet hung off the back. The thing was so huge that only powerful Magic had gotten it loaded in the first place. One eye was closed but the other one Orthus could see was turquoise as it stared sightlessly at the clouds. A bulbous nose the size of a cow pointed skyward. The giant was dead, but everyone tiptoed around it as if it were only sleeping and might be woken at any moment. Dozens of Arcadian soldiers milled about, including some of King Marnoch's elite Dragon Guards.

Nearby Orthus saw Prince Cromartin looking not at the giant but at the Gold Tower. Beyond the Prince of Arcadia and down the hill, wizards of two different Magic Towers were grouped in a circle around a large but short rock platform set in the ground. The rock was only half a foot tall but very wide, its flat top all shiny black and polished. The wizards called it a teleport rock and believed it could be a portal into Sporu Angosta. Eighteen Black Hoods stood there and twenty Gold Hoods stood opposite them, including his father the Gold Mage, Ramanapirus, he whose name cannot be shortened. They were getting ready to cast a spell. But where were the slaves? He cast a *Search* spell and suddenly knew. With a mixture of fear and excitement, he ran past the tower. "Come with me," he ordered Lancemaster Phineas and two soldiers, "and bring collar hooks."

Prince Cromartin happened to see Orthus leave as he surveyed the scene. He watched the boy run past the tall, cylindrical tower that shimmered with a golden color, the most magnificent color he had ever seen. Cromartin had always loved gold, and he longed to walk over and touch those gold bricks. If he could pull down that tower, load up all those golden bricks and take them home to smelter down, he would be rich beyond his wildest dreams. But he knew the tower was well protected. Its Magic shield would stop him cold before he ever got close. With a sigh he turned away. A short distance beyond the tower, rising above a line of trees, stood tall cliffs that ran along the horizon, and he stood in silent contemplation. He wanted to go there worse than he wanted to see the tower. To the west, forested slopes led down to Z Town while more forests blocked the view south towards elvish lands.

Turning back, Cromartin realized he and the giant had the same color of hair. He indicated the giant's long locks to the soldiers. "Hack off that hair so it doesn't get caught in the wheels. Eh, boys?"

More soldiers were hitching a team of forty rupas to a harness to pull the flatbed.

White-haired King Marnoch came over to his son. "Take a company of men and escort the giant back to Ballastro. That giant is a trophy I want to show to my people. Everyone in Arcadia should see what we're doing here in Pandoon."

"I want to go inside Sporu Angosta with you, father," Cromartin said eagerly. "Let McGee take the giant back. I should be by your side."

"I won't risk my oldest son and true heir inside those gates. No, Cromartin. You will return to my capital. It was a mistake to bring you this far and risk your life. If the dragons are unleashed, I want you far away from here. My will is safeguarded in the castle. Should anything happen to me, then you will be King, and I expect you to avenge my death. You *will* leave for home this day."

"I deserve the gold too. Father, please let me go in!" the prince whispered, a certain desperation creeping into his words.

"No. I'll have you tied to a wagon and carted home like a slave if I have to."

Cromartin knew he couldn't press his luck any further. He pulled himself up, bowed, and manfully submitted. "Yes, father my King."

Both had longswords strapped to their waists, but Marnoch wore a beautiful purple doublet of rich material and a purple robe trimmed with ermine fur. A heavy gold pendant hung around his neck. Cromartin wore a purple silk blouse and a cloth-of-gold vest, and he wore no pendant but plenty of gold rings on his fingers.

"I think it wise not to trust the wizards, father," said Cromartin.

"What choice do we have? We need their Magic to get inside. I'll have them dispatched once they are no longer useful."

Cromartin was confused. "Is it possible to kill a wizard?"

Marnoch looked sternly at his son. "Of course. They'll be far away from the protection of their tower, tired and distracted. And we outnumber them." Marnoch walked over to Ramanapirus. "I am ready and waiting, Gold Mage. My son is leaving for Ballastro."

Ramanapirus was younger than the king but his face was lined with concern. "We are at a delicate part of the spell. Soon we will finish casting it and open the vortex. Stay back until I signal you."

"My soldiers and I will be ready."

"See that you are." Ramanapirus rejoined the other wizards. Blocking out all distractions, he reconnected his mind with the others. It would take a group effort of all these talented wizards to cast the spell and (hopefully) open the teleportal to Sporu Angosta. Things had already gone awry when somehow the giant had appeared from somewhere. After the difficult fight to kill the giant, some had suggested they delay the teleportal spell and figure out what had gone wrong before it got worse. And the two top Black Hood wizards had disappeared in the confusion but would surely return any minute, knowing how crucial their presence was at this delicate time in the spell casting. Ramanapirus was convinced it was now or never. They had come too far and stopping the Magic now was too dangerous. So they stood like statues now as the energy flowed between them. An oily ripple ran along the rock's surface, breaking its solid appearance, an effect more felt than seen by the wizards. Each wizard had his part to play. Each phrase must be exact. Each wizard's energy must be properly placed on the rock to turn it to their use. But where was the Black Mage and the Black Rook? He counted the dark figures again to find only eighteen Black Hoods. What was going on? They should have been back by now and without them the spell was weakening. They struggled for several more minutes but the missing wizards never came back. Focused as he was on his own energy, Ramanapirus felt the connection with with the thirty-seven other wizards breaking down. Their collective energy began dropping; the rock stopped rippling. They were losing control and he thought he sensed dragons in motion just inside the Gates. Ramanapirus felt his heart dropping off a cliff.

"This is a bad time to go to the gates," said Woody. They had stopped in a stand of pine trees where they could turn and still see the Gold Tower.

"It's the only time, our only chance," said Kido. "I bet we can find teleport keys inside there."

"Aren't there dragons inside there?"

"I can't remember what the game said."

"Kido, we're not playing the game anymore. I've heard people in the tower talk about that place. No one who ever goes in there comes back out."

"That sounds like something made up to scare people."

"It's scaring me pretty good."

"We're better off going inside the gates anyways," said Domingo. "We can't stay in the tower now."

"Don't say it," said Woody.

"We've passed the point of no return," said Domingo.

"I knew you were going to say that," said Woody. He turned to Kido. "How can we get back in the tower?"

Kido dug an egg-shaped crystal out of his pocket and held it up.

"What's that?" asked Woody.

"A *Hope Crystal*. It lets us pass through the tower's enchantment shield if we need to get back inside."

"Where'd you get that?"

"Orthus has a way of carelessly leaving things lying around."

"You stole it."

"I borrowed it."

"What difference does it make now?" asked Domingo.

"C'mon, you guys," said Kido.

The path left the pine trees and led along a ravine edge and then down a stone staircase cut into the steep slope, across a deep gully and back up another stone staircase to where the land flattened out. A narrow band of swaple trees stood before them and just beyond it the gates of Sporu Angosta could be seen, set in a towering rock cliff that ran forever to their left and right. Kido walked with excitement, eyes forward, when a figure appeared from out of nowhere. He was a tall, middle-aged man dressed in the most ludicrous outfit. His white trousers and shirt were decorated with a harlequin design of large diamond patches in bright colors: turquoise, purple, red, orange, yellow, and green. His shirt had a ruffled collar. His shoes and skullcap were a dazzling white. His face was unpainted except for a black tear tattooed under his right eye. He had a deck of cards in one hand, and he deftly flipped the top card up in the air, caught it with his other hand, and handed it to Kido with a flourish. The man smiled, saluted, and melted back into the trees.

"Who was that?" asked Woody as he and Domingo came up.

"I don't know, but he gave me this." Kido held up the card and they saw a three-dimensional holographic image of a red bird feather.

"I don't get it."

"Me neither, but let's hurry to the gates. We're running out of time." Kido tucked the card into his pocket. The path took them into the trees and ran through a swath of red-leafed shrubs right up to the gates.

The Magical, mystical gates of Sporu Angosta. Inside was supposed to be a fantastic land of dragons and a huge castle full of gold and jewels. Giants were said to be in there, too. The attacking giant probably had come from there. They found the doors were closed and a blue shimmering curtain of energy protected them. The energy hummed and Kido almost thought he heard a soft chanting voice as he waded through thigh-high shrubs. They craned their necks to look up but the tops of the wooden doors were out of sight in the clouds. Walking while looking up, the boys did not see the two kneeling figures until they tripped over them. Lying on the ground Kido saw they were dressed in black robes, their faces hidden in their hoods.

One of the wizards sputtered and shook his fist at them. "You fools! What are you doing here?" Kido saw his smooth white forearm covered in a dragon tattoo that circled up towards the elbow.

The other wizard cried out, "Wait. It is working!" He held aloft in his right hand a cylindrical vial.

The two huge doors swung slowly open and a warm golden-red light poured out like the hot breath of a dragon, silhouetting the towering figure of a giant with his hands on his hips. The giant looked just like the dead one lying on the flatbed except that his suspenders were green. He boomed in a loud voice, "Who dares disturb the peace of my home?" and reaching down he scooped up a hollering Black wizard in each hand and pulled them inside in an instant. The doors began shutting as if of their own accord but not before something tumbled out of the one wizard's hand to land at Kido's feet. He picked it up to see a cylindrical vial, the bottom half metal and the glass top half stoppered up with cork. Inside it a golden liquid glowed through the glass, as if some energy within was trying to get out. Strange runes were raised in the metal and Kido ran his fingers over them. The gates slammed shut with a loud boom and the ground shook. The boys had stood in fear but the boom released them.

"Let's get out of here," Woody said, turning to go. Kido grabbed him.

"No, let's check out those gates first."

"What?!"

With Woody and Domingo following, Kido crept closer. Behind the blue energy curtain the gates looked to be made of ordinary dark wood. On the left-hand door were carved runes and pulling out the vial, he confirmed that the runes were similar. He cocked his head and heard a low hum. His curiosity burned hotter as he got closer. Now he wanted so badly to touch the doors. He wanted to open them and see inside. In his feverish mind it did not matter that he was so small and the doors looked so impossibly heavy.

He stopped when his nose almost contacted the blue energy over the dark wood of the right-hand door. A huge gold pull ring hung right above his head. He paused and listened, hearing only his heart beat.

Woody said, "Kido, don't—"

He took a deep breath and slowly extended his left hand, palm out. It passed easily through the blue energy until it touched the smooth warmness of the wood below the pull ring. He waited. Nothing happened. A keen disappointment welled up inside him. Why did Orthus warn—

A searing vision erupted in his mind. He saw a vivid turquoise sky without clouds, yellow sand dunes, and large stone structures of various colors. He heard creatures murmuring and growling. A strange acrid taste made his mouth salivate while a strong alien smell rankled his nose. In a panic he tried to pull his hand away, but an unseen force held it firmly in place. His legs trembled and he felt the urge to cry, but he could neither move nor speak.

"Kido, what's wrong?" Woody anxiously wrung his hands.

Woody's voice came to him as though through a long tunnel. Something hot and evil crept inside of him, and Kido felt as if he were being consumed from within. But then the feeling moderated and he felt the heat within him cool down, though his hand remained bonded to the door. An alien presence crept inside his head.

P: I sense you open the gates and come inside

A deep, masculine voice commanded, a voice old as the mountains, fierce in its authority. The statements came in one string from some mind into his, and Kido felt an overwhelming urge to obey. His free hand reached up for the pull ring.

P: Leave him alone

A soft feminine voice countered, floating in Kido's mind and quelling the urge to enter. The voices argued briefly.

P: He is mine he is a dragon

P: A dragon outside the gates? That is not possible

P: I can sense him

P: There is something of a dragon outside the gates but it is confusing something is wrong i smell humans too

The male voice growled and hissed, then went away. Kido's fear left him and he released the breath he had been holding.

P: Can you hear me?

The female voice asked gently.

Kido stood trembling, his hand still frozen to the door, his mind overwhelmed by a mixture of fear and curiosity. He tried to speak but couldn't. What was happening to him?

"Kido!"

He heard the voice of Orthus calling from the direction of the tower.

"Uh oh," he heard Woody mutter.

P: You are there i can sense your aura both dragon and human strange you are to my senses i wish to create a bond between us now is not the time but you shall return to us one day here take this amulet and wear it until we meet again take it and go for now

Again the thoughts were jumbled in one continuous rush that poured into his mind like water into a glass, alien thoughts but a pleasant sensation. Kido's hand was released as a spot on the ground glowed and something appeared. It was a necklace with a pendant hung from a thick loop of some animal's hide, the pendant a hollow gold square insribing a silver circular disk covered in strange symbols. The square had a different colored gem at each corner: blue, red, green, and black. The gems shined and the metal glowed warmly. He felt entranced by its beauty until another shout forced him to stuff it into his pocket just as three figures came through the trees. Kido recognized the short gold-robed Orthus, Phineas, and two soldiers with collar hooks.

Orthus strutted up. "There you three are. Why aren't you in the study like I ordered?"

Kido ignored Orthus and stared at the gate. Woody and Domingo stood in shocked silence as Orthus gaped at them. "Well?" He smacked them on the backs of their heads. "You're not supposed to be at the gates." He stood in front of Kido. "You stole something, didn't you?"

Kido clutched the object hidden in his pocket. "How did you know?"

Orthus sneered. "I can sense the Magic coming from it. I am a wizard you know. Hand it over."

Kido gave him the glass-metal vial from one pocket while the dragon's gift remained hidden in the other.

"You're in so much trouble. Wait 'til father hears what you three have done. He'll have you beaten and then sold. Drag them back to the tower for punishment," he ordered.

Phineas and the two soldiers came forward with their hooks at the ready. The three slaves trembled in fear as the iron hooks reached out to grab the eyeholes in their collar flanges.

But then a loud creaking rumble shook the air and the hooks paused. A hot breeze swirled around them and sand struck them. The air grew redder in color.

"What?" a puzzled Orthus said. The soldiers' eyes grew wide.

Turning to look behind them, Kido and Woody were dumbfounded to see the right-hand gate ajar again and craning their necks upward, they saw the giant's head peering out. The door creaked open more and the giant looked down and saw them, and they all took off running, across the gully and through the trees toward the tower. Orthus dropped the vial in his haste, and he and the soldiers headed south towards the teleport rock where the wizards waited. Woody turned to follow but Kido grabbed his arm. "Let us go back inside. It'll be safer there." They looked up at the study window a hundred feet above them. Woody whimpered softly as Kido levitated them up.

The boys landed heavily inside the Wizard's Study and tumbled to the floor. "Sorry. I guess I need practice landing," said Kido with a grunt.

On his hands and knees, Woody looked out the window and gasped. "The giant is coming through the gates. What do we do?"

"Stay here and hide with Domingo." They looked around. "Where's Domingo?"

The Gold Mage and thirty-seven other wizards still stood upon the teleport rock, silent, hoods up. Their spell was dying but this was not apparent to the bystanders. Nearby stood Cromartin and Marnoch with their guards.

"It is time. Get your Aoban and get going," Marnoch growled as he stomped off towards the rock.

Cromartin was staring at his father's back as he was joined by another. Zirmad was his counselor, a man several years older, his large head covered by his hood, dressed in black breeches and a leather tunic emblazoned with a golden dragon's head breathing crimson flames, a Dragon Guard's uniform, though he wasn't officially part of the King's elite bodyguard.

He walked with Cromartin on the prince's right. "Are we leaving, my Lord?"

"Yes. Father is sending us back home, just like I feared."

"What a shame to miss out on the fabled riches of Sporu Angosta."

"Tell me about it."

Zirmad pulled up short. Cromartin was approaching his pet Aoban, Vykar.

Larger than most dogs, Vykar was Cromartin's personal bodyguard, a creature canine in appearance, chained right now to the giant's flatbed. He was a member of the Aoban race, known for their nasty tempermants and tendencies toward violence. They hate all living things, including other Aobans, which meant their numbers stayed thankfully small. His skin was a sickly gray with black splotches, his eyes permanently blood-shot above a canine snout, his powerful jaws full of sharp teeth. He had paws in the rear but clawed humanoid hands with opposable thumbs. His intellect was on a level with juvenile humans, which meant he understood kids and would have gotten along well with them were it not for his tendency to eat them. He spoke the MotherTongue, accompanied by much slobbering. Everyone but Cromartin gave him a wide berth. Cromartin unclipped Vykar's chain from the flatbed and clipped it to his belt. Vykar always stayed close to Cromartin and Zirmad walked behind them, just outside lunging range. Vykar was twenty-one in human years but only three in Aoban years.

Cromartin had known both companions since he was a boy. He looked around, still reluctant to leave. The sun was setting to the west and the woods threw long shadows on them. His father now stood near the teleport rock. The wizards stood like statues.

He gave one last longing look towards the Gates. Marnoch saw his son lingering and yelled, "Go now!"

Cromartin climbed onto his specially-bred, wide-backed horse and Vykar jumped up to ride behind him. They set off leading their party. With them were Zirmad and a squad of the King's elite Dragon Guards, plus a hundred green-clad rangers led by Mio Bushmaster, all riding slowly. In their midst the rupas pulled the great flatbed cart along, its wheels creaking under the load.

They took the sloping ridge going west from the Gold Tower. They passed the stumps of trees that had been cut down to make the flatbed and then onto a dirt road winding through grassy meadows. Progress was very slow and they grew quickly bored. The soldiers grumbled that they should have stayed, for the treasure of Sporu Angosta was legendary.

Cromartin was flanked by Zirmad, their escorts spaced off a respectable distance.

"Think your father will find what he seeks?" Zirmad asked.

"I fear he will, and I will miss out," said Cromartin. "But if not, then this will turn into the greatest fool's errand of all time."

Zirmad smiled. "You do us an honor by taking us into your confidence. This is a long way to come for a fool's errand, though I would gladly travel all the width of Arcadia and Pandoon at the King's bidding."

"I am already weary at the thought of our long journey back home," said Cromartin. "But if my father is right, he will come back with many wagons full of treasure."

"Your father is consumed by his task," said Zirmad.

"Dragons coming," said Vykar in his deep, slobbering voice. "They cannot open the doors so they stand around that shiny black rock?"

"I don't believe in dragons. The wizards' Magic will turn the shiny black rock into a doorway into Sporu Angosta," said Cromartin.

"But how?" slobbered Vykar.

How should I know the ways of wizards?" said Cromartin drily. "But I should be going in there too. I want to see the gold and kill the giants. I want my share. Why should the wizards get to take my place?"

"Ramanapirus *is* the most powerful of his kind in all of the Realm," said Zirmad. "And Astra is the second-most powerful."

"Like that means anything. Who knows if even *they* can get in, or what they'll find," said Cromartin. "If anything," he added.

Zirmad gave a sigh. "I understand your skepticism. People have spent lifetimes arguing about the Prophecy, but I never met anyone with stronger beliefs than King Marnoch."

"Many people want to steal the gold of Sporu Angosta," Vykar said.

"They are fearful of the Guardian Dragons," said Zirmad. "Who can slay dragons but wizards of great power?"

Father believes in dragons, unlike me, but he has full faith in the wizards," said Cromartin, "and so shall we. I just can't stand riding away from all that gold and being forced to escort a dead giant back home."

Vykar said, "Your father won't share any gold with the wizards. I wouldn't."

"Neither would I," Cromartin said, getting angrier as they rode further away. He barely noticed that the sky was growing darker.

A vicious wind now came howling out the gates of Sporu Angosta, between the legs of the giant who still stood there. Colored blood-red and flecked with glittering gold, it picked up the abandoned vial and Domingo where he lay sprawling in fear amongst the shrubs. It swirled on through the trees, across the gully and around the tower. There it split, one current heading towards the south clearing, the other climbing up the tower and carrying the vial and Domingo. Through the window it blew, over the crouching boys and into every nook and crany in the Wizard's Study. "Domingo!" Kido warned, yelling to make himself heard over the howling noise. The evil wind tossed his hair and ripped books open, flipping the pages violently. It tossed Domingo on the floor next to the Butterscotch spellbook. The candles blew out, but the room grew brighter, a strange golden-red light filling the air. A strange indescribable smell assailed them.

The boys watched in shock as the Butterscotch Book shivered and shook, fighting the wind, the amber eye staring upwards in fear. But red tendrils of fast-flowing air brought the metal-glass vial above the book, where blue bolts of energy zapped the book and tore it open. Pages flipped back and forth until it found a certain spot and then a black mist poured out from one page. A giant, pale tentacle came forth from the spellbook, seized a trembling Domingo and pulled him into the book. For a brief moment, the boys locked eyes. "Kiiiiii-doooooo! Wood-eee," Domingo screamed. Suddenly, he wasn't there in the room anymore.

"Domingo!" Kido and Woody yelled and getting up, they stumbled and fought the wind to reach the spellbook. The black mist settled back into the book, and it slammed shut. The red wind sucked itself out of the tower, taking the vial with it. Suddenly released from the wind, Kido and Woody fell flat on their backs. They scrambled over to the Butterscotch spellbook and desperately tried to open it but to no avail. It stayed closed; the eye stayed shut. Crying, Kido, escorted by Woody, carried the book out of the tower to get help for their friend.

In the clearing, the wizards still stood on the teleport rock in their circle, even though the spell had been broken. Ramanapirus stood rooted. "Where is your Mage and your Rook? Treachery!" he screamed at the Black wizards standing on the far side of the rock. Ignoring their puzzled looks, he turned and saw his son and two soldiers running towards them and a giant wall of red-colored wind and sand bearing down on them all. The wind whipped their robes and tugged off their hoods. Blue lightning flashes lit up the dark sky and trees started to burn. The wizards remained rooted to their spots by some unseen force. Orthus paused to look at his father but Ramanapirus twisted his torso and waved his son off. "Run!" he screamed. "Flee from this place!"

Phineas and soldier Gerd escorted Orthus towards a wagon parked nearby. Soldier Emil tried to follow but a massive tree toppled over onto him. Kido with Woody came running out of the tower carrying the big spellbook. "Bring my slave!" Orthus yelled, and Gerd grabbed Kido's collar with his hook and pulled him onto the rolling wagon. It carried Kido, Orthus, Lancemaster Phineas, and Gerd down the hill after Cromartin's party. Woody was pinned by Emil's tree and could only yell in fear as his friend rolled away. The Butterscotch spellbook lay where it was dropped. The vial now floated in the air above the teleport rock. All was chaos.

Still unaware of this chaos, Cromartin's group descended a wooded slope where they could see the walls and towers of Zannalornacopia (Z Town) off aways. Turning southward they attempted to skirt it, though Cromartin would have loved to have explored that fabled city. Anger and resentment churned inside of him. Everything about this trip was turning into a huge disappointment. The road went south and then bent back west around a small lake.

There was a strange rumble and the ground shook. They stopped and looked back up the road to see a fast-moving wagon carrying two boys and two soldiers from the tower. Beyond them, the sky was glowing with colors of green, gold, and reddish-orange against a backdrop of black clouds, and the trees began to sway their branches as the wind picked up. Abruptly, a powerful gust from the direction of the tower roared over them and knocked them off their horses. The air became hot and the glowing sky became brighter. Then a wall of flames appeared, burning the trees they had just passed through. Blue bolts of energy flashed across the sky and thunder boomed in their ears.

The soldiers yelled in fright and ran. The horses neighed in terror and galloped off.

Cromartin looked around in shock. Vykar growled an alarm and said, "Look." He was pointing a claw at the giant. The giant's flesh was melting and flowing off the flatbed to pool on the ground like hot candle wax, exposing stark white bones.

Cromartin looked back and saw the towering wall of red and orange flames moving fast towards them.

"We're going to die," Zirmad shrieked.

They ran to the only possible refuge, into the lake's cool waters, instinctively wading then swimming to where it grew deepest.

The ground opened up in places and swallowed some of Cromartin's soldiers. The boys' wagon teetered a moment at the edge of a sudden chasm where the earth had ripped open. The wagon slid down until it was caught on a pine tree sticking out at an angle. Another earthquake and the wagon lurched upright, tumbling a screaming Orthus into the abyss. Gerd followed. Lancemaster Phineas held on to the back of the wagon, his body dangling above the awful blackness below. Kido clung to the wagon's seat. Phineas and Kido eyed each other, and then the Lancemaster lost his grip and plunged away. The ground shook again, and the wagon lurched and fell into the abyss. Kido levitated himself away at the last second, floating up onto solid ground. He fell on top of a satchel lying there and sat up. He saw the flames coming and jumped up, grabbing the satchel without thinking about it and ran into the lake.

There were several others already there, and the flames swept around them. Kido dived underneath the water, holding his breath until he thought his lungs would burst. Finally he came up gasping for air, sputtering as he drew in sweet oxygen, and then he coughed as he drew in foul vapours. A hot wind was still blowing and making waves. Like frogs in a pond, Kido bobbed with Prince Cromartin, Vykar (doing the doggie paddle), Zirmad, Bushmaster, and what soldiers hadn't been swallowed by the chasm. They stared around them until the wind abated and the air cleared. Slowly then they came out of the lake, their hair plastered to their heads, their clothes sopping wet, and beheld the devastation.

Every tree was laid low and charred like used matchsticks. The forest had been mowed as if by a giant sickle. To the south they could see the forests of elvish Alfheim on fire. Small fires still licked at the fallen trees and unnumbered tendrils of black smoke drifted into the ugly brownish-yellow sky. The beautiful blue color was gone, but this was even worse than the black sky.

In shock, they stared around them at the utter ruination.

Cromartin looked off in the direction of the doors to Sporu Angosta. "What happened?" he asked in hushed awe. "Father?"

Noxious fumes and ever-burning fires prevented them from going back to check on the King or the wizards.

The survivors turned and trudged westward on foot, across the Neeper River and to the safety beyond the Spearhead Mountains. Prince Cromartin returned to Ballastro and waited almost two years for his father to return home, but King Marnoch was never seen again. Nor were Ramanapirus or Astra or any of the forty wizards. As for Kido, Cromartin brought him along and put him in Throg Anvel, a bleak fortress isolated in the rolling plains of Middlerealm, many leagues from anywhere.

Eventually Cromartin led another expedition back across the Spearhead Mountains to search for his father but all he found was the bones of the giant. And he brought back horrific stories of what he found. He never made it to the fabled city of Zannalornacopia or the gates of Sporu Angosta. In fact, he barely made it back alive. Sinister creatures now lurked there, monsters who came out at night and took his soldiers where they camped. Vicious goblins and other, unimaginable creatures hunted them. He returned with less than half his escort from that hellish land, for much of Pandoon had been reduced to rubble and waste by the explosion of Magic.

"The whole land is ruined," he told an audience of people at the palace when he returned. "Ruined and filled with monsters." And so the news spread. People referred to the event as **The Ruination**.

It became a dividing line in their memory. People would say: "My son was born right after the Ruination, or "She passed away two years before the Ruination."

In Ballastro, Cromartin built a large museum right on Obol's Hill and called it the Hall of the Giant. Workers painstakingly assembled the bones and hung the whole from the ceiling with wires so folks could imagine what the giant would've looked like.

Cromartin was crowned King of Arcadia and took his father's place on the throne. But since his return, people say Cromartin had changed, that he seemed happy to be rid of his father and entitled to the throne. He gave up traveling and stayed in his capital. He grew fatter and lazier and indifferent to the world outside his palace. He married many wives who produced many blonde-haired sons.

And you know, funny things began happening in the years after the Ruination. Fish died in rivers and lakes, crops failed in the fields. Strange noxious yellow dust devils swirled everywhere. Clouds came and stayed, covering the blue sky permanently. With no sun, sunrise became cloudrise, sunset cloudset, although the clouds never really rose or set. Now they were always there. No stars or moon meant the science of astronomy died. Food became scarce and some went hungry, while some became sick from some strange disease. It was all too sad and awful to go into further detail.

Refugees came tramping from the east to crowd into the poorer neighborhoods of Ballastro. Calves were born with two heads and snakes with two tails. There was still fish in the faroff sea but some said it was unsafe to eat anyways. And the refugees kept coming, so Cromartin approved a large factory in Ballastro to manufacture food for all those hungry mouths. A wealthy family of entrepreneuers funded and ran Starbolt Foodstuffs, Incorporated. Their motto was *"The most nutritious and delicious thing to ever pass your lips."* The factory's four tall smokestacks dominated the city's skyline, belching smoke into the gray sky day and night. But at least no one starved anymore.

In his grief and overwhelmed by the troubles besetting his realm, Cromartin had forgotten about Kido.

Kido lived in a locked room at the top of the tallest tower of Throg Anvel, in far-off Middlerealm. His only other companion was Jabu. Who is Jabu? Remember the satchel? Turns out it belonged to Orthus, and the Dragon Guards took it from Kido. But one day he was standing at the window in his tower room and saw the satchel lying on a table in courtyard below, and levitating it up found inside a bag of coins and a large Cutknife dagger with a large red ruby set in the gold hilt. The Cutknife Corporation made the sharpest daggers in the Known World. Jabu was a gem genie living inside that ruby. His three wishes had already been used by Orthus so all he could give Kido was advice and friendship.

The guards tried to take away the Dragon's Gift, but when a soldier grabbed it with his hand, the necklace burned him horribly and so the guards let Kido keep it all. They became afraid of him and left him alone. They called Kido a warlock. Orthus's shining *Hope Crystal*, though, they did keep for it did not burn them.

It was at Throg Anvel that Kido began to grow spots on his skin. They were small, diamond-shaped, and colorful, more like tattoos than any skin blemish. A yellow one first appeared on his right palm. A few days later it was turquoise. He assumed it had changed color, but a quick search of his person revealed that the yellow tattoo had migrated to his chest and the turquoise one had replaced it on his palm. By the end of the week, a purple diamond-shaped tattoo was on his palm and the turquoise one had migrated to his belly.

They didn't hurt, but Kido was afraid all the same.

"Have you ever seen anything like this?" he asked.

"Definitely not," said Jabu as he floated in the air.

"I wish I could consult a wizard about them."

"Wizards seem in short supply since the Ruination," Jabu said. "On the plus side, I don't have any spots."

"Meanwhile I'm turning into the Illustrated Man."

"You ain't Ray Bradbury, Kido. I'd say you are turning into the Harlequin."

That reminded Kido of the forgotten card still in his pocket. He took it out and threw it out the window, thinking it was causing the tattoos. But the next morning it had Magically reappeared in his pocket. "I appear to be stuck with it."

"While we're on the subject of being stuck, Kido, how much longer will we be stuck in this wretched place?" Jabu asked in an exasperated voice, crossing his powerful arms.

Kido was sitting on his wooden bed, thinking, Cutknife in hand. "I think I'm about ready to leave, Jabu."

"Thank the dragons." There was obvious relief in the genie's voice.

"I just don't know where to go. Do you?"

"No, I spend all day in a ruby. The soldiers say there isn't much of Pandoon left, so I don't think we can go back."

"I heard the rumors, but maybe the Gold Tower survived. It's supposed to be protected by an enchantment. And the spellbook with

Domingo trapped inside is there somewhere. I have to become a wizard so I can go back and rescue Domingo. But how do I become a wizard with all the Gold Hoods dead?"

"Maybe Chizmo knows if the Gold Tower still stands."

"Who is Chizmo?"

"He is my friend and another gem genie. He lives in a sapphire on the Cutknife of Ramanapirus. He probably heard or saw what happened. He's a nosy genie."

"How do we find him? I need to become a wizard first, but I can't do it at the Gold Tower."

"You could try another Magic Tower."

"I don't know where they are. Maybe I should go to the Red Tower in Ballastro. Wherever that is from here."

"Anywhere would be better than here," said Jabu.

"I was just remembering something. What should I do with the slave boy?" Cromartin asked one morning as he sat on his throne in the huge hall in his palace, a side table full of food at his elbow. An attractive young woman sat on the other side of the table.

"Kill him," said Vykar with a wicked gleam in his eye.

Cromartin dipped a strawberry into a bowl of pudding and took a bite. "You're right, I suppose," he managed as his tongue rolled the food around. "He's a loose end I need to tie up."

A note was sent by Nightshade to Throg Anvel and quickly returned.

Zirmad read, "The note says the weakling guards at Throg Anvel refuse to go near Kido. They say he is a powerful warlock."

Cromartin choked on the frankfurter he was eating just then. "Afraid! Ridiculous. Send some Dragon Guards to kill that boy!"

So several of the King's Own climbed onto the broad back of a giant turgeon and flew to Throg Anvel.

At the top of the stairs, Kido remained unaware.

"How shall we get to Ballastro? Must we walk?" asked Jabu.

"How far away is Ballastro?" asked Kido.

Jabu shrugged. "Don't ask me. I live in a ruby."

"You keep saying that."

"It is a valid defense."

"I don't remember Throg Anvel from the board game, but the Red Tower and Gold Tower were on opposite sides of the board," said

Kido.

Then their eyes went to a corner of the room, to the end of a stone bench that stood in dark shadows. Kido could sense it, an otherworldly presence with them.

Kido crept closer and Jabu too, so that his light chased away the darkness to reveal an old bearded man sitting there on the bench where no one had been a moment before. He was dressed in purple breeches, white shirt, and a black coat, a black top hat on his head, and a large clock embedded in that hat.

"Who are you?" demanded Kido.

The stranger sighed. "Do you require a name? Is it not enough that I am here." The clock's hands spun around.

"Are you a prisoner here, too?"

He gave an indulgent smile. "No one imprisons me. Instead I imprison everyone else."

"Who sent you? The Gold Mage or the Black Mage? Or maybe King Cromartin?"

"I came of my own. I am here to warn you." He stood and approached to stand before them. Jabu fled back to his ruby with a shriek.

Below them the Dragon Guards ascended the spiraling stone stairs.

"Warn us of what?" Kido asked.

The stranger pointedly stared at the door. "Death comes for you on hobnailed boots, Kido."

"How do you know my name? You still haven't told me who you are or why I should believe you."

A grim smile. "Mortals call me Father Time. I mark the passage of every creature's life. I witness the beginnings and the ends of everything. Things will be messed up if your end should come too soon." Father Time unrolled his left arm, pulling never-ending armlengths out to coil on the floor. Hundreds of wristwatches ran all along his arm. He finally came to one he was looking for. "Ah, here is your timeline chronograph. I tell you, it would create all sorts of problems if you die right now. You must leave this tower in the next few seconds. Do not wait for anyone to help you." Father Time pulled a wooden pulley out from his breast and cranked his arm back up into its socket like one withdraws a bucket from its well.

The sound of scuffling boots became audible from the other side of the door.

"Cutting it close, aren't you?" Kido said, now feeling fear.

Father Time arched his craggy eyebrows and coughed, sending a puff of the dust of ages into the air. "I hear you can levitate things. If I were you, I'd levitate myself out of here very soon." He looked pointedly at the large open window. Kido went to the window and looked out. He saw several strange birds roosting on nearby window ledges. They had dark brown feathers, bodies twice as big as vultures, and red eyes, beaks, and feet. The wattles on their throats were also red. When they spread their large wings, they displayed long droopy feathers.

"Nightshades, they are called," said Father Time. "Certain wicked people use them to carry messages. Fastest birds in the kingdom." He looked at the door and then back to Kido. "Good luck," and then disappeared in a puff of purple sparks and smoke.

"Kido!" came the muffled cry from the Cutknife's ruby. Kido brandished his Cutknife as he faced the door, but then his courage wilted and he looked at the window.

The Dragon Guards unlocked the door and burst in with swords raised only to find it empty. "It smells old and musty in here," one complained, sniffing the air disparagingly.

They searched the room and one went to the window and looked down at the courtyard far below. They went back down and searched the entire grounds but found no body.

The guard who drew the short straw made out his will and flew by turgeon to Ballastro with the unfortunate news.

Zirmad told the King, "It's as if that slave boy turned into a bird and flew away. I would have the captain of Throg Anvel flogged, the messenger killed, and the turgeon neutered for this failure. Send out your soldiers to hunt down the boy, my king. He couldn't have gone far."

Vykar growled and gnashed his teeth by the king's side. "Kill! Kill!"

Cromartin glowered and scratched his quivering belly. "Yes, have my soldiers sweep the countryside. He's from the Gold Tower where the Ruination killed my father, so have him killed. Tell McGee and Bushmaster I said so. Right now, I must focus on other things." The King pulled a platter of pastries closer and held up both hands poised to strike, excitedly wagging his fingers, then snatched a yummy treat and bit down hard, sending a puff of powdered sugar over his face.

His seventh wife reached for a danish and he slapped her hand away. "Ask first," Cromartin said in a testy voice, his mouth full.

Vykar stared through the stone walls, wishing he could find that boy and eat him. But no soldier of Cromartin's ever found Kido. It was as if he had disappeared into thin air. In a towering rage, the King proclaimed all wizards as enemies, to be hanged wherever found, and he ordered all the Magic Towers closed even though three of them weren't even in his territory and it was questionable what power he had over the one that was. He ordered a buffet to get him through this troubling bit of news.

The years passed and the folks of Arcadia got by. No one thought too much about Pandoon. It was bad taste to even talk about it, and stories about the gold and the dragons of Sporu Angosta became like childrens' tales or barroom legends. Nobody took them serious except the dreamers and the crazies.

Cromartin sure didn't seem to care. Some people said the King was afraid, and some said they didn't blame him and he should never go east again to risk the same fate as his father.

And yet one fine day, the King finally stirred from his palace and announced plans for a journey to Tempest, northern city of Arcadia. Along the way he begged his friend Zirmad to begin studying sorcery. Cromartin hoped he was wrong, but he had the nagging suspicion that he might have to go himself to Sporu Angosta someday and a sorcerer might come in handy then.

"But you hate Magic and all wizards," Zirmad pointed out to him.

"Sorcery is different from Magic," Cromartin assured him, which was strange since the King knew next to nothing about either. He thought some more and then said, "How else am I to open the gates to Sporu Angosta except by unnatural means?"

"Your father's reliance on wizards cost him his life."

"I know! But you won't fail me the way Ramanapirus failed my father."

Zirmad didn't like it, but one doesn't refuse the King anything if one wants to keep possession of one's head. So he put on a black robe covered in silver nightmare designs that he found in some old closet and took a dusty old tome called *Zeon's Grimoire* from the Royal Library. He also took some strange-smelling gold dust the king had gotten from somewhere. Deep in the bowels of the palace, an old storeroom was cleaned out and made into a lab for Zirmad. But in the back of his mind, he kept turning over the King's phrase...sorcery is different from Magic. *But how? What did it all mean?*

6
THE PEDDLER, THE DRUNK, & THE WIZARD

After leaving Throg Anvel, Kido became a refugee. He stayed off the roads and hiked through forests and up in the mountains. More than a few times he watched from the trees while soldier patrols swept by. In one town, he overheard the town crier reading a King's Proclamation condemning a slave boy from Pandoon and offering a reward for capture. He hid in a haystack behind the stables until cloudset allowed him to sneak away.

Kido avoided villages after that and kept his slave collar covered. He did odd jobs for ranchers and farmers to earn a meal and a dry night sleeping in someone's barn. Occasionally he had to resort to stealing when he became desperate with hunger. His clothes became tattered and filthy, but a kind farmer's wife gave him fresh clothes once belonging to her son.

"He died during the Ruination. You might as well have them." He gratefully accepted the homespun tunic and pants and the broad-brimmed hat. This was a very lonely time for him. Even Jabu grew surly and rarely came out of his gem.

Kido drifted slowly onward through the lands of Middlereach, trying always to travel in the direction of Ballastro and the Red Tower. But with no maps or road signs, he found themselves frequently getting lost. His blisters had turned to callouses and his body grew lean with all the hiking and not enough food. Strangers who gave him directions told him the capital was drawing nearer, but still he avoided the main roads.

Waking up one morning in a thick copse, he walked up to the crest of a ridge to find a huge army encampment spread in the valley below.

There must be hundreds of soldiers, said Kido to himself. *Right smack where I need to go.* He could only groan. So he backtracked down the ridge and spent two days walking in the wrong direction to get around the army, always walking late until cloudset.

The third morning found Kido bone tired but forced to walk because his meager food had run out. Soon he met a farmer and his son on horseback, leading a string of ponies to market.

"Sir, which way to Ballastro?"

The farmer pointed off to their right. "You're headed more toward the river than the city, unless you mean to take the River Road," he said.

"How far away is the city?"

"Oh, about three days walk from here." Kido realized the man was staring at his neck and realized too late that he had forgotten to cover up his iron collar. The farmer spat tobacco juice on the ground. "You from Pandoon, boy?"

Kido was unsure how much to reveal. "Not originally."

The farmer nodded in acceptance. "Don't matter to me where you're from or if you're running. Plenty of kids running around looking for work, food, lost family, whatever. It's all been chaos since the Ruination. You're welcome to come with us as far as the river. Climb aboard a pony."

When they reached it, the river turned out to be a half mile wide from where they stood at the ferry landing. The farmer said, "Cloud River, largest river in the kingdom. Yonder upstream a few days walk is the capital city. Downstream two week's walk is the port and the seacoast."

"What sea?"

The farmer gave Kido a pointed look. "Why, the Never Sea." He spat juice. Kido could tell what the farmer was thinking: *Ignorant slave.*

At the landing were several others, including a peddler and his wagon of wares. They watched the ferry arrive.

Where's the River Road?" Kido asked.

"On the other side," said the farmer.

"Ferry price is ten coppers," said the ferryman, who had opened the gate and overheard them.

"I don't have any coppers," said Kido.

"Looks like you're swimming then," said the ferryman.

Kido looked across again. The far bank was a distant green smudge, and the current looked fast.

"It's a deep river," the ferryman volunteered.

The farmer was accepting money from a man who had arrived with the ferry while another was loading the ponies. "Probably not safe on the River Road by yourself anyways," said the farmer to Kido. Then to the ferryman, "He's from Pandoon, trying to reach the capital."

The ferryman looked him over again. He reached out a hand to pull aside Kido's cloak to reveal the iron coller. Kido jerked away and the ferryman smiled. "You'll never get inside the city anyways. City Guards'll stop ya. The King don't allow Pandooni refugee scum inside his city anymore."

Kido looked around, but the farmer and his son were already riding away, and everyone else was on the ferry. "No money, no crossing," said the ferryman as he began closing the gate. At the last second, the peddler came up. He was tall and thin, with a prominent Adam's Apple. "I'll pay for his passage, ferryman."

"You will?"

The peddler pulled coins out of his pocket and dropped them into the ferryman's hand. "Ten coppers. Into the wagon, boy." The ferryman swung the gate back open and Kido climbed up into the wagon to sit among its wares.

The peddler's name was Burmist, and he and Kido spent one unhappy month together. Kido took on most of the chores. He carried water, scrubbed down the horse, and washed the dishes. He fetched this and cleaned that. And in return, he got the smaller portion of every meal and slept on the hard ground beneath the wagon while Burmist slept up in the wagon, two blankets to Kido's one. Kido took to using the horse's flank for a pillow.

Burmist did not take him to Ballastro, but instead they visited a string of small towns. When they came to a town, Burmist made Kido don dirty, torn clothes and smeared his face with mud before sending him in well before the wagon. Kido would then sit in the town square and beg while people tossed coins in his reed basket. Burmist would ride in separately and sell what wares he could, and then they would meet up again outside of town that evening. If there were too few coins in his basket, Kido would have to trade punches with a cursing Burmist. Sometimes he got robbed by town ruffians, and he quickly lost his Cutknife to a pair of thieves. Now he didn't even have Jabu's morose companionship. But anyone who tried to grab the Dragon's Gift got horribly burned, and so it stayed with Kido, along with the Harlequin's card, which no one thought worth stealing.

One day in some squalid little village, Kido eyed the few coppers in his basket. The townspeople walked by ignoring him. It looked like another beating was coming his way. So he stood and announced in a loud voice that he was going to perform a Magic trick. He waited while a few dozen folk gathered around, eyes full of skepticism. Spotting a young boy in the crowd, Kido announced his attention to lift the boy in the air without touching him. People scoffed but Kido cast the *Levitate* spell. He was a little rusty, but in a few seconds the boy rose up about four feet into the air. People gasped and Kido felt smug at the spell's success, but the boy's mother shrieked. She grabbed his legs to pull him down. That distracted Kido enough to let the boy go, and he and his mother tumbled to the ground.

Feeling proud of his abilities, Kido expected coins to start dropping into his basket, but when he looked around all he saw were hard, suspicious faces. "Maybe this is the wrong crowd for Magic," he mumbled to himself. Before he could stoop to retrieve his basket, strong hands seized him and turned him around.

A big, beefy man held him. "What are you, some kind of con man?" Kido tried to jerk away, and felt the buttons on his cheap cloak popping off. Several others grabbed him, and there was a struggle, during which Kido's shirt was torn away, revealing the Harlequin marks on his torso. The hands released him, and he fell on his back. The crowd gathered around for a closer look, and when they saw clearly the marks, they began backing off.

"He is a freak!"

"He has unnatural skin!"

"He smells like a horse, not a man!"

"He is a half-beast!"

"He is an evil warlock!"

"Mutant from the Ruination!"

And they all ran off, screaming for the town constable and the priest.

Kido ran out of town. When Burmist caught up with him, he was livid. He hadn't seen what had happened, being too far off, but he had heard the stories. Kido was standing there, arms crossed, holding his torn cloak closed. Burmist jerked Kido's arms away and carefully pulled the cloak aside to see the marks for himself. His eyes grew wide in fear, and he backed off. Wordlessly, he scrambled back up onto his wagon, and whipping the reins in a frenzy, he rode off.

Kido watched him go. Standing there in an open meadow, Kido stayed rooted for a long time. Where to go? What to do now? The questions swirled around in his mind like phantasms. He had no idea in which direction lay Ballastro. Finally, he turned and began to walk in the direction opposite where Burmist had gone. For four days he stumbled along, eating grass, dandelions, berries, and whatever else he could find or steal, once small fishes drying on a rack. He noticed a saltier tang in the air, and he began to see seagulls.

On the fifth morning, he crested a hill to find below him a large coastal village with wide beaches, set on the shores of a vast green sea that filled the entire horizon. The Never Sea, he figured.

At the edge of the village was a large wooden sign proclaiming the town as FEATHER BAY. Below the sign was a smaller one hanging by two hooks. It had the picture of a large red feather. Kido dug out the Harlequin's card and compared the two images. They were identical. "How did he know?" he wondered aloud.

Weak from hunger, he staggered into town and begged for food and work. Strangers gave him bread, cheese, and fruit, and they told him to seek out Uncle Oto. "He always has a place for young men like you."

"And where is Uncle Oto?"

They directed him to the road leading northeast, to two buildings on top of the first hill outside of town. On his way, he noticed all the birds on the beach and on the buildings. Besides the usual gulls and terns, he saw small, long-legged birds scurrying along the sandy soil. They were like the sandpipers or plovers he'd seen pictures of back home except they had scarlet feathers. There were many molted feathers on the ground. He picked up a red feather and tucked it into his pocket with the card.

The road was wide and well-maintained, the hill's slopes forested with tall conifers. Past a large tavern the road climbed, and at the top of the hill was a large clearing with a two-story wooden building to the right and a one-story brick building to the left. The first was a shop with living quarters above, and behind which were some small animal pens. The second was an orphanage, and both were run by Uncle Oto and Ludy. Kido was taken in by them.

And so one day soon after he arrived, Kido found himself sitting at the front desk by a window that let in the soft gray light. He stared at the green diamond-shaped tattoo on his right palm. The Harlequin tattoos now covered his torso and were beginning to appear on his thighs. He worked in a shop that sold clothes, candles, walking sticks, lanterns, rope, maps, ands a hundred other things. Kido's favorite part of the shop was the small book section.

Open in front of him with his favorite book, *Growler's Beastopedia* (199th edition). It was open to the page on dragons and showed a picture of a large, winged serpent flying over a village and setting fire to buildings while hapless townspeople ran around in fear. The book was his favorite because it was the only fantasy book in the whole shop, and he was a sucker for dragon stories. He had his head propped in his hand, wondering if all fantasy stories have dragons in them when a middle-aged portly man came in the back door. It was Uncle Oto with his disheveled hair, bewhiskered jowls, foul breath, and bloodshot eyes.

"Ooh, what are you doing, boy?"

Startled, Kido answered, "Just reading."

Kido knew Uncle Oto didn't like him reading. Selling clothes and books to travelers was one thing, but only lazy kids read.

"Reading that nonsense again, I see. And staring out the window, wasting time. Go feed the animals like you're supposed to."

"I already fed them."

"Well, feed them again, and after that sweep up this floor."

"I already swept it."

"Well, sweep it again. I'm sure you missed some dirt."

"I don't want to. I'd rather read."

Oto waddled over and slipped a finger inside Kido's slave collar. "Ooh, ya don't? Remember boy, I can always find a slavers caravan to take you back to the Ruined Lands." He gave the collar a jerk for emphasis.

Kido sighed and got up to head out the back door.

"Chores," he heard Uncle Oto repeat.

Out back, he was teased by some boys hanging out behind the orphanage.

"Hey, there's Iron Neck. Go play with your piggies, Iron Neck!"

"Yeah, run off and play with the chickens. Nobody else wants to play with Iron Neck Kido."

Kido was used to it. There were some hundred or so orphans under the care of Uncle Oto and his wife (never aunt) Ludy. Kido was older than the orphans and could read to boot so he lived apart from them in the kitchen at the back of Uncle Oto's house. The orphans worked in the bakery or else were hired out to craftsmen in Feather Bay or the fishing fleet. Kido was the only one who worked in the shop or fed the animals. He didn't have any friends among the other boys, but he liked the animals.

Before Kido could reply another boy came running up to yell, "They're hanging a wizard down in the town square. They found a wizard!" The news spread fast.

Boys and girls poured out of the orpahanage and ran off, their games forgotten. Kido stood confused for a second. He usually never did anything with the orphans and watching a man hang made him feel sick. But on the other hand, wizards were rare, and he felt a burning curiosity to go see for himself. His feet began moving of their own accord, and he found himself running down the hill towards town, his chores forgotten.

Down in Feather Bay, near the docks, was a small open square and a large wooden scaffold where fish were hung to dry. Now a noose hung from the scaffold and the square was full of people, including boys from the orphanage. Kido came down the hill, past Bolly's Tavern, and into town to breathlessly stand at the edge of the crowd.

Standing on the scaffold with his hands tied was a handsome youngish blonde man, dressed in yellow- and black-striped trousers, white silk shirt with ruffles, and a yellow vest. He had an aquiline nose and intelligent blue eyes. Kido recognized the town's Burgermeister standing on the wizard's left, and on his right a large hairy man wearing a black leather hood with eyeholes while holding a hood without eyeholes. A broken, long-necked lute lay nearby.

The Burgermeister began reading in a loud voice,

> "Puy du Pome, having been found guilty of casting spells and incantations, and attempting to corrupt our children with your seditious songs and poems, are hereby sentenced to be hanged until dead, in accordance with the King's Law. Any last words?"

Puy du Pome looked ahead stoically. "What possible words could I say in this ridiculous situation? What kind of people hang a man for his songs? I am not a wizard, just a traveling minstrel."

"You are a wizard."

"Am not."

"Are so."

"Not."

The Burgermeister grew red in the face. The executioner shuffled his feet impatiently.

"I add the charge of obstructing the King's Justice for arguing with me," the Burgermeister bellowed.

Puy shrugged and began humming absent-mindedly.

The Burgermeister nodded at the Executioner, who lifted the black hood to place on Puy's head.

Kido felt anger at the injustice about to happen and seriouly doubted Puy du Pome was really a wizard, having been surrounded by wizards at the Gold Tower. He hadn't tried any Magic since the squalid village many weeks ago, but he remembered how to levitate. Feeling a little rusty, he worried that he had lost his Magic. But then the words slowly came forth as Kido concentrated on the black hood. He could feel the strange energy begin as a warm glow in his midsection and then flow throughout his body. He cast the spell words softly aloud.

The black hood lifted abruptly and flew out of the Executioner's hands. Cast aloft, it floated through the air towards the sea but then fell on the beach.

"What the—?" sputtered the Executioner.

The Burgermeister was wide-eyed and speechless, but he quickly recovered. "Forget the hood. Just do it quickly."

Some in the crowd gasped at the thought of hanging an unhooded man.

The Executioner reached for the noose, and Kido levitated it to swing away. The Executioner reached again and Kido swung it the other way. Again they repeated the action. Finally in frustration, the Executioner grabbed the rope where it was slung over the scaffold and worked his way down to seize the noose. Kido felt defeated. What more could he do? He wasn't a real wizard after all.

The Executioner began working the noose over Puy's head. Then suddenly the Executioner himself began rising up as if some giant had pulled him off the scaffold. And as the big hairy man flew through the air, his hood popped off and everyone got a quick glimpse of his face. He flew out to land offshore in the sea.

The Burgermeister cried out, and the crowd began yelling.

"It *is* Magic. The wizard is all powerful!" someone yelled, pointing at a bewildered Puy du Pome. Everyone began running away, and the square began to empty. Kido looked around in amazement, wondering what had happened. He certainly hadn't lifted the Executioner like that! Then he noticed a stranger in pale grey robes standing on the porch of the Crimson Plover Inn which overlooked the square, nonchalantly watching the crowd disperse. He was not too young or too old, and Kido felt now a strange sensation emanating from him. It felt like the warm, fuzzy aftereffects of Magic. Kido looked around but the square was empty now but for him and Puy du Pome, who was busily trying to untie his hands. Kido walked down and reached into his pocket for the Cutknife to cut the minstrel free. It wasn't there, and then he remembered it being stolen long ago. And then suddenly there was a large dagger being held before him. He turned to see the stranger in pale grey robes holding it out. He took it, cut the ropes binding the minstrel's hands, and handed it back. "Thank you, lad," said Puy du Pome, rubbing his hands. "What is your name?"

"Kido, sir."

"Thank you very much, Kido. I am at your service. Someday Puy du Pome will repay you, no matter where in the realm our paths may yet again cross. And now if you will excuse me, I must run." He grabbed the lute with the broken neck and jumped down and was gone. Kido watched him disappear up an alley. He turned and looked but the stranger in pale grey robes was gone too. He shrugged and left town.

Uphill he climbed, past the orphanage where the kids had retreated and were watching him anxiously from the windows, back to the chicken coop, goatpen, and pigpen. Disappointed that he didn't get to talk to the stranger and still excited about doing Magic and helping save Puy du Pome, and angry as well that he couldn't just sit and read all day, Kido stood for a moment to enjoy the view. From the high hill he could see back down the road to Bolly's Tavern and beyond to the village. It was a warm day in the Season of Flowers under the usual overcast sky. He could see no ships in the harbor; they were all out on Greenbottom Sound with their nets and lines out trowling for the day's catch, but he imagined the Executioner treading water out there until a giant sharkmouth would eat him in one huge gulp.

Sighing, he turned away from the view. The chicken feed was in a metal cannister, its tin lid held down by a big brick. Still basking in the warm afterglow of Magic, Kido used his mind to levitate the brick two feet in the air and then lifted the lid with his hands to pull out a cup of feed. He went into the coop and scattered seed for the chickens who clucked and pecked around his feet. All the while he kept the brick suspended in mid-air by an awkward mental effort. For some reason, the act of levitation was harder for him to do now. Like the black hood that fell onto the beach because his spell had died before he could get the hood into the sea. This bothered him.

He made for the back of the shop. Sure enough, Ludy had put out a bucket of slops leftover from the kitchen, and he took that up and dumped it in the pigs' trough. Kido had a small book he kept hidden in his pocket, and he opened it to read while the three pigs waddled over and stuck their snouts into the food to eat quickly, grunting with pleasure.

The book held poems, and he began reading one about knights and fair maidens until he felt the aura of Magic intruding. Kido looked up. The stranger in pale grey robes from the inn was standing thirty feet away watching him. His robes covered him from neck to boots and he held a tall walking stick in one hand. He wore no hat and his hood was down. He had a trimmed black beard and bright brown eyes that spoke of great experience.

"Moin moin, young man. My name is Elger. What is yours?"

Kido hesitated at the strange words. "I am Kido, sir."

"You like to read, Kido?"

"Very much, sir."

"And you like to levitate too?"

"Sir?"

Elger looked pointedly at the brick still hanging in mid-air.

With all the distractions, Kido had forgotten to unlevitate. The spell broken, it dropped with a thud on the tin lid. He looked around, but no one else was in sight. Elger looked around with him. When he looked at Kido he saw a brown-haired boy in his early twenties perhaps, dressed in an pauper's unmended clothes.

"I saw you levitating the hood and the noose," said Elger.

"I saw you levitating the Executioner."

Elger seemed amused. "Mind if I ask you a few questions? Have you always lived in Feather Bay?"

"No, sir."

"Where did you live before here?"

"Pandoon."

"Your accent does not sound Pandooni."

Kido did not answer, refusing to admit that he was from another world.

"You live in the orphanage?"

"No, I live with Uncle Oto and Ludy."

"You live with your uncle?"

"He's not really my uncle. That's just what he wants us to call him."

"You are an orphan like the other boys?"

"Yes." The lies started piling up.

"You were born on a farm?"

"No. I was raised in a far off kingdom across the Never Sea. Then I came to Pandoon and lived in the Gold Tower."

The stranger had been leaning casually on his walking stick, but he straightened a bit, and his face took on a new intensity. He rubbed his beard and ruminated, "Now that is the most intersting thing I have heard in a long while. This is before the Ruination?"

"Yes. I was a slave boy there. Ramanapirus was the Gold Mage."

"He whose name cannot be shortened. I knew Ramanapirus years ago when we were both much younger. Did you see the Ruination and what happened to him and the tower? I have heard only rumors."

Suddenly Kido found himself admitting more than he wanted. He told of what he had seen about the Gold and Black Hoods around the teleport rock and the firestorm and the melting giant. His voice faltered when he came to the part about Domingo and the Butterscotch Book. He asked the man, "Are you a wizard and can you help me get my friend back?"

"I do not know if I can help your friend, for you see I am not officially a wizard anymore. I belonged to the Order of Wizards for many years but was kicked out for what is called Magical Mischief."

"What is the Order of Wizards?"

"The Order of Wizards is a diverse group of folks who study Magic at—where else?—the Magic Towers. It is a professional organization, tolerated by the King of the Arcadia, and by the Grand Puttrah of Pandoon, that is when there used to be one. You are legit if you belong to the Order. The rest of us are just Pariahs. I don't admit this to most folks, but I get a good feeling about you, so I feel free to tell you that I, Elger, am a Pariah."

"That means nothing to me. Ramanapirus must be in the Order."

"Indeed he is, if he is still alive. Things aren't the same now of course, not since the Ruination and the King's Condemnation. All the towers are supposed to be closed now. The Order is under extreme pressure, persecution even. I still have friends in it though."

A flood of memories invaded Kido's mind: the tower, his friends and his home in Porterville, the Butterscotch Book, the gates to Sporu Angosta, Orthus falling into the chasm, Father Time at Throg Anvel, Burmist....

Elger stood silently watching Kido, and when the boy returned to the present Elger said, "Tell me, Kido, what are you doing here? Are you going to take over Uncle Oto's shop?"

Kido shrugged. "Most kids in the orphanage end up working on the fishing boats or on farms or in the mine in the hills. I don't want to do any of that."

"Do you want to stay in this village?" Elger pointed with his stick down the hill.

Kido shook his head no. "I want to be a wizard and return to the Gold Tower. I want to go east, find some lost friends, and leave here for good. Uncle Oto says I can have my trust fund next year, so I plan on leaving then."

"Trust fund?"

"Uncle Oto is investing the wages I earn working in the shop."

Elger said, "I can sense your aura. You are no mere slave boy, though it remains to be seen if you can become a wizard. This is not a good time for wizardry, and the Gold Tower might be gone."

It pained Kido to hear this. If the tower was truly destroyed, then what of the Butterscotch Book and Woody and Domingo?" He shook his head stubbornly. "It is protected by Magic. Even the Ruination couldn't destroy it."

"The Ruination, yes. Well, I don't know about the Gold Tower, but there are three other towers still standing, where wizards were made in the old days, although Cromartin has the Red one under siege. That is the closest one, the Red Tower in Ballastro. Do you know where that is?"

"Of course I do. I have studied maps in the shop. It is the capital city, in the Middlerealm, at the southern terminus of the Squark Ear Mountains and on the north bank of Cloud River. It is the seat of the House of Marnoch, capital of Arcadia, and home to King Cromartin."

"I see you know your geography, and you speak in a most articulate fashion."

"I love looking at maps. Sometimes I look at Pandoon too, and wonder how it is now and what I might find there."

"How good are you with books?"

"I read very well."

"Good. Still, it is too bad the towers are all closed. There is no place to formally study Magic anymore in Arcadia or Pandoon."

"Why don't you open them back up?" Kido asked.

Elger smiled. "If it were only that simple."

"How can I become a wizard? Where should I go?"

Elger thought about it. "The Red Tower is closed, that is true. However, I am on my way to see an old friend. I am a Pariah and cannot open anything, but he is a member of the Order of Wizards in good standing. He can help get you into the Red Tower if anyone can. You lived in the Gold Tower. Maybe they will make an exception for you."

They both heard the back door of the shop open as Uncle Oto came out. He looked surprised to see Elger.

Elger said, "I was going to leave today, but I think I will put off my journey for a few more days. It was a pleasure meeting you, Kido." The wizard bowed to Uncle Oto and quickly walked off.

Uncle Oto marched up the hill to Kido. "What did that man say to you?"

"He was talking to me about the Magic Towers."

"What nonsense! Don't talk to such people. That could be dangerous around here, you dumb boy. Have you finished your chores yet?"

"Yes."

"Well, get into the store and sweep the floor then, boy. I have to go change my clothes and see a man at Bolly's about a horse."

That night, as usual, Uncle Oto disappeared after dinner. He woke them up when he returned after midnight, singing off-key and mumbling to himself. He stumbled to the living room couch and collapsed. Soon he was snoring loudly, and Kido could not get back to sleep in his small bed in the kitchen at the back of the house.

It seemed Kido had finally just fallen asleep when Ludy woke him by roughly shaking his shoulder.

"Get up, you worthless boy. Get going and open the shop. You overslept."

Kido stumbled out of bed and dressed after she left. "What about breakfast?"

Her voice floated back to the kitchen, "I'll bring you something later. Now get going."

He came out into the living room to see Oto asleep in his clothes on the couch. His hair was a mess, and his cheeks covered in salt-and-pepper whiskers. The air reeked of ale. "It's going to be one of those days," Ludy said in a bitter voice, shaking her fist at her slumbering husband.

"He needs to stay away from Bolly's Tavern."

She pinched his arm. "You're no one to be giving advice. He's had a tough life, that's all. It's hard work taking care of a bunch of orphans. You kids don't realize that. Now off to the shop with you."

"What about the animals?"

"Feed them later. Those pigs ain't starving to death anytime soon."

Outside Kido smelled the delicious odor of fresh bread baking as as it wafted out the open window of the orphanage bakery. He tried to levitate a loaf out the window, but the bread only jiggled a little and then fell back onto the kitchen floor. The yells of the baker sent him scurrying to the shop, deeply troubled that he couldn't levitate well anymore.

It was late morning when Uncle Oto came into the book shop accompanied by a strange, big man. Kido was still tired from lack of sleep.

"What did you bring me to eat, uncle?" said a hungry Kido.

"Food? I brought you no food." He turned to his friend. "That's the boy for you. Always thinking about himself." He turned to Kido. "This here is Riley. He runs a good boat, and he's agreed to take you on and teach you fishing."

"Fishing! I don't want to learn to fish. I hate fish." Kido got a good look at Riley and realized now that he was the Executioner who had tried to hang Puy du Pome. He shrank back in fright. "I see you didn't get eaten by a sharkmouth," he said to Riley.

A look of confusion came across Riley's face.

Uncle Oto scowled and grabbed Kido's shirt, pulling him closer. "You worthless boy. I ain't gonna keep you in the shop forever. It's time for you to learn a trade and make a living. You're lucky Riley here is willing to make space for you on his boat. And I'm willing to let you keep half your wages."

"Boy seems lazy," said Riley, a fat hairy arm scratching his belly as he looked around, looking out of place surrounded by books.

"Ah, he just needs some hard work to toughen him up."

Now at that moment, the wizard-side of Kido kicked in, and he realized what he must do. He said boldly, "How can I go learn Magic when I'm out on a fishing boat? I'm going to run off and join the Red Tower!"

"You're going nowhere. I told you before. Magic is worthless, so forget about that tower business. You belong to me and you will do as I say."

Riley said to Uncle Oto, "I'm giving him two weeks. If he doesn't work out by then, I'm giving him back."

Uncle Oto rubbed his whiskers. "He'll work out. He *better* work out. You hear me, Kido?"

Kido looked at the floor, feeling his courage ebb away.

Riley to Oto, "I'll give you 300 silver drags for him."

"300! We agreed on 500."

"That was before I saw him. He's a bit scrawny for working on a fishing boat. After a few weeks, if he can do the job and doesn't run away, I'll give 200 more."

Uncle Oto scowled again and rubbed his whiskers. "All right, I reckon I don't have much of a choice. You start with Riley tomorrow, Kido. Now go run along and steal something to eat from Ludy."

After eating his turnips and potatoes washed down with goat's milk, Kido went out to feed the animals. Elger was waiting for him behind the coop.

"Moin moin, Kido! How are you?" he asked cheerfully.

Kido smiled to see him, but his face quickly grew glum again. "Lousy, actually. Oto wants me to learn fishing."

"I doubt he can appreciate what a dismal waste of your talents it is to plop you on a fishing vessel."

"I don't want to stay here anymore." Kido stood there holding a scoopful of chicken feed, staring out to the east, away from the sea. "My friends are trapped in the Ruined Lands, and it's my fault."

Elger leaned on his staff and looked thoughtful. "Knowing when to leave is crucial for a boy who wants to become a man, and for a bookshop clerk who wants to be something more."

Kido looked down at the ground as he thought. "Do you think I can learn enough Magic to help my friends?"

"You can levitate already, and I sense a powerful Magic in you. That is obvious to me. Only time will tell, but I'm willing to take you with me. The future for wizards is uncertain, and who knows if we can reopen the towers, but one thing *is* for sure. You'll never learn proper Magic in this little town."

Kido looked at him and then down at the chicken feed, and then at the cottage. "Can I have time to get my things and say goodbye?"

"I will come by early tomorrow morning."

Kido sat on his small bed in the summer kitchen. Above him was a small shelf holding his tiny library. He took down his leather-bound journal and put it in his backpack. From the box on the floor that served as his closet, he stuffed spare clothes in with his journal. He put in some food he had taken from the larder, just a few apples, biscuits, and goat's cheese. He had said his goodbyes but only to the pigs, goats, and chickens. Not a word had he said to Uncle Oto or Ludy about his plans, wanting to sneak away in the early morning. He took a mental inventory of his meager belongings. Then he remembered. In the stone wall under the window, he pulled out a loose stone and reached in to retract a small box. Replacing the stone, he opened the box to look at the Dragon's Gift of the gold necklace with the jewels, Kido put the necklace on and the box in his backpack. He turned around just as Uncle Oto shambled in.

"Where do you think you're going?"

"Nowhere." Kido iced up at Oto's grouchy bossiness.

"You're not running off on the night before your new job. I'll see to that." And he grabbed Kido's arms and pulled him outside. Oto was bigger and stronger than the boy, and Kido could not wriggle free from his powerful grip.

"I want my trust fund now."

"You haven't been here long. It's still pretty small."

"I'll take whatever is there. I'm going to go east."

"You're going on that boat with Riley tomorrow morning and nowhere else."

Ludy was outside and had the cellar doors open.

"Down you go," Oto said and shoved him down the steps. He stumbled down and fell hard onto the cold dirt floor. The doors slammed shut, and Kido was in utter darkness. He slept that night on a tarpaulin spread on the floor, wondering how he was going to get away to Elger. Several times he climbed the steps and shook, pulled, and pushed on the doors, but it was no good. They had been locked tight.

Finally exhausted, he fell asleep. When he awoke he could see the gray light of predawn filtering through the crack between the cellar doors. He tried them again but to no avail. He paced the dirt floor in despair, feeling time passing and fearing Elger would leave without him. He searched in the pitch-black darkness for an object to use on the doors and eventually by touch found a piece of lumber as tall as himself, and he banged at the doors with it.

But the doors were solid, and the lock still held. He dropped the wood in resignation and sat on a step, his head brushing the doors, the contact reminding him of freedom's proximity. For a moment there in the darkness he let the dregs of defeat wash over him; despair enveloped him. He played with the emotions for a moment until they bored him. Then he felt for and took back up the lumber and jammed it up tight until the doors bulged as far as the lock would allow. Cool air filtered through the crack, and he put his eye to it until satisified that the lock was no answer. The grayness was turning lighter, meaning it was Cloudrise. Elger would be by and Oto would probably tell him that Kido had run away, and so Elger would leave without him!

Crawling over he saw the crack at the one door's edge. Here were the large hinges holding it to the frame. The hinges were solid like the lock, but he perceived the screws that held them, biting into the wood of the frame. A flame appeared in the darkness of his mind, and he tried the *levitation* spell until his head hurt but nothing happened. The despair returned. He sat on the cold stairs and thought of all his experiences since he had left Putnam Castle. All his memories were sad ones except for Akasha. He took a hold of her gift and felt its warm energy pierce the gloom. Kido turned around and tried again, taking long slow breaths. He relaxed and let his thoughts gravitate naturally towards the spell. He began levitating the first screw, feeling it more than seeing it as it slowly rotated out. After it popped out, he levitated the other with growing excitement. With the one corner unhinged, he could prop open the door and crawl out onto the lawn. He was free! Standing up he saw a man sitting on low wall nearby watching him.

"Elger!"

Kido bounded up and hugged him. "I was afraid I would miss you, and you would leave without me."

"If you hadn't gotten out of that basement, I would have."

Kido's smile eased. "What do you mean? How long have you been here?"

"Nearly an hour."

"And you knew I was trapped down there and didn't help me?"

"I wanted to see if you could get out yourself, and you did. You're not going to make much of a wizard if a locked cellar door can defeat you."

Kido looked around. "But where's Oto?" He no longer thought of him as *uncle*.

Elger looked up, and Kido followed his gaze to see Oto sitting on the peak of the cottage's roof.

"He came at me with an axe, so I had to put him where he could do no harm," Elger explained.

"You can't leave! I have plans for you," Oto bellowed down.

"I don't belong here," Kido said with quiet determination.

"You should stay here and be safe, boy. If you go wandering off with wizards, you'll come to a bad end," Oto said.

"I want my trust fund," Kido said.

"There's no fund. I spent what little you made," Oto admitted.

"At Bolly's Tavern, I bet," said Kido.

"Ready to go?" Elger said.

"Just one thing." He ran inside to get his backpack. When he turned to the door, he saw Ludy standing there holding a package.

"I have to go," Kido said.

"Just like that. You're leaving us after all we've done for you."

"Yes, just like that." He took a step towards her. "And you can't stop me."

Her face was drawn and pinched. Her graying brown hair was pulled up into a severe bun, and she wore her usual worn housecoat. She didn't seem like a happy woman, and Kido felt sorry for her. She nodded her head in resignation.

"Here," she said, holding out the package. "I packed you some food. I hope you don't get eaten by a dragon. And one more thing." She reached under the counter and came out with a book that she handed to him.

He read the title, *"Growler's Beastopedia!"*

"199th edition. You were the only one who ever read that book. You might as well take it with you."

"Thank you," he said with glee.

She stared at him and then turned and retreated wordlessly into the living room. Kido took one last look around before he left. "I hope they remember to feed the animals," he said. He passed a startled Riley walking by and came around the house to Elger when a male voice halted him in his tracks.

"You two stand still. That boy is under arrest."

Kido turned to see the Burgermeister and several town guards approaching with drawn swords.

"Arrest? Why would you arrest an orphan boy?" said an unconcerned Elger.

"The boy was seen freeing a condemned prisoner, and who are you, stranger, to question the Burgermeister?"

"I am no one you need to know."

Oto yelled down from the roof, "Arrest the boy! He's going to run off to one of the Magic Towers!"

"Oto! What are you doing on your roof?"

"The stranger picked me up with invisible hands and put me here. He's a wizard, too!" said Oto.

The Burgermeister looked suddenly fearful and stepped back to eye Elger. The guards moved closer and waved their swords threateningly.

"Stranger, don't try anything crazy. I have to arrest you in the King's name. You must be hanged," said the Burgermeister, sounding none too confident. Elger looked like a more dangerous customer than Puy du Pome to him.

"Oh?" said Elger in a tone of exaggerated innocence.

Kido looked in concern from one to the other. The two groups faced off, but then the ground shook with a rumble before a huge animal suddenly came from around the corner, lowered its head and charged the soldiers. They dropped their swords and ran away yelling. The Burgermeister turned to run, and the shaggy beast plowed into him, knocking him over. The Bugermeister struggled up and ran wide-eyed as the beast, grunting all the way, pursued him down the hill towards Bolly's Tavern. Quiet once again descended upon the yard.

Elger turned to a surprised Kido and said pleasantly, "I think we can go now."

They walked along the wide stone-paved road called the Northern Way, through a landscape of rolling meadows full of wildflowers with the occasional farmhouse surrounded by well-tended fields. The Ruination appeared to have not touched these lands. They hadn't gone far when Kido heard a heavy thudding noise, and turning, was frightened to see that same large animal emerging from the nearby trees and approaching at speed.

"Master, that wild animal—"

"He's not wild, just ill-behaved. That's my rupa."

Kido stopped and stared. The rupa was a large six-legged beast of burden as tall as the wizard, covered in shaggy gray hair, swaying a massive head. He had several large saddlebags hanging from a wide belt tied around his midsection. He stopped to return Kido's stare, and Kido saw a bright intelligence in those brown eyes. They formed a special unspoken bond with just a few heartbeats.

Elger had not stopped or even looked behind. "He's my sometimes traveling companion, Kido. You can trust him."

Kido resumed walking and looked back to see the rupa following them. "I have read about rupas in the *Beastopedia*, but they have only four legs."

"That's the common rupa you find everywhere. This one is special. The 200th edition of *Growler's* is supposed to come out with an entry on the six-legged kind."

Kido settled down and concentrated on keeping pace with his fast-walking master, and the rupa brought up the rear. Thus formed, the trio of traveling companions walked by day and camped by night, moving northeast through the rolling hills of Upperealm. Days passed, and the coast fell further behind.

Kido accepted his new relationship with his master and enjoyed his new-found freedom on the open road following Elger. Frequently Elger took dried fruit and nuts from one pouch and munched as he walked. Frequently he passed a handful to the boy. They followed a simple routine like this. The sky was always overcast, but the weather was mild.

One morning the scenery changed and the two stopped. "Look, Kido," the man said and gestured with his staff at a dark green fringe along the southern horizon. "Yonder there is Bremen Wood." The boy dutifully considered the far-off trees. Kido took out his journal and pencil from his pack and wrote:

Master Elger and Apprentice Kido on the 83rd day in the Season of Flowers came in sight of the Bremen Wood while on a journey east, 69 days after leaving Feather Bay.

He put his materials away after Elger nodded his approval.
"Does our path go near the woods?" Kido asked.
"Not yet, Kido."
"Will we...ever go into the woods?"
"Who can say? Strange occurrences are said to happen there. And bands of orphan boys grow up wild in those woods. They're called Bremen Boys. We continue east while those woods stretch south to the mountains," Elger said in his gentle voice. "Our business is in Tempest, but then you must go to Ballastro. *There* is the Red Tower. *There* is a wizard named Numachitura, also known as Numa, or at

least it used to be before it was closed. And *that* is your ultimate destination."

Kido's eyes widened. "I always wanted to see the capital city. I hear the bones of a giant are on display there."

Elger nodded. "Brought back by Cromartin from the Ruined Lands. Cromartin tells the tale that he did slay the giant to save his father."

"I did not see the fight or die in the Ruination."

"You were lucky to get away."

Kido was silent for a moment while thinking about his missing friends. Then he thought of the young blonde prince and said, "I was a slave boy when Marnoch was King. I wonder how Cromartin compares as King."

Elger chewed on some fruit and leaned on his staff. "Mad Marnoch believed in the Prophecy, in his own crazy way. Cromartin does not. If Cromartin acknowledges the Prophecy, it is only because he cannot ignore the stories of treasure and power waiting inside those gates. But they say he distrusts Magic and wizards. I doubt he believes in dragons. Cromartin only believes in gold."

They stood in silence for a moment in contemplation of how the Ruination had changed everything. Then Elger began walking again in his steady, mile-chomping stride and Kido followed. The rupa came last, its head lowered and swaying as it plodded along. The faithful beast needed no leash to follow the humans. As they walked Kido's curiosity gnawed at him.

"Who is the wizard Numachitura, master?"

"Call her *Numa*, for nobody likes to pronounce long names. Perhaps when we are resting in Tempest, I will take the time to explain all that."

"Who will we see in Tempest, master?"

"A friend of mine called Atticus."

"Is he a wizard, too?"

"Yes."

"How long have you known him?"

"Since I was knee-high to a squark. He was my teacher you see."

"And how long will we stay in Tempest?"

"For as long as we need. Maybe he can help you get to the Red Tower, to see if Magic can still be studied there."

"What if we cannot get into the Red Tower, master?"

"Call me Elger, for I am a Pariah. Pray we can, for the other towers are not options. Consider say the Shadow Tower. The Master there as I recall was Astrabanipal, whose name from here on out I will shorten to *Astra,* and I suggest you do the same. But the wizards of that tower all died in the Ruination or went over to Cromartin and became Black Sorcerers. No on knows what happened to Astra, but I would say the Shadow Tower is out, and he is likely dead like Ramanapirus. The Shadow Tower is not a place I would send you anyways."

"What of the other towers, mast—, er Elger?"

Elger stopped and knitted his eyebrows in consternation. "Well, that leaves only two: the Green and Gold Towers. The Gold Tower you already know about, and the Green Tower is run by the elves of Alfheim. The path is unclear now."

"This Astra must also be a wizard?"

"Yes indeed."

"A great wizard?"

"Indubitably."

"The greatest wizard of all time?"

"No, he was not *that* good. Great wizards are few and far between. There are of course the four great wizards of old to consider. And then I would add to them Ramanapirus, as the greatest wizard of *modern times.*"

"The Gold Mage?" Kido thought of the wizard he had met at the Golden Tower, who always seemed cold and aloof.

"Yes, Ramanapirus, he whose name cannot be shortened."

"He may be dead!"

"Or disappeared. So is Astra."

"When did you last see Numa or Astra, teacher?"

"Many years ago, I confess."

"I don't know what to do. I want to be a wizard but I also want to go east and look for my friends. I need to find someone named Chizmo, too."

"You are already a few years past the prime age for entering a Magic Tower, but you have little choice."

"Am I already too old to learn Magic?"

Elger stopped and stroked his beard. "You will find as you get older that life is short, and timing is everything. When you still have time! It seems only a few years ago that I was your age and some sneaky trick that I got so old so fast. Time is a slippery concept. When you are young you want time to speed up, and then the years pile up just as you want them to slow down. It fascinates me; it frightens me.

By the fire of dragons, I didn't know any better when I was your age. Kido, the Magic Towers aren't what they used to be. I haven't been inside one since before the Ruination. You'll have to decide if you want to try and enter a Magic Tower to study or if you will go east to look for your friends. But first come with me and talk to my friend Atticus. He always has good advice. Then maybe our paths can remain joined for awhile longer."

Kido's eyes widened and excitement caught in his voice. "You would help me go east or go to the Red Tower? Like on a quest?"

Elger let out a deep sigh. "We shall see. I have been out of touch for too long, but for now you may consider yourself my apprentice. I have only a modest amount of knowledge to share, but I can at least get you started down the path to becoming a wizard. So we go to Tempest, then maybe get you to Ballastro. After that I will turn you over to someone more competent than I." He turned away and resumed walking, his staff used like a walking stick.

"How much bigger is Ballastro than Tempest or Feather Bay, Elger?"

"Feather Bay could fit in one neighborhood in Tempest, and Tempest could fit in one neighborhood in Ballastro."

"And how many neighborhoods are there in Ballastro?"

"Seems like fifty or more."

"Where is the Red Tower located in the capital city?"

"In an area called Topside."

"Topside." Kido savored the name like a tasty morsel of food. He noticed when Elger said *Topside* that he put a lilt in his voice. Kido copied that inflection.

They walked for a bit, then Elger remembered. "Who is Chizmo?"

"A gem genie."

"Oh, nice."

7
Hearing Voices

They slept that night inside a large tree grove well off the road. In the wee hours before cloudrise, Kido's sleep was interrupted by a feminine voice in his head.

P: Kido, are you still living with the Gold Hood wizards?

He was still in a deep sleep yet the voice found its way through the layers of his mind. Her voice came as if in a dream.

P: I am asleep
P: I just woke up
P: I left the wizards long ago where have you been?
P: I have been asleep too
P: For a thousand years?
P: Where i am i sleep a lot as do my companions there is little else to do here but sleep although i feel more energy now than I have for a long time my sleep is not as deep as it used to be yet I have been here so long
P: Where is here?
P: Sporu Angosta
P: The place of the prophecy?
P: I do not know of a prophecy i only know where i am

Kido turned over and opened his eyes. He was startled to hear the voice after such a long absence and to hear it refer to a place of myth and legend. There were dragons behind the gate that he had touched. His hand went to the pendant lying against his chest.

P: Thank you for your gift

There was no answer. He waited but heard nothing more and rolled back over, his mind too stimulated now to sleep. He vowed next time to ask Akasha if she had seen any wizards in Sporu Angosta.

They stood and watched the sky as darker clouds came in from the east to drive out the lighter clouds that were always there. Kido had already learned what a keen interest Elger took in the weather. He was always commenting on the shape of clouds, direction of the wind, the absence of the sun. Rain was also noteworthy. Right now a soft mist was coming down. Then a flicker of lightning off in the distance, followed several seconds later by the gentle roll of thunder.

Elger nodded in approval. "Nature's energy. Let us tap into it and try an experiment, Kido, my worthy apprentice."

Kido watched as Elger held out one hand while he spoke a spell word. His palm filled with twinkling light that coalesced into a small crystal globe. He went over and placed it on a tree stump and came back to Kido, who was watching expectantly.

"I am the teacher; you are the apprentice. You will learn from me how to tap into your innate Magic," said Elger. "Your basic introduction into Wizardry will begin here, since we don't know if the Red Tower will ever reopen. If Atticus cannot get you inside a Magic Tower, then I will do the best I can in the real world. I can teach you many of the same things you would learn in the Red Tower, up to a point."

Elger squared up on the tree stump, twenty feet away. "Observe." He pointed his finger and spoke a word, and a crooked bolt of purplish energy lept from his fingertip to shatter the globe. He pointed his finger up at the sky and from it a small black tendril of smoke climbed up like a vine. Kido felt the energy emanating from him and smelled something strangely pleasant.

Elger said, "The *Zap* or *Lightning Bolt* spell is very basic, one spell out of hundreds if not thousands. It can have an offensive or defensive purpose. Every wizard learns it as one of their first spells."

Elger cast another globe in his hand and placed it on the stump and returned. "Now your turn," he said to apprentice.

Kido curled his lower fingers until only his index finger pointed out like a pistol. He looked at it, as if mystified how to make it work.

"Did you mark the spellword I used?" Elger asked.

"Yes, Elger, but I've never tried to shoot a bolt of lightning before."

"You have learned your first lesson. You must find the Magic within you and tap into it." Elger leaned over and tapped a finger against Kido's torso. "It's in there, but only you can find it. I can only encourage you, nothing more. This is where the true wizards get separated from the charlatans, whether you can find the Magic within."

Kido still felt the pressure of Elger's finger against his body. He searched within him, curious, wanting to find the Magic. He thought of the one spell he knew, *Levitation*, and felt something familiar stir within him. He could levitate the globe—he looked at his finger—but could he destroy it with a bolt of energy?

He pointed his finger at the globe and concentrated real hard, holding his breath. He grit his teeth and scrunched up his face. He willed lightning to shoot out of his finger with all his might—and nothing happened. He closed his eyes and redoubled his intensity, hoping to hear the crackle of energy and the shattering of crystal, and—nothing.

Elger chuckled, leaning on his staff.

Kido opened his eyes and saw the globe sitting undisturbed. He released a noisy exhalation and looked at Elger. "I don't know if I can do it."

"Doubt kills opportunity. Don't even think like that or else you'll never do it. Try and levitate the globe first. You know you can levitate," said Elger.

Kido faced back towards the globe, focused, and a sparkling energy bubbled in his belly. He made the globe rise slowly three feet and then let it drop back down. The energy within faded away.

"See? Now tap into that same energy but with a different spell. Focus on the storm clouds and think of lightning. Connect with their power, and do not hold your breath or tense up. You're just blocking the energy. Relax and let it flow, don't force it."

"Thanks, Obi-wan."

"What?"

"Never mind."

Kido thought of the energy in the clouds, letting the rest of the world fade away. His eyes remained open but he no longer saw anything but that globe. The bubbling began inside him, and he let it move, visualizing it rising up and flowing into his arm, and feeling it happen. The energy rose higher, paused, then faltered. Kido grew angry and frustrated, and the energy dropped away. So he forced himself to relax, to take in deep breaths while focusing on the energy in an almost casual way, and as he did so, a small locus of awareness formed in his mind. He let his mind expand upward to a cloud full of energy. He smelled the lightning and his hair stood on end. Magic began to boil. It rose up quickly and erupted. He pointed his finger and cast the spell as a red mist formed in front of his eyes. The energy burned hot in his arm and crackled into the air from his finger. There was a huge crack and the sound of splintered wood.

Kido groaned and fell to the ground, his energy spent.

The red mist cleared and he saw the smoking stump split in two. The globe had been knocked to the ground in front of it.

Elger said drily, "I think you used a little too much Magic."

Kido cast again and a greenish bolt scored a black streak in the grass to the right of the globe. He adjusted. Another bolt and the globe finally shattered.

Elger said, "As important as your ability to tap into your Magic is, knowing *how much* Magic is required and how to control it is just as important." He walked off.

Kido looked at his smoking finger in wonder.

Elger peered out between the branches of a tree at the road a good ways down the hill. He turned around and said to Kido and the rupa, "Plenty of people out there, and your Burgermeister's report has had time to reach the King. No doubt the road is watched with unfriendly eyes now that we are close to Tempest. Therefore, we will wait until nightfall."

They retreated back to their campsite at a spot in the woods well away from the road. Elger left Kido to start a fire and walked off into the trees. Soon he came back dragging a long branch and took a hand axe out of one of rupa's pouches. He sat down on a log and began lopping off branches. He switched to a dagger and scraped off the bark, then whittled for awhile. "Do you have a knife?"

Kido thought of Jabu, who he missed very much. "No."

Elger handed over the rough-hewn staff and the dagger. "Try and work on that awhile. Make it straight and true." And though Kido knew nothing of woodworking he tried to emulate Elger's motions. Elger would watch and offer suggestions. "The Upperealm between Feather Bay and Tempest is sparsely populated, but not so the river valley. Now that we are close to Tempest, we will have to be more on our guard."

"From the King's soldiers?"

"Aye and from commoners too."

"Why commoners?"

"Wizards are a rare but instantly recognizable lot. Also, we're unpopular with many. We're blamed for the Ruination, among other things. Also, having a giant rupa with you automatically makes people stare," said Elger.

Kido was only half-listening, admiring the staff that was taking shape. "It's not exactly a proper wizard's staff."

"But it will do as a quarterstaff," said Elger.

"How long does it take an apprentice to earn his wizard's staff, teacher?"

"That depends on the apprentice."

Kido stared at the claw-shaped horn around Elger's neck. "What is that, Elger?"

"A special hollow horn for carrying."

"Carrying what?"

"Ichor."

"What is ichor?"

"Magic dust, made from the blood of a dragon."

"Which dragon?" Kido asked, playing dumb.

"Many dragons once roamed Arcadia until they were driven to Sporu Angosta. Ichor comes from the blood of the *mother* dragon."

Kido loved to talk about dragons. "Tiamat."

"Yes. The mother of all dragons. The Cosmic Dragon. You have heard of her?"

"Sort of." He knew all this from the board game back in Porterville.

"She lived in the ancient times. Her life was forfeited and her blood used to make ichor dust."

"How much ichor dust do you have?"

"Unfortunately, my horn is nearly empty. Since I am a Pariah, I was cut off from the supply years ago. There would be a store of it in the Red Tower. Or hidden elsewhere in Arcadia."

"How many dragons are there?"

"Among the primes there is Pangma the Gold, Ramyre the Red, Sanshinar the Green, and Mazunga the Shadow Dragon. Each has its own tower."

"Any others?"

"There are many others, most of whom don't have names or even towers. Let's see, there is Wingbat the Desert Dragon, Akasha the Blue, Vesica the Horned Dragon, Tailwhip the Tarsus Dragon. That's all I can think of for now."

Kido stared a moment at the horn and then pulled out his journal to record what Elger had said. Elger munched on an apple and waited, and the rupa ate sweet grass until it grew dark. Then Elger got up and kicked out the fire. "March on, Master Kido. Attitcus awaits."

They resumed walking in the same order: Elger, Kido, rupa. It was night but Elger seemed to have a sixth sense that directed his feet. They walked in silence, crossing meadows and farmers' fields. Kido stayed close to Elger's barely discernable dark shape, afraid to lose him. but eventually he began to relax and his mind wandered. He was deep in thought, assimilating all he'd seen on his trek east, so deep in fact that he almost missed a voice in his head.

P: I heard the voice talking to you last night

He looked around trying to see where the voice came from. Elger kept walking as if he had heard nothing.

P: Behind you

Kido turned to see the rupa's big dark shape right behind him. He opened his mouth but shut it again, confused about what to say. Then he tried thinking a thought and directing it at the rupa.

P: Is that you rupa?

P: Yes

Kido was flabbergasted. First the return of the mysterious voice and now this from rupa.

P: How can you hear me and how can I hear you?

P: It is called telepathy

P: What does the *P:* stand for?

P: The *P:* stands for *Ping*. That's what you do when you send someone a telepathic message

P: I never knew

P: Only certain wizards and a few highly intelligent creatures know these things

Kido made a startled noise aloud. Elger turned to look back at him. "It is nothing, master," Kido assured him.

P: Just relax and pretend telepathy is normal

The rupa's thought was full of warm humor.

Kido kept walking.

P: Is this normal for everyone?

P: I dont know i dont try to communicate with most people and even when i do it usually fails but you seem different

P: What can i say?

P: You mean what can you ping?

P: I'm still getting used to that word

P: Not bad vocabulary for an animal eh?

Kido laughed aloud and Elger turned and stopped. "Are you all right?"

"Yes, Elger," Kido said, and they resumed walking.

P: Yes Elger

P: You mock me?

P: I heard that female voice talking to you last night

Kido gasped aloud.

Elger turned and looked but kept walking with a shake of his head.

P: What did you hear?

P: She asked if you live with wizards she sounds nice

P: Shes been talking to me since the ruination i've never met her

P: Of course not one doesn't meet a creature like that

P: A creature like what? Do you know who she is?

P: She is a dragon

Kido stopped cold and brought the rupa up short.

P: Hey keep going the wizard is getting ahead of us

Kido resumed walking but his mind was spinning.

P: How do you know she is a dragon?

P: I have heard their voices before a dragons voice is like no other

P: You hear dragon voices too?

P: From time to time

P: Explain please

P: Some animals can telepathize but most cannot i have had telepathic conversations with rabbits, birds, squarks, other rupas, and dragons there is a whole world going on which most humans remain stupidly unaware of

P: But the dragons are all in sporu angosta they do not even belong to this world

P: Are not dragons Magical creatures

P: Apparently so are rupas but still

P: They can project their voices from far away when they want though sometimes there is some kind of Magical interference that gets in the way and they sleep a lot

Kido was so intrigued by this conversation he could hardly stand it.

P: How many dragons have you heard?

P: I have differentiated all five including your female the others refer to her as akasha

P: Akasha the blue

P: So i understand

P: Have you heard the others elger named?

P: There is a nasty male one who calls himself Mazunga and i have heard the names sanshinar and ramyre at various times

Kido was amazed.

P: Dragons you listen to dragon voices

P: I dont seek them out they float on the air like the wind blowing from the east sometimes it is a babble and sometimes you can hear a single dragon voice quite distinctly the voices come and the voices go last night akashas voice came to you

P: And to you

P: Thats true but she was talking to you

P: But you heard her too

P: I dont think she realized I was listening i stayed telepathically silent what does a dragon need from a rupa?

P: What does she need from a young apprentice who only knows two spells and doesnt even have a proper staff?

P: Or ichor

Kido walked on, confused and excited all at the same time.

P: I must think on this

P: I must lay some droppings

The next day Elger announced that they had reached their destination, although it was hard for Kido to tell because they were still surrounded by trees. Elger led them forward and soon the trees ended at the edge of a large valley. Below them the land was clear and they could see a large town beside a large lake. Tempest was protected by a tall, log wall.

They stopped to contemplate the town, resting on their staffs. "The Northern Way runs right through Tempest. There is a city gate where it enters from the west and exits to the east. Or vice-versa if you're coming the other way," Elger said. "Plus there is the River Gate on the south side, but there is no gate on this side. The gates are always guarded now."

"Who travels from the east this far north, Elger?"

"Not many these days. Used to be that merchants, mercenaries, adventurers, dwarves, elves, all sorts of people would come along this road as it connects Arcadia with Pandoon. But the Ruination put a stop to that. Many humans fled west and filled up Tempest, some going further on to Ballastro, Feather Bay, Port Laphere, and elsewhere. Then the dwarves and elves shut up their kingdoms and hunkered down. Trolls began to appear out of the mountains to prey upon travelers, first making them pay tolls to pass and, if the latest rumors are correct, even capturing and eating people unfortunate enough to be caught. Some have taken to calling the road The Troll Toll Road. Why, it has even been said that goblin patrols have been spotted in the north woods section of the road, when no one has heard of goblins in many, many years. Imagine trolls and goblins! Only the very foolish now use the stretch of the road east of Tempest."

The rain began softly drumming on their hoods again, as if realizing it had been slacking off. A few mosquitos began to drone around their heads in a friendly fashion.

"Back east is where I must go as soon as I am a wizard," said Kido. "I hope I can find my friends."

"Now few good folk remain in Pandoon, except for in the far south at Amphyra and elsewhere along that coast."

"And the elves of Alfheim?"

"No one can say what has happened to the poor elves left in Alfheim. Even the Elvish Warlock was killed in the Ruination."

A thought struck Kido. "How are we going to get into town when there is no gate on this side and the others have guards?"

Elger turned to grin at him from inside his hood. "There is no *official* gate, but there is a way. Come and see."

8
Tempest

Elger led Kido close to the walls of Tempest. There was a wide treeless sward that circled the town, broken only by a tall oak, none too close to the the wall. As Elger passed the oak he glanced up and tapped it with his staff. The last twenty feet to the wall was bare of even grass. Elger turned and slowly walked along, his right arm outstretched to let his hand brush the tall vertical logs that circled the town. The wizard's eyes were closed, and he seemed to be muttering something, but Kido could not make out the words. The boy followed entranced by what his teacher was doing.

Suddenly Elger stopped and opened his eyes. "Here," he said simply. Kido now saw a giant oak was standing next to them where before there had been nothing. He looked back at the sward but the oak was gone. "Did that tree just move?" he asked, but the wizard wasn't listening.

Elger spoke a strange word and the tree bent its branches so the wizard could climb on board. "Well, are you coming?"

Kido stood surprised and Elger laughed. "What's the matter, Kido? Haven't you ever climbed a tree?"

Kido looked back again and saw the rupa quietly watching them from the edge of the forest.

"The rupa stays. He doesn't take to the urban life."

P: He's right

Kido climbed up a branch and held on while the oak lifted them up and deposited them over the wall on the other side. The oak stretched back to its own height and was soon gone.

"I planted that oak years ago and fertilized it with a little Magic," Elger said.

Kido found they were in a narrow dirt street between the wall and a long line of rough wooden houses. He saw a young boy standing nearby staring at them with wide eyes. Elger winked at the boy as they walked by. The boy closed his eyes and when he reopened them a few seconds later, the strangers and the memory of their passing were both gone. He looked down at his hand, and a piece of candy was there.

They walked down narrow alleys between wooden buildings, passing residents of Tempest who gaped at the two but seemed to forget about them as soon as they passed. Elger walked quickly and Kido hurried to keep up. He got a quick impression of the town as they moved. He saw poorly built houses, many with small fenced-in yards with vegetable patches. Some buildings were three or four stories tall. The alleys were crowded and so were the buildings he could look in, for it was hot and doors and windows were left open in the vain search for a breeze. Children were everywhere, as were old people walking with baskets or working in their gardens, and women carrying laundry, but few young adult men were around. The people had a lean, hungry look about them, and they wore ragged, patched clothes.

They came out to where the alley opened onto a wide street and Elger peeked out. He suddenly stiffened and threw a protective arm around Kido. Quickly he drew them both back to crouch behind a large rain barrel. There was a flurry of movement and some startled cries from the street. Trying to peek out around the barrel and past Elger, Kido only saw some large, dark humanoid shapes lumber by.

After they passed, Kido whispered, "What are those things?"

Elger whispered, "I don't know. I've never seen such creatures."

They retreated back the way they had come before turning right and moving cautiously past many houses. This street was empty of people. They turned down a new street. Elger was counting alleys and buildings and soon came to one he liked, knocking on the door. To Kido it looked like all the others. The door opened to reveal the familiar face of a young red-haired woman with beautiful blue eyes.

"Paula!"

"Kido!" They hugged and he whispered, "I forgot you are Pyra, not Paula in this world."

"I am Pyra Flamestar now."

On the royal barge in the middle of the huge Tempest Lake, Zirmad stood in his black robes with silver nightshades and watched a small boat approach, its wake churning the blue water as it came on. And as he waited, Zirmad thought about these younger sorcerers invited by Cromartin. They were wizards of the Shadow Tower, bribed to enter the King's service.

Sailors helped them embark, two dozen black-robed figures. Their leader carried a large bag. He kept his hood up, black gloves on his hands. Rumor had it that some devious sorcery had changed him to something less than human. He was known only as Drecks. Now he stood before Zirmad, who said, "I regret my King finding the necessity to call you from your tower."

"Your confidence in us is overwhelming." The voice was thin and cold.

"How will you serve King Cromartin?"

"With cunning and craft. The King has chosen wisely calling us to service." Each word was icily articulated.

Zirmad snorted and eyed him suspiciously. "The dragons must favor you."

"We only serve the shadow dragon."

"Yes, we'll see about your dragon." Zirmad beheld the bag that Drecks held up, finding it impossible to believe what the rumors said. "Come below and show me what you brought. Then the King will need to see you before you endeavor to contact your dragon."

They went below to Zirmad's elegant cabin and Drecks put the bag on a table. Zirmad hesitated, eyeing bag and sorcerer. Then with suddeness, he grabbed the top and pulled the cord, letting the bag fall away to reveal a strange metallic device the size of his head, as well as a golden robe, a large book with a gold cover, and a beautiful dagger with a huge sapphire in its silver hilt.

Zirmad stood back and stared, afraid to touch anything. He pointed at the device.

"Safed's Shield," Drecks offered up.

"And this must be the spellbook of you-know-who," Zirmad said pointing at the gold book.

"He whose name cannot be shortened," said Drecks.

"And what of the other articles?"

"Supposedly, the robe was what he was wearing when the Ruination exploded into being. The dagger was found with it."

Zirmad rubbed one of his chins. "Interesting that they are not damaged. You would think the robe at least to be nothing but ashes."

"Yet it is as golden and brilliant in color as the day it was made."

"How do you account for this?"

"I have no accounting for any of these mysteries, Master Zirmad."

"But you were there."

"I was not. We brothers were left behind when our Mage and Rook took the others to the Gold Tower. We survived the Ruination."

"And they did not."

Drecks shrugged. "Who knows? We have not seen them since."

"How did you come by these?"

"Our patrol came upon them in our search for our lost brothers."

Zirmad looked into the depths of that black hood and saw nothing but eternal darkness. "Leave me for a moment." After Drecks had gone, Zirmad reached out tentatively and stroked the dagger, then boldly plucked it out and put it in a secret place underneath his robe. He closed the bag and picked it up, noting its heaviness and the Magic radiating off it. He made for King Cromartin's cabin with the Black Hoods in his wake.

Pyra looked very becoming in a flame-colored robe that went down to her calves, her waist wrapped in a wide black leather belt. A pair of gold-colored gloves were tucked into that belt, and she wore red charmet boots.

"We have some catching up to do," Kido to Pyra.

"We all do," said Elger.

"Then come in quickly," said Pyra, "the streets are not safe."

Outside night had fallen while inside the study of Atticus was dim, lit only by a single lamp on the table and the flames in the fireplace. Atticus was sitting in an overstuffed chair, dressed in a long robe the color of deep crimson, two shades darker than Pyra's. He rose to embrace Elger and then held out his hand to let Kido shake it. Kido saw Atticus never opened his eyelids. He tracked them by their voice and Kido realized the old wizard was—

"Yes, I am blind," Atticus said to Kido, guessing his thoughts.

"Kido, go sit over there," said Elger, "and don't touch anything."

Kido went to a chair in the corner, close enough to hear their voices but still out of the way. He took in his surroundings. The room wasn't too large but full of objects: dressers, chairs, tables, and built-in shelves bursting with bric-a-brac. He longed to get up and examine them closely but didn't dare. Looking closer at Atticus, Kido figured the man was in his sixties. Time had delved many furrows in his weathered face. His hair and beard were mostly white though a few black strands still stood the test of time. Dangling from his neck was a horn on a leather necklace, just like Elger's. He must have some

Magic ichor dust in there. Kido focused on their conversation.

"How are you, old friend?" asked Atticus.

"A little shaken. When we were coming here by the front route, we nearly ran into a group of these huge creatures with tusks that walk upright."

"We only recently heard of them. Some vile monsters created by Zirmad. They came up with Cromartin no doubt. People are calling them Tooskers. I hear they have a fondness for human flesh."

They shuddered.

"And what of your wanderings?" Atticus asked.

"I lived for a time with the dwarves, after which I tried traveling into the Last Corner, but I got lost and barely made it back in one piece."

"Did you go into the Ruined Lands?"

"I came to their edge and found a steep drop off."

"A drop off?"

"It is as if the Ruined Lands have dropped several hundred feet below Pandoon's surface. Much of the Eastern Realm is now a sunken realm, at least what I saw of it."

Atticus sighed and shook his head in disappointment. "How bizarre. We've heard only the vaguest of rumors."

"After that, I came west. Just restless, aimless wandering. You see, I am unsure what to do with myself as an Pariah. I struggle with how to study Magic on my own, outside the Order, outside the towers. How to live in this new world, post-Ruination? But then I found someone who might change things."

"Who? Who did you find?"

Elger looked at Kido. "I found a new apprentice, a boy raised in the Golden Tower. I found Kido."

Atticus smiled. "Your new apprentice is from the Gold Tower?"

"Yes, we met at a lynching in Feather Bay. I persuaded Kido to leave his life there with a man named Oto and his job at a bookshop."

Atticus scooted to the edge of his seat and sniffed the air as if smelling out Kido.

Elger said, "He is a stranger in our land."

Atticus said, "As is Pyra."

"These two know each other."

"We are from faraway lands across the sea," Pyra said.

"And we need to find our friends and get back home," said Kido. He told his fake story to Atticus.

"Your tale is truly amazing, but I am not sure if we can render you any assistance," Atticus said. He turned to Elger. "I felt his aura when he climbed into your oak and even now it flows off him like heat from a bonfire. I suspect the lad shows promise?"

"Kido is very bright and shows considerable potential. He can levitate at will. He wants to become a wizard."

Atticus lifted his voice, "Come here, Kido," and patted the spot next to him on the sofa. The old wizard had a warm smile that Kido found comforting. Atticus gave him a long sightless gaze, and Kido got the odd feeling that Atticus was sizing him up despite his blindness. "Think you'd make a good wizard, young Kido?"

"Yes, teacher." Kido settled in on the sofa.

"Hmmm." Atticus stroked his beard. "Why?"

"I can feel it in my bones. I want to learn more Magic. I've always wanted to because I know I have special abilities." Kido felt awkward and didn't know how to express his feelings. "Sometimes I think I want to do something great and magnificent with my talents. But mostly I just want to rescue my friends and go home."

"Of course." Atticus smiled and stroked his beard some more. "Pyra, fetch my spellbook, will you?"

The girl went to a shelf of books and came back with a thick book bounded in red leather that she plopped in his lap. A large eyelid embedded in its cover stayed closed, but the book shivered at its master's touch.

Atticus opened it and transferred it to Kido's lap. The wizard moved close so that Kido could smell him and feel a warmth radiating from him. Pyra sat on his other side and he could smell her hair and perfume and feel her body's warmth, too. He felt flustered and looked at his Master. Elger looked amused at what was going on.

"What page are we on?" Atticus asked.

"Page 14," said Pyra.

"What is the first spell you read, Kido?"

Kido was looking at the spellbook, its vellum pages covered in a dense script of black ink. Each paragraph was written in a strange language but the page headings were all in the MotherTongue. "*BeeSwarm*," he read.

"Can you read any of the other lines?"

"No, teacher."

"Pyra can because I taught her to read Magic from the moment we rescued her from the slavers. First we removed her iron collar and then we taught her to read Magic. And I have the spells memorized so I don't need it read to me. In order to use a spell you need to learn the words that unlock the spell's power."

"Don't I also need the gold ichor dust to cast spells?" Kido asked.

"Ah, I see Elger has mentioned the ichor to you," said Atticus.

"He told me about the horn around his neck, like yours."

"Yes, well let me tell you about dragon's ichor. Not all spells require it. Lower level spells only require the Magical phrase and the intrinsic power of the wizard to successfully cast. Higher spells usually require a pinch of ichor to really work. And a pinch of the ol' gold dust will make *any* spell more powerful. Ichor is not needed to cast the *BeeSwarm* spell, but if you used ichor with the casting, you would get a larger, more powerful *BeeSwarm*, at least until the dust fades. Understand?"

Kido nodded. Then he realized how silly that was to nod to a blind man and said, "Yes, teacher."

"Just call me Atticus. Of course, ichor is very rare. Much of it is hidden or lost. Wizards are searching for it all the time. I used most of my ichor years ago. My horn has only a few pinches left, which I save for emergencies. So you see, I cast only what spells I can on my own. There are also artifacts that imbue Magical powers too, like a wizard's staff and certain amulets, rings, quickdraughts, and so on. But to start with, if you really want to be a wizard, you should learn some simple spells out of a spell book. And so you must start learning the language of Magic. Shall we?"

"Yes, Atticus."

"Lean closer, Kido."

Kido leaned in and Atticus bent and whispered with warm breath into his ear: "*Nuit puala quaralgi.*" Atticus straightened up.

Kido felt a tingle at the words. He opened his mouth and took a breath, wanting to repeat the phrase out loud. Pyra slapped her warm hand over his mouth.

"No, Kido, don't say it aloud," said Pyra.

"If spoken aloud, you may actually cast the spell, inexperienced as you are," said Atticus. "Assuming you have Magic in you, which we all suspect but don't want to find out here."

"Oh, he has Magic in him," said Elger.

"Then you could unleash a swarm of angry bees in my library if you cast that spell," said Atticus with a chuckle. "That's why I whispered the phrase to you, so as to cover up the power of the spell while yet giving you a taste of Magic. Remember that phrase and try it sometime when you are outside and it is safe to do so. Okay?"

Kido nodded and Pyra took her hand away.

Atticus flipped to another spot in the spell book. Pyra read, "Page 133."

"*Zap*. Also called *LightningStrike*."

"I just learned that one, teacher," Kido said.

Atticus flipped again.

"Page 237," said Pyra.

"*Levitation*," said Atticus. He flipped to the last page.

"Page 655."

"*DragonTalk*. Let's you communicate with dragons in their own language. Never been used in my lifetime but perhaps in yours. If you get inside Sporu Angosta. If the Prophecy be true."

Kido could see that Atticus knew by heart every spell on every page.

"Is there a spell for *TooskerTalk*, Atticus?" Kido asked.

"No, they are too new, and I don't think anyone would be interested in talking to them anyways," said Atticus. "But *BeeSwarm* can be your next spell. We could teach you more if you stayed here, but perhaps we should take you to the Red Tower for a proper Magical education."

"I was hoping you would offer to take him there," said Elger. "I can't and won't."

"We can try, though I fear what I might find. Numa has closed the tower to all of us, not on Cromartin's orders but just to be safe."

"You are wizards of the Black Tower?" Cromartin asked the assembled black robes. They were in a large room belowdecks.

"Shadow Tower, and we prefer to be called sorcerers," Drecks said.

Cromartin smiled at Vykar and Zirmad. "I like that." He turned back to his guests. "And this device you have? It is powerful, even against your fellow wizards?"

"Indeed, King."

Cromartin smiled again, looking over the sorcerers like a group of horses he might consider buying. "I will give you a chance to prove yourselves when we return to Ballastro. If you can defeat the wizards of the Red Tower than I will reward you handsomely. I wish also to enroll a few of my sons into your order, to study sorcery with you."

"Of course, King. All this can be done, and more. If you will set your goals higher."

Cromartin's smile faded into confusion. "What do you mean by that?"

Drecks said, "Just this, my King. I have the knowledge to get inside Sporu Angosta. What would you say to that?"

Cromartin was stunned. "What? Inside Sporu Angosta? But how? Did not the Black Hoods fail when they allied themselves with Ramanapirus and the Gold Hoods."

"Yes. But we will succeed this time."

Cromartin drew himelf and crossed his arms, trying to appear regal. "How?"

"With the dragon's help."

Cromartin and Zirmad exchanged glances. Vykar snapped his teeth at the word *dragon*.

Cromartin chuckled. "You are speaking like a Jabber now."

Zirmad mumbled, "He is mad. Breathing the vapors of the Ruined Lands for too long."

"If you will indulge me, I will show you."

Cromartin beckoned with an outstretched arm. "Why not?"

Drecks went over and knelt before a long table with his eyes closed, deep in thought, searching the unknown world for assistance. King Cromartin and Zirmad stood in complete silence watching. On the table a hundred candles were lit and cast a warm glow on the scene. Surrounded by candles sat a small sand-colored figurine of a dragon, its mouth open as if to breath fire, its eyes made of two sparkling red rubies, and its tail was a foot-long, curled up at the end where the tip was barbed.

Drecks was very nervous. Would the dragon talk to him after all this time and with so great a distance from Sporu Angosta? And if so, what would the dragon have Drecks do? Drecks had felt powerless when talking to the dragon before. How would it be now? He had been kneeling there a long time and was aware that the others were watching him and growing restive, fidgeting and exchanging impatient glances. Cromartin was starting to stand when Vykar restrained him, pointing with his scarred muzzle at the wizard and whining.

Drecks had suddenly raised his head and sucked in his breath. He felt a thick wave of powerful emotions seize him in a crushing grip, and a voice in his head heard only by him said:

P: I am mazunga and i have returned to you

The voice was masculine, deep and sinister, as if it came from the foul depths of some hell hole.

P: Where have you been master dragon?

P: Question mazunga not it is difficult to bridge the distance between your world and mazungas an enchantment blocks the way most of the time

P: Forgive me but when its been so long i fear i have lost you forever

P: Mazunga will not let that happen be patient Mazunga has waited almost a thousand years but our time is almost here

P: What do you require of me master dragon?

P: We have enemies who would thwart our designs the wizards who do not wear black must be killed

P: The red hoods cower in their tower and wont come out

P: They are there where you are in tempest

Drecks was startled at the news. He almost opened his eyes, risking losing the connection.

P: Why would they come here?

P: Mazunga cannot read their minds nor guess motives but mazunga knows there is danger there danger to me danger to you and mazunga can sense their presence near you there is something else there too but it is unfamiliar to mazunga mazunga worries about what the unknown Magic can do there is something near you

Drecks could feel the dragon's fear flow over him like a blast from a furnace. The room grew hot and all four of them began sweating. Cromartin, Vykar, and Zirmad could feel awful tension and now saw the dragon figurine changing color, deepening from a sand color to a dusky gray, then a deep purple.

P: Go now and capture the wizards mazunga will direct your movements but you must move fast use your Magic and the soldiers of your king get them and destroy them mazunga commands you only then can we be safe bring the unknown wizard to the gates for your reward

Drecks felt the hot grip of the dragon subside and he collapsed on the floor, panting. The temperature in the room suddenly dropped back to normal, and the others hurried over to help him. Within the black depths of his hood, Drecks's eyes glowed feverishly as he said, "The Red Hoods are here."

"Tower wizards?" said Cromartin. "Here outside their tower?"

Drecks could only nod his head.

"Summon the Tooskers," Cromartin ordered Zirmad. "Get McGee." Cromartin looked back to see the purple dragon figurine was now obsidian black.

Pyra put another log on the fire and brought hot soup, bread, and lemon tarts for them. Atticus and Elger huddled together and kept talking, ignoring Kido and Pyra.

"Cromartin has been conscripting most able-bodied men here in Tempest into a militia of sorts, or to work in his mines," said Atticus.

"We saw few adult men in town," said Elger.

"Even the fishermen have all been rounded up by the King's soldiers. The women and children do all the fishing in the lake now, even though the fishing is lousy since the Ruination."

"Is he assembling an army to march on Sporu Angosta? Does he take the prophecy seriously now?"

"I'm not sure. He's always been hard to read, although his lust for gold is like nothing I've ever heard. And something else. Numa has written about Cromartin's speeches against the dwarves and elves. She thinks Cromartin means to conquer Pandoon and enslave them all. He may just be using the Prophecy as an excuse to march east."

"I wish we had contact with the elves to know what they think."

"That is why a Conclave is overdue. We must summon all wizards and reopen all towers. We must send an emissary east to contact the other people and prepare for the Prophecy to come true. And we must explore what Ramanapirus did to the gates when the forces of the Ruination were unleashed. It may very well be that Sporu Angosta is finally open, and I do not want Cromartin and his sorcerers to seize that throne."

"Without the elves and dwarves, we are the only force standing in his way."

"And we're not much of a force at all. We don't even know if Astra is still alive, and now all his surviving wizards are working for the king. What treachery! As for me, I have been thinking of going to the Red Tower."

"Numa is still there?"

"Yes, and with a full company of wizards. But will she defy Cromartin? Will she accept my scheme?"

"Or will she stay hiding in her tower?"

"We may be the last people she wants to see."

Kido, who had been sitting quietly all afternoon, suddenly said,

"Dragons must get awful hungry after a thousand-year nap."

Atticus said across the room, "Yes, you are right, young Kido. We are caught between a mad king and a horde of hungry dragons. That reminds me, I must send a note to Numa. Pyra, write this down." And he dictated to her, who then rolled the note up in a tiny scroll and went out an arch to a back room.

Kido was on the edge of his seat, wondering where she went. "May I—" he began to ask.

"Yes, by all means go with her," Atticus said.

Kido went back and found himself in a short hall that came to a open door. He went through and found Pyra in an enclosed porch filled with many bird cages. All kinds of birds were there, some squawking and chirping, some preening or climbing their cages. His presence cause a flapping of wings.

Pyra was in the corner slipping the scroll into a tiny metal case. Next to her was a tall wooden stand on top of which perched a large bird with bluish-gray wings, black beak, and a cream-colored belly. It stared at Kido with its black eyes.

"What's the matter? Never seen a Mawker before?" Pyra said.

"Only in *Growler's Beastopedia*. I didn't know they could be used as a pet."

"He's not a pet. He's more a companion. A friend and a helper," she said, stroking his back while admiring him. "His name is Gulmar and he is a Messenger Mawker. She attached the case to one of the bird's legs.

The bird preened himself and then bowed to Kido. "Helper and friend to all wizards and good people," it said aloud in a raspy voice.

Kido started a little. "Did he just talk?" he asked Pyra.

"Yes. He talks," she said simply. She opened a window. "Off you go, Gulmar," she said. It squawked and flew off.

"How did you get here, Pyra?"

"I was bought right away by a man who brought me here from Z Town."

"And did he buy the others?"

"No, just me. I haven't seen them since I left the Slavers Market there. They might still be in Z Town."

"Which means they are still inside the Ruined Lands." They fell silent at the thought of their friends being most likely dead. Finally, Pyra said, "We had traveled far before the Ruination and hid in a cave when the firestorm came over us like a tsunami. I've been in

Tempest ever since. Atticus is very nice. He said his agent picked me out because of my aura. He has taught me spells and gave me this outfit and the Magical gloves. They used to belong to his daughter before she was killed by another wizard. How did you get here?"

He told her the whole story, leaving out only Akasha as he feared what she would think. When he finished, she said, "Poor Domingo and Woody. They're probably gone too, just like the others."

"They're not gone! They're just trapped inside the Ruined Lands. And the others may have gotten away in time like you did."

She felt he was more afraid than angry at the prospect that they were the last two survivors of the Porterville Gang. "Sure, you're right. I'm too pessimistic." She was reassuring herself as much as him. "Did you tell your master of Porterville?"

"No, I said I came from across the Never Sea."

"I said the same thing to Atticus."

"We'll have to tell them the truth eventually."

"Ever since I got here I've been lying about who I am and how I got here. I figure everyone will think I am lying or crazy if I tell the truth."

"But they can't help us if they don't know the truth."

"Trust is hard in a strange land."

"We don't have a choice. I'm coming clean before we get to Ballastro."

"I'll do the same."

Zirmad and Drecks marched up a narrow dirt street of Tempest. Zirmad's staff was lit with a strong blue light that cast a eerie cold glow on the buildings he passed. Behind him tramped four Tooskers, huffing and puffing and grumbling. A dozen armed soldiers of the Dragon Guard brought up the rear. A few concerned people opened their windows at the tramping noises, but hastily shut them when they saw what was passing by. Zirmad held up his staff as he came to an intersection. No one was in sight as he stood there and wondered which way to turn.

Drecks followed the other sorcerer. Suddenly a crushing wave of hot pressure passed through his head that made him stagger.

P: Mazunga says go to the right

Drecks relayed the command after gasping for air. Zirmad obeyed and his ghastly cohort followed.

By now, Kido had disobeyed Elger's command and was walking around the study, examing and touching everything. He saw several shelves full of books, some with titles, some without. And some titles were not in the MotherTongue but strange languages. There was a large table covered with interesting objects: dried plants, animal skulls, strange colored rocks like rough gemstones, various teeth from unknown creatures piled in a jar, several small jars filled with colored powders, and other objects he couldn't describe.

One corner of the study was bare except for a flat rock sitting on the floor. Pyra happened to be walking by and Kido asked her, "You know what that looks like?"

"Of course. A teleport rock, but it doesn't work. It's only a model."

"Does Atticus have any teleport keys by any chance?"

"No, but he said that all the towers should still have some. Maybe the elves have some, too, or maybe we could find some inside Sporu Angosta."

"How many teleport rocks are there?"

"I don't know. We really only need one, the one back at the Gold Tower."

"But how—" Kido began, but she had already walked off. Kido gave up and went back to his chair. He took out his journal and wrote a description of everything he had seen in the study and then carefully tucked it away. In the warm study, he felt drowsy sitting in that comfy chair, flames crackling in the fireplace. The soft voices of Atticus and Elger, still talking, receded in his mind as he felt himself nodding off. Suddenly something in his head shifted, like a window opening to let in fresh air.

P: Wake up kido danger is coming

What? he wondered. His eyes flew open and a strong tide of anxiety surged through his gut. He stood up abruptly.

P: Listen to akasha you and your friends are in grave danger you must leave now hurry

P: What kind of danger?

P: You must not stop to ask questions just leave immediately

Atticus and Elger were making travel plans when Kido ran to the window, frantically trying to peer out into the dark.

"What are you doing, Kido?" Elger said.

P: Hurry please hurry you must make them understand

"Um...please, masters. We must leave this house now. We must flee now." They stared at him in confusion. Kido raised his voice.

"Masters, I have just received a warning. Great danger is coming our way. I think we need to leave this house."

P: You must leave that town flee into the open wilderness quickly kido akasha begs you to move them now

"Flee this house?" Elger asked.

"Actually, flee this town. We must leave Tempest...immediately."

Everyone could sense his fear; even Pyra noticed.

The wizards were men with good intuition. Elger stood and grabbed his staff.

Atticus sat up and took out a small crystal, which he caressed in his hands. "My *Fear Crystal* is hot. The boy is right. Something evil is nearby. I feel like we're being hunted."

P: Mazunga says turn right seventh house on the left run with speed capture before they can get away mazunga commands

Zirmad began running while holding his staff up high, the Tooskers tramping loudly behind him. He could see the house now, warm light coming from its second floor windows. Drecks collapsed after passing on the dragon's commands, too overcome to follow.

"Who gave you this mysterious warning, Kido?" Elger said.

Now they heard the heavy, dull tramping coming up their street. "No time for that," yelled Atticus. "Pyra, grab my spell book. Everyone to the back porch!"

They ran out of the study and down the hall. Atticus stopped long enough to grab a necklace off a shelf and his staff. They all piled onto the porch with the bird cages. Pyra was frantically opening cages and releasing birds.

"What now?" Elger asked.

"We need to take flight. Fritillary and her friends will help us now," Atticus said, and feeling with his hands he located a large covered cage in the corner. He pulled a sheet off to reveal several large, white feathery moths. Pyra was standing on a stool, removing a sliding panel to open a hole in the roof. Several birds flew away.

Outside the tramping was louder and then it stopped. For a split second there was silence, and then an awful crashing noise as the front door downstairs splintered. Some beast roared below them. Akasha seemed to hear it too.

P: Hurry get away

Atticus took the horn from around his neck, uncorked it, and poured some ichor dust into his hands. The gold dust filled the porch with a warm light and the air smelled of something richly organic, which reminded Kido of what he smelled the day of the Ruination at the Gold Tower. Kido stood mesmerized by the sight, feeling something powerful and strange move through him.

"Pyra first," Atticus said, and reaching in, his hand took a moth and brought it out of the cage. He chanted the spell words, and the air around the moth glowed and sparkled with a golden light. He handed it to Pyra and the moth began to grow in size until in a few seconds it was almost as long as Pyra was tall. She climbed onto its back, and they flew up through the hole in the roof and disappeared into the night sky.

"Elger next," Atticus said. And he took another moth and gave it to Elger and with a burst of Magic his transformed moth carried him up and away too.

"You're next, Kido," Atticus said. The old wizard cupped a glowing moth in his hand and held it out.

Kido in shocked delight took it. The moth grew suddenly, and Kido took a hold of it with both hands, sliding onto its back as it became big enough to hold him. Behind him, down the hall, he could hear walls being smashed and some creatures roaring with fierce voices. He felt the aura now, an evil presence moving towards them. It was like the world was going black. He smelled sulfur and heard the creaky wings of bats. Instinctively, he pointed his finger down the hall and let fly a jagged bolt of energy at the dark shapes there and was rewarded with a roar of pain.

Akasha kept up her warnings.

P: Hurry

The moth flapped its furry wings, and Kido felt himself being carried aloft. They cleared the roof, and the light faded into dark. He could feel a cool wind on his face. Looking back, the dark roofs receded, and the warm orange hole in the roof became a tiny square and then a dot swallowed up by the night. He could see Atticus following on a white ghost of a moth. Just then there was an explosion in Atticus's house, and the darkness lit up as flames poured through the roof.

The moth flapped its wings, and they rose higher and higher until leveling off at an altitude where the town looked small. Below them, the Cloud River was a silver thread in a dark land of blues, blacks, and purples. Kido hung on tight to the moth's back and wondered

where they were headed.
 P: That was close be safe kido akasha awaits you
 P: Thank you akasha
 Kido was really beginning to like this dragon.

9
BREMEN WOOD

Cloudrise was visible in the east by the time their flight had ended. After the moths had landed everyone on the ground, a golden glow flared brightly around them and died out. The moths shrank back to normal size, fluttered around them once or twice, and then they dropped to the ground, legs in the air.

Pyra described this all to Atticus, who said, "Goodbye, Fritillary. Thank you, dear friends."

Atticus looked around with his sightless eyes. "Well, describe where we are. I smell pines."

"We are on a bare hilltop beside a rock outcropping," said Pyra. "Below us on all sides are endless trees."

"We are in Bremen Wood," said Elger. "Your moths saved us some walking."

"How much ichor dust do you have left?" Atticus asked Elger.

The wizard opened his horn and peered in. "Precious little, I'm afraid. And you?"

"None at all. I used my last flakes on the moths."

"I bet even the Red Tower doesn't have much either. What do we do when the world runs out of ichor?"

"We slay another dragon for its blood," said Atticus as they began their march.

Elger led, with Atticus and Pyra following, the old wizard walking with his hand on her shoulder.

Kido brought up the rear. "I wish the rupa was with us," he said aloud as he walked.

"He will turn up. He always does," Elger's voice came back to him.

"Why couldn't we have ridden the moths all the way to Ballastro?" Kido asked.

"The Magic doesn't last that long," Pyra said.

"And moths can't fly that far, even under enchantment," Atticus said. "There are limits to Magic."

Elger headed down the hillside. "I think this way is south."

They were walking through a northern forest full of firs and pines, aspens, swaples, and birches. The air had a fresh evergreen scent and the warm weather made for fine walking. The fear of the Tooskers had evaporated like a morning mist.

"We left so quickly we brought no food with us," said Atticus, "and I'm getting hungry as a wolf."

"We shall have to look for fruit and edible plants on the way. Hopefully we'll find some game to hunt," said Elger.

Down one hill and up the next they went. When they found a fast flowing stream, they stopped to fill their waterskins and drink the cold, clean water. They picked berries and dandelion greens and munched as they walked. Twice they saw deer but not close enough for Elger to use his *Arrow* spell. After several hours a general darkening heralded cloudset, and they kept on going.

"Do you know these woods?" Atticus asked Elger.

"I've walked by and around Bremen Wood many times in my travels over the years but never through it," Elger said. "It is an old wood, and the stories one hears discourages being here."

"I have heard the stories, Bremen Boys and ghosts."

Kido looked around and then walked faster until he was right behind Pyra. "Ghosts?"

"Children's stories, Kido," said Pyra.

"Let us hope so," said Atticus.

Kido kept looking behind them.

They came across a small pond and decided to camp there for the night. Elger took a small cobweb from one of his pouches and rolled it out. He spoke a word of Magic and it enlarged into something he could use as a net and he spent some time scooping through the waters of the pond until he had netted several silvery fish.

Pyra and Kido collected firewood from the numerous dead trees around them. Pyra knelt before their small pyre and took a small branch. She put on a gold glove and grasped the branch's tip with it. Instantly the branch caught fire. Soon they had a roaring blaze going, and they gathered around to grill fish, the warm orange firelight on their faces, their backs turned to the growing blackness of the forest.

Kido put his hand near her glove and felt the heat coming off of it. "You want to hold hands," she teased and he shook his head no.

With their bellies full of fish, they lolled around the fire. Pyra and

Elger had that flushed feeling of wizards who had cast spells and Kido felt himself envious of them. He was staring at Pyra, her face radiant in the campfire's glow. Or maybe there was a glow of Magic about her? "Where did you learn to light a fire like that?" he asked.

"The gloves are Magic," she said.

"The gloves were made at the Red Tower by my daughter. Pyra's speciality is fire and heat spells, just like my daughter," said Atticus.

"I heard someone casting a spell as I was climbing onto Fritillary last night," Atticus said.

"A wizard?" said Elger and Pyra together.

"A sorcerer there among the Tooskers."

"Cromartin must have brought him." Elger said.

"It was Zirmad," said Atticus. "He was casting a *Zap* spell aimed at me," said Atticus. "But Kido got him first."

"Obviously it missed you, thank the stars."

"I heard a Toosker bellow and Zirmad yell in mid-spell."

Pyra gasped. "Oh, master. That was too close."

"A near thing yes. I heard another voice, thin and cold. He finished the spell Zirmad started but somehow it went awry. That's what set the house on fire."

"So another sorcerer on Cromartin's payroll. I hear he has some of the Black Hoods working for him now," said Elger.

Atticus sighed. "Yes, apparently some survived the Ruination. What a mess and me with no house anymore. But now that we've got some time, Kido could you explain to me who your friend is who warned you. How did he warn you, because your warning came even before my *Fear Crystal* got hot?"

"Well, sir...." Kido idly picked up a long branch and poked at the embers. "I don't how to describe it. It's strange. You might not believe me. I don't even believe it sometimes."

Elger said, "Kido, just tell us. We're not going to judge you, but obviously you know something important or have some special art. Please help us."

Kido took a deep breath and said, "There is a voice, a female voice, who talks to me, in my head. She warned me of danger coming."

Elger studied him carefully while Atticus appeared thoughtful. Pyra stared at him in doubtful consternation.

"How long have you been hearing this voice?" Elger asked.

"Since I touched the gates to Sporu Angosta, right before the Ruination. " His voice faltered. "Right before my friend Domingo was sucked into the Butterscotch Book. The voice belongs to a dragon."

"Did it reveal its name?" asked Elger.

"Her name is Akasha," said Kido.

Atticus rocked forward and Elger's eyebrows jumped.

"The rupa also knows of her," Kido said.

Pyra scoffed and jumped up and backed off, as if she couldn't stand being close to someone spouting such nonsense.

Elger looked amused and Atticus looked pleased. Atticus turned to Kido, "Communication with a dragon could be useful, though certainly unheard of in *my* lifetime." He turned to Elger, "You have found a most interesting and exquisite apprentice, Elger. I can't wait for us to introduce him to the Order. Most interesting indeed." Atticus rocked back and forth and hummed.

Pyra scoffed again and came back to her place before the fire. She stared intently at Kido until he felt uncomfortable.

Elger patted his knee. "Tell us more, Kido. If you can hear Akasha's voice, can she hear yours?"

"I *can* hear hers, and she can hear mine."

"So a full-fledged conversation. Wonderful," Atticus said. "Can you say something to her now?"

Kido cocked his head and concentrated, searching the aether for Akasha's voice. "Nothing. Not right now. She comes and goes."

Pyra said, "Ha! Can't reproduce evidence when we need it. What a cockamamy story, Kido."

"Pyra, hush. We have no reason to doubt the lad and every reason to believe him," said Atticus. "He did warn us of Zirmad and the Tooskers."

"Hmmph," Pyra said and crossed her arms.

"You say the rupa told you Akasha was a dragon?" Elger said.

"He hears her voice too. And other dragons' voices."

"Does my rupa talk to you out loud or telepathically?" asked Elger.

"Telepathically. He *pings* with me," said Kido.

"He pings you?"

"Yes. To ping means to send telepathic messages."

"I know. I see you're expanding your wizardly vernacular."

Atticus smiled. "Does your rupa ping you as well?" he asked Elger.

"No, I had no clue there was any pinging at all going on. I've never heard anything from the beast except a snort once in awhile," said Elger.

"Interesting."

"Wizard's can use a *telepathy* spell when necessary," said Elger, scratching his chin. "But it is a high-level spell and usually requires a good pinch of ichor dust as well as a competent partner. Most wizards never learn it, including me."

"And me. Even between people it is rare. In my experience no one has ever been able to ping at will. And not with animals, even with a spell," said Atticus.

"Let alone with dragons supposedly sleeping in Sporu Angosta," said Pyra.

"If you cannot find the dragon's voice, can you locate the rupa?" Elger asked.

Kido searched but heard nothing and shook his head.

Pyra scoffed again. "Must be a range limitation to your skill," she mocked.

"He must have quite a range if he and Akasha can communicate," said Elger.

"Perhaps a dragon's telepathic powers are that much greater than a rupa's," Atticus said. "The rupa can hear the dragon, but Kido cannot hear the rupa unless it is close by. Most fascinating stuff." Atticus rocked back and looked off again as if daydreaming.

Kido felt strange to have himself talked about like this, in reference to telepathic dragons and rupas. "Do you know of this Akasha? Is she really a dragon?" he asked the two wizards.

"That name is one of the ones said to be the spawn of Tiamat," said Elger.

"Akasha is not, however, tied in with the Prophecy of Sporu Angosta," Atticus said. "She has no tower and is a lesser dragon."

"I was only a slave in the Gold Tower, but I heard rumors of Sporu Angosta," said Kido.

"What do you know of the Prophecy?" Atticus asked.

So Kido explained what he had learned from the Boardgame.

"I never heard any of that," said Pyra after he had finished.

Because you never played the boardgame, Kido thought.

Atticus sat up. "Because I never told you, Pyra. Anyways Kido, what you say is mostly true. Some say, however, that before Tiamat was killed, that the Fabricator realized his mistake and locked her up and went off to take a nap, putting his assistant, the Demiurge, in charge."

"The Demiurge?" *He wasn't part of the board game.*

"Yes, one of the Immortals. He got bored after a few decades and let Tiamat out to play with her. When he put her back, he carelessly forgot to lock her cage. So she got out while the Demiurge was having cocktails with Apotha Carrie."

"Apotha Carrie?"

"Wife of the Fabricator, another of the Immortals. So the other races got together to hunt Tiamat down and kill her, which they did, led by the four great wizards of old. And of course other dragons were made by the Wizards of old and a few rogue wizards like Antares and Zane. The Fabricator made a separate world called Sporu Angosta, connected with the Known World by a pair of tall magical gates, located in a mountain wall east of Zannalornacopia in Pandoon. People have been to those same gates you were at. And where we may be going some day, but I digress."

Atticus turned towards Kido and smiled. "What do you think of my story so far."

Kido was in awe. "Some of these details are new to me. The Gold Mage always warned us to stay away from the gates, but he never told us what was behind them. The wizards in the tower planned constantly how to get to Sporu Angosta, but I never understood why, being just a slave." Kido took his necklace and held it in his hand, which made him feel better.

Atticus laughed. "But wait, it gets better. No one knows how many Dragons there are. Most name four Primes: Mazunga, Ramyre, Pangma, and Sanshinar. And those four are the ones in the Prophecy."

"Those are names the rupa has all heard pinging."

"So that is an unofficial confirmation of at least part of the Prophecy," said Elger. "Though I wonder if anyone will trust the testimony of a rupa."

"And Akasha?"

"Is one of the Dragonspawn, but she is towerless."

Atticus said, "Anyways, the story goes that the Fabricator built a special palace in Sporu Angosta, out of the bones and hide of Tiamat and within that palace is a great throne in a grand hall filled with gold, silver, jewels, gems, the greatest pile of treasure in the world. It is said that whoever enters Sporu Angosta, defeats the Dragonspawn guardians, and sits on that throne, will rule Pandoon and Arcadia for a thousand years. He will have long life and happiness and infinite prosperity."

"Or *she* will have," corrected Pyra.

"He or she," said Elger.

Atticus slapped both his thighs. "That's it. That's the basic deal about Sporu Angosta. The elves or dwarves might tell variations but that is the essential prophecy according to *our* lore."

Kido said slowly, "So the gates won't open by themselves at some appointed time and let the dragons out?"

"Theoretically, the gates aren't supposed to open themselves. It is debatable whether anyone on the outside has the power and knowledge to open the gates from our side, even Ramanapirus and his band. More likely, it would take someone on the inside to open those gates."

"Who would do that?"

Atticus shrugged. "Any of the Immortals or caretakers or any of the dragons themselves. But the Ruination might have changed all that, and now the gates may already be open. No one knows."

"And the dragons?"

"Could show up anytime."

"And Tiamat?"

"She is supposedly dead and her body parts scattered all over the Known World. Some think she may be resurrected someday. Some *want* her resurrected so she can kill off all but themselves."

"Who would want that?"

"Members of a small, radical cult called The Tiamatists, who believe they are the chosen ones. They are said to have a giant dragon tattooed on their bodies."

Kido thought of the Black Hood he had stumbled over outside the gates. "And they want to go to Sporu Angosta?" Kido shuddered, remembering his hand frozen to the great door.

"Many people do. The lure of treasure and the lust for power is strong," said Atticus. "And there are many problems in the world that could be solved if one had the power and wealth promised once you sit on that throne."

"You *have* to go in if you want to sit on that throne," said Pyra.

"Or prevent someone else from sitting on it," said Atticus. "Not everyone is worthy of the throne. Imagine if Cromartin, Vykar, and Zirmad get the throne."

"Well, what do we do then?" Kido asked.

"We're working on that," said Elger.

"Which is why we need to reopen the towers, and why we need a Wizards Conclave," said Atticus.

Kido fell silent, deep in thought, processing everything he had heard. The fire had died down into soft gray embers while they talked. He felt overwhelmed by it all.

"One more thing, Kido," said Atticus. He stood up. "Stand up and remove your robes." Kido did as he was told. "Just relax and close your eyes." Elger and Pyra watched as the old wizard felt with his fingers to locate Kido's slave collar. "This has been on too long." He spoke the spellwords. There was a soft glow and a hissing sound. The collar snapped off and fell to the ground. "Much better," said Atticus.

Elger picked it up and flung it into the darkness. "Let us get some sleep. We have a long walk ahead tomorrow," he said. "Many long days of walking in fact until we get to Ballastro."

Kido lay on his back and and rubbed his neck while looking up at dark sky, wishing he could see the bright silver stars in the heaven's firmament. He could imagine each star as the eye of dragon, seeing them in his mind even as he closed his own eyes.

In the middle of the night a familiar voice came inside his mind.

P: Where are you?

P: By a pond in the middle of Bremen Wood where are you?

P: On the edge of the wood and away from the River Road I will find you

P: Dont let anyone follow you

P: Dont be silly no one follows this rupa

10
Temple of the Oath

Kido and the others were walking down a grassy slope when he felt tremors indicating something large moving towards them.

P: I am coming

"Rupa!" Kido cried jubilantly.

And turning they saw the familiar shaggy shape come lumbering over the hill, its six powerful legs churning, the big head swaying. The ground shook and Kido said, "I hope I never have to take on a charging rupa."

After some affectionate patting, the beast took its familiar place at the rear. "Now I feel our little company is more complete," Elger said. "Kido, if the rupa has any news to share with you, we'll be glad to hear it."

P: There are many of the kings soldiers on the river road and i even saw some tooskers there not good

Kido passed this on to Elger, who said, "King Cromartin missed us in Tempest so his troops are searching for us."

P: We havent much supplies or any food for you to carry

P: Nature provides my food wherever I go

P: Thats good for you but we dont eat much grass and berries and dandelions only go so far

They had been walking steadily downhill for sometime, where the trees were thinner. From the hilltop that morning they had seen the southeastern borders of Bremen Wood and beyond the open fields and the river and road leading towards Ballastro.

Kido pinged to him about the events in Tempest and who Atticus and Pyra were.

Rupa's reply came in one telepathic jumble.

P: Many enemies a toosker is a match even for a rupa another wizard is good

P: He is blind

P: His eyes cannot see?
P: No
P: Maybe his other senses or Magic makes up for no eyes
P: He is a powerful wizard
P: Good oh look clover

Soon they came to a group of large boulders on a rocky spur where the hillside turned steeper and plunged down into the river's plain. Elger had his spyglass out and was examining the terrain below. "A lot of soldiers down there. A squad of Tooskers as well. And rangers on horseback, too." His spyglass passed to the hillside directly below, where he could see a group of figures moving along a half-hidden trail. "Bremen Boys. Wild orphans. They can be dangerous if in large numbers. They're moving up this way to avoid the soldiers."

"We must find another way," said Atticus. He had his *Fear Crystal* cradled in his hands. "It's warm," he said. "Danger is close but not imminent. For now."

Elger nodded. "We must cross these hills and come in from the other direction. Hopefully there are no soldiers or wild orphans that way."

"Cromartin won't be looking that way either," said Atticus.

And so on they trekked, climbing higher to head southwest, over the ridge and downhill again, towards the far side of Bremen Wood. The pines and firs gave way to oaks and elms, alders and sumacs. They came across some apple trees and loaded up on fruit, and further on picked berries off of the shrubs there.

Since they had left the pond last night they had seen no trails to use, but that afternoon they stumbled across an old overgrown trail. "It looks like it hasn't been used in years," Elger said.

"That means no hunters or woodcutters frequent this part of the wood," said Elger. "I seem to recall a story that some part of Bremen Wood is haunted by ancient spirits. But one can never tell whether there is any truth to these old tales."

"Ancient spirits or not, this is where we're headed," said Atticus.

"Ghosts!" Kido said.

"Lovely," said Pyra, brushing off the leaves of a bush as she followed Elger. Next to her, Atticus kept his *Fear Crystal* in his free hand. Kido followed with his staff and the rupa trailed them, ducking his head and squeezing into the tight spaces between trees. The forest felt like it was closing in on them, forming a leafy corridor, branches arching over the ancient path. An unseen bird chirped at them but all else was silent.

They were on the cloudset side of the hills now, and the trail took them down into a forested valley. The gloom deepened.

"We better find a camp soon," Elger said.

Then they came to where the path split into three.

"Now what?" said Pyra.

They all stopped to consider their choices, but all three paths looked identical, leafy corridors on level ground.

Kido spoke first. "I like the one on the left."

"Why?" asked Pyra.

"It just feels right."

"Left feels right?"

"Yes."

"Lovely," she said as she brushed off a large beetle climbing up her arm.

Atticus held out a hand to feel the air. "I'm with Kido. The other two don't feel safe."

Elger closed his eyes and took a deep breath. "Agreed," he said as he exhaled.

Pyra sighed. "All right."

They went left. The path continued as before for some thirty yards but then began to climb. Soon the dirt path became rocky and uneven, and the forest closed in until the path was a narrow, suffocating tunnel. The rupa at the rear began panting and snorting, breaking shrubbery as it squeezed through the tighter spaces. The still air grew warm, and soon sweat was dripping in their eyes. The grade increased, and their pace slowed as they labored on. They took a break and drank water.

"Still think this is the right path?" said Pyra.

"Yes," Kido croaked.

"Wizard's instinct," Atticus said.

And soon enough as they went on, the path leveled out and the tunnel grew back into a green corridor.

"What's that I see?" Elger said, and craning his neck and squinting his eyes, he saw a structure ahead. "The path leads to some kind of building."

The trees drew back into a clearing, and they saw that they were on the edge of a cliff with a steep dropoff to their right. Before them stood a stone building that rose two stories into the sky. The front wooden doors were hanging on their hinges and yawning open. They approached it slowly, examining every detail. It had an abandoned look about it.

"This place looks ancient," said Pyra.

"Let's have a look," Elger said, passing through the open doorway.

"Yes, tell me what you see, Pyra," Atticus said eagerly.

Pyra didn't look so sure, but she reluctantly led him in and Kido gingerly followed. The rupa snorted suspiciously and stayed outside, searching for something to eat.

The entered a long rectangular hall lit by open windows missing their shutters. Layers of dust and bird droppings littered the floor, along with the bones of small animals. In one corner stood a pile of chopped up wooden furniture, some pieces partially charred. In another corner was a pile of old books. When Kido tried to pick one up, it crumbled into fragments.

"Careful. Don't touch them," Elger said. He went to his knees and turned his head in different angles to try and read the covers. "Most of the lettering is too faded or in some archaic language."

They passed into another room where the roof soared to a cupola far above. The remains of an aged wooden stairway clung to one wall, half the steps missing. It climbed to a dark opening high above. An old musty smell filled the air. Here the only windows were high up and only a dim light reached the ground floor. A spark flew and then a sputtering sound as Elger lit a torch, throwing light on the room.

"I see a painted mural," Pyra said, gazing on the back wall.

Captain McGee led a dozen soldiers and six humanoids as they walked behind the creature and watched. Deepnose walked bent over, his long snout to the ground, sniffing deeply. He'd lift his fuzzy brown head and pan around, sniffing the air, and then drop it back near the ground. "Up ahead, humans passed this way very recently," it said.

A young black-robed sorcerer sat on a rock and cleaned dirt off his boots with a stick. "I can feel them nearby."

McGee looked at Wolfinger. He held out his hand as if to feel the air. "I don't feel anything."

"Of course not. You haven't got my skills," said Wolfinger, walking over and carrying a staff. His face was concealed in his hood. They all stopped to consider their choices. "Let's hurry things up. I'm tired of tramping through the trees."

McGee detested the young mage, but he was one of the King's many sons so what could he do? He heard some snarling and muttering behind him, which made him nervous. He hated working with these creatures of Zirmad too. The King's army wasn't what it used to be. Tooskers and sorcerers. It all boded ill.

He beckoned to 4eyes, a stick-thin tall humanoid. "You see anyone ahead?"

4eyes extended to his full height of nine feet, his squarish head perched on top of his long, thin neck. A large eye occupied each corner of the velvety yellow head. "Not yet, Captain, but I think I see the roof of a building up ahead."

"We are gaining on them," said Wolfinger with certainty, and he held out the broken iron collar with the sigil of a yellow tower. "And the ex-slave from Pandoon is among them."

"Let's move out," McGee ordered to the Dragon Guards and creatures in his company. "Spread out and try *not* to give yourselves away."

Soon they came to where the path split into three.

"I lost the scent," said Deepnose, hunched over and breathing deeply.

"I don't see any tracks either," said the hunched-over Dragon-Guard on point."

"See anything?" McGee asked 4eyes.

4eyes shook his head no. "Only forest."

"The building?"

"Blocked by trees, Captain."

"What do your skills tell you, O Sorcerer?" McGee asked Wolfinger.

The sorcerer came forward and solemnly regarded all three paths. He pointed wordlessly to the right. McGee motioned three of the soldiers to join their comrade on point.

"I sense they are close by," Wolfinger warned.

The soldiers drew their swords and crept forward, followed by the rest. Even the Tooskers were quietly creeping along hunched over. It took quite awhile to cover fifty yards where nothing happened. An exasperated Wolfinger stood up and said, "At this rate we'll never catch them. You there at the front, move out."

The Dragon Guards charged forward, but then the forest opened up, the ground gave way, and the screaming soldiers disappeared. When the rest crept up, they saw a large sink hole. Two hundred feet-down, they saw four broken bodies.

"We'll have to go back," Wolfinger said.

Back at the crossroads, they waited while Wolfinger decided. He scratched his chin and pointed at the middle path. Four more Dragon Guards came forward, spears at the ready. If they had crept forward slowly before, that was nothing compared to the caution now on display. Four Dragon Guards inched forward while McGee, Wolfinger, Deepnose, 4eyes, and the remaining three soldiers followed at a distance. The Tooskers remained back at the crossroads, having lost all faith in their human handlers.

Progress was agonizingly slow, but no one hurried. They tested the ground with their spears before taking a step. Nothing happened. The ground held steady, although the forest on the left now gave way to a rocky cliff that grew higher and higher above their heads. The trail led along the cliff's base, with no sign of their quarry and time running out.

McGee was standing still and contemplating a retreat when loud noises from above startled everyone. An avalanche of large rocks cascaded down and buried the lead soldiers before they could escape. Laughter cascaded down from above and thirty dirty faces of boys beamed down, all holding large branches used to pry rocks loose. The remaining Dragon Guards loosed several arrows but the boys just melted out of sight, hooting and hollering.

"Bremen Boys," McGee muttered. They retreated back to the crosswords and silently contemplated the left-hand path. "If this one doesn't work, we'll have no patrol left," said McGee. Wolfinger pulled down his hood and scratched his head but said nothing as they moved out.

"Describe it to me," Atticus said.

"It is old and the colors are very faded," Pyra said, reaching out a hand to touch the mural.

"Don't touch it. It might crumble," Kido said solemnly, and she quickly drew her hand back.

"It shows mountains as a backdrop and in each corner there is a tall tower with a giant figure in front of each one, although the details are faded." She sucked in her breath. "And there are dragons flying around to form a circle in the center of the mural. In the very center is a temple with four small figures."

"The temple is probably this one," said Elger.

"Mmm, dragons you say? How many?" said Atticus.

"One, two, three, four. Four dragons. They look to be in different shades, but they're so faded now it's impossible to tell what colors they might've been," said Pyra.

"Some look lighter, and some look darker," said Kido.

Elger brought his torch closer. "Could they be the dragonspawn?"

"Possibly," said Atticus. "Is there one huge dragon that could be Tiamat?"

"No, master. Only the four. Four giants, four towers, four dragons, four humanoids. Such fearful symmetry."

"Hmm. Still it is a sign. The towers are obviously our Magic Towers."

"But giants and dragons belong to myths and ancient prophesies."

"Not after what Kido has told us of what he has seen. There is much here to think about."

"Oh, yes, Kido's stories," said Pyra, looking over at her friend.

Kido had taken his journal out and was trying to draw the mural on a spread of two pages. Elger watched him also. "Draw the towers bigger," he suggested.

Looking down, Kido saw a black beetle doggedly walk along the smooth floor and then drop down into a groove in the stone, a groove so straight that it looked man-made. He bent down and blew away the thick layer of dust and saw it was part of a letter carved in the floor. He waved the air and coughed from the dust.

Pyra brushed away more dust. "Letters. Let's see what they spell."

When they finished they saw incised into the stone tiles four large letters:

R-A-M-S

"Rams? They mean male sheep?" Pyra asked.

"You assume the writer was using the Mother Tongue," Atticus said.

"Probably some ancient language again," said Elger.

No one had a clue, so they moved on, although Kido dutifully wrote it in his journal.

Next came a long hallway, both walls showed evidence of large mosaics now destroyed. They walked on thousands of broken shards of painted mosaic tiles that littered the floor like the pieces of two giant jigsaw puzzles waiting for someone with a lot of patience and glue to put them back together.

An archway at the end opened into a large circular room with open windows. At its center lay a massive stone altar toppled over. Upon closer inspection, they saw the alter covered in stone dragon heads, many of them vandalized by hammer blows. Old scorch marks marred the floor. The outer wall to one side had been ripped open by some great force, so that the room was open to the outside. They could see the forest beyond the meadow and the stone building blocks scattered in the grass.

"This place has been desecrated," said Elger.

"And someone burned something," said Pyra.

"Or someone," said Kido.

"Let us leave here," said Atticus. "This room feels evil."

They entered a small room with a shallow empty pool set in the floor. It reminded Kido of an *impluvium* he once saw in a textbook on houses in the Roman Empire.

Beyond the *impluvium* room, they found a long corridor with several small rooms on either side. The doors were all broken or missing and the rooms mostly empty except for some destroyed furniture.

Kido was at the rear and noticed another beetle crawling fast along the floor, except this one was blue in color, and then the blue changed to green. Kido followed it as the green went to yellow, then red, then black. A beetle that could change its colors!

When Kido looked up, his friends were far ahead. He was hurrying to catch up when his eye caught movement. Turning to look into one of the side rooms, he saw a pale ghostly figure of an old bearded man floating there, staring at him with sad gray eyes.

Kido felt the hairs on the back of his neck stand up.

The ghost held up a finger for silence.

"Hey—" Kido turned to the others to point out the ghost, but they were all gone. Turning back, he saw the ghost was gone, the room empty. Intensely curious, he crept into the room but saw nothing and finally he ran after the others.

At the far end, an open archway led outside to a large courtyard paved with old broken stonework, weeds growing up in the cracks. But in the middle of the courtyard was a short, oval-shaped rock, shiny and black, with a polished flat top.

Pyra gasped. "Look, a teleport rock! Here in Bremen Wood!"

Atticus smiled and clapped his hands excitedly. "I had no idea.

What a marvelous find."

"Someone needs to report this to the Order," said Elger.

They walked around the rock without stepping on it and it measured a large oval, about six inches high and thirty feet long, its surface reflecting their faces as they bent over to stare into it. Shiny and new in appearance, it looked out of place surrounded as it was by such decrepitude.

"It's like someone just polished it," said Kido.

"I bet a hundred people could fit on it," Elger said.

"No one knows how many teleport rocks there are in the Known World," said Atticus. "No records from the old wizards survived to tell us."

"How many do we know, teacher?" Kido asked.

"This makes six for sure: one in each of the four Magic Towers plus this one and Kido's in Porterville. There could be dozens more. Who knows? The elves claim there are some in Sporu Angosta even. If only we could find more keys." Atticus clapped his hands again. "Very exciting!" He reached down and touched the surface, his face beaming.

Kido bent and touched the surface, feeling the smooth cool rock. As he gazed at his own reflection, it shimmered and shined with some kind of strange white glow. Maybe there was Magic in that stone after all, and for a fleeting moment, he thought he glimpsed the ghostly buildings of Porterville in the blackness. He strained to see his home and his parents, but then the ghostly shapes disappeared, and he wondered if his imagination was playing tricks.

Feeling homesick, he left the others to talk and wandered further away, where the courtyard ended with a short flight of cracked, slanted steps leading to a sunken grassy area. There Kido was drawn to a line of old statues. Weathered and stained by time they appeared to be tall men, some perhaps in robes like wizards of old, some in armor. Some had their arms held out but their hands empty or broken off, as if their weapons had been snatched away. The forest was encroaching here, too. Branches of trees reached out to embrace some of the statues while others were wrapped in vines. In the crook of one statue's arm was a bird's nest. Most statues were dotted with mold or draped in moss. He bent to read the bases of the statues but most letters were so worn or covered up with lichen as to be unreadable. He found one with discernible letters and traced them with his fingers, moving his lips to try a phonetic pronunciation.

The next base was made of dark green stone and the letters carved in it were of a language so strange Kido had no idea how to read it. But he noticed the statue's feet were not human but rather like large stumps of a reddish-brown moss that didn't look like weathered stone at all. He looked up to see a quick glimpse of a towering, broad figure with powerful arms and a face with an animal's snout and a mouth flanked by sharp, white tusks, all surmounted by dark eyes.

The creature roared as it raised a large wooden mace high in the air. Kido sidestepped as the mace slammed into the ground where he had been. He turned and ran back towards the courtyard while yelling a warning. In his peripheral vision, he saw another creature crash through the underbrush to his right and reach for him with long arms. Kido ducked underneath the grasping limbs and reversed course, while the second creature collided with the first. A third Toosker came at him from out of nowhere, but Kido dodged him. They could run fast in a straight line but were clumsy in changing direction. He kept sprinting away in wild fear.

"Tooskers!" Kido heard Elger's faint voice as he plunged deeper through the trees and further from his friends, twisting and turning to avoid pursuit. He ran for several minutes in a blind panic, fearing the Tooskers were right behind him. Finally, he paused in a thicket to catch his breath. Looking around, all he saw were tall trees, but he could hear two Tooskers crashing through the underbrush nearby. The noises became fainter, and then the woods fell silent. Kido sighed in relief. He had lost them.

Still at the ancient temple, Elger was pouring ichor dust into Atticus's hands and then into his own while Pyra was putting gloves on her shaking hands. Two Tooskers came up the steps side-by-side. Suddenly one of the King's Dragon Guards came through the trees to their right, his sword at the ready. Flanking him were two figures that weren't human. The short one had a huge snout and small beady eyes, the tall one four bulbous eyes, one at each corner of its squarish face.

"We're got company!" Pyra warned, and as she turned, two more DragonGuards came up from behind, waving swords and eyeing her with hungry eyes. "We've got more company!" She thought she saw a dark figure still lurking in the trees.

"I sense a Sorcerer," said Atticus.

Elger did too but he was too busy casting a spell against the two

Tooskers.

Pyra shook her head. She could sense nothing, but what her eyes told her. She rubbed together her gloved hands, nervous at this first real test of her abilities. The five soldiers spread out and took measure of their two opponents. Pyra tugged her master's sleeve and got Atticus turned to square up against them.

The soldiers charged with a yell, and both Atticus and Pyra cast their spells. Everything happened at once in a confusing kaleidoscope of motion and energy. Atticus levitated one Dragon Guard and flung him through the air to tumble over and down the cliff. Pyra's spell caused a *SphereofFlame* to burst into being between her outstretched gloves, which she threw at Deepnose. It exploded against his chest, and he fell over, yelling and moaning. 4eyes charged before they could recast and jabbed his spear, but Atticus parried with his staff, using senses beyond eyesight to ward off repeated blows. Before Pyra was ready, an older soldier with bugged-out eyes swung a sword at her, and she put up her hands in a reflex gesture. A wave of immense heat rose from the gloves to swamp the soldier, and he dropped his suddenly hot sword, staggering back and coughing and gasping deeply. His hair burst into flames, and he ran off yelling into the trees. Pyra looked at the gloves in amazement.

Two Tooskers confronted Elger on the other side of the teleport rock, swaying and making grumbling, growling sounds, opening and closing their mouths and snapping their teeth. They bellowed and charged. Elger flung his ichor into the air and the gold particles sparkled in the afternoon air as he spoke the spellwords.

Elger's spell caused a lightning bolt to discharge from his fingertips and strike the closest Toosker in its chest, shocking it and causing it to collapse and twitch on the courtyard stones. But the other Toosker swung a giant club that struck Elger in the side, and the wizard collapsed in great pain.

Wolfinger entered the fray just then, emerging from the trees and casting a lightning bolt that caught Pyra by surprise. She caught it in her gloves by reflex but the bolt's energy threw her several feet in the air and burned her hair. She landed heavily on the teleport rock and moaned. Her gloved hands sparked and crackled with energy as she rolled over.

"Pyra?" Atticus cried out. Distracted, the old mage fell back and over onto the teleport rock. 4eyes advanced with his spear poised to plunge into the mage's throat. A Toosker stood over the fallen Elger and raised his huge club to bring down on his victim's head. Wolfinger smiled and crossed his arms, letting his minions administer the coup de grace.

Pyra pointed one glove at 4eyes and one at the Toosker, but she did not know the spell to discharge another wizard's energy from the gloves. She shook them violently but that did nothing, so she removed them and flung them in two directions at the same time. The spear and the club began their awful movements. Then two golden gloves flew through the air. One struck 4eyes in his face; the other hit the club. Both caught fire.

The Toosker yelled and dropped the club. Given a respite, Elger cast a spell that turned the Toosker into a pile of sawdust, which the wind blew away. 4eyes danced around in pain, and Deepnose was still trying to put out his burning tabard.

Wolfinger's smile disappeared, and he closed in. Atticus cast a magnetic snake in his hands and flung it in the direction where he sensed Wolfinger's Magic. The Sorcerer, in the act of casting a spell, saw it coming and held up his staff reflexively. The snake wrapped around it and slid down it, causing Wolfinger to drop the staff in a panic. The snake slithered after him, and Wolfinger kept shooting electric bolts at it, which its magnetic field kept absorbing and with each bolt it grew larger. Wolfinger ran off into the trees, the now huge snake slithering after him. An injured McGee and 4eyes and a still-smoldering Deepnose limped off in the same direction.

Pyra was still gingerly picking up her gloves, when she heard a roar. She and the wizards turned to see another Toosker burst from the trees and charge them. Tiredly they braced for its attack when the rupa rumbled into view. Charging with his massive head lowered, he rammed the creature and pushed it over the cliff. It bellowed all the way down.

"How many more Tooskers are there?" Pyra asked, eyeing the woods in fear.

And then Elger remembered. "I saw two of them chasing Kido over by those statues right before we were attacked."

"And one came back," said Atticus.

"So where is the other one?" asked Pyra.

"And where is Kido?" asked Elger.

Kido came out from his hiding place, wanting to quickly return to his friends. But which way should he go? The last Toosker noises had come from his left. He didn't want to go that way. He made a complete circle but didn't recognize anything and realized he had gotten completely disoriented in his mad rush to escape. Tall trees blocked every view and deepening darkness showed that cloudset was close at hand. He started walking straight ahead in the blind hope that he would see something before it got too dark.

So he walked. And he walked. The trees were dense and visibility, already bad, grew worse with the encroaching night. Pines and oaks, hemlocks and aspens, birds and squarks were all he saw. Soon he could hardly see anything. It was getting colder and darker. A veritable Stygian darkness, he thought. He was thinking of hiding under a tree and making a bed of leaves when he abruptly bumped into something tall and hard. Feeling with his hands, for he couldn't really see anymore, it felt like a rock wall. Walking along using his hands, he felt a cave-like opening in the rock. He went down on all fours and gingerly crawled forward, fearful he'd find a bear already in this shelter. But he heard nothing and felt only leaves and pine needles. Grateful for a decent place to spend the night, he piled some leaves up and snuggled in for the night. He would find his friends in the morning.

When he awoke, cloudrise was already up and he could see a soft gray light illuminating the rock wall. He was facing what looked like the back of a small cave. He blinked several times, his eyes noticing the dark rock with reddish cracks in it. Volcanic rock, he guessed?

He rolled over and saw for the first time a row of stalagmites at the cave entrance, and directly above them a row of stalactites that formed an interesting symmetry which his sleepy mind struggled to comprehend. There was a sizeable gap between the two. He lay there for a moment longer, waiting to become more awake. Rolling on his back, he noticed two skylights where water had eroded the cave ceiling near the front. He finally crawled out through two stalagmites, stood, stretched, and yawned.

And there in front of him, fifteen paces away, was another darkish cave complete with stalagmites and stalactites, and two skylights. Skulls! These were giant skulls full of teeth! He walked around the skull he'd slept in to see a long spine of dark bones with attached ribs stretching back into the trees. He took a step and fell over something. Getting up, he saw a large, clawed skeletal foot half-buried in the grass. Here was an entire skeleton of something which was a hundred feet long as he measured it by walking all the way around. It looked exactly like a dragon skeleton.

Excitedly he ran around, discovering dozens more skeletons scattered in the clearing and among the trees. But unlike bleached white bones of dead things back on earth, these bones were dark brown or even black, and shot through with seams or spots of bright crimson. Then he began to find dragon scales in the grass, scales of many varied colors: brown, black, red, blue, green, tan, and in various patterns that were spotted, striped, or solid.

Kido couldn't wait to share his discovery with his friends and ran off to find them, picking a likely-looking direction, when he came upon the biggest skeleton of all. The dragon when alive must have been 300 feet long. He found scales of a beautiful, deep blue color and picked up one to take back. The huge skull was twenty feet tall. He rounded the snout and ran smack into a Toosker.

Kido yelled and the creature roared as two massive hairy arms reached out for him. Kido threw the dragon scale at it, spun around and ran, knowing that the Toosker with its long stride would probably catch him within ten paces. But Tooskers were slow to change directions. The creature was right behind him. Kido turned left, entering a dragon's mouth. He turned left and then back out, not wanting to get trapped inside the skull. The Toosker swiped at him, but Kido was just out of reach. It roared in frustration and charged after him, back out between two tall teeth. Kido turned right and went back in between another two teeth. And so it went. Kido's agility at tight turns kept him just ahead of the tall-striding Toosker as they juked in and out of the dragon teeth. But even a huge dragon like this one had only so many teeth. After the last one, Kido burst out into the open but there were no more places to hide. He turned to face the thing while gasping to catch his breath.

The Toosker came out at full speed, emitting a growl that became a triumphant roar as he saw his prey within reach.

Kido then rememberd he could levitate. He floated up but slowly, too slowly in fact, as if his Magic was somehow weaker. He was almost out of reach when the Toosker leapt up and grabbed Kido's left foot. It fell back to earth and dragged Kido down on top of him. Kido rolled off but not before the thing struck a blow on his head that felt like a sledgehammer. Bright colors flashed in his eyes, and the roaring in his ears deafened him. The pain took his breath away, and he fell like a sack of potatoes.

A dazed Kido sat up as the Toosker came at him again. The creature jerked Kido up and held him high in the air, snapping his teeth and slashing the air with his tusks. It drew him closer and opened a mouth to reveal two rows of sharp teeth. Kido struggled in its powerful grasp and gasped at the stench radiating from it. All he could think of was a phrase that rose in his dazed mind, and pointing a shaky finger at those dark eyes, he said aloud, "Nuit puala quaralgi!"

There was a crackle of energy and bright spots began appearing around the Toosker's head. The spots transformed into large yellow and black bees that began humming and buzzing around the creature, stinging its head and face. The Toosker bellowed and dropped Kido, waving its arms frantically, but the bees kept attacking it. It ran off through the trees until its bellowing faded away.

Elger, Atticus, rupa, and Pyra tramped on through the endless trees.

"How will we ever find him? Should we yell out his name?" asked Pyra.

"I think it unwise to draw attention to yourself in Bremen Wood," said Atticus, holding on to Pyra's arm. "Besides, I vaguely sense an aura in the direction we are going."

"I feel it too. Perhaps we should spread out?" said Elger.

Just then they heard a noise. Faint at first, it came from straight ahead, and soon they could tell it was a roaring noise of some creature fast approaching. They spread out to face the threat. Pyra put on her gloves. Elger poured out some ichor from horn to hand.

A Toosker burst through the trees, yelling and swatting at a dense cloud of bees that encircled it. Toosker and bees ran through their little group and kept going, disappearing off into the trees.

They looked in surprise at each other and then wordlessly began hiking up the Toosker's track. Half an hour later, they found a pale and dazed Kido slowly walking through a glade full of tall ferns.

Elger caught Kido as he collapsed and laid him down with fern leaves for a pillow. Atticus spoke the words of a healing spell with his hand on Kido's forehead. After he revived a bit, they got his story out of him, and after he had rested they followed him back up his trail. But though they searched for hours, they found no sign of the dragon skeletons or scales. It was as though they had disappeared.

"We believe you, Kido," said Elger.

"Hmmm," said Pyra.

"What happened to your hair and eyebrows?" Kido asked her, as they were all burnt off.

She winced as she touched her hair self-conciously. "Don't ask."

They made camp that night still deep inside Bremen Wood.

As the others slept, Atticus sat in silent meditation, only once musing aloud. "A *Beeswarm* spell," he said and then chuckled softly.

11
Ballastro

The next day they retraced their steps back to the ancient temple. Kido found a longsword lying in the grass where one of the King's soldiers had dropped it.

"A wizard sometimes has use for a blade," Elger told him, so Kido stuck it in his belt as they set off.

They walked for hours down into a valley, putting distance between themselves and the ancient ruins. They were still in Bremen Wood, but they had to rest. The fight and the spellcasting had taken a lot out of them and everyone collapsed in a small forest glade. Ever since casting that *BeeSwarm* spell, Kido had not felt himself. He remembered the luxurious cascade of power flowing through him and the satisfaction of seeing the bees come out of nowhere and drive off the Toosker. He also sensed the strange residual smell that ichor left behind. The gold dust that Elger and Atticus had thrown into the air had a lingering effect on him that he could not understand. His whole body and mind tingled with power and enchantment, mystery and knowledge, and that excited him. And he kept smelling the burnt flesh that Pyra's Magic had created. Elger, Atticus, and Pyra also seemed affected by their Magic, drained of energy and requiring extra time to recover. Kido's head still hurt and Elger had a massive bruise on his side and sore ribs. Pyra had three burnt fingers and her hair and eyebrows had been scorched off,

They lolled all afternoon but had found little to eat, and Elger would not risk a campfire. They slept fitfully on and off all through that night, setting a watch in case more enemy returned. "We must leave this wood tomorrow," said Elger.

The next day they wandered for hours under a thick canopy of trees, being forced to backtrack sometimes to get around deep ravines. Elger flew off into the air to reconnoiter and returned with insight about the way ahead. Finally, they came out into the open two days after the fight with the Tooskers and camped by a gentle stream that night within sight of the Wood. Here the land was rolling plains, but not too far off a range of small hills could be seen.

"We're going the longer way around to Ballastro," said Elger.

In the middle of the night Kido woke up. Lying propped up on his elbow, he stared into the smoldering embers of their campfire and thought about this strange journey taking him so far from home, and he wondered about the adventures up ahead. He looked off at the strange Woods and that was when he saw the lights. Small dots of winking lights danced around the trees at the edge of Bremen Wood. They were different colors: gold, red, green, blue, and white, all moving in a hypnotic, swirling fashion and flashing effervescently. Everyone else was still asleep, the rupa snoring nearby.

Kido stared in fascination, mesmerized by the motion and color. He felt they were calling to him and that it would be fun to run over and join the lights, to dance with and follow them. He felt he could run forever within their wonderful warm glow. The pull to get up and join them was so strong, he was standing up and moving forward before he realized it.

Then he heard a voice.

P: Dont go kido ignore the lights they will lead you deep into the dark woods to parts you never saw with your friends you will die if you go there alone at night

Kido felt suddenly foolish and afraid and went back to his blanket. Lying on his back he stared up into the darkness, expecting Akasha's voice to be gone like always. But she was still there.

P: Kido i feel different

A strange curiosity came over him at her confession.

P: What do you mean?

P: I feel less sleepy less constrained something has changed something has shifted in the world where I have been sleeping such a long time

P: You mean spora agosta is changing somehow?

P: The air smells different I sense my siblings the other dragons are waking up too

Kido thought about this for awhile. The dragons of Sporu Angosta were all waking up because of the Ruination? He wondered if Ramanapirus was inside Sporu Angosta. He and the other wizards might be the ones waking the dragons up.

P: Are you talking in your sleep or fully awake?

He waited a long time for her reply, but she was gone again. He slept little the rest of the night, waking from time to time to peer at the woods, looking for lights, but the trees remained dark and silent. And he waited to hear from Akasha, but she too remained silent.

After Cloudrise they set off, walking south now, with tall hills on their left, a gauzy mist rising from their valleys in the morning Cloudlight.

"The Squark Ear Mountains extend from Bremen Wood practically to the north walls of Ballastro," said Elger.

The game was more plentiful here, and the orchards and meadows were full of edible plants, so they did not lack for food. They passed many homesteads and fields full of crops tended by farmers. Nearly two weeks after leaving Bremen Wood, their trail turned southeast to follow the hills. A few days later they saw in the distance small figures moving on the horizon. "Traffic on Marnoch's Highway," Elger said.

They moved almost due east now, paralleling the highway but staying off it. They climbed farmers' fences and passed through orchards. The hills were off to the north now, and the land grew flat. Marnoch's Highway drew closer so they could see individual people, wagons, and animals moving on it. They knew they were visible as well, a strange company of three wizards and an apprentice, all in robes, trailed by a large rupa.

Ballastro appeared on the horizon first as a dark smudge under a leaden gray sky. The great city slowly drew closer. By the next day tall walls and towers emerged from the ever-expanding smudge. Marnoch's Highway diverged away to swing around the south side of the capital, but they kept walking straight at the huge city on a smaller gravel path. The path was rising above Marnoch's Road as it began climbing a ridge. Other people joined them off the main road so they no longer traveled alone.

"The main city gate is on the south side, facing the river, but you will enter using one of the western gates," said Elger.

"How many gates are there in Ballastro, teacher?" asked Kido.

"Ten," answered Atticus for Elger. "I was born in Ballastro," he explained.

"How will we get past the city guards?"

"There shouldn't be any, or at least there never has been any in my lifetime," said Atticus, "but we'll cover up just the same and try to be inconspicuous. Ballastro is an open city. We should be able to slip right in." The road they were on led to one of the western gates.

"Do the gates have names, teacher?" Kido asked.

"They are named after the first animals of creation," said Atticus. "The main gate in the south wall is the Dragon Gate. The others are named Fox, Raven, Bear, Fish, Horse, Eagle, Frog, Deer, and Snake Gates."

P: No rupa gate

The animal snorted loudly.

"This road leads to Bear Gate," said Atticus.

As they kept walking they could see a white cliff coming down from the north and turning to go around the upper city. The cliff marked the end of the hills, and the beginning of the Cloud River's floodplain. At that point the city walls split as the upper walls terminated at the cliff's edge and the lower walls began from the bottom of the cliff.

Kido could see now that the city of Ballastro was built on two levels separated by the cliff. The upper city stood on a huge terrace, the lower on the river's floodplain. They were moving on the upper.

"Ballastro is like two cities," said Kido.

"The upper city is called Topside, and the lower is called Riverside," said Atticus.

They stopped to stare more closely at the city. The massive walls were made of a dark brown stone and looked thirty feet high, crowned with battlements. Numerous towers were spaced out along the walls. Further back but above it all, a very tall, rectangular, reddish structure rose up high into the sky. It too had battlements.

"Is *that* the Magic Tower?" asked Kido.

"Yes, that is the Red Tower," said Elger.

"It must be huge to be visible from so far!"

"Wait until you are standing next to it.'"

They put on peasant's cloaks to cover their wizardly attire and drew up their hoods to hide their faces.

Elger said to Atticus, "I will give you the last of my ichor."

"Are you sure?"

"I think you will need it more than I will."

There was a transfer of a few precious golden flakes from one horn to the other. Elger looked at the rupa and then at Kido. "Time to say goodbye to me and the rupa. He doesn't like cities anyways, and Pariahs aren't allowed in Ballastro. I don't know how long you'll be in the city or when we'll meet again."

Kido patted the rupa.

P: I guess this is goodbye

P: Goodbye then friend

P: Where will you go?

P: Probably east towards the mountains we have trampled all over the west

P: Will I see you again?

P: I think yes if you leave the city you must go east I will be out there

Kido stroked his neck and patted his massive flank before turning away. He felt sad to see his new friends go off for who knew how long.

He clasped arms with Elger. "Thanks for the staff."

"Next time I see you, I expect you'll be carrying a real wizard's staff."

"Will we meet again?"

"I'm sure of it." The two parties went their separate ways.

As Kido, Atticus, and Pyra drew closer to the city, she said, "Uh, oh."

"What?" said Atticus.

"The gate is closed," said Pyra.

"It can't be. Ballastro is an open city."

"How long has it been since you were here?" Kido asked Atticus.

Atticus sighed. "Before the Ruination. I guess things have changed."

Already they could see several of the others who shared this road turn at the closed gate and follow a secondary road that led to the right and ran along the walls. Walking up to the base of the wall they craned their heads up to see the top. It looked so high. Over the gate two bears were carved into the very stones of the wall, standing and facing each other, paw on paw. But the stone door that the road went under was closed. Kido tried pushing on the gate with all his might but it wouldn't budge. "Barred shut."

Atticus said, "We are forced now to take the long way, down, around, and then back up to the tower. I was hoping to avoid Riverside."

They turned right and an hour later came to the cliff where a steep stairway cut into the rock descended some hundred feet to the lower level. They carefully climbed down, assisted by an iron handrail bolted to the wall. More walking and they reached another closed gate, this one with two large ravens carved above it.

"The Raven Gate is also closed," said Kido.

Atticus sighed. "We must go around to the front. We have one more gate before the Dragon Gate."

They kept walking but found the next gate also shut tight. Two foxes were carved above, touching noses. "No good."

The road carried them around, curving with the wall, skirting the bases of towers. Eventually it merged with Marnoch's Highway, and they found themselves in the midst of a thick stream of people walking towards the main gate. The Cloud River was nearby on their right now, and they could see boats moving up and down her, sails out and billowing in the breeze which bore along the scent of fish to their nostrils. Fishermen were casting their nets while at the docks other boats were loading and unloading. The road widened and merged with another from the east and together they turned north and swept in towards the main gate to the capital city of Arcadia.

The Dragon Gate was much larger than the others. It's massive iron-shod doors were wide open and people freely flowed in and out. Looking up Kido could see a large dragon carved into the stones above the doors, its wings spread out wide to both sides, its mouth open to reveal large fangs. Above the dragon, he could see soldiers walking along the parapet. They entered Ballastro easily, letting the flow of people carry them inside.

High up on the parapet, a figure in black robes watched them enter. "Warn the king," he said in a cold, thin voice to the Captain of the Gate before descending to the street.

In a long room with high ceilings sat a tall, wide wooden throne on a dais, upon which King Cromartin reclined on pillows. Chained to the throne was Vykar, his snarling pet Aoban. Zirmad in his black robes covered with silver nightshades stood safely on the other side.

"My Lord, you have 3000 new conscripts now added to your army. They are training right now in the Field of War if you wish to review them," said Zirmad.

Cromartin waved a lazy hand and yawned. "Not necessary. I'll take your word for it."

Zirmad looked at Guard Lieutenant Bangalore, in charge of security that day. "Is the army ready?"

"We could be ready to march within a fortnight, Grand Sorcerer."

Zirmad paused, looking at his king. "I think we need to start our campaign soon."

Cromartin patted his fat belly. "I'm ready for my next meal."

Another silent pause and then Zirmad said, "Rumor has it the dwarves are ready to strike for the gates."

Cromartin sat up, which took quite an effort. He was wearing an orange velvet robe that went to his big feet. "The dwarves! Their kingdom has been shut up since the Ruination! What could Leadbeard have in mind?"

"The throne and treasure of Sporu Angosta, perhaps?"

"But how does he think he'll force the gates?"

"I fear a union between the elves and dwarves," said Zirmad.

"The elves historically have shunned any attempt on Sporu Angosta. What could possibly make them conspire with dwarves?" Cromartin rubbed his triple chins.

"The riches of Sporu Angosta are a powerful motivation, my liege," said Zirmad. "Even for elves."

Cromartin's eyes widened. "The dwarves and elves in league. Our worst nightmare, Vykar."

"I know, sire." Vykar snapped his teeth and drooled.

"But you know, even together I doubt they have the power." Cromartin was so agitated he nearly got up out of his chair.

"With dwarvish might and elvish Magic, who knows?"

"The Elvish Warlock died in the Ruination, it is said. Who among the elves could take his place?" said Cromartin.

"Presumably he had trained wizards waiting in the wings to replace him. It is hard to say since the elves closed their kingdom after the Ruination," said Zirmad.

"Even my rangers have had no contact with them," said Cromartin, standing up. "Where are my rangers?"

They fell silent as the great double doors to the hall creaked open to admit the Chamberlain. "My Liege, Mio Bushmaster returns."

"Ah, perfect timing, almost as if I had planned it that way."

And in strode the leader of the Rangers of the Realm. Bushmaster was a tall human, strong and quick, with black hair and a bushy black mustache. He was dressed in brown pants and green jerkin, with a long sword on his belt, and a bow and quiver on his back. He wore a yellow kerchief around his neck.

"What news of the East, Ranger Mio?" hailed Cromartin.

"My King, the news is confusing and troubling. My rangers penetrated all the way to the borders of Pandoon. We rode south along the edge of the Ruined Lands and felt an unknown evil lurking there. Our horses would not go any closer. I sought volunteers to climb down into the Ruined Lands and explore, but a great fear gripped my men and none would go."

"My rangers were afraid?" asked Cromartin.

"Normally they are the most fearless men in Arcadia, but even they would not go into the Ruined Lands."

"Any sign of dwarves or elves on the march?" said a worried Cromartin.

"We interviewed some wayward adventurers who reported seeing dwarven war parties on the march, and supposedly dwarves are building steps down into the chasm to reach the Ruined Lands, although we were kept away so I cannot confirm such reports," said Bushmaster. "Of elves, we saw and heard nothing."

"Most disappointing that you come back with so little information, Ranger," said Zirmad in disapproving tones.

"I *had* expected more," said Cromartin.

Bushmaster knelt on one knee. "If I have failed my King, it is not for lack of trying."

"But even I penetrated into the Ruined Lands, far enough to find the bones of the giant," said Cromartin.

"Excuse any impertinence, but were the Ruined Lands collapsed into a great underworld when your kingship went there?" asked Bushmaster.

"Well, no, it was mostly flat then," Cromartin admitted.

"My King, the Ruined Lands have collapsed down into a great sunken underworld which contains much of Pandoon now. Something has happened out there," said Bushmaster, "in the lands beyond the mountains."

"Collapsed?" said Cromartin, sinking back onto his throne, which groaned in protest.

"Sunk down in, my King. Deeply sunk. We came to the edge, many week's ride beyond the last mountain pass. We looked down and saw the land far below and far wide; it must be hundreds of leagues across. We stood and watched birds flying on our eye level, far above Pandoon's bottom," said Bushmaster. "The climb alone would be quite a feat just to get down there. Whatever could cause such a horrifying change to the land can only be imagined. Also, strange trees are growing now in Pandoon."

"Trees?" Cromartin squeaked.

"Yes, sire, trees. We saw them. They have dark bark, as hard as iron and impossible to chop down. Their branches are crooked, and their red leaves and berries never fall. Also, the berries are poisonous. Locals we questioned said they started spreading after the Ruination. Some call them Dragon Trees and some Everreds. They are spreading this way."

"Towards us? Towards Arcadia?" Cromartin croaked.

"Yes, sire."

There was silence as the king silently mused, his face etched with concern. Cromartin finally roused himself from his thoughts. "Very well. I must ruminate on this. You are dismissed for now, Ranger Mio."

Bushmaster bowed and exited. After he was gone, Zirmad turned to Cromartin. "We must go at once and reconnoiter the Ruined Lands."

Vykar said, "Sire, we must go at once and invade the dwarves and elves. Kill them all, then take Sporu Angosta."

Zirmad nodded his approval at this.

Cromartin licked his thick lips. "I would then have control of both Arcadia and Pandoon, except perhaps Alfheim, Amphyra, and the Never Coast."

"More ripe fruit for the plucking, sire." said Zirmad.

Cromartin got a far-off dreamy look in his eyes. He smiled at Vykar and Zirmad. "I like that."

The great double doors creaked open again. The chamberlain said, "My Liege, your patrol returns."

"My patrol?"

"The one sent to the far side of Bremen Wood, my Liege," the Chamberlain reminded him.

"Oh, yes."

In came a bedraggled Captain McGee and the soldier Deepnose, his arm in a sling. Behind them came Wolfinger without his staff. They'd obviously had a rough time of it.

"Well?" Cromartin snapped.

"My King, we were ambushed by a group of wizards in Bremen Wood. We lost the fight, sire," said a crestfallen McGee.

"It sure looks like you lost. Describe what happened," said Cromartin.

So McGee described the fight.

When he finished Cromartin said, "So you two were injured and three of my Tooskers were killed?" The king shook his head. "Amazing."

"Hard enough to kill one Toosker, let alone two," said Vykar in the hard voice he used when he wanted to wreak violence, which was most of the time.

"And all at the hands of two old men and two kids?" asked Cromartin.

"Powerful wizards they were, sire," said McGee.

"Was one of the old men blind?" asked Zirmad.

"Maybe. He wore a red robe and had a young woman with red hair by his side," said McGee.

"My Liege, that would be Atticus, an old master of the Red Tower," said Zirmad. "No doubt traveling with some fellow spellcasters. They are outcasts from the Red Tower."

"And a rupa," said McGee.

"A rupa?"

"A very large, six-legged one," said McGee.

Vykar said, "Rupas have four legs."

"Not this one."

"Where is 4eyes?" asked Cromartin.

"3eyes, sire."

"3eyes?"

"Yes sir. 4eyes is now 3eyes as he lost one in battle, I'm afraid. That red-haired tart burned him with some flame spell. He's resting as comfortably as can be in the infirmary."

"And the fourth Toosker?"

"His face is swollen from all the bee stings."

"Did you capture any of the Red Tower scum?"

"No, sire."

Cromartin snorted. "Some patrol that was." He turned to Wolfinger. "And what of you, my son?"

"They were powerful wizards, father. By myself it was too unequal a struggle," said Wolfinger.

"He was attacked by a snake, my King," said McGee.

"A snake?" said Cromartin.

"A magnetic snake," said Wolfinger. "I killed it."

"How?"

"*Guassian Purge* spell, father."

"Hmmm." Cromartin rubbed one of his chins.

The Chamberlain returned and passed on the report from the Captain at the Dragon Gate.

"The wizards you let slip away are here in my city," Cromartin said to his patrol. He turned to Zirmad. "Your sneaky Drecks is on the case. Personally see to it that they're captured."

My Drecks? Zirmad thought as he left.

Cromartin raised his voice to the court. "There has been a colossal failure, and someone must pay." He dropped a pudgy hand to unclip Vykar's leash. The Aoban rushed forward with a growl as screaming people scattered. In less than three seconds, Vykar had McGee down and his throat torn open. Servants drug the body out and spread copious amounts of sawdust to soak up the blood.

Cromartin addressed a shaken Bangalore. "I promote you to Captain. Prepare the army according to plan. We march east after the Festival of the Dragon."

"Yes, sire." Bangalore mumbled as he stood watching the blood soak into the sawdust.

"Bring me food," Cromartin ordered.

Servants scrambled while the king daydreamed.

12
Fear & Hope

Ballastro was the largest city known to man, elf, or dwarf. It was like no place Kido had ever seen since he had left Putnam Castle. The streets of Ballastro just went on and on. And there were so many people filling up this city. People were everywhere. As they walked, Kido felt as if he were swimming in a river of people. Old and young, men and women, poor and prosperous, dressed in rags or finement; they were all here.

The streets were paved in cobblestones. Most of the buildings here were made of brick or stone, not wood. In fact, the city *looked* new, its buildings little weathered by time. A young city. And this was only Riverside.

They passed a fish market and then a produce market. They passed under a wide stone arch which had carved in it:

Welcome to Ballastro, capital of the realm

Beyond was a wide street between tall buildings, identified by its street sign as Dragon Street. Pyra would describe where they were, and Atticus would tell them where to go next.

After struggling against the crowds for a short while they ducked into a covered doorway to talk. "I think we should go straight away to the Red Tower," said Atticus. "We are in the lower level, the area called Riverside. We need to continue north, and then up the cliff to the upper area, which is called Topside. The Red Tower is in the middle of Topside."

"You have your *Hope Crystal?*" Pyra asked.

Atticus patted one of his pouches. "Right here. Numa knows we're coming although not when."

"And she will let us in?"

"I would think so, even if the tower is officially closed. I *am* a wizard in good standing still with the Order."

"Lovely. Well, let's go. I won't relax until we get to the tower."

"Here, wait." Atticus took a crystal out of one pocket. It was wrapped in red cloth, and he handed it to Kido. "I want Kido to carry this since I'm concentrating on our movements. Kido, this is my *Fear Crystal*. It grows warmer when danger approaches. It grows hot when danger is on top of us. Warn us before it gets hot."

"Yes, teacher." Kido held the smooth crystal clutched in his right hand.

Atticus and Pyra started out but Kido didn't. "It feels warm already," he called out.

They stopped. "It's warm?" Pyra came back to stand next to him, looking at the crystal, and then they nervously scanned the crowds. Atticus tilted his head up and sniffed the air. "Anybody see anything?"

"No."

"Well, let's keep going. Whatever it is, hopefully we can avoid it or at least beat it to the tower," said Atticus. "Once inside the tower, we will be safe."

"This feels like a trap," Pyra muttered, casting her eyes about as she took her teacher's arm. They moved out.

Behind them, Drecks followed at a distance, ducking into doorways and dodging between people. Every fifty feet or so he would drop a shiny red rock the size of a poker chip. Each *Glow Rock* blazed a cherry red where it lay on the pavement. Passerbys were attracted to the bright color, but anyone foolish enough to pick one up was burned and quickly dropped it.

They passed rows of shops and then elegant brick rowhouses. The street began to slope gently uphill. After several blocks of nice, tall houses, there were more shops, their windows full of fine food, household furnishings, or clothing. Signs hanging above each shop advertised their wares. The street led directly to a t-intersection, beyond which broad stone stairs climbed up a flat-topped hill.

"That is Obol's Hill," said Pyra.

"You've been in this city before?" asked a surprised Kido.

"Atticus has described this city so many times, I feel like I was born here," she said.

A wide street went around the hill in both directions, lined with more shops to the left and right. The street sign read: OBOL'S CIRCLE. Kido looked to the right. "There's another hill over there. Let's go that way. What's over there?"

"The King's Palace on Asper's Hill," said Pyra.

"And the flat area between the two hills?" Kido asked.

"The King's Gardens," said Pyra.

Kido pointed to the far side of the gardens. "And is that—"

"It is an aqueduct, bringing water to the gardens."

"Just like ancient Rome."

"Let us go in the *opposite* direction from Cromartin's palace," said Atticus.

As they moved left, Kido asked about the two large white stone buildings on top of Obol's hill.

"The Temple of the Dragon and the Hall of the Giant," said Pyra.

"Wow. Can we see them?"

"No. We will avoid them at all costs. We must get to the Red Tower," said Atticus. "How is the crystal?"

"Still warm."

"Keep moving," Pyra said through clenched teeth.

Drecks hurried to keep pace with them. They were in a hurry, he thought. When he saw them heading around Obol's Hill, he knew he was right in guessing they were headed for Topside. And he knew the only reason these reprobate wizards would want to go to that part of the city. He kept looking around, wondering when soldiers would show up. He dropped another *Glow Rock* and hurried after his quarry.

Atticus was walking fast for a blind man, letting Pyra be his eyes. They passed more houses, these not as high or as nice but still respectable. The land was flatter here but the streets still crowded. Up ahead they could see a lofty cliff face now rising above the houses. To the right and way back still, the Red Tower rose above all else, its head in the clouds. The cliff drew near, but the city's neighborhoods kept coming on. Kido stood and gaped at the tower, still far off but easily visible. He looked around at the bustling city. "This is such a huge city," he said aloud.

Finally, after walking forever, they came to the cliff's base where the shops and houses stopped and left an open, paved plaza. Before them now was a huge stone ramp which ran up from Riverside to Topside. It looked too steep to comfortably walk up, but men with ropes were pulling up flat carts of bundled objects along its incline.

"Do we go up that?" Kido asked.

"We have two better options," said Pyra. "Climb the Stairs of

Vadda or use the Lazy Lifts."

"I'm pooped. I vote for the lifts," said Atticus.

"Fine with me. Where are they?" said Kido.

"East."

It took two hours to reach the first Lazy Lift, which was a system of thick ropes hung from a massive crossbeam jutting out from the top of the cliff. Attached at each end of the rope was a large iron cage. When one went up, the other came down. At the base was a group of men coordinating the on-loading and off-loading. There was also a long line of people waiting to use the lift.

Pyra groaned. "We'll wait forever."

Atticus said, "Shoulda taken the stairs. It's a heck of a climb but quicker than this wait."

"Let's use the stairs," said Kido.

"We would have to completely backtrack to reach it now," said Atticus. "It is clear west of the ramp."

"I could try a *Float* spell and you've got your staff," said Pyra.

"But Kido has neither, and nothing would mark us out as wizards faster than if all these people saw us in the air," said Atticus. "That is only a last resort. No, let us try and get to the tower without warning Cromartin of our presence."

"Actually, I can *Float*," said Kido.

"It's too dangerous," said Atticus.

"We better hurry whatever we're doing, because the crystal is getting warmer," said Kido. It was starting to hum too.

They began retracing their steps. "It's getting hot," Kido warned.

"Turn in here," Pyra said, drawing them into a small alley in between two shops where they melted back into the shadows. Pyra put on her gloves and Kido took his sword out. They watched townspeople go by. Then a dark cloaked figure came into view. He was half-crouched and walking fast but then he stopped. They held their breath as they waited to see what he would do. Kido felt a cold dread come over him as he watched.

The figure looked left and up the cliff, then back the way he came. Stealthily his thin, gloved hand went to his pocket and dropped something on the cobblestones before he hurried on towards the Lazy Lifts. The object he dropped began to glow a cherry red. As they continued to watch, a man attracted by the bright light bent to pick it up but then yelled loudly, dropping it. Pyra whispered it all to Atticus.

"*Glow Rock*," Atticus murmured.

They waited to make sure he was gone and then crept out of the alley and headed back west. After they passed DRAGON STREET, the townspeople there parted to reveal a large group of Dragon Guards headed towards them. Captain Bangalore was at the front, bent over and following the trail of *Glow Rocks*.

Hurrying away, Pyra led Atticus and Kido west.

Bangalore saw a cherry red glow and turned right, heading east.

"Did you recognize our pursuer?" asked Atticus over his shoulder as they hurried along.

"Hard to say," said Pyra. "His hood covered his face. He was wearing black gloves and a plain black robe."

"He was short and kinda skinny," said Kido.

"He sounds new to me," said Atticus. "Definitely not Zirmad. Probably a survivor of the Shadow Tower. Kido, how does that crystal feel?"

"Still warm, Atticus, but not as hot as before."

After awhile they came to the base of a tall stone stairway cut into the side of the cliff. Several people were using it. To Kido it looked about a hundred feet to the top of the cliff. "A lot of stairs in this city," he said. They began ascending. The stairs were wide enough to let people in both directions pass, but there was no hand rail. As they climbed Kido got a good view of Riverside. Off in the distance he could see the hilltop square with the temple and hall with its giant's bones that he wished he could visit. Further off he thought he saw the dark walls and the Dragon Gate. But then he felt vertigo as they climbed and concentrated on the steps. He heard humming and took out the crystal. "It's getting hot again," he said.

They stopped and looked around. Pyra called out, "Look!" and pointed at the top of the cliff. They could see several soldiers wearing gold star & moon symbols on their white tabards. "The City Guard."

"Ouch!" Kido said. The *Feur Crystal* was so hot, he had to put it in a pouch, where its hum was still audible. "Oh, no." He looked down and saw the dark hooded figure, Bangalore, and another group of soldiers approaching the base of the stairs. These soldiers wore black breeches and brown tabards with dragon heads. "Dragon Guards. We're trapped," he said.

They threw off their outer cloaks. Pyra put on her gloves and Atticus poured golden ichor into his palm. The old mage pushed back his hood, spoke a word of Magic and shot a lighting bolt upward from his staff. It missed the soldiers.

"Six feet to the right," Pyra told him.

Atticus shifted his staff and shot again, this time toppling two soldies on top of the cliff.

Kido said, "He's casting a spell," and indicated the hooded figure whose arms were outstretched. He was looking up but no face could be seen in the depths of the hood. "He is a wizard."

"He is a Black Hood," said Pyra.

She rubbed her gloved hands together, spoke a spell phrase, and a glowing golden ball of light the size of a grapefruit appeared. She held it aloft with one hand, and with a grunt, threw it down with all her strength. Her aim was good but the hooded figure blocked it. On deflection, the ball o' fire struck a nearby guard square in his chest. He screamed and ran trailing smoke and jumped into a nearby fountain.

Atticus blew gold dust into the air and chanted a phrase that caused two soldiers at the top to levitate up into the air and then plunge yelling past them to the ground below.

The strange smell of ichor hit Kido's nostrils. Then a dark blur came at Kido's head, and he ducked instinctively as a crossbow bolt clattered against the cliff behind him. He looked down to see several soldiers wielding crossbows. Another bolt was shot and Pyra yelled, pulling her teacher aside. The bolt narrowly missed Atticus and as he turned he lost his balance and began windmilling his arms and teetering near the edge. Kido grabbed him and pulled him back. Atticus embraced him. "Thank you, my boy. I'm in no shape to go flying today."

Bangalore and his soldiers mounted the stairs and ran up towards them. The cliff face right below them exploded with a lightning bolt from the sorcerer.

"We need to go up, not down!" Kido said.

"Quite right," said Atticus. He held his staff aloft and called out a spell and a thick gray smoke poured out and up into the soldiers above, enveloping them. "Pyra, go up. Keep climbing."

They ran up the stairs and found everything obscured in a thick cloud of smoke. A City Guard suddenly appeared and Kido batted him with his sword, knocking him off the cliff. Another loomed out of the smoke and came at him, and Kido waved his sword, but the soldier was in a panic and ran away on his own.

When they came out of the smoke there were no soldiers in sight, only curious townspeople watching. They were standing in a small paved plaza. The smoke cleared a little, and Kido, looking off, got a good glimpse of the tower, rising above rooftops until its top disappeared in the clouds. "How tall is it?" he murmured aloud. Pyra broke his reverie by tugging his sleeve as she hurried past.

They ran between buildings and up a street. They moved deeper into Topside. Topside looked so different from Riverside as to be a different city.

Here the street upon which they hurried was dirt. The buildings were of wood and looked aged and weathered. The people had a scruffier look, too. They passed a lot of children and dogs running around in the street. They came to a small paved courtyard with a statue of a stone creature, legless and winged. Pyra described where they were to Atticus.

"We should be nearing the Manta Zirkus," said Atticus. He was panting some and holding his side. "Let me rest a minute."

Kido could see Atticus looked tired, and he wondered how spellcasting sapped one's energy. He admired the statue and ran his fingers along its smooth stone wing. "Have you ever seen a manta?" he asked Pyra.

With a toss of her red curls, she said, "No, supposedly they disappeared after the Ruination. But people used to fly on them."

"Mantas can fly?"

"Sky mantas they are called."

People walking by stared at them. One little boy said, "Look, mommy," and pointed at them.

"Wizards," the mommy said in disgust and dragged her boy away from them.

"We're not popular here," said Pyra.

"Are we anywhere?" asked Kido.

"Pyra, come here," Atticus said. He took out a small object wrapped in green silk and handed it to her. When she unwrapped it, they saw an egg-shaped crystal similar to the *Fear Crystal*.

"That is my *Hope Crystal*. I want you to carry it. It identifies the holder as a friend to the Red Tower. Hold it high as you approach the tower, and it will recognize you and allow you in. Otherwise, you'll never penetrate the enchantment that protects it. I want you to carry it in case something happens to me."

"Oh, Atticus," she said tenderly.

"Take it, my dear," he said, folding her hand over the crsystal and holding it for a moment.

"Yes, Atticus," Pyra said.

Atticus took a deep breath and put a hand on her shoulder. "Let's go. Straight ahead, Pyra. We turn east at the Manta Zirkus and that's close by now." Sure enough, at the next cross-street, the buildings opened up and they saw on their left a massive stone structure that rose six stories high and extended for three city blocks.

"What is *that*?" Kido asked in awe.

"*That* is the Manta Zirkus, a stadium where they used to race Sky Mantas," said Atticus. "I used to go there as a boy back in the day. Back when I had my sight."

"It's huge," said Kido.

"It holds 80,000 people," said Atticus.

Kido took out the *Fear Crystal* and held it in both hands. "It's only slightly warm now," he said.

"Still, we better keep moving," said Pyra, her eyes shifting nervously about.

A wide paved street intersected their dirt one, and they turned on it. The street sign read: TOWER STREET.

"Only paved street in Topside. This street leads straight to the Red Tower," said Atticus. "Only eight blocks away now."

Kido looked ahead and saw the Red Tower looming high over the other buildings, dominating everything in sight.

"Almost there," said Pyra.

The crowds on the street thinned out as they went along. There were trees lining this street, full of brightly colored fruit. The trees grew taller and the fruit more abundant as they went along. The cobblestones began to change color, growing more vivid. Kido commented on the change.

"We are entering the tower's sphere of enchantment," Atticus said.

Kido lifted his head and smelled. The air smelled cleaner, and he felt some kind of tingle on his skin. He felt more alive, more in tune with the world. Then he heard a humming and pulled out the *Fear Crystal*. "Much warmer," he said with a moan. There was a commotion behind them as people back near the Manta Zirkus scattered.

"Dragon Guards!" Pyra warned, holding onto her master's sleeve as they burst into a sprint towards the tower.

Kido stopped and looked back to see a sea of brown tabards with fire-breathing dragons, sprouting swords and spears. Kido ran to-catch up to Pyra and Atticus. Their feet pounded the pavement as their hearts pounded in fear. The trees ran past them, and the air grew sweeter.

The Dragon Guards yelled and gave chase, the links of their chainmail armor making chinking sounds.

"Just got to...reach...the tower," Atticus panted.

Time slowed down and the air began to blur. The tower loomed high overhead but something was wrong. There was a loud, unearthly moan and a howl of anger as numerous dark figures lurched out from the left and the right to block their path. They pulled up abruptly to confront six snarling Tooskers.

"I don't need to see to know. Tooskers is it?" Atticus said grimly. He waved his staff and took off his ichor horn and pointed it away to the side. "Pyra, Kido, run! Get away! I will hold them off."

"No, master. I'm staying with you," said Pyra. She turned and handed the *Hope Crystal* to Kido.

Kido hesitated. There were Tooskers in front and Dragon Guards closing in from behind. The trap was closing, but he didn't want to leave his friends. He tried to take a step and his legs faltered.

Pyra whispered fiercely, "Run, you silly boy!" She pushed him away and then took out her golden gloves.

Kido looked at the Tooskers, tall and dark, growling and snapping at them. They raked the air with their tusks and lumbered closer. He looked to his right at the closest structure, a tall house of faded turquoise with wooden steps leading up. He looked back once more as the creatures were closing in, two black-hooded figures now visible behind the Tooskers, the short, slight one and a taller one.

"Run, Kido, run," Atticus said while facing the Tooskers, and his calm filled Kido, and he knew he had to escape somehow. He ran off the street and into the narrow space between two buildings. He could sense a tall dark shape moving swiftly towards him from the left; he heard a Dragon Guard yell close by on the right. Up the wooden stairs his feet pounded, two at a time. At the top was a door he crashed through as the steps shook. The steps lurched and fell away as he toppled heavily onto the floor inside. He tried to remember the *BeeSwarm* spell but the words were blocked by his own fear.

Feeling more frightened than he ever had in his life, he got up and ran, bounding down an inner stairwell and towards the back of the house, paying little attention to the fleeting glimpses of decaying, deserted rooms. Behind him, the front door and window blew open with a noisy crash. Kido flew through a living room, a kitchen, and out the back door. There was no one in the yard as he lept a fence and went down an alley.

Popping out into a small dirt street he turned left and ran as fast as he could. He was all alone on an empty street lined with old frowning houses. Counting side streets he went six blocks and then turned left. The tall red tower rising above rooftops was his guide, and he kept homing in on it, glancing up and then around him, expecting a Toosker to appear at any moment. He came back out on TOWER STREET. In a quick glance, he saw a tall Toosker roar at its prey and come bounding towards him on tree-trunk legs. With it ran Captain Bangalore waving his sword madly. The tall Black Sorcerer followed them.

Kido sprinted away. In front of him he could see the street widening and a large, open space ahead. And there in front of him was the base of a massive, tall building made of red bricks. He put every ounce of energy into his motion, arms and legs pumping. The buildings were a blur now.

Strange currents of air eddied and flowed before his eyes. The tower shifted and danced a little. He sucked in huge draughts of the sweet air but felt his limbs dragging. He thought he was tiring and then realized the air was thickening. It was slowing him down! He felt like he was wading through chest-high water, his feet dragging in thick sand. He looked down where the brick-red cobblestones looked solid but felt like quicksand to his struggling feet.

The Toosker bellowed behind him. It was getting closer, fighting through the thick air with its immense power.

"We got you, boy. You can't get away," he heard the distorted voice of Bangalore sounding as if it was coming through a long tunnel.

"Get him quick before he gets any closer," said an urgent male voice that had to belong to the Black Sorcerer.

The enchantment was slowing them down too. Their movements came to a crawl. It was becoming almost impossible to move forward. Kido's legs felt like lead. Turning his head with considerable effort, he saw the sword of Bangalore reaching out to him, almost touching him. The blade's tip was so close now. He felt the hot breath of the Toosker on his neck. It would catch him in another few seconds.

Then he remembered.

In maddeningly slow motion, Kido reached into his pouch and pulled out the *Hope Crystal*, holding the smooth hard object in his hand. It felt warm, not the angry warmth of the *Fear Crystal* but a soothing warmth. He held it high, and in an explosion of light, the air instantaneously became thinner and his feet felt light as feathers. Kido exploded forward to cover the last twenty yards to the base of the tower.

Bangalore yelled and collapsed, unable to come any closer. The Toosker, being bigger and stronger, continued to fight forward, roaring as Kido pulled away from it. Kido looked back and saw the tall creature outlined in bright energy that turned to flames. It fell rolling and writhing, consumed by fire. The Black Sorcerer had halted further back and was staring at Kido.

Kido came to a stop before a short flight of red brick stairs that led up to a set of wide, double doors of wood bound in brassy metal. He looked up at the great height of the tower and while the top was still covered by clouds, he did notice the green climbing plants that grew up its brick flanks, sprouting blue, yellow, white, and pink flowers in a colorful profusion. Clusters of succulent purple berries peeked out from amidst the vines. The building was so massive, Kido couldn't see where it ended. It looked like an endless, tall brick wall.

He mounted the stairs to the doors still holding the *Hope Crystal* aloft, feeling its gentle pulsing warmth in his hand. The doors opened on their own to reveal an older bald man dressed in red jerkin and trousers held up by gold suspenders. His lidded eyes beheld Kido for a silent moment, and then he said in a gentle voice, "Who are you to reach the tower?"

"I am Kido. I am...a friend of Atticus."

"Atticus?" The eyelids raised a bit to allow blue-gray irises to look around.

"He's down the street, fighting Tooskers with Pyra," Kido supplied.

The man gave Kido a second look. "Oh, you are the one the Mawker mentioned. You are the Witness to the Ruination."

"Gulmar."

"Yes, the Mawker bird." The man stepped aside. "Well, I suppose you should come on in..."

Kido hesitated, still clutching his crystal.

"...or not, as you wish."

Kido looked back to see that the Toosker was nothing but a pile of smoldering ashes. Through the haze beyond he could see the Black Hood already back up the street and Bangalore slowly trudging be-

hind him, dragging his sword.
   Kido went in, and the doors closed themselves.

13
The Red Tower

Kido was inside the Red Tower, standing in a long narrow hallway, where the man stood silently waiting. He realized he did not know what Numa looked like, or even if Numa was a man or woman.

"Are you Numachitura, sir?" Kido asked.

The man showed no emotion but spoke in the patient long-suffering voice of butlers everywhere. "Most certainly not. I am Farstaff, sir. I am part of the staff here at the tower. You may hang your things there." He pointed at a long line of knobs running along the wall.

Kido took off his pack and held it up, but the knobs were all too high. "I can't reach," he was about to complain, when two knobs obligingly slid down and accepted the pack and his gray cloak. Then they slid back up to their spots.

"And your sword, sir," Farstaff said.

Kido took it out of his belt and held it up to the knobs. Two slid down and morphed into a pair of hands held palm up. He laid his sword on them and they slid back up out of his reach.

"Please sir, my friends need help down the street," Kido said, but the man ingored the comment and began walking slowly down the quiet hallway.

"This way," said Farstaff. A few feet further on, he gestured with one hand to an archway on the left. "You may wait in here, sir."

'Here' turned out to be a large room with tall ceilings. The walls were red brick, adorned with pictures of fantastic creatures. There was a unicorn, a snake forming a circle by holding its tail in its mouth, a two-headed giant carrying a bag, a large golden rooster with a red comb, a silver pegasus, a smiling sphinx, a centaur, a minotaur, a sky manta, a mermaid with blonde hair, and over the fireplace a large red dragon. A large clock on the wall showed it was midafternoon. Several overstuffed chairs lined the walls and Kido sat in one. The room was as quiet as a crypt, and he felt overwhelmed by such a strange, alien environment. He felt the urge to jump up and run screaming for help for his friends outside and wondered if he could get his sword back. He had expected to find help and wondered why the tower seemed quiet and empty.

Time crawled and Kido grew restless. Finally he heard soft footfalls approaching and looked at the doorway, expecting to see a wizard but was startled to see a beautiful cat with lustrous red hair enter and jump up to sit on a cushion on top of a trunk in the corner. The cat regarded him with golden eyes. He was twice the size of household cats we see today.

"Hi," Kido said to it. "Are you Numa?"

"He is not. That is Curiosity, the alpha cat of Red Tower. And I am not Numa either," said a stern masculine voice from the doorway.

Into the room swept someone wearing a red robe. He pulled down the hood to reveal a very long, very thin face dominated by luminous globed eyes that bulged out. Kido wasn't sure what race he was.

"I am Codface, Senior Wizard in the Order of Wizards. I am called the Red Rook, and you are the Kido person Atticus mentioned in his Mawker letter?"

"Yes, sir," said Kido with confidence, trying not to be intimidated.

"How did you get past the King's guards? This tower is officially closed."

"I ran past them."

"But how did you get past the tower's shield of enchantment?"

Kido held up the *Hope Crystal*.

Codface frowned ever more seriously. "And where is Atticus and Pyra?"

Kido told him about the Tooskers and Dragon Guards.

"Hmm." His ears flapped gently like gills as he regarded Kido intently. "And this just happened?"

"Indeed, sir."

"Well, let us go have a look then."

Kido eagerly followed him out, hopeful now that it seemed they might go down the street and help his friends. He wondered where everyone else in the tower was.

Outside they walked quickly.

"Give me your *Hope Crystal* for safe keeping," Codface said, and Kido handed it over without thinking. He wanted to run down the street with this powerful wizard with the strange eyes. Codface grabbed his arm and steered him forward. Kido began to trot, scanning eagerly down the street at far-off figures to see what was happening. It was hard because of the ripples of thickening air.

Something wasn't right. He could feel the air resisting him. He looked back to see Codface had retreated to the tower, still holding his crystal.

"Hey!" He tried to go back, but the enchantment shield stopped him. The air grew stifling hot.

"You cannot stay in the tower," Codface's voice came to him as if from a great distance. "We are closed. No more young wizards, you must understand. Numa has ordered me to tell you that we cannot take you."

"But Atticus and Pyra?" Kido sputtered, confused and afraid.

"We did not think they would really come. The King's soldiers must have them by now. In fact, you should run away before they get you too."

"Aren't you going to help them?" Kido cried out.

Codface shook his head no. "They are beyond help. Run away, little boy."

Kido felt anger flare up inside him, mixed with Magic. His Magic felt stronger outside the tower. Without thinking, he cast a *Levitate* spell at the *Hope Crystal*, and it flew from Codface's hand to his in a flash.

A shocked Codface looked at his empty hand, and then his eyes glowered at Kido. "Why you little—"

Kido walked triumphantly forward, crystal held aloft. He passed the wizard and went inside the tower. Farstaff with surprise-popped eyes watched him go by, and Codface's angry-slapping feet followed him deep into the tower.

In a large deserted dining hall, with long tables to one side, a kitchen to the other, and a wooden stairwell beyond, Codface caught up with him.

"I suppose you think you're pretty clever, getting back in here like that," he said.

Kido shrugged. "I had to do something. I was told this is where I go to become a wizard."

"Nobody becomes a wizard here anymore!" he snapped. Then he paused and took a deep breath to compose himself. His ears slowed their flapping and he tucked a stray strand of black hair behind one.

"Look here, Kido-wizard-wannabe. The sad fact is Atticus and Pyra are no doubt prisoners of King Cromartin by now. And I repeat, this tower is closed. Why should we open it for you? Things aren't the same here anymore. The world has changed. Half of Pandoon is ruined, and everyone hates us. The King can make things quite difficult for the Order if he finds out we let a young wizard in. There's nothing for you here, and frankly we don't want you. Can you see things from our point of view?"

Kido looked around at the deserted hall. "Are there wizards here? I mean, besides you and Numa."

Codface crossed his arms. "We have numerous young wizards working upstairs and that is it. They are holdovers from before the tower was closed, but now since you have forced your way in, we have to decide what to do with you. You understand, we have accepted no new wizards in a long time. You may have a bed here for the night, but that is all I can promise you. In the morning you shall be summoned before the tower's company where we shall decide your fate."

Kido was given a cot in the corner of a storage room on the ground floor, sleeping next to a mop bucket.

A female elf woke him the next morning. She had long straight gray hair tucked behind pointed ears and purple, almond-shaped eyes, the most beautiful eyes he'd ever seen. A shy manner and graceful movements soon became apparent. She was shorter than him and slender of build in her red robes. "I am to escort you to the tower meeting." She spoke in a soft, accented voice and kept her head bowed.

He was totally fascinated. "Are you a wizard?"

She gave a soft laugh at the question but wouldn't look him in the eye. "Yes. Can you not see the color of my robes?"

"What is your name?"

"I better not say."

"Why?"

"You are wearing drab clothes and look like a street urchin. Wait here." She soon returned with clean pants and undergraments and a clean gray robe and then waited outside while he changed.

He came out and said, "Is this better?"

A shy smile was her reply.

The Red Tower was deserted in appearance except the elf leading the new boy. Kido followed her up the back stairs onto the second floor and into a huge auditorium built like an ancient Greek theater, semi-circular rows of wooden seats rising up from the stage. The seats were partially filled by people, mainly kids with a smattering of teenagers, young adults, and a few older folks up at the front. Only a small minority of the assembled wore red robes. On the stage a long table stood before the mural of a huge red dragon with green eyes. The elf indicated he should sit in the front row.

A gong sounded and a side door opened, admitting five figures wearing red robes, their faces concealed under their hoods. They slowly and silently walked in to sit at the table.

"Unhood," commanded an authoritarian female voice from one of the five.

Four men and one woman were revealed, the men looking much older than everyone else. The woman had black hair with straight bangs above a pale face accented with bright red lips. She looked neither young nor old. *Mature.* That was how Kido saw her as she shuffled some papers and, lifting her voice for all to hear, said with considerable gravitas, "Red Rook?"

Kido recognized Codface coming forward from somewhere behind him. "Master of the Tower," he acknowledged with a reverent bow.

"Is *this* the person who somehow entered our tower yesterday?" She nodded at Kido.

"Yes, master."

"And he has a *Hope Crystal*?"

"Yes, master."

Kido sat there feeling strange, watching this unfold with great uncertainty.

The woman studied him briefly, as if he were a strange animal stumbled upon while on safari. She consulted a document.

"You are Kido from Feather Bay?" she asked him directly.

"I am from across the sea, but I more recently came from Feather Bay, ma'am."

"Call her 'master,'" Codface ordered him.

"Yes, master," Kido said.

"You are a Witness to the Ruination?"

He hesitated, hating to associate himself with that event. She lifted her cool gaze, and he finally said, "Yes, master."

"From Feather Bay?" She sounded incredulous.

"I was in the Gold Tower before coming to Feather Bay."

She blinked several times. Gasps and shocked murmuring swept through the assembly.

When it died down, the woman said, "I am Numachitura, the Red Mage and therefore Master of the Red Tower. Tell me, where did you come by the *Hope Crystal*?"

"Atticus gave it to me."

"Atticus the wizard?"

"No, Atticus the lion-tamer. Of course it was Atticus the wizard."

Codface hit the back of his head.

"Ouch."

"Hmmm," she said. "Insolent little one. Are your parents wizards?"

"Hardly. They are back home. Master."

"And you so far from home." She studied him again. "I am told you wish to become a wizard?"

"Yes, master."

She lifted her eyes to the assembled. "You come to us in bleak times. Normally, a young aspirant is sponsored by an established wizard. I am told that Atticus is a prisoner of King Cromartin. I have here his Mawker message, but he can hardly sponsor anyone whilst busy rotting in the King's dungeon. So, who else then sponsors this aspirant?"

There was much muttering on all sides. Kido looked around but didn't see too many friendly faces. Codface was smirking at him. The female elf stared at the floor. Numa looked haughty.

Then someone stood up. It was the figure at the far end of the table, an older man with a long gray beard, long gray hair, and wire-rim spectacles.

Numa looked surprised. "Master Shippleglass? You are willing to sponsor this unknown boy?"

"Yes. Yes, I am. Any friend of Atticus is a friend of mine. I see no reason to cast him out without giving him a chance." He sat back down.

"Hmm." She gave Kido a prim smile. "Very well, we have a sponsor. Therefore, I nominate Kido of Feather Bay to join the company of the Red Tower on a provisional basis. Can I have a second?"

The tower was silent.

"I must have a second or his application is disqualified."

Kido's heart dropped as the quiet continued.

"Anyone?" asked Numa. She looked around. She looked up.

The female elf slowly stepped forward. "I second him," she said in a small voice. She stepped back.

"You?" Numa said sharply. She sat back in her chair, looking put off. "The Tower Elf has given us a second. However, Summer Wind, being an elf, doesn't count. Will any *human* wizard step forward?"

Summer Wind. Kido knew her name at least.

"Oh, do give the boy a chance," said Shippleglass to anyone.

Numa rolled her eyes and sighed, crossing her arms. Then she thought of something. "The tower is technically closed, all normal procedures suspended. But there may yet be a chance." She looked around at her red-robed assembly. She asked them, "What do we do when we cannot decide whether to keep someone in this tower or not?"

There was a pause, and then several people answered in soft voices. A chant began, picking up support as it grew louder.

"Tower walk...tower walk...tower walk...TOWER WALK!"

Numa nodded and smiled smugly. "Tower walk," she said to Kido.

They all left the auditorium, Kido guided by Codface now. Back down on the first floor, Codface led them down a long hallway to a large iron door guarded by a big man wielding a cat 'o' nine tails. The man reminded Kido of Lancemaster Phineas except he was taller, hairier, and tattooless. He wore black leather breeches and black boots. His naked torso was covered in thick, coarse black hair, and he had a black beard. He must've been half-bear.

"This is Black Bob," said Codface. "He helps me maintain order and discipline."

Black Bob pulled out a large ring of skeleton keys to unlock the iron door. It creaked ominously as it swung open. They descended stone stairs that circled down into darkness. A red light appeared and the air grew warmer. Eventually, the stairs terminated in a huge circular chamber dug from the very rock. And there a narrow stone bridge crossed the giant chasm where a floor should be. The heat and red light emanated from the chasm.

Numa said, "This is the very core of the tower, Kido. The source of its enchantment lies here. Walk around to the other side of the chasm."

Reluctantly Kido went to the left, in the direction she indicated, and saw a narrow ledge circling the chamber's wall. He walked along it, trembling at the sight to his right, a dizzying fall that looked to go down thousands of feet into a sea of flames and lava. Kido heard the grind of stone in motion and looking back saw the ledge behind him disappearing into the tower's wall as they went along, cutting him off from going back. Finally he reached the other side and saw the stone bridge spanning the chasm and leading directly back to Numa and the stairs. As many spectators as could fit stood on those stairs watching him.

Numa called out, "Now, cross over the bridge to join us. If the tower accepts you, it will allow you to cross. If it does not accept you, it will retract the bridge and...well, in that case it's been nice knowing you, Kido."

Kido stood there shaking in fear, as anyone would in such a situation. He felt some strange enchantment in operation here and just knew that he could not levitate himself here. He could only rely on the bridge. What would the tower do?

And then he thought of everything that led to this point, his friends teleporting with him, the Gold Tower, the dragons in Sporu Angosta, Elger, the rupa, Pyra, and Atticus. If he was to succeed at anything, it had to start here. It was now or never he realized, and taking a deep breath, he stepped onto the bridge. It shivered but held. He could took another step. And another. A shudder went through the tower, shaking its core. The bridge seemed to retract just a bit, opening up a small space. Dust and rock chips fell like rain into the chasm.

Kido could see the warmly-lit faces on the far side, the eyes of Numa and some of the others joyful at what they hoped to be his imminent demise, still others showing suspense or curiosity. Summer Wind looked scared to death. Heart thumping, Kido took another step. The bridge shuddered as it retracted, opening up a wider gap. He took another, wondering if it would be his last, holding his breath, and the bridge retracted almost to his feet so Kido teetered on the edge of the chasm. Kido paused. Looking back, he saw the bridge had retracted behind him too; by some enchantment it just hung in empty space. He could hear Codface laughing loudly at his predicament. He held his breath and inched forward. The wizard kids were yelling at him, but a roar in his ears was all he could hear now. He couldn't go any further without plunging off. He closed his eyes. Not knowing what else to do, he reached inside his robe and felt the Dragon's Gift, holding it in his hand but keeping it hidden. He felt the bridge hesitate. And the bridge held steady. In fact it returned to its initial position, closing the gap it had just opened.

With joy, he realized the tower was accepting him. He ran the rest of the way, to stand before a shocked Numa. "Well," she said crossly.

"It looks like you're in...for now."

"Congratulations," said Shippleglass, smiling at him. Several other young wizards also smiled and shook his hand. Kido was in. He tried to go up the stairs and out of that accursed cavern, but Codface stopped him.

"What now?" Kido said.

"You get to stay down here."

"I thought I got to stay in the tower. I survived the tower walk."

"This is technically part of the tower."

Kido looked around in confusion. "How can I study Magic down here by myself?"

"In the past you would have had an older wizard who would have become your teacher and mentor, your master."

Kido thought of Elger, who was too far away, and Atticus, who was too old and a prisoner to boot.

Codface continued, "You'll have to learn Magic on your own, if you can. I don't think anyone cares if you learn anything at all. But you'll sleep down here."

Wizard kids filed past Kido, ogling him with wide eyes. Codface led him to the right to a wooden door beneath the stairs. He opened it and lit a torch to reveal a small rock chamber with a bed and table. "You are to stay here."

"Here?" Kido said, looking around at this dismal little cell. It smelled musty. A large spider web spanned one upper corner.

"Yes. Maybe you can move up later on." Sarcasm.

"I'd rather have the cot in the storage room back."

"No. Numa says here," said a voice from the doorway. It was Numa herself with the elf.

"And what am I to do down here in the dark?"

"You can have free run of the tower during the day, outside of a few restricted spaces. This is just for sleeping at night. But be careful you don't interfere with the other wizards' work. And obey the Tower Rules. Too many demerits and I'll have an excuse to kick you out. And don't go wandering down in the catacombs."

"Catacombs?"

"Yes, they are beyond the chasm room. Don't go in there. There are tunnels all over the place beneath the tower, but I'd avoid them if I were you. Few of them are explored. Dangerous things lurk in the catacombs."

"Like ghosts?"

"And worse. Or so they say. I've never been in them. I remember a young wizard from Bear Floor who went in there five years ago on a dare. No one has seen him since."

"I'm afraid down here," Kido admitted.

Numa stood over him. "You should be. You're lucky you get this." Then she seemed to reconsider. "But I don't want you to die." She bent and spoke some strange words and traced squiggles in the air in front of the door. "There, I put a ward of protection on your door. Do not leave this room until morning and you shall be fine. Nighty night." Numa flew off, leaving only Summer Wind with Kido.

Kido said, "There are ghosts down here?"

Summer Wind said, "They say the ghosts of wizards of old roam the catacombs, Pognip Oldcastle's spirit among them. Of course there are ghosts in other parts of the tower, too, and maybe more than ghosts."

"Ah. Tell me, Summer Wind, can anyone here help me learn Magic?"

"Try Professor Shippleglass. Or the wizards on Frog Floor. That's my floor. Otherwise be careful who you trust." She regarded him solemnly with her beautiful purple eyes and then left with a final, "See you in the morning."

The next morning Summer Wind came for him, and Kido was ushered upstairs to the third floor and a large, windowless room dominated by a giant wood desk covered in curious objects. A skull of some unknown animal stared at Kido with empty black sockets as he sat down. The master wizards sat off to one side, and Codface stood before the closed door.

Kido noticed for the first time the ichor horn around Numa's neck. She sat heavily behind the desk and closed her eyes, meditating for a moment. She opened them and studied Kido anew. "Ahem. Now, are *we* to believe that *you* were a witness to the Ruination?"

"Yes, master," Kido said.

"Tell us about you and that day and leave out nothing."

Kido left out plenty. He left out Domingo's disappearance and their visit to the gates of Sporu Angosta. He left out the Butterscotch Book and the strange metal-glass vial of bright golden liquid. He left out the second giant. He left out his surreptitious reading of Orthus's spellbook. He left out the telepathic conversations with the dragons and the Dragon's Gift. He left out Father Time, Elger, and the rupa.

He even made up a chance encounter with Atticus and Pyra. And of course, he left out Putnam Castle and Porterville.

But he told everything else. They all seemed most interested at the description of Gold Hoods and Black Hoods around the teleport rock. They seemed troubled to hear about the first giant. And they seemed confused about the red wind and blue energy.

He was fined 50 demerits for saying aloud the name of the Gold Mage and dismissed with an admonition to go read the Tower Rules.

After they left, Numa turned to the others. "Did any of you know of this collusion between the Gold Hoods and the Black Hoods?"

"Of course not, Numa. We all thought Astra and his boys were destroyed by chance, lingering after the last Tower Cup," said Bothros with a snort of derision.

"We knew of no nefarious purpose," said Longtuth, nodding solemnly.

"Who could have even guessed they'd try to teleport into Sporu," said Pontazar.

"They must've found some *Essence of Dragon*," said Shippleglass.

They all turned in shock at him.

"The *Essence*? Impossible!" said Bothros with indignation.

"It's all gone by now," said Longtuth.

"How can you be so sure?" said Shippleglass to them. "How else could they hope to teleport inside Sporu Angosta?"

"The boy mentioned nothing about it," said Numa, "but he wouldn't recognize it for what it is. Could any of us I wonder?"

"The gates could be open," said Shippleglass.

"This is the worst possible news. To think the Gold Mage and Black Mage dead is one thing, but who knows where they went and what happened to them, if they had the *Essence* and if the gates are now open," said Pontazar. "This gives all new meaning to the Ruination."

"They might still be alive, trapped in some strange dimension, maybe even inside Sporu right now," said Bothros.

"Mad Marnoch would be with them then," said Shippleglass, "and his bodyguard."

"Maybe we should tell King Cromartin of all this?" said Bothros, who wasn't very bright as far as the others were concerned.

"Tell him what? We have no proof of anything. This is all irrational speculation," said Numa. "Do you want to go to Cromartin with some crazy ideas? He would have no concept of the *Essence* anyways."

"He doesn't even believe in dragons," said Pontazar.

"I would've thought the Black Hoods had consumed all the *Essence* by now," said Bothros.

"There are other vials out there," said Shippleglass.

"Maybe," said Numa.

"What should we do then?" said Longtuth.

"Perhaps we should use interrogation spells on Kido, probe his memory for every little detail. He is the only living witness to the Ruination," said Bothros.

"If you believe that. He has quite the aura, but he understands nothing of what he saw," said Numa. "He is ignorant, and I still resent the fact he's in my tower."

"But what then?" Pontazar and Bothros said together, wringing their hands.

"I will think on it," said Numa as her eyes narrowed, staring at the door where Kido disappeared. Shippleglass said nothing but appeared thoughtful as he got up and left.

After his departure, Pontazar asked, "Are you going to tell Cromartin any of this?"

"I think he would find this information most valuable," said Longtuth.

"He will reward us," said Bothros with a greedy smile.

"If only he could reward us with ichor," said Numa.

"We don't have much left," said Pontazar, wagging his jowls in concern.

"Tell me about it," Numa said drily. "But you know what else I am thinking?"

"What?"

"It is clear now that someone needs to teleport into the Gold Tower and find out what exactly are the conditions there. We can't go in blind later on."

"Teleport into the Ruined Lands!" exclaimed Longtuth. The three masters looked fearfully at one another and began to hem and haw.

"Relax. Relax! I wouldn't ask any of you to go. I will go by myself."

Silence descended. Numa dismissed them and brooded a long while after they were gone about one concern above all others. *The gates could be open. Is the Prophecy coming true?*

14
CREEPING IN DARKNESS

Kido lay in his bed in the dark chamber below the Red Tower. Awake in the eerie blackness, he wondered what time it was. He had been dreaming of dragons with shiny scales, claws scratching on stone, leathery wings stretching, softly rumbling voices. Was it Akasha talking? He couldn't be sure, and then something had woken him.

He listened for the sound again and after a time he heard the distant soft grinding of stone against stone. He lay frozen in fear, Summer Wind's warning echoing in his mind: "And don't go wandering down in the catacombs."

He strained to hear, wondering if some huge vicious monster was slinking towards him, only a thin wooden door between them. Moving very quietly, he got up and crept to the door, putting his ear to it. He heard nothing, but he sensed something terrible waiting out there, and running back to bed, he pulled the covers up to his head and closed his eyes to wait until morning. He wished for Jabu and his friendly red light. He wished for Woody, Trailhog, and the others, but he was all alone.

"This is almost as bad as Throg Anvel," he whispered to no one.

Sleeping down here, Kido discovered that during the night the fires from the chasm burned lower and lower, until they seemed to go out. But by morning, the fires grew brighter, and a thin red line appeared at the bottom of his door. It was his sunrise. He'd dress in his plain gray robes and go upstairs to eat in the cavernous, half-empty dining hall. A tall, skinny man with a red beard manned the kitchen. The kids called him Garlic John, and with a booming voice he'd chase them out of his kitchen, swatting their rear ends with a giant wooden spoon. There was always an array of factory-fresh food: Starbolt cereal, Starbolt steak, Starbolt soup, Starbolt salad, and so on. Everything tasted rich and satisfying, salty or sugary or juicy. He didn't remember the food in Pandoon being this rich. He always ate alone, having no friends in the Red Tower yet. He wandered the many huge rooms of the tower's ground floor, amazed at its size. Room to room he went, seeing no evidence of any Magic study. Indeed, all the kids he saw were the younger ones, running around and playing or languidly reclining on the furniture. It was more like a nursery than a place of study. The real wizardly work must go on on the upper floors, he decided.

He noticed a slender boy a few years younger than him. The boy had short blonde hair, fuzzy blonde eyebrows, a weak chin, and a quizzical smile that he wore as he watched the others. Kido walked over to him. "Hi, I'm Kido. Can you tell me where the Tower Rules are posted?"

"I'm Imple. You're the boy from Pandoon, aren't you?"

"Yes."

The boy leered at him. "Follow me if you must." Imple walked fast on the balls of his feet, swinging his arms confidently, his head on a swivel as if he were keeping tabs on everyone. He led Kido to the front entryway, just inside the double doors. He pointed high up on the wall. Kido looked past the cloaks hanging on knobs and his own sword still suspended there. He saw nothing.

"Where?"

"Tell the tower what you want," Imple explained.

Kido raised his voice, "Tower, I want to read the rules."

There was a moment's hesitation, then Kido saw faint black marks milling about high on the wall, marks that rapidly descended to his height. They were all jumbled up and it took a moment for them to sort themselves out, but eventually they formed the following list:

<u>TOWER RULES</u>
1. NEVER MENTION THE RUINATION!
2. NEVER SAY THE OLD MAGES' NAMES ALOUD!
3. NEVER LEAVE THE TOWER WITHOUT PERMISSION!
4. NEVER CAST A SPELL WITHOUT PERMISSION!
5. NEVER TELEPORT!
6. NEVER GO INTO THE CATACOMBS!
7. NEVER TALK TO GHOSTS!
8. REPORT ANY GUFFINS IMMEDIATELY!

"That's it? Eight rules?"

"That's it," said Imple, walking away on the balls of his feet.

"Wait a minute. What's a guffin?"

"You'll know it when you see one."

"How am I supposed to recognize something I've never seen?" Kido muttered to himself.

Kido wanted to explore more, but he felt suddenly lethargic, despite having a big breakfast. So he found a nice overstuffed chair near a potted plant and took a nap. He woke up and it was mid-afternoon. Imple was there with a tray.

"You missed lunch so I brought you some Starbolt pudding and Starbolt crackers."

"Thanks. I'm starved." Kido ate fast because it tasted so good. He noted that Imple also wore non-red robes and remarked on it.

"I'm not a fully-fledged wizard yet," Imple said. "I've only been here 18 months."

"I thought the tower's been closed since the Ruination?"

"They make a few exceptions if you're the child of a wizard, like me. Were your parents wizards?"

"No." Kido thought of his parents and felt homesick.

"Oh that's right. You are a slave."

Kido felt the condescension and his face reddened. "*Was* a slave."

Imple looked away, but Kido caught his quizzical smile. He wasn't sure if he liked Imple, but he was the only one to show the slightest interest in him.

"We are both novices," said Imple. "We get our red robes when we pass a test." Imple sounded bored with it all.

"What do we do to get to take the test?"

"Train and study for a bunch of years."

"How long?"

Imple shrugged.

"Train where and with whom?"

Imple pointed at the ceiling. "All the labs and study rooms are on upper floors."

"I haven't been above this floor except my first day when I was in the auditorium. I know nothing about the Red Tower."

Imple brightened up. "I'll take you on a tour if you must. Come with me and learn about the Red Tower," he said.

They transversed several huge living rooms and went down the broad central corridor, stopping in another large room, this one near the dining room. Looking up, Kido saw a large circular hole cut into the ceiling.

Imple said, "Now to go from floor to floor, wizards *float* up and down using these drop holes. So I guess the first thing I need to do is teach you how to *float*."

"I learned to *float* in the Gold Tower."

"Okay, let's go up to the next level then." Imple rose up effortlessly in the air through the drophole and landed on the second floor. He bent over and talked back down to Kido. "Now you."

Kido tried to follow Imple up through the drophole, but his body wouldn't budge. He closed his eyes and focused on the self-levitating spell he'd cast many times before, but he couldn't lift off the ground. He tried again and again but nothing happened. "I can't *float*," he finally admitted.

Imple *floated* down and grabbed Kido's arm. "This is going to be awkward, but I will try to help you." They floated up slowly, Kido being just dead weight now. He felt embarrassed.

On the tour, Kido discovered there were many levels to the Red Tower. Each had a drophole cut in its floor, all lined up so one could *float* all the way from top to bottom if necessary. He found out that the wooden stairwell at the back was only used by Farstaff, Garlic John, and the tower's many cats. The wizards all found it quicker to *float* up and down.

Levels 2-3 were the offices and sleeping quaters of Numa, Bothros, Longtuth, and Pontazar. Level 4 was storage space, but also featured a large mural map on one wall. Here a few of the older wizards were studying. Kido studied the map, comparing it to ones he knew by heart from Oto's shop. The mural showed the huge Spearhead Mountain chain separating Arcadia from Pandoon. A blue twisting line of paint cleaved the former where the Cloud River ran from Lake Tempest down to Port Laphere. Bremen Wood was a green patch, Marnoch's Road and the Troll Toll Road dashed orange lines running east and west. The Ruined Lands was a huge blackened circle covering much of Pandoon, separating the green forests of Niflhem and Alfeim. At the center of the blackness, a gold tower was optimistically painted in. A red tower was painted over Ballastro, a green tower on the coast of the Never Sea near Amphyra, and a black tower in the extreme southwest near the Rockfire Canyon. A second blue line labeled the Neeper River ran from the north into the black circle, only to come out of the bottom of the Ruined Lands and flow through Alfheim to Amphyra.

As Kido stared at the Gold Tower, thinking of the teleport rock to Porterville made him homesick again. And then he noticed something. "I wonder why the gates are not painted on this map," said Kido.

Imple looked nervous. He said, "Numa does not let us talk about the gates. If they are not on the map, we won't be reminded of them. Don't mention them again, Kido. It is an unofficial tower rule"

They floated higher as the tour continued with brief glimpses of each floor. "Level 5 is the Magic Warehouse. All Magic ingredients for spells, and all Magical rings, potions, weapons, amulets, and so forth, are all here," said Imple. "Rumor has it, the ichor gold dust is here, although none of us has ever seen it. We can only visit this level during daylight hours, and only one at a time under Codface's supervision. They are very strict about this floor."

The Magic Labs were on Level 6. "Where wizards learn and practice spells, always under the supervision of a senior wizard. Level 7: tailor's shop and Wizard's Laundry. Level 8: armory for non-magical arms and armor, little used since the tower has no soldiers anymore, and we have no one to fight anyways. Level 9: botanical gardens."

Here they landed where they were surrounded by tall plants and Kido could smell some deep organic odors.

Imple said, "Levels 10-19 are where all wizards sleep and hang out. Each is named after an animal like the city's gates. I am on Horse Floor, which is Level 14."

"What about the higher floors?" he asked Imple.

"I'm not allowed to go any higher, Kido. I can't show you those."

Numa came in, followed by Codface. "I will show you those," she said. "Only higher wizards are permitted above Level 19. A novice like you is forbidden."

"Am I not considered an apprentice now that I passed the tower walk?" he asked.

"No, Kido, you are a still very much a novice," she said.

"Is that like an apprentice?"

"No. You see, we are an orphanage as well as a Magic Tower. Many children seek sanctuary here," she said. "But most of them will never study Magic. Only a select few will ever enter the Order of Wizards and wear red robes. Eventually most will be booted out of the tower to fend for themselves when they get a little older."

"What will happen to them?"

She shrugged. "They'll scatter like seeds in the wind. They could wind up in Cromartin's army or in a religious order, or working in the mines or on farms. Some will go to the coast and the fishing boats. Some will no doubt stay in Ballastro and find a trade, or become thieves or beggers. So could you if you fail to win a red robe."

"How do I stop being a novice?"

"You must survive your first class and a test," said Codface. With a smirk he added, "If you can."

"You must prove you are worthy of being a wizard," said Numa, "by showing your courage and ability while avoiding demerits. You and Imple are novices and wear the plain gray. But once you pass your test at the end of the first class, you are formally admitted into the Order of Wizards. Then you will be an apprentice."

"Then I will wear the red robes?"

"No. You must pass a test at the end of the second class to become a junior wizard. Then you get a red robe. Then there is the third class and test to become senior wizard, and fourth class and test to become a master."

"And how long does each class last? A whole year?"

She laughed at his naivete. "Oh, it could take many years to finish just one class. Most study 30-40 years to become a master, if they make it that far at all. Wizardry is a lifetime program."

Kido felt deflated. He didn't have 30-40 years to spend in this world. "Excuse me, but about this tower. How many floors are in the Red Tower, Master?" Kido asked, changing the subject.

"How many?" she put her finger to her chin and looked up at the ceiling as if counting. "I don't honestly know. When you float higher than Level 21, it gets confusing. The floors just keep coming and some seem to change position from day-to-day, switching and swapping so it's hard to count. I'm sure there's another fifty or so, at least. Sometimes the tower seems taller and sometimes shorter."

Kido couldn't believe it. "It changes its height?"

"It has a mind of its own. Very independent for a tower, and I bet the Gold Tower was the same way. But there *is* a top, I know that for sure. I'll show you. I understand you cannot *float* yet—and you must correct that if you will have any chance to become a wizard—so I will help you. Come."

She took his arm and they *floated* higher at a leisurely pace past Dragon Floor, Eagle Floor , Fox Floor, and so on.

"Which floor will I eventually be on?" The thought of Rupa Floor went through his mind, and he smiled at the suggestion, thinking of the animal he was missing more and more. And Elger.

She cleared her throat and waited, expecting Kido to append the required *Master* to his question, but Kido ignored that and she finally answered, "That is yet to be decided. For now you must remain in your subterranean quarters."

Kido felt depressed at the thought of returning back down there tonight.

They *floated* up through successive dropholes, past more floors. "Even when you become an apprentice, if you do, you will need permission to go above Manta Floor."

Kido counted carefully as they rose. Manta Floor was Level 19. "Beyond here you are forbidden unless you need to go all the way to the roof."

And upwards they continued, *floating* faster now. At most floors some unknown light source would turn on, but some floors stayed pitch black. Kido got only glimpses as they rose higher. Some floors held corridors lined with closed doors, while some floors were wide open. Some were empty and some held tables full of objects too small to see. Some were empty save for large objects draped with sheets that lined the back walls. Every floor was huge, and he knew he was seeing only a small part of each one. Kido soon lost count of the floors.

Eventually they landed on a floor that appeared mostly empty. Kido saw a wooden ladder leading to a door in the roof, and at the opposite end was a drophole up to the roof, which did not line up with the other dropholes. A large cistern sat underneath.

To one side stood a dozen wooden perches, seven of which were occupied by large birds with brilliant yellowish-orange feathers, including their throat ruffles. They had red beaks and looked like ravens except for their color.

"We are in the highest room in the tower," Numa whispered. "Called the Raven Room. We are just below the roof."

"If this is the Raven Room, why aren't they black like ravens?" Kido said in his normal voice. He thought he could detect a Magic aura from the birds.

"Gronk," a bird articulated.

Numa whispered, "Try to whisper up here, so as to not disturb their repose. These are Sun Ravens. Each hour throughout the day, one flies in here to mark the passage of time. There are twelve total for the twelve hours of the day. At sunset they fly off and the first Moon Raven appears. And at each hour another Moon Raven flies in to roost and thus mark the passage of night. They are midnight blue in color, and only a wizard can tell them apart from the common ravens. At sunrise, er Cloudrise, the Moon Ravens fly off and the first Sun Raven of the new day arrives. *At first raven* is a phrase for the beginning of the day. *Last raven* is the end of daylight or cloudlight. Right now there are seven birds so that means it is the seventh hour of the day."

"Wow. Raven Chronology. You have to fly all the way up here to get the time?"

"No, the tower sends telepathic time updates. You just have to learn to be attuned to its voice. Let's climb onto the roof." They climbed the ladder and opened the hatch. There was a loud squawk and a bluish-gray bird dropped past them to the floor.

"Gulmar! What are you doing up here? Go down and onto your perch," Numa said.

"Okay," said the Mawker and flew down the drophole.

They climbed up onto the roof and into a cloudy world. The top of the Red Tower was just barely out of the clouds.

"Well, this is it. This is the top of the tower," said Numa.

"Do these clouds ever go away?" asked Kido.

"Sometimes they lift a little higher but they never go away. The sky is never blue anymore since the Ruination." Curious the cat had made his way all the way up to join them, walking around their feet in a figure-eight.

"Isn't that right, kitty?" Numa said to him.

The tower's top was very wide and covered by a huge—

"A rooftop garden!"

"Yes, many things are grown up here. Some of our wizards are gardeners and some eat this stuff although I never understood why when our pantries are full of delicious Starbolt food made right here in Ballastro."

He walked on, exploring, and she followed in silence. There were orchards of trees bearing orange and yellow fruit. Grassy paths wove between the trees and beyond were rows of vegetables and then an herb garden. Kido wondered how they grew if the sun never shined. It must be the tower's Magic.

The tower's top was huge and they walked for a very long time before crenellated battlements suddenly appeared out of the clouds. Kido peered out at the city. "Wow. You can see all of Ballastro."

"You can even see all the way to the Spearhead Mountains from here if you have good eyes. Although the clouds rarely lift high enough to see much these days, since the Ruination."

The Ruination. No comment ever gets too far from its mentioning. Kido noticed a large gray building in Riverside with four tall smokestacks belching black smoke into the sky. "What's that?"

"The Starbolt Factory. They make most of our food now."

Climbing back down the ladder, Numa saw there were eight Sun Ravens now. "Gronk, gronk," they said.

"It's nearly time for Garlic Jon to start cooking dinner. You should watch that. Why don't you go to the kitchen?"

As Kido descended the stairs through the second level, Imple saw him. "Going to watch Garlic John roast the meat for dinner?" he asked.

"I think so."

"I'm coming too. I never get tired of that."

Kido and Imple arrived in the kitchen to find a crowd there. "Everyone enjoys watching the Fenix," said a senior wizard called Spindrift.

"The Fenix?" said Kido.

"Just watch."

Kido felt something brush against his ankles. A black and yellow tomcat was there to watch too.

Against the back wall was a deep pit dug into the floor, with iron stands on both sides at waist height. The backside of the bottom of the pit was open to the outside. Peering down into the stone pit, Kido could Garlic John down there messing around at the edge of a pile of wood logs and kindling. "What's he doing?" Kido whispered.

"Putting spices around for the fire," Imple whispered back.

"Then he's going to light a fire?"

"Not him. Just watch."

There were rungs in the side of the pit and Garlic John climbed out. Then he grabbed Kido's sleeve. "I ask ye, help me with the meat." Kido helped him with carry two long metal skewers of meat over to place on the metal stands so the meat was above the pit.

They all waited. After a moment, a bright warm glow appeared outside and grew brighter. Then a bird about the size of a turkey appeared, but it was no turkey. It had beautiful plummage: a gold head, red and purple feathers on its wings, and blue feathers on its belly. It chirped loudly and slowly walked into the pit to climb up and lay on the wood pile like it was a nest. It spread its wings, shook them several times, and folded them. The bird closed its eyes as if in a trance. Motionless it sat, then shivered. A rush of air came into the pit, and the bird burst into flames, burning brightly, its image visible in the fire. A heat rose and drove them back, and they watched the meat began to sizzle and cook.

"The Fenix will burn for a good hour, long enough to cook whatever we're having. Then he'll arise from his ashes and fly off, only to return tomorrow night for the same ritual," said Imple.

Every now and then, Garlic John turned the skewers and basted the meat. "Dinner'll be ready soon," he announced.

"What time is it, Imple?" Kido asked him.

Imple smiled and went over and placed his palm against the tower's brick wall. Kido copied him. He closed his eyes and felt a vibration of energy flow into him. In his mind came the image of nine golden Sun Ravens on their perches. "It *is* nearly dinner time," he said to Imple. He looked at the seemingly normal brick wall. "It's like the tower is alive."

Imple grabbed a Starbolt scone and saluted him with it. "You're beginning to learn."

15
A Bone in the Eye

Drecks went to visit the Grand Sorcerer in his study. Zirmad wore his black robes with silver silk nightshades and sat in a tall chair with his right leg propped up, the foot swathed in thick bandages. A female servant hovered nearby, ignored. Drecks remained hooded as always. Zirmad had a big, bald head, slits for eyes, a bulbous nose, and a misshapened mouth with thick lips. Of Drecks no features could be seen. Even his hands were covered with black gloves, but under his robes his body appeared slight.

The room was dimly lit. Behind Zirmad's chair was the frosted glass of his aviary where he kept his pet nightshades.

"The boy apprentice made it into the Red Tower, master," Drecks spoke barely above a whisper and with no emotion.

"That's ridiculous. How could you and Wolfinger capture the old wizard and the girl but let a young boy get away?"

"The tower let him in. The tower's enchantment protected him."

Zirmad shook his head in disgust. "Grolk and goblin, I wanted them all. Could one more apprentice in the tower mean more to Numachitura than one more prisoner to the King? The King has Bangalore setting a watch on that tower every minute of every day. If we can keep them bottled up so much the better, and if they leave there, we'll know about it. Soon the King plans to move east. East, Drecks. Just think of it! I can finally get back to the Ruined Lands."

"And Sporu Angosta."

"Of course Sporu Angosta!"

"Will you be able to travel by then?" Drecks looked pointedly at the bandaged foot.

Zirmad coughed and pointed at his foot, looking at the servant. She hopped up and lit an oil lamp, then came over to slowly, carefully unwrap the bandages. Drecks saw that she had spiked black hair, black lipstick and eye makeup, and wore a short black tunic. She too was skinny. The fingers that unwound his master's foot had long fingernails painted blood red, but then he saw.

"Wow," said Drecks.

The right foot of Zirmad was flattened like a duck's webbed foot and twice as long as the left foot. Its flesh was pale so that blue veins stood out. The toes were splayed out as thin as paper.

"Never...ever...let a Toosker stomp on your foot!" said Zirmad.

"No, indeed."

"I'll never dance again, that's for sure. Tried every healing spell in the book. Nothing helps."

"I never studied any healing spells. Pain and suffering are merely things to be endured."

"Healing has never been a strong suit in sorcery. I can quell most of the pain, but I cannot reform the shape and walking with it is awkward as hell. It seems permanently deformed."

Drecks bent close over the damaged foot to inspect and reached out a tentative gloved hand as if to touch it.

"Ah!" Zirmad grabbed his staff and backed off Drecks.

"Hmm," said a chastened Drecks. "Apparently, Toosker stomping is Magic resistant."

"And I had to find out the hard way." Zirmad moaned and sighed as the servant rewrapped it. Behind the frosted glass came the rustling of wings and a nightshade's tortured cry. Drecks could see dark bird-shapes silhouetted.

Zirmad slowly stood up, using his staff like a crutch. He snapped his fingers and six mice came scuttling out of a hole in the baseboard. They came over and assembled as a group and Zirmad laid his injured foot on them, so they carried its weight on their backs. Thus with the mice and his staff to support him, Zirmad made his slow painful way with herky-jerky motions towards the aviary. He grunted and groaned with each step. Then he paused. "I'm going to feed my pets," he told Drecks over his shoulder. "Prepare a report on whatever information you Black Hoods know about Sporu. Our good King will want a full briefing before our expedition heads east."

"And what of our prisoners?"

"The Red Tower rabble? The King I'm sure has plans for them."

The herky-jerkyness resumed.

King Cromartin waddled his way through the Treasure Room, huffing and puffing as he went. Vykar followed, his claws clicking on the marble floor. This was a regular ritual, for the King loved to visit his treasure. The Treasure Room was long and tall, with no windows, and armed Dragon Guards stood around its locked door. It was dark inside except for the lanterns carried by servants that accompanied them. Numerous woodens chests lined a long table along the back wall, and as Cromartin unlocked them and opened them to look, the lantern light fell on sparkling treasure. Gold drags, silver drags, rubies, diamonds, emeralds, sapphires, pearls, the finest jewelry anywhere in the realm. It was all here, sparkling in the King's eyes.

"Ah, my treasure!" Cromartin held out his arms as if to hug all that gold and silver. "Gold and silver! Jewels and gems! All mine!" He dug his hands into a chest full of gold coins and let them rain through his fingers, clinking back into the chest. He fondled the gemstones. Holding up a beautiful small gold eagle to his chest, he said, "I'll have to make that into a brooch for the new lady."

After feasting on his treasure for a long time, Cromartin closed up the chests and locked them, depositing the key in his pocket. He sighed. "I'm going to have to part with some of my gold to fund this expedition to the east." He seemed sad at the thought, but then his face brightened. "But I will capture even more treasure in the east. Once the elves and dwarves are defeated, I will gain *their* treasure." He stroked the lid of one chest. "And then there's Sporu Angosta."

"The greatest treasure of all, my King," said Vykar.

"Yes, then I will have most of the gold in the world, which I alone deserve." He looked around at his guards and servants. "Eh, boys?"

"Yes!" was their enthusiastic reply.

Cromartin stood and daydreamed for a moment. And then he came back to reality, stroked the chest once more with a sigh, and waddled out. "I shall visit my new guests now."

The king and several soldiers left the Treasure Room and went through the Throne Room, down a wide, marble hall lit by crystal chandeliers and hung with large colorful paintings of the kings of old. Past several rooms and outside into the bailey they went, past the summer kitchen and then the Servants Hall. The king had to stop and rest several times as they made their slow way to the far side of the Imperial complex and inside the White Keep. At the back of the keep was a guard room with a large door in the floor guarded by an ogre. Down a wide flight of stone stairs they descended. It was damp and musty here, dark but for a fitful glare of light coming from torches in wall brackets.

At the bottom, in the deepest, darkest, nastiest part of the palace, they came to a wood door bound with iron and knocked. Creaky hinges stirred the silence. On the other side, two short, ugly dungeon guards snapped to attention. Gob and Galt were their names, and they never left the dungeon.

"Where is Snather?" Cromartin asked.

"Put away for now, sire," said Gob.

They went down a rough-hewn passage, so narrow that the King had to be pushed through when he became stuck, then through a room with a table, down another, longer passage, to a small antechamber. In a corner leaned a wizard's staff and on a table were two red robes, a pair of wooden horns on drawstrings, some leather pouches, and a pair of gold gloves.

Beyond was a long corridor lined with cages on both sides. The occasional torch gave inadequate light in this dim world. They walked past prisoners both human and non-human who slept on straw strewn on the stone floor and muttered and snarled at them until soldiers back them off with spear points and sword blades banged against metal bars.

At the end was a t-intersection, and beyond it two large cages sat side-by-side, separate from the rest and facing the corridor. In the right-hand cage Atticus sat on the floor, his leg chained to the back wall. Pyra lay on a bench against the right wall. There was straw and old bones scattered about on the stone floor. A faint blue shimmer of energy formed a barrier just inside the bars. The left-hand cage appeared empty but for a large pile of straw.

"Enjoying our leisure, are we?" Cromartin laughed at them. They looked tired and dirty, the bright torchlight making their eyes blink. "The King's dungeons not so bad, eh?" The prisoners sat mute. "Ah, dragon got your tongue?" He waddled closer, pressed his big belly against the iron bars, and looked at Pyra. "And you, my dear, having fun yet?" She turned to wall. "Ah, not the friendly type I see." Deepnose and 3eyes laughed at this and leered between the bars at her.

Cromartin looked at Atticus. "You can make your time easier by telling me everything you knew about Ramanapirus and those Magic doors to Sporu Angosta. What do you know about Zannalornacopia and that tower there? What is Numachitura, the elves, and the dwarves up to?" He paused and waited. Nothing. "Well?"

Silence.

"I'm going east, you might as well know. Exactly what lies behind the doors I will find out. What remains of the Eastern Realm will soon belong to Cromartin, and there's nothing you good wizards can do about it. The dwarves and the elves, they can't stop me." He waited for a reaction but got none. "Fine. You can stay here the rest of your lives on my charity. Or until I get tired of you, and then I will find your deaths amusing." Cromartin walked away, his merry laughter echoing down the stone corridor, the warm torchlight of the guards retreating, darkness closing behind them. "Let them rot for now," his faint voice floated back to them.

They waited until their keepers disappeared, and the locked door clanked shut. Soon their eyes adjusted to the returning gloom of the dungeon. High on the wall above them, a small barred window let in the tiniest bit of faint outside light.

"I figured he'd never go east. He never believed in the Prophecy," Atticus said. "And he's too lazy."

"Plus, he's already rich," said Pyra.

"Even the non-believers can't afford to ignore the Prophecy, especially someone as greedy as Cromartin," said Atticus. "There's never enough gold for a man like Cromartin. Sounds like he wants the elves and dwarves too."

"He wants to conquer everyone and everything."

"We gotta do something, but first we have to get out of here."

Atticus got up and walked to the front of the cage, the long chain softly clinking as it stretched out to its full length. It allowed him to reach the Magic barrier in front of the bars. He could sense the blue shimmer and feel its energy. Atticus leaned closer and could hear it hum slightly. He reached out to feel for it with his hand and the contact caused a sharp crackle of energy and a flash of light.

"No good, Pyra. Even ichor wouldn't break that barrier," Atticus said, slowly retracing his steps. "Safed's Shield is all powerful."

They sat in silence and eventually nodded off.

Unnoticed, an eye opened under the straw in the cage next to them. It was a large, amber-colored eye that belonged to no human. It had been quiet and still for a long time. It had listened to their voices, though it did not understand the Mother Tongue of humans. Now it slowly shifted its great weight and inched a little closer to the bars separating its cage from theirs. It was so hard to see, and the movements were small and slow and careful. It kept crawling closer until it was right next to the bars. Now it could see the chain attaching the leg of the nearest human to the wall. It was a long chain and a loop of it came close to the bars. It had moved its head around to face them and now watched with one large amber eye peeking out of its straw-like fur, an eye that detected no movement, no sign of awareness from its prey. It was patient, waiting and watching.

Cautiously it stuck out a hairy paw and slowly extended it through the bars to touch the chain. Carefully it picked up a few links and held them, enclosing them in a firm grip. It reached another paw through and repeated the process, trying hard not to hoot and growl in response to a growing excitement. It was hungry and hadn't eaten fresh meat in a long time. It paused, tensing its muscles for action.

Something inside of Atticus stirred, a Wizard's Instinct. Half-asleep, his anger over their situation was pushed aside by a vague sense of danger. He was beginning to wake up when he thought he heard a soft grunting noise to his right. Pyra of course was to his left. His eyes flared open.

In an explosion of straw, the monster leaped to its feet and roared, giving a mighty tug on the chain. Atticus was pulled to the right, closer to the bars. The monster dropped the chain in its left paw and reached, but the human was still out of reach. It pressed its face to the bars, opened a toothy maw, and roared in hungry frustration. Atticus grabbed the chain in both hands and began pulling back with all his strength, but the creature was stronger and managed to pull him ever closer.

Pyra had jumped off her bench and ran over, screaming at the monster and picking up straw off the floor to throw at whatever it was that was attacking Atticus. All she could make out was a tall mound of hair with two arms, one eye, and a large mouth full of teeth.

Showered with straw, the powerful monster kept pulling Atticus closer. It got excited and started hooting, sensing its next meal almost within reach. In desperation, Pyra bent to throw more straw and saw an old white bone fragment of some long forgotten creature who'd died here. It was about a foot long, knobby at one end, and with a sharp point at the other where it had been broken off. She seized it and ran to the bars.

The monster was intent on its prey and didn't see Pyra, didn't see anything until it was too late, and the white point plunged into its eye. The bone pierced the amber surface and went deep into the socket, forcing vitreous to spout out and splatter Pyra. The monster roared in pain and dropped the chain. Reeling backwards, it bounced off the walls and bars, roaring and bellowing in an awful racket. Atticus and Pyra yelled back at it.

Quickly Gob and Galt ran to the cages, half-dressed and brandishing spears. The sight they saw made them stop and go no further. Zirmad had to send down a pair of Tooskers to remove the wounded beast.

After the dark and the quiet returned, Pyra said, "Yep. We gotta get out of here."

"Patience. Numa will come for us," said Atticus.

"What was that thing?" Pyra asked.

"*That* was a grolk," said Atticus.

"I hate grolks," Pyra muttered, kicking a bowl of rancid meat off her bench to clatter on the stone floor.

Back in his chambers, far from the dungeon, Cromartin waited alone, smoking on a cigar. The room was dimly lit, the thick drapes drawn over every window. A door at the far end opened and bright light briefly pierced the gloom so he could see his Chamberlain letting in a cloaked figure.

The figure made its way down the long carpet to his desk, keeping its face concealed beneath the hood. From the light of a nearby fire, the cloak looked red in color.

"You risk much in coming here," he said.

Numa took down her hood and walked closer. "I have ways of remaining unseen, and I thought you should know something."

"Oh? Do tell?" Cromartin puffed away while the chamberlain poured him a brandy.

"There is a new novice wizard in our tower."

Cromartin coughed twice. "I thought I closed the tower."

"I did close it, but this one has friends amongst our Order, and he was in possession of a *Hope Crystal*. He is...unusual."

Cromartin caught the change in tone and cocked his head, eyeing her through the cigar smoke. "How so?"

"There is a certain aura about him. He seems gifted. He is an orphan from far away."

"So? Just boot him out, and the rest of those orphans you are sheltering as well. Aren't you tired of them under foot?"

"Of course, but this one is different."

"How?" Cromartin's eyes narrowed, wondering where she was

going with this. He lifted the glass to his lips.

"He is from Pandoon, an ex-slave."

Cromartin choked on the brandy he was drinking and coughed it up on his silk doublet. "What?" he managed to croak.

She repeated the information and then described Kido when he asked her to. Cromartin thought for a moment, his head wreathed his smoke like a dragon. "Get rid of him," he demanded. The chamberlain was busy cleaning his king's doublet with a napkin.

Numa said, "He is a teenager with no spells, a novice with no ability. He's no threat at all."

"Get rid of him."

"You mean expel him?"

"I mean *get rid of him*. Permanently. Or else."

Our deal is still in effect?"

"Of course, and the time is fast approaching. Just make sure there are no complications on your end."

"Very well." She put her hood up and left quickly and quietly.

Vykar came out of the shadows to curl up at Cromartin's feet, but the King seemed not to notice. He was consumed with brooding about the reappearance of this Kido person.

Back in the Red Tower, Numa became visible in front of Codface and Black Bob. "Is our new novice resting comfortably in his new bedchamber?" she asked them.

"But of course, due to your protection."

She looked off as if remembering something and then looked back. "Remove that protection." She floated off.

Codface went invisible and slipped past the iron door that Black Bob opened for him. He went visible for a moment, for a wizard cannot cast other spells while invisible. Then he quietly removed the spell of protection on Kido's door.

After Codface and Black Bob were gone, Spindrift went down using a *Door Ajar* spell and placed his own protection spell on Kido's door while Summer Wind acted as lookout. They left and Kido was on his own, unaware of all this activity outside his door.

16
GLOW BALLS & MONSTERS

Kido heard the creature coming for him. His fear of the thing kept him awake and sitting on the edge of his bed. His door was shut and bolted, but Kido worried if it would hold. The creature's approach saved him from answering. Outside his door he heard its claws scratching on stone and then on the door's wood. A shadow could be seen blocking the chasm firelight at the bottom crack. He stayed perfectly still and quiet, holding his breath. Kido knew his spells wouldn't work down here, but he was ready with his sword in hand.

Something struck the door, once, twice, a pause, and then a third time, very hard. The door shook violently but held. It was caved in and more light shone around its edges. One more good push would shatter it. The creature outside hissed several times, but then there was a pause before the clicking claws receded and all was quiet.

Sleep was impossible. Later in the night, something else could be heard moving around somewhere out there, something making ponderous noises, stone scraping on stone, something that sounded massive. Wrapped in cold fear, the young man waited for his doom, but whatever it was, it did not try to break down the door. Later still, there were softer distant stone-scraping noises to keep him on edge. Only in the last hour of night did quiet return.

It was with immense relief that Kido dressed and went up when the chasm fires burned bright at the bottom crack. He ate some Starbolt gruel and passed out in a lounge chair in a quiet corner off the dining room. He woke up, ate some more, and slept on, too tired and afraid to care about Magic or what anyone else was doing. Imple tried to wake him once but gave up and left him alone.

Kido's life took on this strange routine of frightening, sleepless nights, followed by eating and sleeping binges during the day. He gave little thought to anything else. He even stopped bathing. Eating the factory food after unwrapping their bright cellophane wrappers gave him his only comfort. In fact he couldn't seem to eat enough or sleep enough when he was upstairs. He began developing a paunch on his once lean physique, but nightmarish creatures prowled around in his sleep the way they prowled around in the dark every night outside his door. Bags formed under his eyes, and he carried his sword with him everywhere. Everyone avoided him except Imple, but even he did no more than to laugh at Kido.

"Eating and sleeping. Sleeping and eating," Imple would say and shake his head at Kido, and then laugh as he went off. Kido just rolled over in his big overstuffed chair and closed his eyes, trying to find peace in sleep. He knew that all too soon he would have to go back down into his subterranean bedroom for another long, dark night. Maybe tonight would be the night when the door would fail to hold. With no friends in the tower, Kido was quite alone now.

One day as he lay sleeping two figures came toward him, kicking away the bright cellophane wrappers—The Most Delicious and Nutritious Thing to Ever Pass Your Lips!—that littered the floor around his chair. The figures looked at Kido curled in his chair, hair all tangled, dark circles under his eyes, a half-empty jug of Starbolt juice still clutched in his hand. One of them pulled the jug free and dumped its contents all over Kido.

Sputtering in surprise, Kido bolted upright, sticky reddish juice spilling off of him. "Hey, what gives?" Through the juice his eyes beheld the female elf and a tall, broad-shouldered young man who wore breeches and tunic, not a wizard's robes. He had a familiar face that Kido hadn't seen in a long time.

"Trailhog! How did you get here?"

The man grimaced. "I'll never get used to that name."

Kido tried to hug him, but Trailhog accepted a handshake instead. "You need a bath and a change of clothes first."

So Kido did as he was told, and when he came out, he saw Trailhog but not the elf.

"Where did Summer Wind go?"

"Back up to her floor. She wants us to meet her there."

Trailhog couldn't float either so they walked up the back stairs, climbing, climbing, all the way to Floor 18. Kido saw brick walls and corridors. He was led to a doorway behind the stairs that led outside the tower. Summer Wind was sitting on a balcony jutting out from the tower, and Kido felt outside air for the first time in weeks.

"Now you look and smell better," she said with approval as Trailhog gestured Kido to sit on a stone bench opposite her. "We need to talk to you."

"I didn't think anybody cared about me in this tower," he said with bitterness. "Or even noticed me."

"On the contrary, everybody in this tower is aware of you, although not everybody wants you safe. But we care."

"Why did you wait so long?" Kido asked.

"We weren't sure about you. Some of the people in this tower are spies for Numa or Codface, and some are spies for the King. Your sudden appearance and entry into our closed tower is suspect, to say the least. But I'm a good judge of character, and I have a feeling about you," she said. "Also, I don't think they'd put you in that awful dungeon cell for so long if you were a spy for them. You are lucky to still be alive. Most who are put there do not survive their first night," Summer Wind said, her voice tinged with sadness. "I must talk to you to find out something. Rumor has it you were a witness to the Ruination."

"I was there. I saw…a lot, a lot I wish I could forget."

"Please tell me what you know."

So Kido told her and Trailhog the same story he told Numa and the Professors, leaving out the same details. He still did not know who to trust.

They listened in rapt silence to his story.

Summer Wind inhaled deeply to break the silence. "Okay, Kido, that's all for now. Thank you for taking us into your confidence. I will talk to you again soon when I introduce you to the rest of my floor."

After Kido and Trailhog left, two wizards who had been invisible and standing nearby, appeared on the balcony. Summer Wind asked them, "What do you think?"

"He's lying," said one wizard.

"Or at least he's not telling everything," said a second wizard.

"We haven't given him a reason to trust us yet," said Summer Wind.

"His story of the Ruination is a doozy," said the second wizard. "The world needs saving, that's for sure."

"We need to do something, but I don't know what," the first wizard said softly.

"I know what I'm doing," said Summer Wind.

Kido caught up with Trailhog as they walked back down the eighteen flights. "How did you get to Ballastro?" Kido asked.

The big man said, "One of Cromartin's agents bought us in Z Town and brought us to Ballastro. They removed our iron collars and made us servants in the King's palace. One day Woody and I got sent on an errand. We escaped the guards escorting us and wandered the city until we got jobs at the Starbolt factory."

"Wait a minute. Which of the gang is in Ballastro?"

Me, Woody, Holly, Dahlia, and Misha all got to the King's palace. Woody and I escaped there. We didn't know about you, Pyra, or Domingo."

"Domingo is trapped in a Magic spellbook in the Gold Tower."

"What?!"

"It's...weird. I'll explain later. Pyra is, I think, being held in the King's dungeon with a wizard named Atticus."

"What?!"

So Kido spent a couple of floors explaining things. Then he asked, "So you and Woody are at the factory?"

"I still am but he's not. He's close by, though, and something tells me you'll be bumping into each other real soon."

"What?!"

"I don't want to spoil the surprise."

"Okay. And the girls?"

"Still in the palace as far as I know. Kido, how are we ever going to get back home?" They had arrived on the ground floor, kids running everywhere.

"I'm trying to find a teleport key here in the tower. Then we get everyone together and teleport home."

"Make it soon, will ya? I'm getting tired of this place."

"Just one more thing: how did you get into the tower?"

Trailhog smiled and punched Kido's shoulder. "I deliver Starbolt food to the tower every week. See you in seven days."

Kido rubbed his shoulder and watched his friend walk out the tower's doors. He touched the wall and counted sun ravens. One more hour til it was time to head downstairs. He decided not to wait, gathered his sword and trudged back downstairs. Black Bob leered at him as he opened the iron door for Kido.

Kido automatically turned to head under the stairs when he stopped. He had some time to explore before it got dark so he pivoted. Straight ahead of him was the main chamber, its walls rough-hewn rock, its ceiling a hundred feet high. The fiery chasm with its rock bridge was in front of him, and the narrow ledge went around the chasm's left edge. To the right was a wide area that led past the chasm and into the darkness beyond, and this is where Kido went. Where the chasm ended, the chamber became like a large tunnel. The ceiling was still a hundred feet high, but the walls narrowed until they were only twenty feet apart. The floor was paved with smooth stone tiles, as if to facilitate locomotion. He entered the tunnel and walked briskly, still unsure how far he wanted to go.

It grew darker as the chasm's fires receded behind him, but soon Kido detected warm light up ahead. He came to a fork where the tunnel split into two. The light came from the right-hand tunnel. Kido went right.

The tunnel slanted upward and it grew brighter and warmer, and he could feel a gentle current of air brush past him. After walking for a good while, he found the tunnel opened up into another huge chamber split by another fiery chasm. Kido thought he was experiencing deja vu until he peered over the edge and saw this chasm was narrower than the first, though just as deep. And there was something else. About twenty feet down was a wide ledge which was littered with debris: bones, dead branches, dried heather, and the bone-white shards of what looked like the remains of a giant egg.

An upward-slanting tunnel on the far side of the chamber was the only other way out. Kido went up it until it turned a corner and opened into a massive chamber three hundred feet high and twice as long. On the left was a huge nest of rushes and grass, on the right was an iron stairs bolted to the wall and climbing to a door near the ceiling. Above the nest was a large circular indentation in the wall where it looked like something had been removed. Then turning to look directly ahead, Kido saw a large, rectangular opening to the outside. He could see the buildings of Topside out there and realized he was standing in Ramyre's Lair. Somehow he had traveled underground from one side of the tower to the other and was back up at ground level.

Kido knew the rumor that the Gates were probably open and Ramyre might show up any minute. He quickly retreated back down to the fork and took the other tunnel. It was dimmer and cooler, but even with his eyes adjusting it was getting too dark to see. Just when he was ready to turn back he spotted two doorways: one on each side and both obviously man-made. He tried the left opening and found it to be some kind of storeroom with shoring timbers, rope coils, stacks of red bricks, and a wooden table. It was lit by some strange source coming from a wooden bucket sitting on the table.

Investigating the bucket, he it found full of tennis ball-sized globes that emitted a soft greenish glow. Reaching for one he found they all glowed brighter with his hand nearer. Pulling his hand back in surprise only subdued their glow but did not extinguish it. Waving his hand several times confirmed they were somehow keying on his presence. He reached in and grabbed one. It was soft and yielding to his touch and glowed now about half as bright as a lantern. Opening his hand, he found it floated up to hover in the air near his head.

"You must be some kind of Magical Glow Ball. What other tricks can you do?" Kido said to it. He waved up with his hand and the Glow Ball dutifully floated up higher. He waved it back down. He waved it left and right and in a 360 degree circle. The Glow Ball followed all of his commands. Then Kido thought of a different experiment. He held his hands by his side and tried mental commands. He thought of *up* and *down*, *left* and *right*. The Glow Ball executed every command. "You are keying on my thoughts, not my hand gestures," he said to the Glow Ball. "You are pretty handy to have around. I think I'll take you with me. Now what to name you?" Kido thought for a moment before he had it. "I know. I shall call you Egon, after a character in one of Grandma's old movies."

With Egon leading the way, Kido investigate the other opening. This led to an small rectangular room with a marble altar and nothing else. Beyond was another doorway which Kido sent Egon through. Egon quickly came back, and then Kido heard soft clicking noises. Looking down, he realized there were thousands of little black insects crawling across the floor from the next room. He scrambled up on to the altar and watched them go by in Egon's greenish glow.

He was sitting with his legs dangling, ready to jump down when he heard clicking louder than before. He stood up atop the altar and drew his sword just in time to see a insect the size of a Saint Bernard enter the room. It had six legs, a black head with large mandibles, and a brown body. Two tall, hairy antennae waved at him as it paused to study the situation. Then it charged with a hiss.

It reared up its head and tried to climb up onto the altar. Kido swung with all his might but his sword bounced off its hard exoskeleton, and he nearly dropped it. The insect was almost on him and in desperation he stuck his sword in its mouth. That stopped it, and it swung its head side to side before backing off, spitting out the swordblade. It circled around to the back and came again with a hiss. Kido had circled with it and was ready to strike another blow at the vulnerable mouth. The sword had damaged a mandible, and it withdrew to wave its antennae some more, giving Kido an idea. When it raised its head again above the altar, he gave a mighty swing and lopped off an antennae. Another hiss and a partial retreat. It circled and came on again, and Kido lopped off the other antenna. "You're not very bright, are you?"

In reply, it rushed with a loud hiss. Kido stabbed at the mouth, but this time the insect kept coming and pushed Kido off the altar. He felt the sword pulled free from his grasp, and he fell on the stone floor and rolled over, scrambling to get back on his feet. Egon hovered anxiously over him.

The hisser came scuttling around the altar, Kido's sword halfdown its throat, and charged. Kido braced himself and seized the hilt to plunge the blade deeper. The insect stopped and shivered. It backed up, dragging Kido until he yanked the sword loose. The thing just stood there making spasmodic jerking motions, so Kido began chopping off legs until three of the original six were severed, and it tipped on its side and flailed the air with the remaining appendages.

Kido paused to catch his breath. "Geez, they got a real bad insect problem down here."

Egon finally led him into the room beyond, and that was where he discovered the crypt. It felt colder and deathly quiet in here after all the hissing and fighting. In Egon's green glow two rows of stone sarcophagi flanked a central aisle that ran back as far as he could see. All the sarcophagi were closed except one: the one closest on the right. Kido called Egon down close and bent over to read the name carved there:

POGNIP OLDCASTLE, RED MAGE

Kido could see the lid to Poggy's sarcophagus was leaning against the back wall and covered in dust, as if never used. He got a bad feeling standing there in the crypt and backed out, past the still-struggling bug, until he was back in the central tunnel. Looking left, he could no longer see any of the chasm fire. He knew he was running out of time but wanted to see what else was here since he was this far out. He sent Egon to a spot ten feet above the ground and ten feet in front of him, ten and ten, and together they continued on.

Soon he saw niches carved in both tunnel walls. The niches were full of the bones of the dead, piled haphazardly. Some niches held only stacked skulls, others long femurs and humerus bones. Even the ones with full skeletons were jam-packed. Sometimes the bones spilled out onto the tunnel floor. This tunnel was a crypt for the poor. He kept walking and found further on only empty niches for the future dead. He hesitated, realizing he had strayed far from his bedroom, but something pulled at him. He could sense something up ahead, something dangerous. He had to know, and so he kept walking, despite a growing feeling of dread.

Another long stretch and his feet felt a difference. The smooth tile floor had ended and now there was only a rough rock floor to walk on. The niches had stopped, too, and the ceiling had dropped until Egon was barely below it. Kido felt a fear growing inside of him that slowed his steps. Even Egon sensed it and circled anxiously over Kido's head.

"Just a little further," Kido whispered softly to the Glow Ball. A loud voice seemed a bad idea right now.

Soon enough the tunnel ended in a steep, rocky set of stairs. They were as broad as the tunnel and went down as far as Egon's light could show. Kido stood on the top step, wishing he could know what was down there but not wanting to go any further. He thought of sending Egon further down, but he had no way of seeing what Egon could, if the Glow Ball could indeed 'see' anything at all. Worse, there might be a range limitation in their connection, and Kido feared losing him if he sent him too far down. Kido had already grown quite fond of Egon.

But there was something down there, a large, evil presence somewhere below that made his whole body cold with fear. He had had enough. He summoned Egon and turned to go, and that was when he almost walked into the ghost.

Only shock prevented him from screaming. It was the ghost from the shattered temple in Bremen Wood, the old bearded man staring morosely at Kido with sad, gray eyes. It floated in the air, six inches away. Kido raised his sword but it passed right through the ghost, so Kido stood rooted, unable to breath. His skin crawled, and he wanted to run but couldn't. After a long moment, during which the ghost did nothing but hover and stare, Kido summoned the courage to slowly sidestep around the apparition and move away. The ghost did not follow.

Kido ran several feet and then turned to see what it was doing. The ghost had moved to the top step and was staring down into the gloomy depths. Kido was shocked to see the ghostly hilt of a dagger sticking out of its back.

Kido kept backing away while keeping his eyes on the ghost. Back, back, back he went, his useless sword in his hands and Egon circling helplessly overhead. He knew he had a long way to go to reach the comforting fires of the chasm, and so he was surprised when he backed into something that stopped him. Turning he found himself confronted by thirty or more skeleton warriors armed with swords. He was not too frightened to scream this time as the skeletons closed in, skulls leering at him with empty sockets. A quick glance to the right confirmed that many niches had been emptied. He looked back to see the ghost gliding towards him. He was trapped in between.

The skeletons attacked. Kido had time to swing his sword twice. He cut off the fingers of one bony hand and decapitated the next skeleton before he was overwhelmed and dragged down. Many cold bony hands pinned him to the floor and ripped open his clothes to expose his chest. A tall skeletal warrior loomed over his head. It wore chain mail and a conical helm and a golden necklace dangled on its chest. It smiled a toothy smile, reversed its grip on the hilt, and raised a longsword.

Kido screamed and closed his eyes to wait for the cold steel to plunge into his chest. And nothing happened. He opened his eyes to see the skeletons staring at him, but the bony hands had released their grips on him. The tall warrior had lowered his longsword and was staring at Akasha's gift and the Harlequin markings on Kido's chest. The skeletons got up and backed off. Kido sat up and turned to see the tall warrior wore a Dragon's Gift too. It backed up and gave a short bow. The skeletons moved aside to open a path back to the chasm.

That was all Kido could take, and he jumped up and took off running as fast as he could up the tunnel, Egon barely keeping up. A few times he stopped and turned around while catching his breath, but there was no sign of anything else pursuing him. Finally, after what seemed like forever, he arrived back in the chasm chamber.

He dropped his sword and stood bent over, waiting for his pulse to return to normal. An hour later, he picked up his sword and went under the stairs. Already the chasm fires were dying and the gloom growing. Then the low grinding noises started again.

Kido closed his damaged bedroom door with care and sat on his bed cradling his sword. He fully expected the ghost or some skeletons to finish him off that night, and his door wasn't going to stop them. His door couldn't stop a mouse. He was tired of running and hiding. He would face whatever was there and fight it with all he had. He got up and opened the door, and it fell off its hinges, crashing on the stone floor and shattering in several pieces.

"Figures," Kido muttered.

He walked over to the tunnel entrance and brandished his sword. "Come on! Come and get me!" He yelled down the tunnel in his loudest voice.

The iron door at the top of the stairs behind him grinded open. Down the steps came several red-robed wizards.

"Who are you yelling at?" Summer Wind asked.

"Ghosts and monsters," Kido said.

Black Bob went to Codface, who went to Numa. The Red Mage floated down to the iron door and scampered down the steps. Through Kido's open doorway she saw the assembled company all crammed inside his sleeping chamber.

"Just what is going on here?" she demanded.

"As long as Kido sleeps down here, so do we," Summer Wind said. The others nodded in agreement.

"You've got to be joking." Numa regarded them with pursed lips before relenting with a sigh. "Fine. Let him stay on Frog Floor then. What do I care?" She floated off in a huff.

"You Froggies are Pariahs in all but name," Codface said to them as they triumphantly filed by. Then he remembered where he was and quickly floated up after them. The iron door clanged shut on the darkness.

The chasm fires were at a low ebb, and the tunnel beyond was pitch black. Far back there and far down those stairs, quite aways beyond where Egon had stopped, two kobold brothers named Wrathbone and Gnawmark stood looking up in silent contemplation. Finally they turned to each other and spoke in High Goblin.

"I saw a green light up there," said Wrathbone.

"Me too, and I smelled human stink," said Gnawmark.

"I heard a human voice scream."

"At least one. But why was he so far from their tower?"

"Because they are stupid. Let us run them down and kill them. They are so slow."

"They might have weapons." Wrathbone was the older and smarter of the two. "They should if they are down here."

Gnawmark was bald save for a tuft of dark hair above each pointed ear. He also had pale-colored teethmarks on his forehead that stood out against his black skin, as though bleached and scarred by some creature that had clamped its jaws on his head but he had escaped. "They are too stupid. We could jump them in the dark."

"Maybe." Wrathbone massaged the warts on his face as he thought.

"Hurry up, before they get away!"

"No, no. We make no move yet. Better we report it to the boss."

"Aaaagh!" Gnawmark's voice cracked and gurgled in disappointment.

"Soon enough there will be time for jumping and killing."

Wrathbone turned and descended the stairs in nimble hops. Gnawmark reluctantly followed his brother after one last look up above.

17
NOVICE WIZARD

Kido's new home in the Red Tower was a windowless ten-by-twenty brick-walled room with a real bed, dresser, desk, and chair. Down the hall was the bathroom. He was eighteen floors up. His first morning waking up on Frog Floor, Kido rose early and hurried out, eager to explore, and nearly collided with someone. The person was a very old man with blue eyes that stared straight ahead. He had a long gray beard, and gray hair that cascaded down to his knees, as if he hadn't had a haircut or shave in years. He was barrel-chested and dressed in the red robes of a tower wizard. Kido took him for a teacher, but the man just ignored Kido's friendly 'Hello' and just kept slowly shuffling along and mumbling to himself.

Passageways stretched out in three directions from Kido's room, all in straight lines. He decided to follow the long-haired mumbler, having no better reason to pick a route.

Frog Floor was like all the other Red Tower floors in size, that is to say *huge*. Kido wondered at how many wizards were meant to be working here. They passed a large stone cell with bars and the mumbler altered his straight shuffle to shy away. Kido wondered why until he saw a large hairy hand extend through the bars and just miss grabbing him. A large creature covered in long, shaggy, brown hair growled as he scurried by. If it had a face or eyes, Kido didn't see any.

Kido grew restless with the mumbler's slow pace and passed him. Wandering on his own now, he discovered that floor-to-ceiling brick walls segregated the 18th Floor into a warren of small rooms off numerous passageways. A few of the passageways were wide and straight, but others were narrow and winding. It got confusing, and soon Kido realized he was lost and could not even find his way back to his cubicle. Pressing on he came after awhile to a large rounded chamber with two dropholes, one in the floor and one in the ceiling.

He knew the dropholes were located in the exact middle of the Red Tower, and so he must be at the center of Frog Floor. In the floor there was a wooden ring carved with frogs surrounding the drophole. The rest of the floor was red brick. Looking up and down, he could see that the dropholes of all the floors combined into a vertical tunnel of air that ran through the entire tower. He wished he could still float.

He explored further, eschewing side passageways. Eventually he came to the backstairs and a door on either side that led out to the same balcony where yesterday he had met with Summer Wind. It jutted out from the tower's south wall and offered stellar views from its eighteen floors above Topside. Outside he breathed the air of a cloudy, warm day. Faroff he could see the roofs of the King's palace, and he wondered about his friends forced to work as servants there. That made him feel homesick, and he wondered if his parents were still trying to find him or if they had given up. The thought of the grief he was causing them made him physically ill, and he could only stand and stare sightlessly out over the strange city.

A touch on his shoulder startled him. He turned to stare into beautiful purple, almond-shaped eyes. "How long have you been there?"

"Long enough. Your tears are still drying," said Summer Wind.

"I miss my home."

"You are so far from your home, as I am from mine. Come, we're having a floor meeting. It is time you met the other Frogs, and perhaps we can help you return home."

They went inside and just up the corridor they met a wizard in his mid-thirties with black, curly hair, brown eyes below thick eyebrows, and a pleasant face. He was walking with a long staff in hand and wore a red robe. Kido suddenly felt a cool draft and sensed the man's aura of Magic. He recognized him from the Fenix cooking show. "Good morning," Kido said in a cheery voice.

"Good morning," Spindrift replied. "Here, hold out your hand."

Kido did and the man waved the tip of his staff over it, intoning a strange phrase. Blue light swirled in Kido's palm, light that solidified into a snowball that grew to grapefruit size.

"Have a snowball," he said.

"Thanks," Kido said in astonishment. Then the snowball grew cold, and he jerked his hand away to let it fall to the floor. The man walked before them, a few icy sparkles followed in his wake.

"You are Spindrift," Kido called fter him.

"And you are Kido," the man said over his shoulder. "The newest resident of Frogland." The air warmed back up.

Kido mentioned the old mumbling wizard he saw.

"That's Old Man Wizard," said Summer Wind.

"Who is he?"

"He is the oldest person in the tower."

"But why does he mumble and behave like that?"

"Magic has taken over his mind," said Summer Wind.

"Worst spell creep in the history of wizardry," said Spindrift. "He wanders all over the tower like that. No one quite knows what to do with him. They say he was a master of old."

They were approaching the cage, and Spindrift turned around. "Here hold out your hand again."

Kido kept his hand by his side.

"I won't give you another snowball. I promise." Spindrift smiled.

Kido held out his hand and Spindrift placed two mangoes in it. "Why fruit?"

"For the grolk."

"What is a grolk?"

"Watch." Spindrift tossed a banana into the cage and while the big hairy creature with no face was busy retrieving it, the wizard stepped through the wall right next to the bars.

Kido gasped. "Where did he go?"

"There's no wall there. It's just an illusion. You just have to distract the grolk." She tossed a papaya into the cage and disappeared behind the 'wall.' Her head ducked back out. "Your turn, and hurry."

Kido tossed in his two mangoes and ran through the wall, closing his eyes right before impact but hitting nothing but air. He found himself in a dim passageway before some steep stone stairs.

"Did you keep one mango?" Summer Wind asked.

"No, I threw them both in."

"Oh, dear. You're going to have trouble getting back out."

He followed them up a steep, narrow set of stairs into a round stone chamber with a low ceiling and a large wooden table in the center. Summer Wind whispered in his ear, "This is our Secret Meeting Room. Tell no one about it." There was only a little light from a single torch as he took a seat on a stone bench. As his vision adjusted, he could make out several figures seated around the table.

Summer Wind spoke softly, "I call to order this meeting of the Frog wizards to introduce the novice Kido and to discuss pressing business. We begin with introductions. "I am Summer Wind from

Alfheim.

A second torch was lit and the faces became more visible. Next to Summer Wind sat a tall humanoid with a thick head of spiked wheat-colored hair and a long but thin face crowded with freckles and a long, aquiline nose. He regarded Kido with a benign curiosity.

Summer Wind introduced him. "Thistledown, Junior Wizard. He doesn't speak much."

Kido had never seen anyone like him. "What—"

"He's a Flibken. Yeah, I know. Thistledown's the only Flibken I've ever seen either. But he's nice. Though where exactly his kind comes from I can't say."

"Yes," said Thistledown solemnly with a slow blinking of his luminous turquoise eyes. Kido noticed Thistledown had six long, thin dextrous digits on each hand, working away on some mechanical device placed on the table. He soon found out that the Flibken only used the words 'yes' and 'no' and 'oh' but sucessfully communicated his feelings with facial expressions, especially his thick fuzzy eyebrows that arched, lept, and wiggled in tune to his thoughts. He hummed constantly.

Next was a young man bent over a book. When he raised his head, Kido was shocked to see it was his dear friend. "Woody! What are you doing here?"

I am the Tower Librarian, believe it or not." He was wearing grey robes. He and Kido were the only ones not in red robes.

"Woody's endorsement is one reason we've invited you to join our floor. As for the rest of our group...." Spindrift beckoned to the far side of the table where sat another tall person of an unknow race. His phantasmagoric hair was long and wispy, his eyes bright and merry above a prominent, broad nose. "Hello, Kido. I am Mosshair, Junior Wizard from Pormaritsa. Welcome to Frog Floor."

Next were five boys with black hair and brown eyes. "We are the Bremen Quints, identical quintuplets. We were raised in Bremen Wood," said the first of them. "I am Bastian. Boys, your names...."

"Burl."

"Berry."

"Boykin."

"Bryce."

Lastly came another familiar face. "Spindrift, Senior Wizard from Tempest. As you can see, we are from all over Arcadia."

"Thank you all for accepting me," Kido said.

"We know where you and Woody are from and how you got here," said Spindrift. "Can you fill in the gaps for us?"

"Since the Ruination I have lived in Throg Anvel, a Feather Bay orphanage, and with an itinerant Pariah."

"Did you really see the Ruination?" asked Mosshair, his eyes bright with curiosity. "Because that would be really amazing and bizarre."

"It's the truth, although sometimes I wish I hadn't seen it."

"Tell everyone what you saw," said Summer Wind.

And so Kido told the story again. He left out nothing this time. He felt the need to share all his experiences, not only to connect with his new friends but to release the burden of all that knowledge he had been carrying around by himself. He even told them about his *BeeSwarm* spell and the Tooskers in Bremen Wood.

Afterwards there was a stunned silence.

"What does that all mean for us?" Summer Wind asked softly.

"We have to figure that out," said Spindrift.

"We have to do research," said Mosshair, nodding emphatically.

"How can we research something like the Ruination?" asked Bastian.

"Esoteric Magic was obviously at work that day. Esoteric, arcane Magc by high-level wizards," said Spindrift. "If only we knew what they were up to."

"Who would know?" asked Bastian.

"The elves maybe," said Spindrift. "If anyone cares to travel to the Green Tower."

"That would take months to get there, and you'd have to go near the Ruined Lands," said Mosshair.

"Hmmm. Oh. Umm," said Thistledown, his bright eyes dimming in concern.

"Alfheim is closed, need I remind you," said Summer Wind. "I'm not even sure if I could get in."

"The Red Tower is closed, and I got in here," said Kido.

"Under the most unusual of circumstances. You can't count on making it past the elves like that," said Bastian.

"Numa and the teachers would know," said Mosshair.

"They wouldn't tell us anything," said Spindrift. "The Black Hoods that defected to Cromartin might know something."

"Maybe or maybe not, but good luck gaining access to them," said Summer Wind.

"Why bother anyways?" said Burl with a shrug. "What does it matter to us? We can't change the past. We are not even allowed to cast spells in the Red Tower."

"It matters to me. I need to rescue Domingo," said Kido. "It's my fault he's not here. And me and my friends need to get back home."

"Atticus and Pyra are still in the King's dungeon," said Summer Wind. "We need to get them out."

Spindrift said, "I doubt Numa will let us risk a rescue attempt, even for fellow Red Hoods."

"So what should I do?" Kido asked. He felt confused and discouraged.

"Don't run away or do anything rash, Kido," said Spindrift. "You can still study Magic here. You just can't *do* any Magic since you are a novive."

"I can study Magic?" asked Kido in disbelief. "Without demerits?"

"Numa and Codface won't care, "said Spindrift.

"They don't think you can learn it," said Summer Wind. "Prove them wrong."

"First, you have to learn to float," said Mosshair. "I will show you." He threw an arm around Kido's shoulders."

"Good," beamed Spindrift.

"This Butterscotch Book...you say it had a tawny animal hide and oozed black smoke when it opened?" said Summer Wind to Kido.

"Yes."

Summer Wind said to Spindrift, "Does this ring a bell?"

He paused at length before answering. "No, but there are many great grimoires left over from long dead wizards. It could be anything. One thing I can say is it is probably very old. I should love to look it over someday, but only if it is safe to open."

"That means we must get to the Gold Tower," said Kido.

"Sure, let's just travel hundreds of leagues across Arcadia, across the mountains, across Pandoon, through the Ruined Lands, and to the Gold Tower," said Bryce. "You can count me out. I'm staying put."

"The Red Tower is so safe," said Bastian in a patronizing voice. "Just read safe little books, never casting a spell, never seeing the world. Just sit around getting fat eating Starbolt slop while the world goes by."

"You're mocking me." Bryce crossed his arms in defiance. "You go if you're so enchanted by adventure."

"So quick on the draw," said Bastian.

"I can cast a *LightningBolt* twice as powerful as yours," he said.

"How do you know? You haven't cast anything in years."

"Neither have you."

"Knock it off, you two," said Spindrift.

"Kido's right. We have to travel to the Gold Tower," said Summer Wind.

"Of course, he's right. When are we leaving?" said Mosshair.

"Hold your dragons. I agree we have to do something," said Spindrift, "but exactly *what* and exactly *how* is yet to be determined. There is a lot going on here that we don't know about."

"That much is for certain," said Woody.

Bryce turned to Woody. "You're going east, too?"

Woody drummed his chin with his fingers and looked thoughtful. "I am as homesick as Kido, but we need more knowledge of what's going on. How can we free our friends? How can we teleport back home?"

"If Numa finds out about all this, she will turn us in to the Order's Council. We will be made into Pariahs," said Bastian.

"There isn't much of the Council left," said Summer Wind.

"Nobody's leaving yet. Everybody think on it and we'll meet again soon," Spindrift. "Say nothing to anyone else."

Summer Wind said, "One last thought before you go. All this may mean the Prophecy has come true and dragons have returned to our world."

No one said anything after that, each lost in his own thoughts.

On their way out they fed the grolk. Kido tried to duck by, but the grolk caught his shirt and grabbed the Dragon's Gift as well. There was a discharge of energy, and the grolk roared in pain and released Kido. It retreated to the back corner of its cage and held its injured hand to its chest while growling and snorting. The stink of burned fur hung in the air. Kido dodged around Old Man Wizard and returned to his cell with his mind full of dreams of rescuing his friends and saving the world.

The next morning Kido was out on the balcony where Summer Wind found him.

Said Summer Wind, "So, what do you think of the Red Tower so far?"

"It is amazing. I can't wait to learn Magic, but I did see something weird. I saw a face in the window of that building nearby. I thought all the houses near the tower were deserted." He indicated a two-story weathered gray, old house that stood just outside the tower's enchantment shield.

"They generally are, except for the King's spies," said Summer Wind.

"The King spies on us?"

"Oh, yes. All the time. He'd like nothing more than to wipe us out. The only wizards he likes are the ones on his payroll."

"Like Zirmad?"

"He's the big baddy daddy, but he's homegrown. I was thinking of all the Black Hoods who abandoned their tower to live in the King's Palace."

"Are there always spies watching us?"

Summer Wind shrugged. "I don't often look or pay much attention to the outside world. We're safe inside the tower so it doesn't matter if the King had an army of Tooskers surrounding us."

Kido's eyes grew wide at the thought of Tooskers everywhere. Summer Wind smiled in reassurance. "I'm joking about the Tooskers. You rarely see them Topside. But you do often see a face in one of those windows—like you did this morning—and that's normal. Sometimes you'll see a patrol of Dragon Guards marching up and down the streets just outside the enchantment shield. The king messes with us."

"Maybe it was someone living there."

"Impossible. No citizens occupy the houses close to the tower."

"Why did they build those houses so close to the tower to begin with?"

"They didn't. The houses were here first. The tower came later."

Kido was surprised. "You mean there was a time with no Red Tower in Ballastro?"

"I see you have much to learn."

"Do you think that was a Black Hood spying on us?"

"The King has many servants. He uses soldiers, sorcerers, and ordinary citizens, but if you think about it, this is his capital. He is paranoid about maintaining peace and security for Arcadia. He uses the Ruination as an excuse to persecute us. These are troubling times, but we are safe here in the tower." she said. She sighed. "Too safe in fact. Nothing ever happens here."

"Do you ever want leave the tower?"

"I think of going back to Alfheim, more everyday, but my situation would be complicated back home."

"Does anyone ever leave this tower?"

"No. Trailhog brings us news of the outside world but that is precious little. We're not supposed to know anything. Or do anything. That is why it is a blessing that you came into the tower. You've shaken things up. Great things are to come, Kido. I can feel it. Now I want you to meet someone."

He expected her to lead him inside but instead she lead him to the railing. "We're going to float up."

"Up where?"

"You'll see." She grabbed his arm and rose up into the air, taking him with her. She counted floors. "19...20...21." They landed on another balcony and went through an open door into a dim corridor. No one was in sight. Summer Wind whispered, "This is Shippleglass's floor. He lives apart from the other teachers. Don't let Numa or Codface see you. Massive demerits if they catch you on this floor. But Shippleglass is our biggest ally. You must talk to him. Bye."

"You're leaving?"

"Yes."

Kido was nervously looking around when the import of her words hit him. He looked back, but she was already floating off the balcony.

He stood rooted by uncertainty. He could see the door and eventually crept down to it, stopping frequently and listening. He was afraid of getting caught and expelled before he'd even begun his training. Finally he reached the door but before he could knock a voice entered his mind.

P: I know you are there kido you cannot come in until you are worthy of being here

It was telepathy, but he did not recognize the voice.

P: This is shippleglass

Kido was frightened. Was he in trouble? How did Shippleglass know he was here?

P: You may only enter my quarters when you are judged worthy

Kido quietly hurried away and searched for the stairs, feeling bad that he'd been judged unworthy.

Back on Frog Floor, he bumped into Woody and they hugged. "How did you escape the King and get here?" Kido asked.

"Trailhog and I were let out of the King's palace on an errand, and they sent only one guard with us. They underestimated us because they thought we were stupid ex-slaves. Trailhog overpowered him and we escaped. We were hiding in the city when Summer Wind met us. She brought us here because it is the safest place. We told her the truth about where we're from."

"How did you know to trust her?"

"She is an elf! You can always trust elves, unless they are drows."

"Drows? This ain't Dungeons & Dragons, Woody!"

"It feels like it. Anyway, she has this way about her."

"So, you are the Tower Librarian?"

"Yes."

"Is the library here better than the Porterville Library?"

Woody laughed. "Come and see."

Kido could hardly contain himself as he followed his friend. Woody led him down a wide corridor, and they walked some distance. Eventually he could see a faint blue light that grew brighter as they approached. As they came up to it, Kido could see the blue light was a shimmering curtain of energy covering an arched opening in the red brick wall. "What is that?"

"That is a sort of shield, a protective enchantment over the whole library," said Woody.

"It keeps us out?"

"No. It keeps Magic books in."

"The library is beyond?"

"Yes, Kido." Woody was starting to sound exasperated at these simpleton questions, but Kido failed to notice.

"How do we get in?"

"You just walk through. It won't hurt you or stop you."

Kido looked skeptical. "Really?"

"I do it all day long. Watch." Woody turned and walked through the curtain as simply as if there was nothing there. There was a slight crackle of energy but nothing more. Kido could dimly discern his shape on the other side. "Now it's your turn."

Kido still hesitated.

"Come on," Woody encouraged.

Kido reached out to touch the blue curtain, and his finger passed easily through it. Then he suddenly remembered the blue energy curtain in front of the gates to Sporu Angosta, and this gave him courage. He plunged through and found himself standing next to a bemused Woody.

"Welcome to the Library of the Red Tower," Woody said and he beckoned to the space beyond with an expansive gesture.

Kido turned to look and was overcome with awe.

They were in a corner where two wide hallways intersected. Both walls of each hallway were covered, floor-to-ceiling, with bookcases full of books. The ceiling looked thirty foot high, and the hallways seemed to run forever.

For a moment, Kido couldn't speak. "How big is this library?" he finally said in a breathless voice.

"Bigger than you can imagine. I've been here several months, I think. Time's passage defies measurement in this strange world, but anyways, I have only seen a fraction of the library. And I am the librarian."

"Does the library cover this whole floor?"

"Kido, the library covers many floors. In fact, almost all the East Tower is devoted to the library."

Kido had been staring around in wonder as he listened, but now he turned back to face Woody. "East Tower?" he said.

Woody smiled. "Yeah. You may not have realized it, but the Red Tower is actually made of two towers joined together: the West Tower and the East Tower. The West Tower has the kitchen, dining room, front parlor, Magic labs and the Magic Warehouse, living spaces, sleeping cubicles, offices, laundry, garden, the Raven Room, etc."

"Frog Floor?"

"Yes, Frog Floor, Eagle Floor, Fish Floor, and so on, all in the West Tower."

"And the East Tower?"

"The bottom five floors of the East Tower are combined to make the dragon's lair, Ramyre's place when he was here, and the very top floor is another Raven Room. Everything in between is the library."

"And how many floors is that?"

"Nobody knows. You can't count the floors. There are many, many floors holding many, many books: millions of books, tens of million, hundreds of million. Every book that has been written or will be written is here, Kido."

Kido's mind was spinning. "*Will be written?*" he repeated in disbelief.

"Yeah. Past, present, and future books, all here."

"How is that possible?"

"Future books can't be read until they are written, but they are here. It's like Schrodinger's Cat, I guess. Future books are both readable and unreadable, until the day when they are written, when both possible states collapse into a definable, readable condition like we are used to. Weird, I know.

"Schrodinger's Library?"

Woody laughed. "Yeah!"

"I'll just stick to reading the readable books. I'm here only to learn enough Magic to get back home."

"So am I, now that I am free from King Cromartin. We are safe here in the Red Tower."

"You and I are here. We know where Trailhog is. Pyra is a prisoner of Cromartin along with the wizard Atticus."

"Last I saw Dahlia and Misha, they were lowly servants of Cromartin working in his palace," said Woody. "And Holly is some kind of princess now."

"Princess Holly?"

"Don't ask me how it happened."

"Domingo is trapped inside a Magic Book of some kind in the Gold Tower. So we just need to rescue our friends, find the right teleport key, get back to the teleport rock now buried deep inside the Ruined Lands, and go back home."

"That should be a piece of cake."

Kido tried to ignore the feeling of being overwhelmed. "We need to find out everything there is to know about teleportation. Show me where the Magic book section is." Kido pointed down the nearest hall and began walking that way until he saw that Woody was not moving. He stopped. "You can do that, can't you?"

"Well, there is something else about this library."

"What?"

"When I arrived at the Red Tower, they weren't going to let me stay, despite Summer Wind's endorsement. Numa and Codface were going to force me out, until Shippleglass came to my rescue. He suggested letting me stay if I agreed to be the new librarian. Numa laughed and agreed. I found out why when I got here. You see, when the Ruination hit here, it was like a hurricane of Magic. It shuffled books around. It wrecked any organization. The powerful Magic forces unleashed made the tower unlivable and it was abandoned for awhile until the storm subsided. The wizards fled out into Ballastro, and there the old tower librarian caught the epidemic that was going around and died. When the rest came back to the tower and saw the chaos, no one wanted to take over the library, until I came along."

"So the books are out of order?" Kido looked around. All the books looked neatly lined up on the shelves.

"They look lined up, but there is no rhyme or reason to their location."

Kido closed his eyes and rubbed his forehead.

"There's more," said Woody.

Kido let out his breath with a sigh. "What else?"

"I'm told that only about one percent of the books in the library contained Magic dating from pre-Ruination times. Not only did the Magical hurricane move books around, but it lifted passages from Magic books and blew them around like confetti until they landed inside non-Magic books. Snippets of spells and partial passages of wizardly instructions are now hidden inside random texts. Even if you found a book on teleportation, it would likely be incomplete, parts of it ripped out and plopped down inside other books."

"Great."

"One more thing. Don't be in the library after dark."

"Why?"

"After darkness falls, the creatures come out."

"Creatures?"

"The ghosts of long-dead wizards and the creations of many failed spells are said to haunt the library at night."

There was a heavy swaple table with chairs nearby. Kido pulled out a chair and sat down, feeling overwhelmed and frightened. "Have you seen these creatures?"

"No, and I don't want to. I'm always back in my sleeping cubicle long before night hits. I suggest you do the same."

18
Shippleglass

Summer Wind found Kido lounging in a hammock in his cell. Bright cellophane wrappers littered the floor, and the remains of a Starbolt roast chicken sat on his desk. She kicked the wrappers aside. "You ever clean up around here?"

Kido yawned like a lion. "After my nap."

"You're getting fat and lazy on that Starbolt slop."

"Doesn't everyone eat it?"

"No, not everyone eats it, if they're smart."

"What else is there?"

"I'll show you." She took him out on the balcony in the fresh warm air. The thick vines that climbed up the tower's side stirred in the warm breeze. Summer Wind pushed leaves aside and plucked some of the Purpleberries that grew there. She ate one and gave two to Kido. "Eat."

He did and found the fruit delicious. "I remember seeing these vines and berries the first time I came to the tower, but I never thought about eating them."

"Well start eating them. I eat them all the time. The leaves too. And the fruit growing on the trees on top of the tower. Also, the vegetables and legumes growing up there. The meat Fenix cooks at night is okay, and the bread and rice Garlic Jon makes every day. All these things are healthy. Just don't eat that disgusting factory food."

"No more Starbolt slop."

"No more Starbolt slop."

He smiled and was pleased to see her smile in return. "I haven't yet gotten to talk to Professor Shippleglass." He told her what had happened.

"Until you are worthy?" she said.

"That's what he told me, whatever it means."

She shrugged. "You'll have to figure that out yourself." She favored him with another smile before leaving.

He paced around on the balcony and wondered. Gulmar flew in and landed on the balustrade. "Gulmar, when will I be worthy?" Kido asked him. He had long ago gotten over the novelty of talking to animals.

"When?" The Mawker bird seemed to consider the question. "Now."

Kido said, "Now? Just like that? All I have to do is declare myself worthy and I am?"

Gulmar bobbed his head up and down.

"I'm not sure you understand what I'm asking."

"Now."

"I don't have to be a member of the Order of Wizards or wear red robes, do I?"

"Yes. Uh, no. Gulmar means no."

"Gulmar means no to what?" It was Mosshair, a red-covered book under his arm. Kido explained his predicament. "You'll have to figure that out for yourself. In the meantime, you need to learn to float. This tower is too tall for you to keep walking up and down those stairs, and really, if you cannot float, then you have no hope of becoming a wizard." He took the book out and opened it to a marked page. Handing it to Kido, he said, "That is the *Float* spell. It is the simplest spell there is, and the first one every young wizard learns. Memorize it. I shall give you some time."

Kido promptly handed it back. "I know the spell. I learned it months ago—it seems like years ago in fact."

Mosshair was surprised. "You know the spell, and yet you cannot float?"

"I learned it out of a spoiled brat's spellbook, back in the Gold Tower. I floated many times back then. They called it the *Levitate* spell, and you guys call it the *Float* spell, but it is the same thing." A note of pride crept into his voice, but then he lost it. "I can't float anymore."

"When was the last time you floated?"

Kido thought about a moment. "In Bremen Wood, months ago."

"And now you can't."

"Now I can't."

"You last did it outside this tower?"

"Yes."

"You cannot do it inside the Red Tower, but you could outside it?"

Kido's eyes widened in understanding. "The tower is blocking my Magic!"

Mosshair nodded. "All Magic done here is under the influence of Ramyre. We Red Hoods draw our energy from him. He is our totem. Your totem must be another dragon, which the tower blocks."

Kido felt deflated again. "How am I going to study Magic *inside the tower* then?"

"You can *study* Magic inside the tower all you want. You just cannot *do* Magic inside the tower."

"So I have to come outside to cast spells?"

"You are outside right now." Mosshair rubbed his chin and thought about Kido's situation. "You are going to have to figure out your totem. Ramyre isn't it. Pangma might be since you lived in the Gold Tower and first floated there, but you also have a connection to Akasha." Kido pulled the Dragon's Gift out from his robe. "Yes, that thing," Mosshair said. "If the blue dragon be your totem, that would be awkward, since there is no blue tower. I don't know how much more I can help you, given your strange situation." He patted Kido's shoulder as he headed back inside. "But I wish you luck."

Kido sat on a stone bench out on the balcony and noticed Gulmar was still there. He didn't know if the Mawker had listened to their conversation, but it was watching Kido intently now. Kido thought about it some more until he made up his mind. "You're right, Gulmar. I am worthy. There is no reason I can't talk to the man. I'm just going to do it and whatever happens happens."

Gulmar remained silent and began to preen.

"You're such a good listener."

Kido closed his eyes and thought of dragons. How to pick a totem? He barely knew about Pangma, not surprising since he'd been only a slave at the Gold Tower. He knew he couldn't stand the evil Mazunga, and Sanshinar seemed the exclusive totem of elves. If he had to pick a totem dragon, he wanted Akasha. Akasha had treated him well and had talked to him kindly. Maybe she was deceiving him, but from what little he had to go on, Akasha was the only dragon for him. It was so obvious a choice that he gave it no more thought. He was now and forever a follower of Akasha the Blue. Even if she didn't have her own tower.

Now how to connect with her? He thought of how far away she was, hundreds of leagues to the east, beyond the high mountains and deep into the Ruined Lands. Were the gates open now and were the dragons loose in the Known World? Would Akasha come looking for him? Could she track him by the gift?

He tried to visualize a huge dragon with brilliant blue scales. He spoke her name aloud, "Akasha?" He tried telepathy.

P: Akasha are you there?

Nothing. He opened his eyes with a sigh. Gulmar was still preening. Kido just sat there and thought of nothing. After awhile one thought did come into his mind like a single cloud drifting across a blue sky. He closed his eyes, visualized a blue dragon, and took ahold of the gift in one hand as he did so. The metal felt smooth and warm.

P: Akasha?

P: Yes kido?

Tingles coursed through his body. It was her!

P: It has been a long time

P: Not to a dragon but i suppose to a human you sound very distant

P: Can you sense me?

P: Right now yes but oftentimes you are nowhere to be found

P: Where are you?

He wondered if she would reveal anything about her or the other dragons whereabouts.

P: Right behind you

He gasped and wheeled around but there was no dragon. And then he heard her gentle laugh.

P: Just joking I am where I have always been

P: You are not free yet?

P: The world is changing I feel it

P: When will I meet you?

P: Someday

P: Can you help me perform Magic?

P: Magic is what I know best

P: I need to float higher up the side of this tower

P: Then feel the power of akasha and you will float

He took a deep breath and felt a surge of confidence as the spellwords came tumbling out his mouth. He felt lighter. He opened his eyes to see himself in midair, the stone bench falling away. Floating up, he counted balconies, landing twenty-one floors high, through the open door, to land awkwardly, tumbling to the floor. "I got to work on my landing." He got up and slowly walked, knowing he was breaking his connection with Akasha by being inside Ramyre's tower. He tucked his gift back under his robe. The corridor was empty, and his footsteps sounded loud as he took that very long walk to the professor's door, which he found open.

He entered and found a large room with high ceilings and no windows. Torches and a large brazier provided orange light. To the right, tall shelves lined the wall. The shelves were full of pale white skulls of various creatures, small- and medium-sized. He looked to the left and was startled to see a huge skull, as tall as him, its gaping mouth full of long sharp teeth. The legs and feet of what looked like a human skeleton dangled out of the toothy maw. Looking closer, he could see the rest of the human skeleton inside the 'mouth.' The large eye sockets seemed to follow him as he went deeper into the room.

He went past glass tanks half full of dirt. One had green ants scurrying around, another red and black ants. A third held large, pale termites. Beyond was a tall corridor of shelves on both sides, holding a large variety of knick-knacks and curiosities. The room opened up beyond. A man with his back turned was dropping flakes of something into a glass tank of water on a pedestal. The water looked ordinary except for the pair of large pale eyes staring out at him. There was no body, just eyes.

The man turned to reveal he wasn't Shippleglass but one of the other teachers.

"I'm sorry. I thought you were Master Shippleglass. I—"

"I am clearly not Shippleglass. I am Master Bothros. What are you doing here?" he asked in a cold voice.

"I made a mistake," Kido said in a small voice.

"You certainly did. Don't you knock?"

"I'm sorry."

"Fifty demerits for your impudence. Leave now or I will pile on more, and don't ever come back in here." He turned his back to Kido.

Kido stumbled out, and stood for a moment to regain courage. Further down the hall was another door that he approached with some trepidation. He raised his hand to knock but then paused in mid-motion. He looked down and before his feet floated the words COME IN in smokey letters that drifted out from the crack under the door, only to evaporate as he read them. He carefully pushed the door open and went in.

This room was just as large as the other but very sparse in decoration. A far wall held a single bookcase full of titles and next to it stood a small, empty table. Mounted on the wall above the table was a picture of a strange sigil painted in bright red. In the center of the room was an overstuffed chair and a long couch facing each other, both covered in white fabric and perched on a white shag rug. Shippleglass sat in the chair. There was nothing else in the room. High windows in the back wall let in ambient light from the cloud-shrouded world outside. The room appeared very bright, clean, and pure.

"Kido, our young novice. It didn't take you too long to come up here, did it?" Shippleglass said in dulcet tones. "Come and sit." He beckoned to the couch.

Kido felt at ease and obliged. "What did you mean, suggesting I was unworthy to visit you?"

"That was just a little test to see how you felt about yourself. You'd be surprised how many novices assume they're unworthy. Some wait months or even years to approach me but not you."

"I wanted to meet you," Kido said.

The professor regarded Kido with frank appraisal. "And I you."

"How did you know I was coming, Professor?"

"I could sense your aura."

"My aura?"

"All Magic exudes a field of energy that is discernable to those attuned to it. Wizards, dragons, elves, Magic devices, spellbooks all generate auras, unless they have been cloaked. You have the strongest aura I have ever encountered."

"Really? How...how far away can you sense me?"

"I suspect you would have to exit the tower and go halfway to the Zirkus before I would lose you."

Kido was so surprised to hear this. "Can others sense me?"

"The senior wizards and all the masters can. It is a lost art now, so the junior wizards never learn it and the kids have not the ability. Non-wizards also have no clue."

"So Numa and Codface...."

"...know you are here in my study, without a doubt."

"Will I get in trouble?"

"No, because I will say I invited you here. Uninvited, you would be burdened with new demerits if caught on this level, but I will protect you. I will lose some of their respect, of course, but that matters little to me."

Shippleglass adjusted his wire rim glasses and clasped his hands on his belly. He regarded Kido with curious interest before speaking.

"Kido, I wonder if you realize what an amazing thing it is that you gained entrance into the only functioning Magic Tower in the Known World. Not to mention how you got to Ballastro. Somehow you escaped the Ruination. Somehow you met Atticus and received a *Hope Crystal*. Somehow you survived the tower walk even."

"*Float* is a spell I learned way back in Pandoon, but I wonder if it would've worked."

"Actually, you don't know the half of it. That chasm you were hanging over is part of the spawn cave of Ramyre, token dragon of this tower, and the source of the tower's enchantment. The Magic down there would've overwhelmed your little spell and sucked you down to your doom. You would've flown like a lead zeppelin. So you owe your life to the tower."

Kido lowered his eyes and thought about that, feeling gratitude, awe, and fear at the same time. Neither spoke for a long moment.

"Please tell me *everything* about the day that the Ruination happened at the Gold Tower."

So Kido told again the story he was used to telling, with all the details.

Shippleglass identified the vial of golden liquid as something called *Essence of Dragon*. "The unadulterated Magic drawn from the blood of Tiamat, possibly the last remaining drops in all the Known World. Wizards have been searching centuries for more vials. Now, please show me the Dragon's Gift, Kido."

Kido took out the pendant and held it up so it sparkled in the cloudlight. Shippleglass let out a soft gasp, got up and came around to study it closely. He was careful not to touch it. He sat back down. "It is beautiful. However, accepting a Dragon's Gift is fraught with danger, Kido, I must tell you. It may confer some special abilities on you. It may be contributing to your aura, too. But at some point, the bestowing dragon will most assuredly ask of you a favor, and you may not like it, but you cannot refuse it. I bet you didn't realize that when you picked up that pendant."

Kido felt his stomach sink. Now he wasn't so sure about having a totem dragon. "No, I didn't know anything about it. Wouldn't I have to be inside Sporu for Akasha to prevail upon me?"

"Perhaps that is your destiny?"

"I'm beginning to feel that way."

Shippleglass said, "No doubt the dragon has established a link with you. You have telepathic powers to begin with, but no one can-communicate with a dragon unless the dragon makes it happen. At least it's Akasha and not Mazunga. I used to teach Dragonology to our wizards when the tower was open. Now I focus on Wizard Psychiatry. How do you feel about dragons, Kido?"

"They fascinate me. I think I saw the skull of one in the office next door."

"Bothros is a cold fish, is he not?"

"He didn't like me being there."

"He doesn't like anybody. And that large skull you saw by his door?"

"It's huge."

"That's nothing compared to a Prime Dragon or Tiamat. That skull belonged to a Lesser Dragon called Fumar, killed at the end of the Age of the Empty Towers."

"So Fumar lived centuries after the Prime Dragons had been banished?"

"Quite. As far as we know, the only dragon ever to exist in the thousand years since the Prophecy was born, was Fumar."

"And the skeleton inside its mouth?"

"The remains of a wizard named Null Ack Zane, known as Zane for short. An unfortunate accident. He created the dragon but from an incomplete manuscript attributed to Antares. Null failed to gain control of it, and the dragon ate him. Somehow the wizard cast a spell to inflate his body as he was being chomped on, and he choked the dragon. They both died and were found that way. The rest of Fumar's skeleton is up on, I think, the 27th floor. Fumar was a Swamp Dragon, all green and black scales, blue eyes. Dragons are a fun subject, except we're not supposed to talk about them anymore. Maybe Cromartin will open up Sporu and let them out again."

"Do you think he can?"

"No, I don't think *he* can. What concerns me is if the Black Sorcerers can for him. You yourself said they were at the teleport rock with the Gold Hoods. What did Ramanapirus and Astra know? How were they going to teleport into Sporu, and how was that vial of *Essence of Dragon* to be used? And as for that giant, did they uncover some kind of vortex to teleport him out, or did he merely open the gates from inside and let himself out? Most crucial of all is whether any of the Black Hoods at the teleport rock survived and are now in Cromartin's hands. There are rumors of such a thing. Then there is the possibility that the gates were opened as part of the Prophecy, and thus it is only a matter of time until dragons begin appearing. I must think on this some more. In the meantime, you should work on cloaking your aura."

"Can Spindrift teach me that?"

"No, and anyone in this tower who could teach you won't. You must teach yourself from a book in the library."

"I have been to the library and seen its size and heard all about its chaotic organization."

"It is difficult to find anything in there, that is true. But it it not impossible. Spend some time there, if you truly want to get back home."

Kido didn't head straight to the library. Instead he went down to the first floor and outside, checking first to make sure the *Hope Crystal* was in his pocket, just in case.

Ever since Woody had told of the West and East Towers, Kido had wanted to walk around the outside of the tower to gauge its size and structure. He went out the west double doors and started walking clockwise. It was still midmorning on another cloudy, hot day.

It was a long walk, and he counted his paces. The north and south sides turned out to be twice as long as the western and eastern sides. So the Red Tower was rectangular. All sides were covered in flowered Purpleberry Vines. There were only two ground-level openings: the doors he came out and the dragon's hole.

The latter was on the east side, a massive opening 300 feet tall and half as wide. He had peered inside to see a cavernous space whose details were lost in a vast gloom. He was reminded of a similar dragon hole in the Gold Tower. The air here had a stale, musky smell that wrinkled his nose. Somewhere back there was a passage that connected to the chasm chamber. He noticed the cobblestones before the hole had been worn by the countless passages of something large and heavy, marred in spots by claw marks. The neighborhood houses on this side of the tower stood far away.

When he got back inside, he touched the wall and counted sun ravens. It had taken him five hours to walk around the Red Tower, and he had missed lunch. He was headed to the kitchen when he changed his mind, went back outside, and ate Purpleberries and leaves instead.

19
Books of Magic

At first raven, Kido always went now to eat Purpleberries outside the tower on the 18th balcony, dressed still in his sleeping tunic. He plucked berries from the vine, amazed that their abundance never slackened no matter how many he ate. Often he floated up to the roof for more food. Afterwards, he would wash up and put on his gray robe, his *Hope* and *Fear Crystals* in one pocket, Egon in the other. He regretted not having a staff but only true wizards were allowed one by the Order.

Then it was to the library to look for Magic books. Inside the tower of course he could not float, so he traipsed up and down the backstairs, trying to explore as many library floors as possible. When in the library, he would slowly walk along and read the spines, or reach out a hand and let his fingertips lightly brush the spines.

Often he would stop and pull a book out as a brightly-colored cover, an unusual script, or a bold design would catch his eye. However, these unusual books were few in number. Most books were nondescript or had darkly aged covers under a layer of dust. In fact, most looked like they hadn't been used in decades. Most were in the Mother Tongue, but some were in Elvish or other, strange languages. He knew Magic books were written in the language of Magic (which he could recognize, even if he couldn't read), but Kido was yet to find any of those. He did pull books out at random and wiped dust off their covers. With great disappointment, he discovered they were all about boring topics: metallurgy, psychology, cooking, crop cultivation, heraldry, genealogy, temple architecture, stonemasonry, meteorology, and so forth.

He tried to search a new floor each day but that got overwhelming, so he concentrated on his floor, the 18th. He just walked east from Frog Floor, passed through the blue energy shield as if passing through a dry waterfall, and there he was.

One of the first things he did was to test Woody's statement that the books move around. So he took off the shelf the first book he found on the 18th floor that was in the Mother Tongue. It was called *Of Shoats, Stoats, and Boats*. Kido sat down in a chair and read some of it. It was the memoirs of a wizard of long ago named Jorgander. From historical references, he had lived in the last years of The Age of the Tower Builders and the first twenty years of The Golden Age. He had been through the Goblin Wars. Before entering the Red Tower, the youthful Jorgander had helped raise pigs on his family farm, and in his spare time trapped weasels and fished in boats on the Cloud River, thus the title. As an old wizard, Jorgander had penned his memoirs. His body now lay in the catacombs below the tower. Memories of that place made Kido shudder.

He carefully shelved the book on the bottom shelf at the near end of the first bookcase he came to when entering the 18th from Frog Foor. The next morning he discovered it was not where he had put it. Three weeks later he found it again, still on the 18th but far removed from its original spot. Woody was right. The books do move, but what force does the moving? It was yet another tower mystery.

It was lonely in the library. Most of the wizards were working in their labs, and the kids never came into the library at all. Woody's office was on the 6th floor. Up on the 18th, Kido was all alone. Then one day he saw four young wizards together on the 18th. He watched them for awhile and noticed how they systematically examined a bookcase, top-to-bottom, book-to-book. He mentioned it to Woody when they lunched together on the west tower's main floor.

Woody said, "They're from the Horse Floor. Periodically, junior wizards do a little sweep of a portion of the library looking for lost spells."

"Do they find any?"

"Rarely. That's why they don't waste much time."

"Or enthusiasm."

"The odds of finding anything are astronomical. It's like winning the lottery back home. But still just finding part of one spell is a huge thing, so they keep trying when they can."

Not too long after that, Kido did find a book with part of several spells written in the language of Magic. Feeling excited, he took it to Woody, who summoned Numa to the library. She referred it to Pontazar and Longtuth. They looked it over carefully for some time before announcing these were first class spells they already had. The book was returned to Kido without comment.

"Where should I reshelve it?"

"Anywhere. It doesn't matter because it will just move around anyways."

But Kido didn't reshelve it right away. Instead he sat down at a swaple table and copied the spells into a notebook. Then he had Spindrift help him with the pronounciation. By learning the language of Magic, he was taking the first steps towards becoming a true wizard.

Another language he was learning was Elvish. He had found a book that had the Mother Tongue on every left-hand page and Elvish on every right-hand page. He showed it to Woody.

"That's a dual-language book," said Woody.

"Can I take it out of the library?" asked Kido.

"Sure. It's not a Magic book."

"How long can I check it out?"

"As long as you want, so long as no one else asks for it."

So Kido kept it in his cubicle, along with a textbook on Elementary Elvish that he also found. Soon he was spending an hour or two everyday on Elvish. One morning he met Summer Wind and greeted her in Elvish as they passed. When he looked back she was staring at him with her purple eyes wide with wonder. Her reaction gave him a thrill that lasted all day long.

The next morning she somehow crossed his path again and was ready this time. She rattled off a long line of Elvish at him.

He grinned sheepishly. "I don't know what you just said."

"Come back when you do."

Kido began a second search at this time, in addition to looking for Magic books. The next morning he asked Summer Wind where the tower's teleport rock was, and he asked in Elvish.

"Teleport rock?"

He switched to the Mother Tongue. "Yes. Every tower has one, right?"

"Nobody teleports, except maybe the masters. I have never teleported."

"Okay, but you know where it is, don't you?"

"No."

"No? It's never come up in conversation? You've never come across it in all your time here?"

"No, the masters are very secretive about stuff like that, although

I've always wondered about it. The masters always restrict us to our quarters when they want to do something secretive."

"Could it be with the Magic Labs on the 6th?"

"No, I spend enough time there to know that."

"The Magic Warehouse?"

"Nope."

"Well, it's not on the roof, like Putnam Castle, because I've been all over the roof. And it's not outside, like the Gold Tower, because I've been out there, too."

"We're prohibited from certain floors. It's probably on one of those."

"So yet another tower mystery."

He took a welcome break from the library to hunt for the teleport rock. He searched the pantry until Garlic John brandished a giant wooden spoon and chased him out. He searched the laundry and the tailor's shop. No teleport rock there, but he left his dirty clothes to be cleaned.

After he left, Codface took Kido's clothes from the startled laundress and carried the basket, as a waiter balances a tray, to a secret location, all the while humming pleasantly. There he found Bothros and Pontazar building something big. Codface shook out Kido's clothes on a table until he had acquired several of Kido's hairs. He placed a few of these in a slot on the thing's head along with a slip of paper on which was written the word KILL. Bothros used the remaining hairs to cast a delayed *Sleep* spell. They exchanged wicked smiles.

Kido meanwhile tried the botanical garden next. Coming off the back stairs onto the 9th, he rounded a tall wall and found himself confronted by a sea of greenery. There were potted plants and plant beds everywhere. A huge bougainvillae with bright purple flowers stood right in front of him. The air was full of the sweet smells of so many flowers, and there were different colored butterflies fluttering around. He saw more plant species than he ever knew existed. He wandered and found a bee hive in one corner next to a very tall heliconia plant with dazzling yellow flowers, fruit flies all around and also many caterpillars and spiders. Twice a bat flew overhead. There were little green lizards hunting shiny black beetles through the underbrush. Occasionally a frog would croak. He saw a green snake with white bands slither by. Some mysterious light source in the ceiling substituted for the sun. The 9th floor was warm and humid, and

Kido was soon soaked with sweat as he pushed his way through the thick and overgrown vegetation. He decided this floor was more like a jungle than a garden, but there was no sign of a teleport rock anywhere.

Kido tried the armory next, but Codface blocked his access. The armory seemed a likely place for the teleport rock but then so did the many higher floors where he was also forbidden. He gave up and the next day went back to the library.

It seemed like another fruitless day spent looking for elusive books on the 18th floor.

Kido said aloud, "It's a Magic Tower with a Magic library full of every conceivable book. Where is the Magic? I'm talking to myself, just like Gollum, precious."

He was alone again, sitting cross-legged on the floor near the back stairs. It was late afternoon, and he was feeling tired and discouraged. As he was examining the books that went along the bottommost shelf against the back wall, his body leaned over until he was half-reclining. None of the books appeared Magical, of course. He propped his head in his hand and slipped into a daydream where he was a great wizard with a spellbook full of powerful spells. He created a dragon in his lab and flew off on his dragon to rescue his friends. Kido stretched out his legs as he savored his fantasy. The dragon seemed so real that Kido could feel his hot breath.

He woke up in pitch blackness with no idea how long he'd been asleep. Rolling over on his back, he winced at the stiff aches caused from lying on the hard brick floor. He wondered what had woken him and then felt warmth from his pocket and pulled out a hot *Fear Crystal*. He heard a noise in the faroff darkness and suddenly remembered Woody's warning. It was the distant, ponderous thumping of something heavy coming closer. The crystal's whining sounded unnaturally loud in the darkness, and he stuffed it back in his pocket.

Kido lay there with his senses taut and heart beating. The thumping grew louder, the floor vibrated, and when he could hear it very plainly, he surmised that the thing had turned the far corner and now there were no bookcases between them. There was a brief, silent pause, and Kido sensed it was somehow sizing him up in the dark. It made no vocalization. Then the heavy footsteps resumed, faster and louder, and with it was the strange noise of grinding rocks or bricks. He still couldn't see the thing, but it clearly knew where he was and meant to run him down. Galvanized into action, Kido jumped up, and fumbling for the stairs' railing, he mounted the backstairs and raced upwards as crashing footfalls sounded close behind.

The staircase shook violently as the thing blundered up the stairs after Kido. Floor after floor the two raced up. Kido sensed he was more nimble at turning the corners, and he pulled ahead as the thundering steps fell further behind. But it still kept on coming, and Kido was panting loudly and his leg muscles were starting to burn. *I am such a couch potato*, he berated himself. He knew he couldn't make it all the way to the roof, so at the next landing he reentered the dark library. He slowed his sprint to a steady loping stride, and swung left with his arm outstretched. Contacting bookspines, he used them as a guide as he made his way down the long, dark hall.

He hoped the thing would miss him and keep climbing up the stairs, but all too quickly he felt the floor vibrations and heard the heavy thumping behind, gowing faster and louder. Kido realized the thing could outrun him in a straight race and desperately began sprinting again. It was gaining on him, still making no sounds except those thundering steps and brick-on-brick grinding.

It was almost on top of him now. In desperation he was pulling books off of the shelf onto the floor, hoping the thing would trip, but on it came. Just another few steps and it would have him. And then Kido felt empty space to his left. It was an intersection of hallways, and Kido cut left. He felt the air of the thing blowing by behind him and heard a loud crash as it couldn't negotiate the abrupt turn. Kido stopped and looked back but saw nothing in the dark. In his mind though he could visualize a giant with its legs turning left but its momentum still carrying its upper body forward. Physics took over and it crashed. Quickly though it got back up.

Hands on his sides, gasping for breath, Kido was forced to resume sprinting. He figured he was heading for the west tower now, but this was another long hallway, and it was gaining on him again. It would catch him for sure now.

He gave up running and stopped to face his pursuer. He opened up his pocket. "Light, Egon." A soft green light emanated from the Glow Ball as it floated up, and Kido could see the thing now. It was humanoid and fifteen feet tall, shuffling quickly towards him with that strange grinding noise. It must be made of rocks or bricks. As it got closer, he could see its massive arms that ended in sledgehammers, nothing that resembled true hands or articulating fingers. It raised both arms over its block-shaped head, and Kido ran in the only safe direction, through its legs and behind it. Sledgehammer hands slammed into the library's brick floor, raising a cloud of brick dust where Kido had been.

The Brick Golem—for Kido had now surmised that he was facing a golem—looked around. Whatever brain or sensory organs it had must be rudimentary. Ponderously it clomped around 180 degrees. It perceived its prey and raised the sledgehammers. Kido ran through its legs again. Another empty blow and another cloud of brick dust. They did this several times. Each time the golem got closer to hitting Kido. Clearly this wouldn't last.

Kido had an idea, based on what he had read about golems. The next time he ran east through the golem's legs, he kept running. Egon followed. Sprinting madly, they made it to the intersection and turned right. The thundering and brick-grinding noise followed. It was going to be close. For a moment, Kido feared he was going end up as pulverized jelly on the library floor, but then the backstairs loomed up in the greenish light. He ran part-way up the stairs and stopped.

The Brick Golem entered Egon's circle of light and slowed up to avoid plowing into the wall. As its head came abreast of him, Kido perceived the slot on top. He reached through the bannister and plucked out the piece of paper. The golem stopped abruptly, shoulders sagging, arms dangling uselessly and swaying gently until all momentum was gone. Kido waited several minutes to make sure it was dead. Then he held up the paper to read it in Egon's green glow. It read: KILL.

Just then a small flash of energy came down swiftly from above. It was colored bright orangish-gold and passed through the slip of paper to disappear in the blink of an eye. Kido gasped and dropped it as it began burning. It fell to the floor by the golem's right foot, and by the time Kido got down there it was nothing but ashes. He edged around the golem and into the library, walking slowly. His mind was now occupied by the cold realization that someone in this tower wanted to kill him. He knew he was unpopular with some of the wizards and most of the masters, but he hadn't feared being murdered, until now.

Not knowing what floor he was on, and not trusting in the safety of his sleeping cubicle, he just kept walking, past the spilled books, turning towards the west tower, shuffling through brick dust. He walked for some time before perceiving a pale light up ahead. As he drew closer, he realized it was the same ghost he'd met twice already.

Pognip Oldcastle's ghost, dagger in his back, eyed Kido wordlessly as he passed but did not follow.

Eventually Kido passed through the blue-energy curtain and out of the library. Egon's light showed this floor was wide-open, with many brick piers. It looked mostly empty, but here and there were large shapes covered in white sheets. He kept walking to put distance between himself and the library. Then he came across a huge pile of white sheets, and pocketing Egon, he crawled inside and soon was asleep.

20
THE PRINCESS & THE SCULLERY MAIDS

Holly Hawk sat in the king's carriage and watched as a 400 pound pink pig ran around its pen grunting. Cromartin dangled an ear of corn over the fence from a string tied to a stick, keeping it just out of reach. The pig ran back and forth chasing the corn. Cromartin was sitting on the low fence, laughing whenever he pulled the corn away just as the pig was going to bite it.

They were all outside the city walls in the Field of War. Behind them was a tent city where soldiers were training. After the king had inspected his troops, their procession had moved on to the livestock pens so Cromartin could pick the unfortunate victim for this evening's feast. The smell of dung was making Holly sick.

Captain Bangalore, Ranger Bushmaster, and General Phalanx were standing nearby and watching. Two black-robed sorcerers sat in a second carriage, one with his duckfoot propped up. Apart from them all stood a big man in a leather apron with a large boning knife in one hand and a meat cleaver in the other. She could see the men's lips moving but was too far away to hear their voices. They were probably talking about the upcoming campaign to the east. She had heard enough rumors about that going around the palace.

Cromartin drug the corn ear along the pig's back as it passed underneath and laughed as it grunted and poked its snout in the air. In a frenzy now, the pig backed into the fence with all its weight, trying to get around at the corn. The collision almost made Cromartin fall into the pen, and he dropped the stick. In an instant the pig grabbed the ear in its mouth and began eating. Cromartin said something to the butcher and began his slow walk back to the carriage. It took several soldiers to push him up into the carriage, and the springs groaned in protest. Cromartin probably weighed more than that pig. Holly scrunched over as far as possible from him. Finding him repulsive, she felt like Princess Leia with Jabba the Hutt whenever he was in close proximity. He smiled and patted her leg. "Getting along all right in your new home?"

She forced a smile and tried not to squirm. "Yes, my lord."

"Good. I have plans for you."

She wondered if the king was going to make her a princess, or worse, a mistress. She felt like vomiting at that. They rode in silence the rest of the way, for the king seemed preoccupied, and Holly had time to ponder her situation.

She had been living in the Royal Palace for some time now. How long she could not say. The chamberlain had picked her out of a line-up of the Porterville gang, saying the king "would like her looks." She was given a private apartment and a wardrobe full of nice clothes, even some jewelry. An austere, skinny, middle-aged woman named Lady Remora rode herd over her and taught her court etiquette. Some days Holly spent hours sitting at the king's court, listening to the most boring talks. She knew Dahlia and Misha were scullery maids and had it harder than her. They saw each other nearly every day but never had the privacy to talk. Trailhog and Woody had escaped the palace some time ago, and she wanted badly to follow them. She had no idea where Kido, Domingo, and Pyra had gone but feared they had died in the Ruined Lands. Porterville seemed such a long way off. Riding through Riverside, her eyes lifted to see the cliffs and the Red Tower standing above everything. It was all an alien landscape to her, like being on the moon. And then the carriage climbed up Asper's Hill and the castle walls blocked her view. The carriage passed through the Gatehouse, and Holly looked up at the murder holes in the roof thirty feet above. Up ahead loomed the Great Hall of the King of Arcadia, his yellow flag flying above its door. From behind the heavy portcullis clanked into place, closing her off from the outside world.

Dahlia had seen the king's retinue returning to the palace as she stood in the hallway, awaiting the king like everyone else. Fat Cromartin waddled by, wheezing loudly and sweating with effort. Behind him came slobbering Vykar, Dragon Guards, a pair of black sorcerers, then Holly, followed by servants. The two girls locked eyes, and for the briefest of moments they were just two girls from Porterville again, before the throne room swallowed Holly up.

Cromartin heaved himself onto his seat with a massive groan followed by a sigh. The great wooden throne chair creaked loudly but held. The many wives and mistresses who had been standing and waiting now sat. The king called for food and drink. Dahlia hurried forward, bearing a wooden platter with bread, yellow butter, orange cheese, and roast beef. A second maid followed with a flagon of wine. The two maids left quickly, knowing their presence was barely tolerated here.

She had just cleared the kitchen door when someone grabbed her ear and pulled it sharply. "And where have you been?"

She knew who it was before turning around. It was the hunch-backed kitchen troll, hunch-backed yet still taller than her. And Dahlia was six-foot-five.

"Ouch! I was helping Brinn carry food to the throne room."

"You ain't supposed to be anywhere near that throne room unless it's to get dirty dishes. You're a scullery maid. Get back in the scullery and start washing them dishes." He tried to boot her but she moved too fast. In the huge main kitchen she had to turn quickly to dodge a team of men carrying in a trussed pig carcass, bound for the huge fireplace at the center of the kitchen.

Rubbing her ear, she passed a thirty-foot long wood table made out of a wide cross-section of a giant lorch tree cut down in Bremen Wood long ago. The table and fireplace were centerpieces of the palace's huge main kitchen. Brinn was there mixing a baste for the pig and smiled at her as she passed. The smell of the herbs made Dahlia hungry. She kept walking, past Carly, who was wiping away meat juices and bread crumbs to reveal the warm lorchwood in all its beauty. Carly winked at her. Both girls had befriended her and helped her get along in the king's kitchen. Brinn was black-haired and petite, Carly brown-haired and a little bigger.

She finally reached the scullery in the back, a room with two huge iron sinks and a long counter piled high with pots, pans, and crockery. With a sigh she rolled up her sleeves and plunged both hands in the warm, sudsy water. Fantasizing about washing dishes with her mother back home, she was jostled by Misha carrying in another stack of dishes.

"We have *got* to get out of this place, " Misha said with a fierce urgency. "The king has been eating again."

Dahlia turned to look at her friend and was again taken aback by her appearance. They had hacked off her long dreadlocks when she had arrived at the palace, claiming they made her look like a witch. Those beautiful long dreadlocks she had sported for years, now replaced by the short, crudely hacked hair. Dahlia made to reply but Misha had stacked the dishes too close to the edge, and they fell to the stone floor with a loud crash.

Misha bent to pick up broken pieces, muttering, "He better not call me *Darkie* again."

"What was that? Was that Darkie?" The troll's angry voice boomed out as he came stomping back.

Misha cursed under her breath. The troll grabbed her dress collar and yanked her up. Pointing at the broken crockery, he said, "Look at that! Breaking the king's dishes, eh? You'll pay for that. I should whip you, but I have a better idea. Come with me." He drug her over to a table, still gripped in his nasty big paw, and made her pick up a heavy stewpot and a loaf of bread. "Follow me." He finally released her hair, and she dutifully tramped after his hulking form.

They went out the back door, past the summer kitchen and the servants quarters, to the north side of the bailey. Having always been locked indoors, she realized for the first time just how large Cromartin's Palace was. They walked and walked.

The White Keep loomed up before them, and the kitchen troll led her inside. They crossed an octagonal room with a marble floor, down a long corridor past closed doors to a door at the end. The Kitchen Troll knocked and a Dragon Guard let them in. Misha found herself in a large room. To the left was a table with a half-eaten plate of food and a tankard. To the right was a fire burning in a small fireplace. A large iron ring was set in the floor. At the back a large ogre squatted on his haunches and ate with his hands the food on a large platter. The ogre wore a brown tabard with a dragon's head breathing flames. He stopped eating and stared at Misha with unhuman eyes. Misha wanted to drop the food and run from the Keep but the guard had already closed the door. He went to the fireplace, dipped a wooden torch in a bucket of pitch, lit it, and gave it to the kitchen troll. The ogre dropped his platter with a clatter and came forward, forcing Misha to back up to the wall in fright. The thing grabbed the iron ring with both hands, and groaning and grunting, yanked open a door in the floor to reveal a broad stone staircase descending into darkness.

The kitchen troll began descending, pausing to wait for Misha to follow. The stairs curved around and down. After about twenty feet, a large opening appeared to the right, even as the stairs continued down. The troll went through the opening and Misha followed. They were in a torch-lit small room with three brick walls and a rock wall at the back with a human-sized hole at its base. That was where he pushed her.

"Climb down there and deliver that food to the dungeon guards," he snarled.

"Down there?"

"There's an iron ladder attached to the wall. Use it."

Fear made her hesitate. "Down into the dungeon?"

He smacked the back of her head, almost making her drop the stewpot. "Stop stalling or else."

She turned and stepped down into the hole, gingerly feeling for the first iron rung with her feet. She had to tuck the loaf under her arm so as to free up one hand, then slowly descended. The air grew warmer and the light darker, and there was a stale, mineral smell that wrinkled her nose. It felt like a good thirty feet before she touched solid ground.

At the bottom she turned to find herself in a large chamber cut into the rock. Several torchs provided a hellish orange light. In the center of the chamber was a wooden table with two chairs, three bowls, and two wooden spoons. To her left was a large, dark opening. To the right was another opening into a smaller passageway fitfully lit by a few faroff torches. On the wall next to her was a wooden rack holding several spears, leather whips, and an iron mace. She stood frozen in fear, afraid of what would happen to her down in this awful place. From the Kitchen Troll up above there was neither sight nor sound. Misha had just decided to set the food on the table and climb the hell out of there when she heard something in the dark opening to her left. It was moving her way.

From that dark opening emerged a large, loathsome creature. It was humanoid and about seven feet tall. It had an oversized, hairless head, and powerful limbs. Its rotund torso was covered by a tattered and filthy tunic over which it wore a short, ringmail shirt. A huge belly stretched the clothes and mail-shirt out as if it had been dressed this way years ago and had grown too big for its outfit. Small ears sprouted from the sides of its head, and the facial features were clustered together at the center of its wide face. The nose was two small slits but the eyes were large and the irises a light greenish-gray. Upon seeing her, it smiled to reveal large, jagged teeth. "What this?" it said, the voice scratchy as if little used. It shuffled her way.

Misha let out a scream and dropped the stewpot, which landed on its side and spilled out half its contents. Upon seeing the stew, the creature swiftly knelt and crawled over to lick stew off the rocky floor until it was all gone save the remnant still in the pot. It stood, stewpot now in hand. Misha handed it the bread, and it took it, standing and staring at her for a long moment, as if it couldn't make up its mind what to do next. It wheeled and shuffled to set the food on the table and returned to stand before her. It stood looming over her, silently devouring her with hungry eyes, breathing loudly and swaying gently. She cringed and backed up to the wall, but it stepped close again and continued its studied inspection of her. It smell fouled, and she was on the verge of panic.

"What your name" it asked. It spoke slowly, annunciating each word carefully.

"Mi—Mi—Misha."

It moved its head back and forth to see her from every angle. "Me Snather, Dungeon Keeper." It seemed in no hurry. "Pretty thing," it said. "All for me, yes, yes."

She shrieked.

Snather smiled at her. "Funny noise."

Abruptly it straightened as if remembering something. Going back to the table, it dumped stew into a bowl, inserted a spoon and broke off a hunk of bread to add to the bowl's contents. It brought the bowl to Misha and shoved it in her hands. "Give Galt."

"What?" She was too frightened to comprehend and could only focus on getting back up that ladder.

"Give Galt."

"Who's Galt?"

It pointed down the smaller passage. "Galt there."

"You want me to feed Galt?"

"Yes, yes. Gob on errand. You go."

"Galt and Gob are also guards?"

It poked her hard with a fat finger, and its voice grew more insistent. "Feed Galt. Gob not here. I no go." Another finger poke. "You go."

She didn't want it to get angry. "Okay, I'll feed Galt." She entered the passageway as behind her Snather gave a satisfied "Yes, yes."

The floor of the passageway was uneven and sloped down at a twenty degree angle. Two torches spaced far apart gave inadequate illumination, so she walked carefully. Half way down, she looked back to see the dark bulk of Snather blocking all light. No way he could fit down this tunnel.

After about a hundred feet, the passageway came out on a small antechamber. On the right was a large fireplace with a blazing fire. On the left wall hung many iron chains and collars, grappling hooks, and what looked to her like torture devices. Below them was a small table upon which were placed several accoutrements which she barely noticed, for her attention was now focused straight ahead.

The cavern beyond was long, with ten-foot high ceilings. Numerous lamps gave enough illumination to see a row of cages made of iron bars on either side of a central aisle. She saw no Galt and guessed he was somewhere down at the end. She could also see that her presence was causing a stir amongst the occupants of those cages and not wanting to linger, she began walking fast past the bars. Occupants of all the cells rushed to the bars and made noises, speaking in a babble of various languages. Arms were thrust out through the bars, hands and claws groping for her. Misha looked back, wondering if all this noise would bring Gob.

She kept to the center to avoid the searching hands, but curiosity forced her to glance sidelong as she passed by. Some cages were empty and some had humans in them, but some had strange creatures she'd never seen or heard of before, all making vile sounds.

She passed one creature shaped like a humanoid with bulging dark eyes and skin the color of sickly green mottled with blue splotches. It smelled like rotten fish and the briny sea as it reached out a webbed hand and grabbed at her, hissing and snarling.

Some cages were larger and in one she saw a group of twenty or so humans who stared at her silently. She was shocked to see women and children and wondered why they were here. She pushed on.

At the end of the aisle was a t-intersection and beyond it two large cages sat side-by-side, separate from the rest and facing the aisle. The left-hand cage appeared empty. In the right-hand cage an old man sat on the floor, his leg chained to the back wall. A bald, young woman lay on a bench against the right wall. Both wore plain tunics, but the woman had on bright red boots. There was straw and old bones scattered about on the stone floor. A faint blue shimmer of energy formed a barrier just inside the bars on all three sides. The blue light came from a cube-shaped metallic device placed on a stool in front of the cage.

The woman awoke, rubbed her eyes, and sat up to stare at Misha. "Misha?" she said.

Misha at first didn't recognize her until she spoke her name a second time. "Pyra?"

Pyra jumped up and rushed forward. Misha almost cried out to see her friend, but Pyra put a finger to her lips and pointed to her left to a spot outside the cage. Misha turned and saw a soldier with eyes closed, sitting on a stool and leaning against the wall, snoring softly. He cradled a spear and wore a sword and a conical helm, plus the usual dirty tunic under ringmail armor and black breeches. This, she assumed, was Galt.

Misha tiptoed up to the bars and whispered softly. "Pyra."

"Misha," her friend whispered back. "Don't touch the blue light," she warned.

"How are you?"

"Lousy. I'm in a dungeon."

"So am I."

"At least you're on the right side of the bars."

"What happened to your hair?"

"It got burned in a fight with the king's soldiers. What are you doing here?"

"I am a scullery maid. So is Dahlia. Holly is a lady-in-waiting at the king's court."

"Cool. Maybe she can help us get out."

"I dunno. There are always guards around her." Misha scanned around at the blue light. "What is this?"

"Some anti-Magic shield. Because of the wizard."

Misha looked at Atticus, and Pyra said, "Atticus, my teacher."

"Are you a wizard, too?"

"I am in training. Do you know of the others?"

"Woody and Trailhog escaped some time ago. I have no idea where."

"We were caught in Topside trying to get to the Red Tower with Kido."

"Where's Kido?"

"Hopefully in the Red Tower."

"Where's Domingo?"

"Trapped in a Magic book in the Gold Tower."

"Oh my god. What a horrible mess. I—." Misha stopped when Pyra's eyes went to Galt.

Misha saw the soldier was stirring. She backed away from the cage to face him. His eyes fluttered open, and he jumped up when he saw her. Brandishing his spear, he said, "Who are you?"

"I am Misha. I brought your food."

His eyes narrowed in suspicion. He was short and old, with a bony, hardscrabble appearance. "Where's Gob?"

"On an errand. The Dungeon Keeper sent me, or actually the Kitchen Troll sent me."

"He must hate you to send you, a pretty young girl, down here."

"What do you mean? I'm going back to the scullery after this."

"You think you're going to get by the Keeper? He's waiting up there for you. You're lucky you made it this long. Nobody who comes down here leaves alive. You're meant to be trapped here forever, prisoner of the king, which means prisoner of the Keeper."

"What!"

"You're Snather's new toy. He'll keep you down here until he gets tired of you."

"Then he'll let me go?"

Galt laughed. "Then he'll eat you."

"Aiieeey!"

"You mentioned food."

She held it out with shaking hands.

Galt snatched the proffered bowl of food, peered inside it, sniffed appreciatively, and began eating after setting his spear aside. Then he remembered his guest and pulled his sword out. "You better leave. You don't belong here."

Misha looked at Pyra, then back to Galt, who waved his sword. Then she turned and gave a quick wave to Pyra before reluctantly heading back through the dungeon and the usual commotion. There was no sign of guards at the other end, and she took the time now to study the accoutrements. There were two red robes, two belts, two pouches, and a pair of gold gloves. A tall wooden staff was leaning up against the wall. She checked the pouches, but they had been emptied, as had the pockets of the robes. She was considering taking the staff to help fend off the Dungeon Keeper, when she noticed something odd. The two robes, which had both seemed the same shade of crimson red at first glance, now looked different. One had turned a deep burgundy and the other a flame-kissed scarlet. They had both just changed color. She was sure of it. Clearly one belonged to Atticus and one to Pyra. A quick peek up the tunnel confirmed that Snather was waiting for her up there.

Misha agonized over what to do. She wanted to leave the dungeon but feared the Dungeon Keeper. She wanted to free Pyra but feared Galt, and Gob was lurking somewhere, too. There were weapons for her to use: the wooden staff, grappling hooks, and torture implements. She fished through a jumble of the latter and found thumbscrews, leather straps, iron pokers, and a large boning knife. She also noticed a long iron pole with a long loop of rope at the end, some kind of catchpole. She had to hurry before Gob showed up.

She decided Galt was easier to defeat than the Keeper. She chose her weapons. Strapping on one of the belts, she tucked the boning knife in it. The she grabbed the catchpole. She had a plan but she would have to be quick. She took a deep breath and tensed her body to spring forward, but just then a powerful blow struck the back of her head, and everything went dark for her.

21
Numa teleports

A gong sounded and Kido woke up in a white-shrouded world. *I must be sleeping in the clouds,* he thought. He lifted the sheet over his head, half expecting to see a ruddy-brown Bespin filling up the sky below him, but there was only the brick floor, open spaces, and brick piers of this floor in the west tower. Whichever floor it was. Morning gray light came through a few frosted-glass windows. He lay back and tried to clear the sleep from his mind, remembering now the Brick Golem and the Guffin. He should report both, but to whom? He didn't trust Numa or the masters, except Shippleglass. He decided to tell Spindrift. He would know what to do.

He stretched out to give himself a moment to get fully awake and his foot struck something hard buried under the sheets. He got up and pulled them off to reveal a white object four feet high. It was egg-shaped except for its flat base and sat perched on a cart with wheels. There was a dial near the top and seams running along its whole length. Kido was careful not to touch it.

Then he heard faint voices from somewhere. Peeking out from behind a pier, he saw small figures on the far side of this vast floor. He couldn't see who they were from this distance, but he could discern five figures. Kido left his hiding spot and crept closer, moving from pier to pier. Peeking out again, he now saw Numa, Codface, Bothros, Pontazar, and Longtuth. And he could hear their voices.

"If you are not back in twenty-four hours, we are coming after you," said Pontazar.

"If I'm not back by then, you should flee to the most remote corner of the world and find a safe cave to hide in," said Numa.

"If there is such a thing," said Bothros.

"If you do not return, may we have your permission to carry out-the Zane plan?" asked Codface.

"If something happens to me, you can do as you like," Numa said. There was grave concern in her voice.

No one else said anything. Kido watched Bothros uncoil some rope. Numa tied one end to herself and Bothros tied the other to a pier. Numa chanted a spell and the air shimmered until a teleport rock appeared before them. Kido gasped. So that's where it was! Numa stood on the rock, dropped a key, and plunged from sight. Kido smelled the Magic. The rope was pulled through the rock's surface after her, until it drew taut. The three figures stood for a moment staring silently at the black surface.

Longtuth sighed loudly. "Well, that's it."

"I'll take the first watch," said Pontazar.

"I will come relieve you in four hours," said Bothros.

Kido watched Pontazar remove a white sheet from a chair and move it over to sit by the rock. The other three walked off, but at the last second Codface looked over directly at him. With a start, Kido remembered his aura and realized they knew he was there. He got scared at the trouble he was probably in now.

Figuring he had nothing to lose, he walked over. Pontazar glanced at him but said nothing, and for a few moments they stared at the glossy black surface in silence. Kido studied the rope next. It was as thick as a garden hose and made of braided gold. Wonder Woman's Golden Lariat, he thought.

"It is a Yar Rope. It will help her find her way back through the portal," said Pontazar. "Safed Yar's last contribution to the world of Magic. Hey, you're supposed to be in your room like everyone else."

"I was hunted by a Brick Golem in the library last night."

"Serves you right being in the library after dark."

"I did see a Guffin."

"Report it to the Red Rook. He's in charge of Guffin Control."

Kido went to find the back stairs and counted as he descended. Nine floors down to Frog Floor he went, so the teleport rock was on the 27th. The hallways were empty except for a housecat-sized black scorpion scuttling by. After the All Clear gong sounded, he went to find Codface, leaning as usual on the front counter and staring out the window of the Magic Warehouse. "I saw a Guffin."

His impassive face did not change as he stared at Kido. "Where and when?"

"In the library last night."

"In the library? They're never in the library."

"One was last night."

Codface gave him another stare and then left, returning in a few minutes to hand over two items, a glass tube and a glass cap. The tube was two feet long and three inches in diameter. "Next time you see a Guffin in the library, or anywhere, catch it in that and bring it to me."

"Catch it! How, when they move so fast?"

"You figure it out."

"What bait do I use?"

Codface leaned closer and his bulbous eyes glowed at Kido. "Magic. Also, that's 100 demerits for being in the library overnight, 100 for being out of your room during restricted time, 100 for spying, and another 100 for being above the 19th Floor. You should be expelled any day now from racking up demerits."

Feeling dispirited, Kido returned to Frog Floor, but he wasn't ready to return to the library yet. He saw Spindrift in the study lounge and went in. The senior mage sat at a table with his spellbook open, and he was concentrating on a live, green frog sitting on the table before him. The frog had one blue front leg. Kido kept quiet and didn't approach. He watched as Spindrift spoke some spellwords and pointed his finger at the frog. There was a puff of smoke and one of the frog's back legs turned a bright yellow.

"Hey, cool!" Kido said.

Spindrift noticed him for the first time. "Yeah, except the whole frog was supposed to turn red." He peered at his spellbook. There is a lacuna in this spell I am trying to bridge with educated guesswork. So far no luck."

"They let you do spells up here instead of in the labs?"

"Us older Spellheads can play with simple spells outside the labs as long as we don't use any ichor dust."

"Where is the ichor dust kept?"

"In a locked room in the Magic Warehouse."

"Would it have helped?"

Spindrift looked up and saw the tube. "You Guffin hunting?"

"Yeah, in the library."

"Good luck with that. As for the ichor, it always helps any spell. This would be so much easier with ichor."

"Then why not do this in the labs where you can use the dust?"

"There is so little dust left in the tower that they ration it out. Senior wizards get two pinches a day, enough for two spells. I've already gone through my quota for the next three days. I get no more until Dunnersday. They track our usage meticulously. Junior wizards get none at all. In fact, we are told repeatedly that the day will soon come when the ichor dust will be all gone."

"What happens then?"

Spindrift shrugged. I guess we'll all teleport into Sporu Angosta, kill the dragons, and make more. As soon as we find the recipe."

Kido told him about the Brick Golem.

Spindrift shook his head. "That is insane. I bet I can guess whose Golem that was, too."

"They have it out for me."

"Not all of them. They can't threaten a novice. Even though you don't wear the red, you're still a member of the tower."

"They don't care about me. They want to get rid of me. Don't tell anyone, please."

"Okay for now, but the rest of the Frogs should know."

Summer Wind came in as Kido was talking about Numa teleporting somewhere. He was always happy to see her. "I bet she went to the Ruined Lands," the elf said. "She's reconnoitering to see what shape the Gold Tower is in and if the Gates are open."

"She has to get more ichor dust," said Spindrift, "or this tower is dead."

"I wonder what she will find," said Summer Wind. "I wonder if she will make it back."

"Who knows if all the rumors you hear are true, but if anyone could make it out it is the Red Mage," said Spindrift.

"What about the Gold and Black Mages? They didn't make it out," she said. Spindrift fell silent.

Kido said, "As for the ichor, is it possible to sneak in at night when Codface is sleeping and take a little for our own purposes?"

"They would know how much is missing by the next morning, and the Warehouse is guarded at night by WhamBam anyway."

"Who is WhamBam?"

And as Spindrift answered, Kido thought of a plan to steal some ichor.

"Stealing ichor will get you instantly expelled from the tower," Summer Wind said.

"They're going to do that anyways. At least I'd have some ichor."

It was Market Day and Trailhog brought his double-cart full of Starbolt factory food to the Red Tower under the watchful eyes of the King's spies. After unloading, he joined his Porterville friends on the 18th Floor balcony. They could feel the spies' eyes on them from below, so they went inside to Kido's room.

"Imple is gone," said Woody.

"Gone?"

"Just plain disappeared. Everybody thinks he was a spy for the king."

"Speaking of disappearing, I think we should leave the tower as soon as possible.

Trailhog said, "When?"

"Tonight or early next morning, as soon as I can steal some teleport keys and ichor dust."

"And how are you going to do that?" asked Woody.

"I'm breaking into the Magic Warehouse. Tonight. And then I'm leaving."

"That's short notice, Kido," said Trailhog. "Why now?"

"Numa has diappeared into the Ruined Lands."

"I know. Everyone in the tower knows by now. She hasn't come back," said Woody.

"Not yet," said Kido.

"Maybe something got her."

That means the Red Rook is in charge now."

"He hates us, especially you."

"Believe me, the feeling is mutual, and it was already hard enough trying to study Magic here under Numa. But with her gone, everyone will be distracted. Right now is the perfect time."

"So what is your plan?" asked Trailhog

"We know where everyone is. We steal some keys, we break into the palace, we get everybody together, we head east, we get Domingo out of that spellbook, we teleport home. Done. And we never come back."

"It'll be tricky to pull all that off. Also, the best library in the universe is right here," said Woody. "I would miss it."

"I know, but what good is it if I can't find Magic books there, and the Masters won't teach me anything? I gave up on becoming a wizard. I just want to go home now," said Kido.

"How are we going to get Domingo out of that spellbook?" asked Woody.

"There are Magic books in the Gold Tower that should be easier to find than the ones here. One of them has to have a spell to get Domingo out. Especially if I have some ichor."

"And how long will this all take?"

"I dunno. A few days, a few weeks." Kido shrugged. "We'll stay in the Gold Tower no longer than necessary."

"Isn't the Gold Tower in the Ruined Lands?" asked Trailhog.

"Yes," said Kido and Woody in unison. All three exchanged looks.

Trailhog switched gears. "How do we get the girls out of the palace?"

"You deliver factory food there, yes?" asked Kido.

"Yes."

"Woody and I hide in your wagon to get on the palace grounds. Then we blend in with the staff. Find the girls, and sneak out that night," said Kido.

"Then I'll have the wagon waiting outside the walls for you," said Trailhog. "The security is pretty lax there. The guards never check my wagon. They're always bored, and you can tell nobody *ever* expects anything. This thing just might work."

"Can you draw us a map of the palace?"

Trailhog grimaced. "I'm not a good artist, but I'll try." He sat down at the desk and put charcoal stump to paper.

As they watched him, Kido said to Woody, "It's too bad we won't get to see dragons. That would almost be worth staying."

"But this world is dying. The Magic is all but gone," said Woody.

"It's not gone, just well-hidden. Call it entropy. It is merely the end of a cycle."

"I'm not sure thermodynamics operates correctly in this world, and I know I don't want to be a part of the Prophecy, especially when it involves dragons!"

"All worlds renew themselves eventually. We arrived here at the end of one world and at the beginning of another, like the Fenix from its ashes. Can't you feel it?"

"I can *feel it* all right, but I don't want to get caught up *in it*. The old world first has to be dstroyed before the new one can be born. Hence the dragons."

"Well, let's get out of here before things get too hot then."

"Let's!"

"There!" Trailhog held up his crude map with pride. The boys made him add more details with questions like: *what's this?* or *where does this corridor go?* In particular they made him mark all known guard posts.

Then the big man left to make arrangements for tomorrow. Woody left to pack, leaving Kido alone to fret. Their hasty plans could go wrong in so many ways. He needed someone to talk to but knew he'd have trouble finding any of the few he trusted. That was the problem with the Red Tower. It was so massive and underpopulated that it took forever to find anyone. He did think of someone and floated up, but Shippleglass wasn't in his office. A gong sounded while he was there. He went to exit the room but found the door blocked by Black Bob and Codface. "Come with me," Codface ordered.

They went to Numa's office where Bothros was already seated. Codface sat at *her* desk and glared at Kido with his cold fish eyes. "Kido, from the transgressions you have committed in the last twelve hours, you have earned enough demerits to be permanently expelled from this tower."

"Magical Mischief on an egregious scale, young man," Bothros chimed in.

"Yes." Codface continued to glare at Kido for a full minute, until his hard face softened a little. "Yes, *but* we will let you stay, provided you do a small favor for us first."

"What favor?"

Codface took a deep breath and his ears flapped. "We want you to visit the Ruined Lands and bring back information."

Kido felt a wave of fear. He thought of monsters and his voice dropped. "Visit the Ruined Lands?"

"Yes, the teleportal is still open."

"That's the same one Numa used."

"Yes."

"She never returned!"

"Well, not yet."

"But why me? Why not one of you?"

Codface paused and looked at the Masters. "None of us want to go, to be honest."

"But you're going to send me?"

A note of anger crept back into Codface's voice. "You don't have a choice, if you want to remain in this tower. We have you at a disadvantage, now don't we?"

Kido suddenly felt very small. "I don't know many spells. I'm no great wizard. I'd be helpless there."

"We are not sending you there to use Magic. We just want some information. We need your eyes."

"You want me to find Numa?"

"No."

Kido was shocked. He assumed that finding the missing Red Mage would be their first concern. "What then?"

"We assign three tasks to you: assess the condition of the Gold Tower, find out if the Gates of Sporu Angosta are open, and check for signs of any wizards lying around, that means Gold Hoods, Black Hoods, Numa, elves, anyone at all."

"And let us know if you see any dragons," added Bothros.

"That's four tasks. Wait, dragons?" said Kido.

"There may be none. The Gates may still be closed and the seals still intact. But just in case you happen to notice any," said Codface in a dismissive tone, as if dragons were some trifle concern hardly worth mentioning. "Do we have your cooperation in this?"

"How long do I have to think about it?"

"None," said Bothros, crossing his arms.

"We'd like you to go right now, actually," said Codface.

"Right now?" Fear had his throat and his voice could only croak. Kido looked at both in turn.

"Time is of the essence," said Bothros.

"I'm afraid so, Kido," said Codface, who had an unreadable look on his face. "You may select a friend or two to accompany you, whatever fools you can find. We will meet you on the 27th Floor, in say, twenty minutes."

"I'm not staying in your tower, but before I go I want several pinches of ichor dust for my reward when I return."

"Ichor dust? What for?"

"Magic."

Codface rolled his eyes. "Whatever."

22
THE GOBLINMASTER

In an underground lab, four Black Sorcerers stood around a long, stone-slab table, upon which lay a silent, motionless Toosker. Drecks, Wolfinger, and Ipso watched as Zirmad was inserting the tusks. All but Drecks had their hoods down. From within his hood's black depths, Drecks watched the process unfold, knowing that all that was left now was the *Animation* spell. Zirmad was teaching the process to the king's sons, per his request, and presumably to Drecks, too, though Drecks did not care at all to learn. He had his mind on other things.

Beads of sweat had formed on Zirmad's high forehead, furrowed in concentration, and his thick lips were pursed. It was delicate work, and they had been at it several hours already. Finally he let out a long exhale. "I need a break," he said. "Meet back here in an hour."

The two young men bounded up the rock stairs, glad to escape the dungeon for awhile. Wolfinger Drecks knew well, but Ipso was new to him. He had heard the young man bragging about spying inside the Red Tower for the last year. Drecks filed that important information away.

Zirmad paused at the bottom step. "You coming?"

"No, I wish to remain," said Drecks. "There is much to absorb here."

Zirmad shrugged. "Suit yourself, just don't touch anything."

After he was alone, Drecks headed towards the back. He knew the layout of the lab well. For instance, there were two other exits besides the stairs. In the direction where the Toosker's head pointed there was a tunnel, but that led to Snather's lair. Drecks knew not to go down that way, so he walked in the other direction. Since his arrival at the palace, Drecks had spent many nights roaming the hallways and tunnels, learning as much as possible about the king's palace while everyone else slept. If Cromartin or Zirmad knew how much he knew about the palace's layout, they might start worrying.

He had also heard rumors of important prisoners in the dungeon that he wanted to confirm.

Deeper in the lab, he passed more cluttered tables and old equipment. The further he went, the deeper the dust that covered everything. Thick dust even covered the floor, as if no one had walked back here in decades. But he was looking for something. He weaved first left, then right, then began to circle back around until he found it. There was a clear path in the dust on the floor that led to the back of the lab. He followed it and eventually came to the back wall and the third exit. He entered the tunnel without hesitation.

After two hundred feet, a chamber opened up. He saw two beds to the right, and both looked recently used. He crept out and saw a small chamber to the left furnished with a toilet and bathtub. Past the beds were some old wooden wardrobes and a pair of desks with chairs, then some old boxes and piled junk. Beyond that was an exit tunnel. Drecks pressed on, knowing from previous observations that it was unlikely either dungeon guard would be back here during the day.

He went down the tunnel straight for twenty feet before leaving it and turning right onto a side tunnel. After one hundred feet, there was another chamber, a very large one. Stepping out, he saw to the left were two large cages made of iron bars. To the right were more cages. A path separated the left and right cages, and at the end, a short, old human dressed in a guard's uniform was sleeping in a chair, cradling a spear. The far left cage was outlined by blue energy from a Safed device, but two figures could be discerned inside. He could hear someone whispering. In the nearer cage lay the prostated form of a young woman who had the darkest skin he'd ever seen on a human. Fascinated, Drecks drew closer, even as the guard snored on.

Pyra knelt in the straw by the bars and agonized over Misha in the next cage. The guards had carried her unconcious body in several hours ago, and in all that time she had remained unconcious. Indeed, she had hardly moved, although she had often moaned aloud. Pyra had called her name softly many times, but Misha never responded and never awoke.

"What are we going to do, Atticus?"

The old wizard stood behind her, keeping careful distance from the blue shield. "Nothing, my dear. I can't do a cursed thing with this energy curtain between us." He sighed heavily.

Pyra tried softly whispering again. "Misha? Misha honey, can you hear me? Misha—" Pyra saw something in her peripheral vision and straightened up, catching her breath. Atticus sensed a presence and stiffened. He took two steps back. Both had perceived Drecks but did not know how long he had been standing there. The Black-hooded one stepped closer. Gob stirred and his eyes fluttered open. Upon seeing Drecks, he jumped up and pointed his spear. "Who are you?" Drecks ignored him, entranced by the sight of the young female. Gob came closer and threatened with his spear, but a sudden feeling of fear washed over him like a cold bucket of water. Thinking better of it, he raced away and came back a few minutes later with Galt. They both waved their spears.

Drecks casually turned towards them. "I am a Black Sorcerer in the king's service. Ask Zirmad if you don't believe me." His voice was as cold as ice.

At the phrase *Black Sorcerer*, the two guards muttered and backed up, their spears still at the ready.

Drecks turned back to the cages to examine things more closely. Then he picked up the Safed device and the stool it sat on and moved them to a spot exactly midway between the two cages. He adjusted the device until its blue curtain wrapped around both cages as if they were one, removing the energy barrier between them.

He turned back to the guards again and pointed to the device. "Touch this and you will pay for it with your miserable lives." Drecks began to leave when the hand of a humanoid in the far cell reached through the bars at him, and the creature spoke in its strange tongue. Drecks pointed a finger at the hand and shot a bolt of energy. A cry of pain and the smell of burnt flesh filled the air. Drecks vanished into the darkness, and the dungeon fell silent save for the whimpers of the injured creature.

Misha knew she was asleep and couldn't wake up. Instead, she was trapped in the most awful dream, reliving a traumatic moment from last year. Their family was solidly middle class, the kids born and raised in Porterville. But that day she was visiting cousins in the big city with her little sister and mother. The two sisters were going with their cousins to the corner grocery store for treats. "Do *not* go any further than the corner," their mother had warned them. "We won't, mom. Geez." It was a safe neighborhood. But down there they met some cute boys who knew a better store a short drive away. One had an older brother with a car who was going that way anyways. Soon they were driving north, and that short drive then became a twenty-block jaunt down the expressway to the edge of a housing project.

When they got out, the girls saw only black people, graffiti sprayed everywhere, and metal bars on the windows. A crowd of kids hung around like they had nothing to do and nowhere to go. Meekly, the girls went inside and bought their treats. Back outside, the cute boys wanted to hang out and talk, so the sisters stood around feeling awkward and nervous, like they had just landed on a strange planet. Some boys started flirting with them, so the sisters didn't notice the car at first. It was a late model Monte Carlo, electric blue, all tricked out with shiny chrome rims, driving slowly by and blaring loud rap music out its windows. Then suddenly: *pop, pop.... pop....pop, pop.*

Kids either hit the ground or took off running. The girls dropped. Bullet casings tinkled as they dropped. *Tink, tink....tink.....tink, tink.* The car sped away with the squeal of tires. Misha and her sister got up. So did everyone else, except for one boy. There was something wrong with him, lying motionless with his limbs akimbo, like a broken doll. Then she saw the hole in the back of his head and the blood starting to pool. Her little sister was crying and pulling at her arm, but Misha kept staring at the boy, dumbfounded at the sight. It was so surreal and so unlike the movies.

They did make it back home safely and got the lecture of a lifetime from their parents. "You coulda been killed!" Grounded for three months. Thinking about that boy, though, Misha thought that a head wound must really hurt. Lying where she was now, not really sure where, her own head hurt badly, as if in sympathy for that boy who died in a parking lot in the projects. In fact, it hurt a lot, pain like she never felt before. Waves of pain hammered her skull. She felt sick and weak. This must be what torture feels like, she decided. Then she noticed the loud moaning. Was it the boy in the parking lot? No, she realized. It was *her*.

Somebody else heard, too. She now registered a soft voice from close by that slowly penetrated through the pain. A woman's voice, very soothing and gentle, calling her by name.

"Misha? Misha honey, can you hear me? Misha—"

The voice stopped for a few minutes but then started back up again. "Misha, crawl closer. Crawl towards us. Can you hear me?"

It took a few minutes for the words to register. The voice was familiar, though she could not place it. But Misha could tell she had to move. The voice was right. She instinctively knew somehow that she had to obey it. She tested things by moving an arm. Good so far. She moved her head a little. Pain, instant and overwhelming. She nearly blacked out. The urge to give up and surrender was so tempting, but the voice pulled her back.

"Keep trying, Misha. Keep trying. You can do it. Please. We can help you, but you have to move closer. Please, honey."

Misha wiggled a little, and then more. The pain made her suck in her breath and clench her fists, but she kept at it. Using her whole body, she squirmed slowly forward, inch by inch, always toward the voice that was so soft, soothing, and gentle.

"That's great, honey. A little more. Come closer. That's it. A little more. You're doing it. Almost there."

Without the blue energy curtain in the way, Pyra could see Misha's hair on the back of her head matted with blood. Her progress was agonizingly slow. Pyra described it all to Atticus, and the wizard, lying on the ground like Misha, had his right arm through the bars in full extension. Finally Misha's head contacted Atticus's hand, and he softly chanted the healing spell. Another wiggle and Pyra was cradling Misha's head in her hands. After a few minutes the lines eased in Misha's face, her fists unclenched, and her ragged breath became soft and and regular. She stopped moaning.

"You're gonna be all right, Misha. Everything's okay, honey," Pyra cooed. She turned to Atticus. "Isn't that right, teacher?"

Atticus sat down slowly on the wooden bench against the back wall and let out a long sigh, hands on his knees and his back arched. "As well as can be expected in such a place," he said.

Galt and Gob had watched the whole scene play out in wordless surprise. Now they just turned to each other and shook their heads before returning to their posts.

Drecks returned to the lab in time to watch Zirmad reanimate the Toosker and escort it away. He volunteered to clean up the lab, and Wolfinger and Ipso happily ran off. Left alone again, Drecks retraced his path out of the lab and through the guards' quarters. But this time, he did not turn right at the tunnel intersection but continued straight on. After a long walk, the tunnel merged with a perpendicular, wider tunnel. Drecks turned left and walked along a ledge while in a channel below dirty water flowed out of the palace. The air smelled bad here to his goblin nose, but he expected that from any place associated with humans. He had explored here before and knew no humans came down here, just their dirty water.

There were numerous side tunnels. He counted them and took the eighth one. It went level aways and then began a gentle downhill slope. Down and down he went for a long time. Finally he came to a large, rocky chamber. It was pitch black, but his goblin eyes could see good enough.

Wrathbone and Gnawmark rose from where they were sitting and greeted the Goblinmaster. Here, for the first time since leaving Sporu Angosta, Drecks took his hood down, revealing his large goblin head. It was a head striped in both goblin green and kobold black, with one green eye in a black stripe and one black eye in a green stripe, a long nose dangling down, and skin covered with big warts.

The three exchanged head slaps and talked in their gutteral speech.

"Your report?" asked Drecks.

"Climbed the Great Stairs, O Filthy One," said Wrathbone. "Made it nearly to the Human Boneyard."

"The crypt. Good."

"Yeah, but we couldn't make it no further," said Gnawmark. "My feet no work."

"The tower's Magic stopped you."

"How can we take the tower then, Your Grisly Eminence?"

"Don't you worry. I have a plan," said Drecks.

"We smelled a human," said Gnawmark.

"When? Where?"

"On our way back, only part way down the stairs," said Wrathbone.

"They smell awful," said Gnawmark.

"But they taste good," said Wrathbone.

Drercks nodded in agreement. "I often wonder how they can stand each other. I can barely tolerate their stink when I consort with them in the Fat King's palace. But their flesh is tasty."

"Consort?" a puzzled Gnawmark asked.

"Did you see the human? Was there only one?" asked Drecks.

"Unsure of the numbers, but we saw a light," said Wrathbone.

"Torch light?"

"No, Your Filth. It was a green light."

"Green? This puzzles me. Anything else?"

"I want to go back and eat humans," Gnawmark said.

"Me, too," said Wrathbone.

"Soon, my kobolds, soon you will feast on more humans than you can count."

They all made horrible gurgling sounds that passed for laughter for such wicked creatures. "Go back to the others and wait for my command. Tell them to work harder." Drecks sent them away with a few more head slaps. And as he took the long walk back to the palace, he thought not of the Red Tower, but the young female human with the wonderful dark skin. A wicked idea was forming in his fiendish mind.

23
And Then There Were Five

The three stood next to the teleport rock: Kido, Woody, and Summer Wind. No one else wanted to go. They all wore longswords in leather scabbards, a parting gift, although none of them knew how to use one. They also had *Hope Crystals*. The golden Yar Rope stretched from the pillar where it was securely tied down through the glossy black surface like a fishing line disappearing into a lake's dark depths. It appeared very taut. Close by stood Codface, Bothros, Pontazar, Longtuth, and Shippleglass. On the other side were assembled as many tower dwellers as could fit, including Spindrift, the Quints, other wizards both young and old, Gulmar, Farstaff, Garlic John, and numerous cats.

Codface addressed the three. "When you are ready, take firm hold of the rope with both hands and walk onto the teleport rock. Let the rope slide through your hands but *do not* let go under any circumstances while in the portal."

"What if we do, I mean, on accident?" asked Kido.

Codface shrugged. "We don't know. We've never used a Yar Rope, but that's what the old masters always told us."

"You will probably be lost forever in the dimension-less, time-less void between portals," said Bothros.

"No one can find you there, except maybe one of the Immortals," said Pontazar.

"If even that," said Longtuth.

"Just don't let go," said Shippleglass.

"Numa will have tied the other end to some anchor. You will use the rope to return to us, and thus you will not require any teleport keys. Remember what you are looking for. Any questions?" said Codface.

The three exchanged serious glances but stayed silent. Kido simply nodded at Codface. Codface addressed the crowd across the rock. "Anyone else still want to go? Now's your last chance."

There was a silent moment and then a rustle of activity as Gulmar flew over to land on Kido's shoulder and Curiosity the Cat ran around and jumped up to land in Summer Wind's arms.

"Splendid. Now you have pets to keep you company. Are the five of you ready?" said Codface. The five nodded. Codface wordlessly beckoned to the rope.

Kido took hold with both hands. The Yar Rope felt alive with energy and warmth, smooth in his hands. He paused, took a deep breath, and stepped up onto the teleport rock. He immediately began sinking but kept on moving his feet. The sensation was like walking in a lake from the shallows into deeper water. His legs disappeared and then his waist. He didn't have time to look back at Woody, but he risked a quick peek to his left to see Shippleglass watching him intently. Then Gulmar squawked and Kido's head went under, and they entered the blue, watery-yet-dry world of the teleportal vortex.

When they arrived at the other end, they were on that same rock cut in the hillside where they had first arrived in Pandoon so long ago. There was a steady wind blowing downhill, and the air was quite warm and humid. A musky animal smell lingered in the air. Gulmar took off with a squawk and flew a circling pattern.

Human figures surrounded them, frozen like statues around the rock's outer rim. Their robes fluttered in the wind, but their bodies did not move. Nineteen wore gold robes, and eighteen black robes. A thirty-eighth figure wore no robes at all, only his tunic and leggings. Kido walked over to him and recognized the Gold Mage, his eyes open but unblinking, his beard blowing in the wind.

"Someone took his robes," said Kido.

"Or they blew off," said Woody.

"Ramanapirus, he whose name cannot be shortened," said Kido. He waved a hand in front of the wizard's face, but there was no response. All the wizards looked unharmed but frozen and unresponsive. "After all this time, they are still transfixed by some powerful Magic. Weird."

"Look at those trees," said Woody, the first off the rock. "They weren't here before."

And now they all noticed a belt of strange trees that ran down the hillside between the teleport rock and the tower. The trees skirted around the fringes of the Alfheim forest and headed west and southwest. They varied in height, from saplings to towering monster trees, all with crooked branches, dark trunks, and bright red leaves. "Have you ever seen trees like that?" Kido said to Summer Wind.

"No, never, but I hear they're called Dragon Trees."

"Or Everreds. They never lose their leaves," said Woody.

The Yar Rope was tied to a nearby Everred. They walked through the trees on a wide path covered with huge footprints that filled them with wonder. Beyond the trees they could see the Gold Tower. "It still stands," said Summer Wind.

"Yeah, but it looks funny," said Woody.

Kido studied it for a moment. "You're right. Something's wrong with one side." The tower's left side had clean, straight lines like normal, but the right side looked blobbed and distorted at the base. It was not lost on them that the distorted side faced the gates of Sporu Angosta.

They looked around but saw no one else. Gulmar flew overhead to announce "Nobody here," and then flew off towards the tower. Curiosity retreated inside Summer Wind's hood, where she peeked out.

The clearing they stood in had been devastated. All the grass had been burnt away and the pine trees knocked over and scorched. Summer Wind looked south towards Alfheim, where the devastation continued as far as the eye could see. "Oh, my homeland," she moaned.

"I'm sorry," Kido said and rubbed her shoulder.

Kido and Summer Wind held hands as they went uphill with Woody. On the bare hillside between the trees and the tower were several large, shallow divots, as if something had scooped up the topsoil for some strange purpose. The three marched up to the tower, and here they made a remarkable discovery.

The gold brick facade on one whole side of the tower had melted off and flowed down in molten heaps on the ground where it had cooled like an old lava flow. And where the gold bricks were gone, brilliant sapphire blue bricks showed.

Gulmar had perched on a nearby tree stump. "Blue Tower," he squawked.

Summer Wind gssped. "Underneath the Gold Tower is a Blue Tower?"

"It must be Akasha's Tower," said Kido, feeling pleased at the discovery.

"Akasha doesn't have a tower," said Summer Wind.

"She does now," said Woody.

"She always did. It was just covered up," said Kido. "Someone had stolen her tower."

"But who would do that? And why?" asked Summer Wind.

"Whoever would stand to benefit from it," said Kido. But there their line of reasoning ended.

"Do we go in?" Woody asked. The great wood door had been blasted off and was nowhere to be found. The dark opening beckoned.

"We still need to look at the gates," said Summer Wind. They all turned north at the frowning cliffs, but a heavy mist blocked their view in that direction.

"Wait one." Kido spent some time walking around near the tower's base, where he remembered dropping the Butterscotch Book during the Ruination. The book was nowhere to be seen. *Did someone carry it back inside the tower or did it blow away somewhere?* he wondered.

"I want to go look inside the tower," Kido said.

"I don't," said Woody.

"Domingo may be inside there," said Kido.

"He could be anywhere."

"We have to find out."

"Do you think it's safe, after what the Ruination did to it?" asked Summer Wind.

"Perhaps we should just check the gates and then go back, wait for a larger expedition to return and check the tower," said Woody.

"I'm going in but not through the front door." Kido walked around to the north side of the tower, and the others followed. They knew from before that the hillside just beyond this side of the tower slopes down into the valley of the fabled city of Zannalornacopia, Z-Town. None of the three had ever been there, but they had heard stories. Now they ignored the tower and walked past to the valley's edge, and saw something that took their breath away. Where before there had been a valley, now there was deeply-sunken world that extended far beyond the old valley. Where they stood was a precipitous drop of several hundred feet straight down where all they could see were clouds. They all bent over and peered down.

"Where is Z-Town?" asked Kido.

"Below those clouds, I guess," said Summer Wind.

"What happened?" asked Woody.

"The Ruination did this?" Kido guessed.

"How could it do *that*?"

"It isn't just the valley, but half of Pandoon is deep, deep down there!" said Woody. "Can you see the other side?"

"No," said Kido. He turned to Summer Wind, with her keen elvish eyes.

She stared and she squinted. "No? Maybe? I don't know."

They went back to the north side of the tower, which had a window several floors up. Here the line between gold bricks and blue bricks ran up the side. "Wait here if you want," he said, and then he *floated* up and disappeared through the window.

"I can't *float*," said Woody.

"I can. You want me to take you up?" said Summer Wind.

Woody thought about it. "Sure," he said in a small voice, so she took his arm and they *floated* up after Kido.

Gulmar watched them all go, then shook his head. "Nope. Not going in. Nuh-uh."

The 27th floor of the Red Tower was deserted. Codface had said Kido's mission could take hours and he'd alert everyone as soon as they had returned. Codface had walked out with everyone but slipped away as soon as he could and circled back. He walked over to where the Yar Rope was tied to the brick pier. He looked around and saw no one. It took a few minutes to untie the snug knot before the golden rope snapped free and disappeared down the teleportal. Codface wiped the dust from his hands and walked off whistling a merry tune.

Spindrift watched it all from his hiding place ten piers away.

They all landed inside a dark room where the air smelled heavily of smoke and ash. Without the wind it was preternaturally quiet as they waited several minutes for their eyes to adjust. Kido sent Egon aloft. "Nice," Woody said of the Glow Ball. "Where did you get that?"

"Found it in the catacombs."

"You're not supposed to go there."

"It's not that bad, once you get past the bugs and the skeletons."

In the soft green light, they could see the room was the Wizards' Study. Everything in it—the long pine table, the bookshelves, books, chairs—had been reduced to ash. The empty walls were stained with soot. Ash was piled deep on the floor. Kido began kicking around the ash." What are you looking for?" asked Woody.

"The Butterscotch Book, or anything else that survived," said Kido.

"You took that book outside."

"Somebody coulda brought it back in before the final catastrophe."

So they joined him, kicking around until their robes' hems were colored black but found nothing.

"If it was in here, it probably got burned to ash like everything else," said Kido. They all looked at each other but didn't say what they were thinking.

"I'm sure somebody took it to a safe place," said Summer Wind.

"Yeah, I'm sure," said Woody.

"Let's keep looking," said Kido.

They exited through the open doorway where the door had been destroyed.

"You know this tower. Where to now?" asked Summer Wind.

"I only knew the laundry and kitchen," said Woody.

"Let's search for the Mage's Quarters and any storerooms," said Kido.

Egon led the way, ten and ten. All the doors to all the rooms had been blown open by some tremendous force, but the interior rooms had less fire damage than the Wizards' Study.

"This tower is much smaller than the Red Tower," said Summer Wind.

"This is the seventh floor," said Kido. "Orthus's room is one floor down. Whenever he went to visit his dad, he said he'd be on the ninth floor. So let's go up two." They came to a stone stairway and ascended.

The ninth floor was eerily quiet and empty. The doors were blown open here too, but there was no fire damage. Peeking in doorways, they saw living quarters in disarray: clothes, bedding, and personal effects strewn everywhere. A spacious and well-appointed apartment at the end of the hall was in the same condition.

"The Mage's Quarters," said Summer Wind. They searched carefully but found no spellbook or Magical items. Back outside Kido sighed. "Well, let's keep going up until we find something."

They went back to the stairwell and ascended. On the tenth floor, they found a body lying on his stomach. It was Tower Clerk Dulcinata. He looked like he was sleeping, but he wasn't breathing. Curiosity gave the body a wide berth but then hung back to clean himself as the others moved on.

The doors on this floor were all closed and locked when they tried them. At the end of the hall was a set of double doors.

"This place looks important," said Woody.

Kido tried the handle. "Locked."

"I know an *Unlock* spell," Summer Wind said.

"Try it."

She closed her eyes to concentrate and spoke the casting words. Kido jiggled the handle. "Nope."

She tried again.

"Nope."

"Maybe the Gold To—Blue Tower is blocking my Magic," she said.

"We could find an axe and just hack our way through," said Woody.

"These doors look thick and solid. We'd be hacking forever," said Kido.

"Let's just go then. We'll peek at the Gates and then head back to the Rope," said Woody.

Kido thought for a moment. "Hold on. I have an idea. You remember that scene in *Wizard's Revenge*, when the heroes were confronted by an unlockable door in the castle's keep?"

Woody thought for a second and then his eyes widened in recognition. "Find a key on a nearby dead body!"

"What are you guys talking about?" asked Summer Wind.

The boys raced back to Dulcinata's corpse, while the elf stood with arms crossed and a perplexed expression on her face. They rolled the body and rifled its pockets, finally brandishing a large key ring. They ran back and began trying brass skeleton keys. With key number fourteen, they heard a click.

"All right, let's see if we get lucky," said Kido.

He turned the handle, and the door burst open with an explosive force and out surged a ten-foot high sticky wave of goo that instantly engulfed them all. Kido had the impression of some translucent, gooey matter that completely covered him. He felt like a fly stuck in glue. He struggled mightily to break free but found it hard to move. It seemed the more he moved, the tighter the goo stuck to him. He closed his mouth to avoid swallowing any of the stuff and his eyes to protect them, but still he felt a burning sensation on the exposed skin of his hands and face. The goo seemed toxic. He wasn't going to last long like this, and so he began using all his strength to pull backwards away from the goo, but it held him tight and his skin burned worse. His lungs were starting to hurt too, and he ached to breath. He could sense Summer Wind and Woody struggling too. Only Curiosity had escaped by hanging so far back.

What was this thing that seemed so soft and yet so dangerous? He forced back down the panic welling up inside and tried to remember where he'd read about such a thing. And his mind went back to Oto's bookstore and *Growler's Beastopedia*. The Ectoplasm. That's what it's called, a gelatinous, semi-sentient creature of Magic. It was impossible to defeat with steel weapons, but it did have a weak spot susceptible to fire. But where? Kido couldn't remember. He'd have to open his eyes and look for it.

His eyes began to sting as soon as he opened them, but he forced himself to look around. It was a bit like looking while submerged in the ocean without a mask, except the 'fluid ' was clear, not blue. There was a dim light source somewhere in the background that backlit the Ectoplasm. Kido could now make out small blue blobs distributed throughout the transparent goo, like raisins in rice pudding. Then he noticed something else. A few feet deeper, in the Ectoplasm's core, was a sizeable object, a yellowish blob that seemed to pulse with energy. Looking to the right, he was shocked to see a human arm bone stuck in the goo, then more skeletal parts stuck in different parts of the Ectoplasm. He began to swim towards the yellowish blob. It seemed to be easier to move inward than it was to move outward through the Ectoplasm, as if it were sucking him in. The yellowish blob glowed brighter and pulsed faster as he neared it. Bright spark-like lights cascaded across it. The stinging sensation increased as well, until his skin and eyes were on fire. He was close to asphyxiating now, desperate to breath.

He raised his right hand and pointed a finger at the yellow blob, only inches away. His mind searched for the spellwords to cast the *Zap* spell, but it found *Beeswarm* instead. Dozens of yellow and black bees shot out of Kido's finger and slammed into the yellowish blob, but it absorbed them all. All that stinging did nothing,

Bright spots danced before his burning eyes. Kido was out of air, his reeling mind fluttering about like a dying moth. It found memories of his grandma, schoolmates, their old house, walking with the rupa, role playing games with Woody, rolling dice, casting spells, his blue wizard's robe, a wand, a sword, the *Zap* spell. The *Zap* spell!

The words came forth unbidden, and a bright bolt of energy followed the path of the bees, shattering the yellowish blob. There was a slight pause as the Ectoplasm quivered violently and then it all disintegrated. They all fell to the floor into a thin, wide puddle of liquified goo. For a long moment, they sat on the floor gasping like fish out of water, sucking in deep draughts of sweet air. Eventually they became aware enough of their surroundings to get up and find a sink with running water, and they rinsed their skin and eyes and plucked gobs of goo out of each other's hair.

Only then could they fully explore the room they were in, albeit with bloodshot eyes. The large room had stone floors, stone walls, and a high ceiling. There was a shallow floor basin of stone near the sink, and a dozen wooden tables scattered about. The tables were empty, but the floor was cluttered with many objects lying under a thick layer of dust. The dust had furrows like it had been plowed for planting. Kido began shuffling through the dust with his feet. When he kicked something, he picked it up and cleaned the dust off it to examine it. The other two copied his movements but their search turned up nothing interesting. Then they heard impact tremors getting closer.

On the outer wall was a large opening where a window had been blown out. Going over there, they found a commanding view of the meadow, teleport rock, the strange trees, and the destroyed forest of Alfheim off into the distance. Something came at them, making them jump, but it was only Gulmar landing on the window sill with a fluttering of wings. "Giant coming," he said simply.

"What?"

"Giant." Gulmar looked back outside, and what he saw made fly into the room and land on a table. They could feel the impact tremors now. Then into their view lumbered a giant wearing blue pants and black suspenders. He was shirtless, shoeless, and bald, carrying a giant shovel. He was walking downhill with huge strides when something made him abruptly stop to look back over his shoulder at the tower.

Kido, Woody, and Summer Wind ducked away. There was silence and then impact tremors closing in. A huge hand with hairy knuckles reached through the window and raked the dust to scoop up debris and pull it back outside. Kido risked a peek and saw the giant examining the debris in his hand before dumping it on the ground with a rumble of disappointment. Up came the head again. Kido ducked back. The giant's hand gripped the window sill and he must've been on his tippy-toes to look in. All he saw was Gulmar on a table. The Mawker squawked and flew out of the room to land in the hallway by Curiosity, who was lying on his side taking it all in with mild interest.

"Bird," the deep voice rumbled. Impact tremors walked away.

When they looked again, the three intrepid explorers saw him digging down the hill. Presently, the giant returned and passed the tower, the tremors fading away.

"Well, that tears it. Let's go check out the gates," said Kido.

"You don't want to check out the higher floors?" asked Summer Wind.

"No. I'm looking for three things only: The Butterscotch Book, the spellbook of Ramanapirus, or teleport keys," said Kido.

"All those could be on the upper floors."

"Maybe, but I feel that if they were here, we would've found them by now. If we had more time, we could keep searching, but I think we have wasted too much time already."

"We might run into the giant out in the open," said Woody.

Kido shrugged. "We still gotta go."

They made their way down the stairs, passing several more bodies. Most of these had arrows in them and dried pools of blood stained the floor. Summer Wind pointed out that all the fletchings were green and black. "Goblin arrows."

"How did they get past the tower's shield?" asked Woody.

"All those wizards out there frozen to the rock would've had *Hope Crystals*," she said.

There were several dead bodies piled up just inside the front door, but no sign of the giant outside. The path uphill soon took them inside the grove of Everreds. The trees covered the upper hillside and ran down into the ravine. Further on, they discovered both doors of the Gates flung wide open, and the Everreds continued inside Sporu Angosta. The three paused just outside the gates, regarding it with wonder. Gulmar perched on a nearby stump. A golden light poured out, only to be swallowed up by the drab grayness of Pandoon's sky.

"They are open," Summer Wind said.

"Very open," said Woody, mimicking her hushed voice. "Now let's go back to the Yar Rope."

Kido looked around but they were quite alone. "I'm going in."

"What?"

"To look around."

Woody couldn't believe it. "We saw all we came to see. Let's go back."

No, I'm going in."

"For how long?"

"Awhile."

"How far?"

"A ways."

Woody rolled his eyes.

They walked into Sporu Angosta, first Kido, followed by Summer Wind with Curiosity riding inside her hood. Gulmar flew in after them, and a reluctant Woody came last.

Inside Sporu Angosta, the golden light was dazzling to those whose eyes had not seen sunlight since the Ruination. They stood still and blinked repeatedly while their eyes adjusted.

Kido was expecting a large rocky chamber with four large dragons lying on piles of treasure around a golden throne while a few giants lurked in the background. What he saw instead was another world with wide open vistas.

Sporu Angosta had a cloudless turquoise sky and a seemingly endless space. If there was an end to it, they couldn't see it. What they could see was a single line of Everred Trees running from the Gates off into the distance without break. Nearby to the left of the trees was what looked like a refuse pile in an area the size of a football field, a space of churned up dirt and sand with objects sticking out. Nearby to the right was a massive teleport rock. Off in the distance were the vague suggestions of features too remote to discern. The air was warm and humid.

Boys and elf looked at each other, unsure what to do now. Curiosity lept down and ran over to the refuse pile and began digging. They followed her and found all manner of objects deposited there: clothes, furniture, wizards' staffs, candlesticks, books, jewelry, and so on. Kido then turned up something shaped like one of those tiny plastic treasure chests people put in the bottom of aquariums. It was only three inches long. "Probably not much in here, but let's open it up and see." He fingered the clasp and the top popped open. Out came a giant shelving arrangement much larger than could physically fit inside the chest. Each shelf held dozens of large marble-shaped teleport keys in many colors, all exuding little wisps of smoke. The smell of Magic hit their nostrils.

"Jackpot!" He sang out.

Summer Wind came over and gasped at what she saw.

There were black, red, green, blue, and gold keys for the towers, plus white keys for whatever. And there were other keys that swirled with multi-colors.

"Very nice. Hey Kido, look at this," said Summer Wind. Kido saw she was holding a large, thick book covered with tawny hide. He gasped and took the book. "You found it!"

"Yes!" They were happy.

"Your friend Domingo is in there?" asked Summer Wind.

"Yes, but how do we get him out?" Kido stroked the cover but the amber eye opened and glared at him.

"Perhaps we should just take it back to the Red Tower and let the masters look at it," said Summer Wind.

"I think you're right." Kido let her place the Butterscotch Book inside his backpack next to the *Beastopedia*. "You keep the keys for now."

"What else is here?" They spied some low, black shapes nearby. Only when they got closer did they realize they were staring at charred, unrecognizable bodies. None of them voiced what they were thinking. Were these people killed in the Ruination? Or by dragonfire? Was one of them Numa?

They next went to the teleport rock, only to discover that what had looked like *one* massive rock was, in reality, *five* normal teleport rocks clustered close together.

"Five rocks," said Kido. "I wonder where they go?"

"Anywhere you want," said Summer Wind. "It's the keys that specify the destination. Right?"

Kido shrugged. "Unless these are different."

"Why would they be different? They look the same as the other ones."

"Then why put five of them here if one should suffice?"

Now it was her turn to shrug. "Maybe they're special rocks for inside Sporu only?"

Kido looked around at the vast horizon. "That would make sense."

Woody said, "Maybe that's what the white keys are for?"

"Maybe."

"Should we should go back and teleport home?"

Kido was still looking off into the depths of Sporu. "Maybe we explore further," he said in a preoccupied tone. They looked around. They looked at each other. They furrowed their brows.

Woody said, "I'm not going any further. I'll stay here and wait for you two to get back."

"Have it your way, Woodmeister," said Kido.

Then Gulmar flew in and landed on one of the rocks. Within a few seconds the surface rippled and Gulmar sank out of sight with a startled squawk.

"He disappeared!" said Kido.

"And he didn't need a key!" said Summer Wind.

They walked over to the one rock where Gulmar disappeared, and bending over, they could see the ghostly image of an egg floating beneath its shiny, obsidian surface. Checking the others, they found other images: a single tower that looked like a rook chess piece, a diffuse star-like object, a pair of gates, and a blob. The last image gave off evil vibes that took their breath away.

"We're not going there," she said.

"Let's follow Gulmar," he said, and a few seconds later they popped up out of a new teleport rock cluster.

Gulmar was perched on a sand dune near a long line of Everreds. Some distance off were some very tall cliffs and something at their base that couldn't be discerned from here, something shrouded in shadow. The trees stretched the other way as far as could be seen. There was no sign of the gates. Gulmar said, "Eggs," and pointed his wing behind them. They turned and saw a landscape of thousands of rolling sand dunes. They stepped off the rock into deep, soft sand and walked over to the first dune. It was about ten feet high, and they climbed it to only see more dunes stretching to the horizon. The air here was warmer yet and very humid. A musk smell was strong.

"It's like the Sahara," said Kido, feeling sweat bead on his forehead.

"What?"

"We call this a desert back home, a place that is very hot and sandy."

"In Elvish we call it a *khedil*," she said. She suddenly seized his arm. "Look!" She pointed where a giant figure bent over a dune. He was far off but they could see he was dressed in blue pants and green suspenders. His name was Baugi, and he appeared to be digging. They fell down on the dune's summit and watched the giant manipulate something and then cover it back up.

"I'm starting to not like this place," said Kido, his anxiety leveling rising fast.

Gulmar landed next to them and said, "Eggs." The Mawker began scratching at the sand.

"Eggs? What eggs?"

"Dragon eggs," said Gulmar.

"Gulmar, I don't want to dig up any eggs," said Kido. "Especially here."

"If every dune has an egg, and every egg has a dragon inside," said Summer Wind, shading her eyes and staring off into the distance. "But why haven't they hatched yet?"

"Because they're covered up in sand?"

"But how long ago were they laid?"

"I have no clue. Too bad Shippleglass isn't here."

"He wouldn't know either."

"He knows a lot more than I do about dragons."

"I'm just thinking if they all hatch and fly out of Sporu and grow up, then the Prophecy is true."

"And what about the prime dragons? Something had to lay all these eggs, and I don't want to meet Mazunga." He looked back at the teleport rocks. "I wonder where Akasha is?" He closed his eyes and tried to ping her but got no response.

Woody wandered around the refuse pile, hands in his pockets. He was aimlessly kicking at objects stuck in the sand and singing to himself. He really didn't expect to find anything and was just waiting for Kido and Summer Wind. His foot contacted a small piece of clay, and turning it over, he uncovered something else. The glint of gold caught Woody's eye. He brushed off sand and picked up a ring. He held it in the palm of his hand and studied it. It was plain gold and his mind went to some books he'd read and movies he'd seen about a ring.

"It can't be," he muttered. He looked around, but he was all alone.

He looked some more at the ring and thought about it. Should he try it on?

He put it on and felt nothing. He looked down but he was visible. The ring didn't work. "All the Magic must've been used up." He tried to pull it off and throw it away, but it wouldn't budge. He pulled and twisted and pulled some more, but the ring would not come off.

He went and stood underneath a tall Everred near the gates, feeling very nervous and alone. He wished now he had gone with the others. No, wait. He wished they would hurry back so they could get out of here, and the strange ring on his finger didn't help. He was so scared he was shaking, his body literally vibrating. Then he realized the ground was vibrating. He looked down to see the ground beginning to split open right next to him, and he took off runnning. When he stopped and turned back, he saw trees sprouting from the very ground. They had pale grey trunks and black leaves and black berries. They were growing fast. There were two lines of trees now, one red and one black, side-by-side.

Summer Wind and Kido felt the ground shaking too.

She said, "We've been here long enough. We need to go back and report this."

He said, "All right. Let's go."

They slid back down the dune only to discover a large egg now sticking out of the sand. It was light green with dark green and black speckles.

"Gulmar! Look what you've done!" Then they saw Curiosity had joined Gulmar in digging.

"Not you, too. Cover it back up quick."

But both animals kept digging.

"Oh, why did we bring animals?" He said as he and Summer Wind began frantically scooping sand back on the egg. There was an avalanche of sand, and the egg popped out. Kido tried to stop it, but it was too large and heavy. It rolled away downhill to strike a rock. There was an audible crack and the shell split open. A dragon the size of a horse unfolded itself and emerged. Actually it was longer than a horse if you counted the tail. Kido had fallen down to land right next to the egg. He looked up to see a creature with jungle green scales streaked with brown and black. Strikingly blue eyes stared back at him.

"Great! Now we have a dragon. Correction, a baby dragon."

Summer Wind said, "He's cute, but we can't take him with us."

"Did you think I was going to?"

"Giant coming," said Gulmar from the top of the dune.

They scrambled back up to confirm that the giant, while still a football field away, was closing in fast on them. They slid back down.

"What now?" Kido said.

"We'll hide in the sand," she said.

"He'll see the dragon."

"Let's run then." She scooped up the cat and took off for the teleport rocks. Kido and Gulmar followed. Back at the gates, Summer Wind and Curiosity popped up, followed by Gulmar, Kido, and the baby dragon.

"It followed us!"

"Doesn't matter! Keep going!"

They ran the short distance to the gates, where they met Woody. "I got tired of waiting. What took you so long?"

"I'll explain later," said Kido. "We're leaving."

"There's a couple giants hanging around the tower," said Woody. Then they noticed the black trees. "What's with the trees?"

"I don't know. They just grew out of the ground."

They heard a rumble and turned to see Baugi from the *khedil* emerge on the teleport rock and run after them. They fled out the doors and across the ravine. They could hear him crashing through the Everreds right behind them. They burst out of the trees and ran between the legs of a giant with blue pants and black suspenders. This giant, whose name was Friggi, was so startled that he could only manage a hasty grab that missed and sent him sprawling on the ground where Baugi tripped over him. Their fall caused tremors, but they were up quick to resume the chase, shaking the ground with their huge feet.

Kido was running as fast as he could downhill, past the tower and through the Everreds and Everblacks, but Summer Wind was faster and she was pulling away. She was the first to spot the problem. "The Yar Rope is no longer connected to the teleportal!"

"What?" Kido looked and now he saw that it was still tied to the Everred, but it was no longer stretched tight to the rock. Instead it was lying slack on the ground like a long golden snake. "Hold up then. Let me get the keys out of your backpack!"

She slowed up, and he began unbuckling her straps while still running. Curiosity was riding in the hood and face-to-face with him. He could see her watching the two giants chasing them from behind. Then her head swiveled to the right where a third giant emerged from the burned forest. He had blue suspenders and a huge shovel which he raised above his head with a roar. This giant's name was Bergelmir. Summer Wind cut left and ran through his legs, Kido and Woody right behind her. The unexpected maneuver threw off Bergelmir's aim, and the shovel's blade struck empty ground. He roared in frustration and lurched around, but his prey cut back to the right and angled towards the teleport rock, now only fifty yards away.

Friggi and Baugi plowed into Bergelmir and all three went down in a tangle of arms, legs, and shovel. Kido, digging around in Summer Wind's backpack, finally found the little treasure chest and pulled it out. Still running, he opened it up. Shelves popped open, and the smell of Magic filled the air. Kido reached for a red marble as Summer Wind abruptly stopped. Distracted as he was, Kido plowed right into her, spilling all the marbles into the dust and ash on the ground. "I'm not leaving that rope behind," she said as she ran over to the Everred.

"Oh no, oh no, oh no," Kido mumbled and fell to his knees, when Woody tripped over Kido and fell too. The shaking ground told them the giants were back up and coming on. In mounting panic, the boys were digging for marbles.

The Yar Rope coiled over her shoulder now, Summer Wind raced back and jumped up on the teleport rock between two frozen Gold Wizards. She waved frantically at the two boys, her eyes on the three giants running their way.

"Hurry!" she pleaded with them.

Gulmar landed beside her. "Hurry!" he squawked.

"We're trying to find a red one!" said Kido.

Everything was happening fast and everyone was yelling in fright. The ground was shaking like crazy. "I keep finding the wrong colors," Woody said.

"There's no time left. Grab one and jump on board!" she yelled.

Kido plunged both hands in the dust and ash and felt a small hard sphere in one hand and something else in the other. "I have one!" He jumped on the rock. Woody tried to follow but lost his balance and started falling back, windmilling his arms. Summer Wind reached out and missed the first time but then got a hold of his robe and pulled him onto the rock. "Drop it!" she yelled at Kido.

Kido dropped the marble and saw it was black.

Three towering figures loomed over the teleport rock as its surface rippled and the kids plunged out of sight. A massive shovel blade cleaved the waters of the teleportal, missing them but created a swirling vortex. Kido felt himself tossed around like a boat in a hurricane, but gradually the waters subsided, and soon they popped up onto a new teleport rock inside a strange tower.

"Kido," Summer Wind said after she had caught her breath.

"I know. We're in the Shadow Tower," Kido said.

"No, not just that," she said.

"It followed us," said Woody, and he pointed behind Kido.

Kido turned and looked into the strikingly blue eyes of a baby dragon. It came up and rubbed against him.

"Great."

THE END

The Magic Towers continues with
Book Two,

Shadow Tower, Green Tower.

A map of the Known World follows.

Milton Keynes UK
Ingram Content Group UK Ltd.
UKHW032110220224
438319UK00010B/727